Tales of the Cthulhu Mythos

Cthulhu is the vast, terrible being from beyond time and space who lurks in his loathsome lair beneath the ocean in sunken R'lyeh, symbol and actuality of inconceivable nightmare, the greatest creation of this century's master of adult fantasy, H.P. Lovecraft.

The Cthulhu Mythos inspired many authors to write stories using it as a theme. *Tales of the Cthulhu Mythos* contains the best of these tales of ultimate terror, together with key Cthulhu stories by Lovecraft himself.

D1460665

ALSO BY H.P. LOVECRAFT

The Shadow Over Innsmouth
The Outsider and Others
Beyond the Wall Of Sleep
Marginalia
The Lurker at the Threshold (with August Derleth)
The Case Of Charles Dexter Ward
The Dream-Quest of Unknown Kadath
The Survivor and Others (with August Derleth)
The Shuttered Room and Other Tales of Horror
The Dunwich Horror and Others
Dagon and Other Macabre Tales
At the Mountains of Madness and Other Novels of Terror
The Horror in the Museum and Other Revisions (with others)
The Haunter of the Dark and Other Tales

H. P. LOVECRAFT
and others

TALES OF THE CTHULHU MYTHOS

Collected by
August Derleth

HarperCollins*Publishers*

HarperCollins*Publishers*
77–85 Fulham Palace Road,
Hammersmith, London W6 8JB

This paperback edition 1994
1 3 5 7 9 8 6 4 2

Previously published in paperback by Grafton 1988
Reprinted four times

First published in Great Britain by
Grafton Books 1975

Copyright © August Derleth 1969
Published by arrangement with Arkham House

ISBN 0 586 20344 3

Set in Century Schoolbook

Printed in Great Britain by
HarperCollinsManufacturing Glasgow

Acknowledgements

Contents

The Cthulhu Mythos

'All my stories,' wrote H. P. Lovecraft, 'unconnected as they may be, are based on the fundamental lore or legend that this world was inhabited at one time by another race who, in practising black magic, lost their foothold and were expelled, yet live on outside ever ready to take possession of this Earth again.' When this pattern became evident to Lovecraft's readers, particularly in the stories that followed publication of 'The Call of Cthulhu', in *Weird Tales*, February 1928, it was named 'the Cthulhu Mythos' by Lovecraft's correspondents and fellow-writers, though Lovecraft himself never so designated it.

It is undeniably evident that there exists in Lovecraft's concept a basic similarity to the Christian Mythos, specifically in regard to the expulsion of Satan from Eden and the power of evil. But any examination of the stories in the Mythos discloses also certain non-imitative parallels with other myth-patterns and the work of their writers, particularly Poe, Ambrose Bierce, Arthur Machen, Lord Dunsany, and Robert W. Chambers, who afforded Lovecraft helpful keys, though it was from Dunsany that Lovecraft admitted getting the 'idea of the artificial pantheon and myth-background represented by "Cthulhu", "Yog-Sothoth", "Yuggoth", etc.'; yet he got no more than the idea from Dunsany's work, for none of the major Lovecraftian figures of the Mythos has any existence in Dunsany's writings, for all that on occasion a Dunsanian place-name makes its appearance in Lovecraft's tales.

As Lovecraft conceived the deities or forces of his Mythos, there were, initially, the Elder Gods, none of whom save Nodens, Lord of the Great Abyss, is ever identified by name; these Elder Gods were benign deities, representing the forces of good, and existed peacefully at or near Betelgeuse in the constellation of Orion, very rarely stirring forth to intervene in the unceasing struggle between the powers of evil and the races of Earth. These powers of evil were variously known as the Great Old Ones or the Ancient Ones, though the latter term is most often applied in the fiction to the manifestation of one of the Great Old Ones on Earth. The Great Old Ones, unlike the Elder Gods, are named, and make frightening appearances in certain of the tales. Supreme among them is the blind idiot god, Azathoth, an 'amorphous blight of nethermost confusion which blasphemes and bubbles at the centre of all infinity.' Yog-Sothoth, the 'all-in-one and one-in-all,' shares Azathoth's dominion, and is not subject to the laws of time and space, being coexistent with all time and conterminous with all space. Nyarlathotep, who is presumably the messenger of the Great Old Ones; Great Cthulhu, dweller in hidden R'lyeh deep in the sea; Hastur the Unspeakable, who occupies the air and interstellar spaces, half-brother to Cthulhu; and Shub-Niggurath, 'the black goat of the woods with a thousand young,' complete the roster of the Great Old Ones as originally conceived. Parallels in macabre fiction are immediately apparent, for Nyarlathotep corresponds to an earth-elemental, Cthulhu to a water-elemental, Hastur to an air-elemental, and Shub-Niggurath is the Lovecraftian conception of the god of fertility.

To this original group of Great Old Ones, Lovecraft subsequently added many another deity, though usually lower in rank – such as Hypnos, god of sleep (representing an attempt to link an earlier tale with the Mythos, as Lovecraft did also by describing Yog-Sothoth as 'Umr At-Tawil in the Lovecraft–Price collaboration, 'Through the Gates of the Silver Key'), Dagon, ruler of the Deep Ones, dwellers in the ocean depths allied to Cthulhu, the 'Abominable Snow-Men of Mi-Go,' Yig, the prototype of Quetzalcoatl, etc. Adding appreciably to the Mythos were other beings sprung from the fertile imagination of Lovecraft's creative correspondents

– the Hound of Tindalos and Chaugnar Faugn, by Frank
Belknap Long; Nygotha, by Henry Kuttner; Tsathoggua and
Atlach-Nacha by Clark Ashton Smith; Lloigor, Zhar, the
Tcho-Tcho people, Ithaqua, and Gthugha of my own inven-
tion; and by such later inventions as J. Ramsey Campbell's
Glaaki and Daoloth, Brian Lumley's Yibb-Tstll and Shudde-
M'ell, and Colin Wilson's Mind Parasites.

The trappings of the mythology necessarily came into
being. Pre-human races were evolved to serve the Ancient
Ones; place-names were invented to establish the 'homes' of
the beings – sometimes actual places, such as Aldebaran,
and Hyades, sometimes mythical places like the Plateau of
Leng, or the Massachusetts towns and villages of Arkham
(corresponding to Salem), Kingsport (corresponding to
Marblehead), Dunwich (corresponding to the country around
Wilbraham, Monson, and Hampden), etc. To further
implement the Mythos, Lovecraft wrote of and sometimes
quoted from a shunned and terrible book, the *Necronomicon*
of the mad Arab, Abdul Alhazred, which contained shuddersome and frightening hints of the Great Old Ones who lurk
just beyond the consciousness of man and make themselves
visible or manifest from time to time in their unceasing
attempts to regain their sway over Earth and its races. For
this book Lovecraft drew up a 'history and chronology' so
convincing that many a librarian and bookdealer has been
called upon to supply copies. In brief, the book, originally
entitled *Al Azif* was written circa A.D. 730 at Damascus
by Abdul Alhazred, 'a mad poet of Sana, in Yemen, who is
said to have flourished during the period of the Ommiade
Caliphs.' Thereafter, its history was as follows:

'Translated into Greek as the *Necronomicon*, A.D. 950 by
Theodorus Philetas.

'Burnt by Patriarch Michael A.D. 1050 (i.e. Greek text . . .
Arabic text now lost).

'Olaus Wormius translates Greek into Latin, A.D. 1228.

'Latin and Greek editions suppressed by Pope Gregory IX,
A.D. 1232.

'Black letter edition. Germany – 1440?
'Greek text printed in Italy – 1500–1550.
'Spanish translation of Latin text – 1600?'

To supplement this remarkable creation, Lovecraft added the fragmentary records of the 'Great Race,' the *Pnakotic Manuscript*; the blasphemous writings of the minions of Cthulhu, the *R'lyeh Text*; the *Book of Dzyan*, the *Seven Cryptical Books of Hsan*, and the *Dhol Chants*. Members of the Lovecraft Circle added to the bibliography – Clark Ashton Smith with the *Book of Eibon* (or *Liber Ivoris*), Robert E. Howard the *Unaussprechlichen Kulten* of Von Junzt, Robert Bloch the *De Vermis Mysteriis* of Ludvig Prinn, and I the *Celaeno Fragments* and the Comte d'Erlette's *Cultes des Goules*. Brian Lumley later added the *G'harne Fragments* and the *Cthaat Aquadingen* and J. Ramsey Campbell the *Revelations of Glaaki*.

The stuff of the stories belonging to the Cthulhu Mythos, those of the followers in the Lovecraft tradition as well as those by Lovecraft himself, usually concern the ingenious and terrible attempts of the Great Old Ones to resume their sway over the peoples of Earth, manifesting themselves in strange, out-of-the-way places, and affording glimpses of blasphemous horrors, those dislocations of time and space Lovecraft liked so well, or, on a secondary level, some related evidence of the existence of the Great Old Ones and their terrestrial minions.

The primary stories of the Cthulhu Mythos, written by Lovecraft, include thirteen definite titles – 'The Nameless City', 'The Festival', 'The Call of Cthulhu', 'The Colour out of Space', 'The Dunwich Horror', 'The Whisperer in Darkness', 'The Dreams in the Witch-House', 'The Haunter of the Dark', 'The Shadow over Innsmouth', 'The Shadow out of Time', *At the Mountains of Madness*, *The Case of Charles Dexter Ward*, and 'The Things on the Doorstep'. In addition, Lovecraft worked into many of his 'revisions' (which were actually far more Lovecraft than the work of his clients) allusions to the Mythos; such stories, 'revised' by Lovecraft, as Zealia Brown-Reed's 'The Curse of Yig' and 'The Mound', Hazel Heald's 'The Horror in the Museum' and 'Out of the Eons', and some few others properly take secondary place in the Cthulhu Mythos, together with the tales of the writers who were contemporaries of Lovecraft or came after him – such tales as these gathered here, ranging from Smith's 'The Return of the Sorcerer' to the most recent of them, Colin Wilson's 'The Return of the Lloigor'. The unfinished novel, *The Lurker at the Threshold*, which I completed and saw published in 1945, is also part of the Mythos.

Interestingly enough, while most writers have elected to utilize the Lovecraft settings, some – notably Ramsey Campbell and Brian Lumley – have simply transplanted the myth-pattern to the English countryside and added milieus of their own to the growing body of work, in which the Lovecraft books have been supplemented by such books as my own *The Mask of Cthulhu* and *The Trail of Cthulhu*, Ramsey Campbell's *The Inhabitant of the Lake and Less Welcome Tenants*, Colin Wilson's *The Mind Parasites*, and Brian Lumley's *The Caller of the Black*.

It would be a mistake to assume that the Cthulhu Mythos was a planned development in Lovecraft's work. There is everything to show that he had no intention whatsoever of evolving the Cthulhu Mythos until that pattern made itself manifest in his work, which accounts for certain trivial inconsistencies among the stories. The roots of the Cthulhu Mythos are readily recognizable: Poe's *Narrative of A. Gordon Pym*, after reading which, compare the being which cried out *Tekali!, Tekeli-li!* in the Antarctic wastes in *At the Mountains of Madness* (though the Poe scholar, J. O. Bailey, points out that Lovecraft, like Jules Verne, misunderstood Poe's destination for Pym, adding in extenuation that 'very few people did know what Poe had in mind for the rest of his story until the relationship to *Symzonia* was uncovered and published'); 'The Yellow Sign', in *The King in Yellow*, by Robert W. Chambers, which gave us a Hastur and a Hali in mystic form, to be given additional substance later by Lovecraft's adoption of them; Ambrose Bierce's 'An Inhabitant of Carcosa', whence came Carcosa in the Mythos; and the tales of Arthur Machen, particularly *The White People*, from which came the Aklo Letters, the Dols (Lovecraft made them Dholes), the Jeelo, the voolas. Little by little, these were assimilated into the structure of the Cthulhu Mythos as Lovecraft slowly put it together.

In point of time, the mad Arab Abdul Alhazred was the first character of the Cthulhu Mythos to make his appearance; this was in the strongly Dunsanian tale, 'The Nameless City' (1921), fashioned about the 'unexplainable' couplet:

> '"That is not dead which can eternal lie,
> And with strange aeons even death may die."'

The second tale to carry on the pattern was 'The Festival' (1923), in which Lovecraft drew upon the more familiar New England background for the first time, tying up the Kingsport of his Dunsanian tales with the Mythos, bringing the mad Arab back once more, and for the first time mentioning the *Necronomicon*.

The next of the tales, chronologically, was 'The Call of Cthulhu' (1926), in which, for the first time, the pattern of the Mythos began to emerge. Lovecraft begins this tale with a significant quotation from Algernon Blackwood: 'Of such great powers or beings there may be conceivably a survival . . . a survival of a hugely remote period when . . . consciousness was manifested, perhaps, in shapes and forms long since withdrawn before the tide of advancing humanity . . . forms of which poetry and legend alone have caught a flying memory and called them gods, monsters, mythical beings of all sorts and kinds.' The concept of Cthulhu, the first of the Great Old Ones, comes out of this tale of horror rising from the sea; here also the *Necronomicon* reappears; and the mad Arab's couplet is echoed for the first time in that chanted ritual, 'Ph'nglui mglw'nafh Cthulhu R'lyeh wgah'nagl fhtagn,' which Lovecraft translates as: 'In his house at R'lyeh dead Cthulhu waits dreaming.' Ancient 'Irem, the City of Pillars,' from 'The Nameless City', reappears briefly in 'The Call of Cthulhu'. From this story Lovecraft began deliberately to construct the Cthulhu Mythos, and for the remainder of his life all his major work developed the Mythos.

The present collection, therefore, is headed by 'The Call of Cthulhu', and contains, in rough chronological order, other developments of the Mythos by friends and correspondents of Lovecraft's, as well as by more recent writers, whose tales in this anthology have not been previously published. One other Lovecraft tale has been included; that is 'The Haunter of the Dark', which was written in reply to Robert Bloch's pastiche on Lovecraft, 'The Shambler from the Stars', the publication of which was followed by Bloch's 'The Shadow from the Steeple'; these three connected tales appear here for the first time together in chronological order. The tales here collected are but representative of the host written for the Mythos by Clark Ashton Smith, Frank Belknap Long (notably his short novel, *The Horror from the Hills*, based on a dream of Lovecraft's), Robert Bloch, Henry Kuttner, Robert E. Howard, myself, and others. Stories by J. Vernon Shea, Ramsey Campbell, Brian Lumley, James Wade and Colin Wilson appear here for the first time anywhere.

The Cthulhu Mythos, it might be said in retrospect – for certainly the Mythos as an inspiration for new fiction is hardly likely to afford readers with enough that is new and sufficiently different in concept and execution to create a continuing and growing demand – represented for H. P. Lovecraft a kind of dream-world; and it ought to be pointed out that Lovecraft lived vicariously in a succession of dream-worlds, sometimes only peripherally attached to reality – that of ancient Greece, that of ancient Rome, that of eighteenth-century England (he was all his life a pronounced Anglophile), and the domain of fantasy and 'remote wonder' which led him into the world of the Cthulhu Mythos, where he indulged his predilection for the fantastic, and the strange and terrible in a series of memorable stories of such strength that even today, more than three decades after his death, they command the respect and admiration of readers throughout the world.

AUGUST DERLETH

Sauk City, Wisconsin
November 27, 1968

The Call of Cthulhu

H. P. LOVECRAFT

I. *The horror in clay*

The most merciful thing in the world, I think, is the inability
of the human mind to correlate all its contents. We live on a
placid island of ignorance in the midst of black seas of
infinity, and it was not meant that we should voyage far.
The sciences, each straining in its own direction, have
hitherto harmed us little; but some day the piecing together
of dissociated knowledge will open up such terrifying vistas
of reality, and of our frightful position therein, that we shall
either go mad from the revelation or flee from the deadly
light into the peace and safety of a new dark age.

Theosophists have guessed at the awesome grandeur of
the cosmic cycle wherein our world and human race form
transient incidents. They have hinted at strange survivals
in terms which would freeze the blood if not masked by a
bland optimism. But it is not from them that there came the
single glimpse of forbidden eons which chills me when I
think of it and maddens me when I dream of it. That glimpse,
like all dread glimpses of truth, flashed out from an accidental piecing together of separated things – in this case an old
newspaper item and the notes of a dead professor. I hope that
no one else will accomplish this piecing out; certainly, if I
live, I shall never knowingly supply a link in so hideous a
chain. I think that the professor, too, intended to keep silent
regarding the part he knew, and that he would have
destroyed his notes had not sudden death seized him.

My knowledge of the thing began in the winter of 1926–27 with the death of my grand-uncle, George Gammell Angell, Professor Emeritus of Semitic Languages in Brown University, Providence, Rhode Island. Professor Angell was widely known as an authority on ancient inscriptions, and had frequently been resorted to by the heads of prominent museums; so that his passing at the age of ninety-two may be recalled by many. Locally, interest was intensified by the obscurity of the cause of death. The professor had been stricken whilst returning from the Newport boat; falling suddenly, as witnesses said, after having been jostled by a nautical-looking Negro who had come from one of the queer dark courts on the precipitous hillside which formed a short cut from the waterfront to the deceased's home in Williams Street. Physicians were unable to find any visible disorder, but concluded after perplexed debate that some obscure lesion of the heart, induced by the brisk ascent of so steep a hill by so elderly a man, was responsible for the end. At the time I saw no reason to dissent from this dictum, but latterly I am inclined to wonder – and more than wonder.

As my grand-uncle's heir and executor, for he died a childless widower, I was expected to go over his papers with some thoroughness; and for that purpose moved his entire set of files and boxes to my quarters in Boston. Much of the material which I correlated will be later published by the American Archaeological Society, but there was one box which I found exceedingly puzzling, and which I felt much averse from showing to other eyes. It had been locked, and I did not find the key till it occurred to me to examine the personal ring which the professor carried always in his pocket. Then, indeed, I succeeded in opening it, but when I did so seemed only to be confronted by a greater and more closely locked barrier. For what could be the meaning of the queer clay bas-relief and the disjointed jottings, ramblings, and cuttings which I found? Had my uncle, in his latter years, become credulous of the most superficial impostures?

I resolved to search out the eccentric sculptor responsible for this apparent disturbance of an old man's peace of mind.

The bas-relief was a rough rectangle less than an inch thick and about five by six inches in area; obviously of modern origins. Its designs, however, were far from modern in atmosphere and suggestion; for, although the vagaries of cubism and futurism are many and wild, they do not often reproduce that cryptic regularity which lurks in prehistoric writing. And writing of some kind the bulk of these designs seemed certainly to be; though my memory, despite much familiarity with the papers and collections of my uncle, failed in any way to identify this particular species, or even hint at its remotest affiliations.

Above these apparent hieroglyphics was a figure of evidently pictorial intent, though its impressionistic execution forbade a very clear idea of its nature. It seemed to be a sort of monster, or symbol representing a monster, of a form which only a diseased fancy could conceive. If I say that my somewhat extravagant imagination yielded simultaneous pictures of an octopus, a dragon, and a human caricature, I shall not be unfaithful to the spirit of the thing. A pulpy, tentacled head surmounted a grotesque and scaly body with rudimentary wings; but it was the *general outline* of the whole which made it most shockingly frightful. Behind the figure was a vague suggestion of a Cyclopean architectural background.

The writing accompanying this oddity was, aside from a stack of press cuttings, in Professor Angell's most recent hand; and made no pretence to literary style. What seemed to be the main document was 'CTHULHU CULT' in characters painstakingly printed to avoid the erroneous reading of a word so unheard-of. This manuscript was divided into two sections, the first of which was headed '1925 – Dream and Dream Work of H. A. Wilcox, 7 Thomas St, Providence, R. I.,' and the second, 'Narrative of Inspector John R. Legrasse, 121 Bienville St, New Orleans, La., at 1908 A. A. S. Mtg. – Notes on Same, & Prof. Webb's Acct.' The other

manuscript papers were all brief notes, some of them
accounts of the queer dreams of different persons, some of
them citations from theosophical books and magazines (notably W. Scott-Elliott's *Atlantis and the Lost Lemuria*), and the
rest comments on passages in such mythological and
anthropological source-books as Frazer's *Golden Bough*, and
Miss Murray's *Witch-Cult in Western Europe*. The cuttings
largely alluded to outré mental illness and outbreaks of
group folly or mania in the spring of 1925.

The first half of the principal manuscript told a very
peculiar tale. It appears that on March 1, 1925, a thin, dark
young man of neurotic and excited aspect had called upon
Professor Angell bearing the singular clay bas-relief, which
was then exceedingly damp and fresh. His care bore the
name of Henry Anthony Wilcox, and my uncle had recognized him as the youngest son of an excellent family slightly
known to him, who had latterly been studying sculpture at
the Rhode Island School of Design and living alone at the
Fleur-de-Lys Building near that institution. Wilcox was a
precocious youth of known genius but great eccentricity, and
had from childhood excited attention through the strange
stories and odd dreams he was in the habit of relating. He
called himself 'physically hypersensitive', but the staid folk
of the ancient commercial city dismissed him as merely
'queer'. Never mingling much with his kind, he had dropped
gradually from social visibility, and was now known only to
a small group of aesthetes from other towns. Even the
Providence Art Club, anxious to preserve its conservatism,
had found him quite hopeless.

On the occasion of the visit, ran the professor's manuscript,
the sculptor abruptly asked for the benefit of his host's
archeological knowledge in identifying the hieroglyphics of
the bas-relief. He spoke in a dreamy, stilted manner which
suggested pose and alienated sympathy; and my uncle
showed some sharpness in replying, for the conspicuous
freshness of the tablet implied kinship with anything but
archaeology. Young Wilcox's rejoinder, which impressed my

uncle enough to make him recall and record it verbatim, was
of a fantastically poetic cast which must have typified his
whole conversation, and which I have since found highly
characteristic of him. He said, 'It is new, indeed, for I made
it last night in a dream of strange cities; and dreams are
older than brooding Tyre, or the contemplative Sphinx, or
garden-girdled Babylon.'

It was then that he began that rambling tale which
suddenly played upon a sleeping memory and won the
fevered interest of my uncle. There had been a slight earthquake tremor the night before, the most considerable felt in
New England for some years; and Wilcox's imagination had
been keenly affected. Upon retiring, he had had an unprece-
dented dream of Cyclopean cities of titan blocks and sky-
flung monoliths, all dripping with green ooze and sinister
with latent horror. Hieroglyphics had covered the walls and
pillars, and from some undetermined point below had come
a voice that was not a voice; a chaotic sensation which only
fancy could transmute into sound, but which he attempted to
render by the almost unpronounceable jumble of letters,
'*Cthulhu fhtagn*'.

This verbal jumble was the key to the recollection which
excited and disturbed Professor Angell. He questioned the
sculptor with scientific minuteness; and studied with almost
frantic intensity the bas-relief on which the youth had found
himself working, chilled and clad only in his nightclothes,
when waking had stolen bewilderingly over him. My uncle
blamed his old age, Wilcox afterwards said, for his slowness
in recognizing both hieroglyphics and pictorial design. Many
of his questions seemed highly out of place to his visitor,
especially those which tried to connect the latter with
strange cults or societies; and Wilcox could not understand
the repeated promises of silence which he was offered in
exchange for an admission of membership in some widespread mystical or paganly religious body. When Professor
Angell became convinced that the sculptor was indeed ignorant of any cult or system of cryptic lore he besieged his

visitor with demands for future reports of dreams. This bore regular fruit, for after the first interview the manuscript records daily calls of the young man, during which he related startling fragments of nocturnal imagery whose burden was always some terrible Cyclopean vista of dark and dripping stone, which a subterrene voice or intelligence shouting monotonously in enigmatical sense-impacts uninscribable save as gibberish. The two sounds most frequently repeated are those rendered by the letters 'Cthulhu' and 'R'lyeh'.

On March 23, the manuscript continued, Wilcox failed to appear; and inquiries at his quarters revealed that he had been stricken with an obscure sort of fever and taken to the home of his family in Waterman Street. He had cried out in the night, arousing several other artists in the building, and had manifested since then only alternations of unconsciousness and delirium. My uncle at once telephoned the family, and from that time forward kept close watch of the case, calling often at the Thayer Street office of Dr Tobey, whom he learned to be in charge. The youth's febrile mind, apparently, was dwelling on strange things; and the doctor shuddered now and then as he spoke of them. They included not only a repetition of what he had formerly dreamed, but touched wildly on a gigantic thing 'miles high' which walked or lumbered about. He at no time fully described this object but occasional frantic words, as repeated by Dr Tobey, convinced the professor that it must be identical with the nameless monstrosity he had sought to depict in his dream-sculpture. Reference to this object, the doctor added, was invariably a prelude to the young man's subsidence into lethargy. His temperature, oddly enough, was not greatly above normal; but the whole condition was otherwise such as to suggest true fever rather than mental disorder.

On April 2 at about 3 P.M. every trace of Wilcox's malady suddenly ceased. He sat upright in bed, astonished to find himself at home and completely ignorant of what had happened in dream or reality since the night of March 22. Pronounced well by his physician, he returned to his quarters in three days; but to Professor Angell he was of no further assistance. All traces of strange dreaming had vanished with his recovery, and my uncle kept no record of his night-thoughts after a week of pointless and irrelevant accounts of thoroughly usual visions.

Here the first part of the manuscript ended, but references to certain of the scattered notes gave me much material for thought – so much, in fact, that only the ingrained scepticism then forming my philosophy can account for my continued distrust of the artist. The notes in question were those descriptive of the dreams of various persons covering the same period as that in which young Wilcox had had his strange visitations. My uncle, it seems, had quickly insti-tuted a prodigiously far-flung body of inquiries among nearly all the friends whom he could question without impertinence, asking for nightly reports of their dreams, and the dates of any notable visions for some time past. The reception of his request seems to have been varied; but he must, at the very least, have received more responses than any ordinary man could have handled without a secretary. This original corre-spondence was not preserved, but his notes formed a thor-ough and really significant digest. Average people in society and business – New England's traditional 'salt of the earth' – gave an almost completely negative result, though scattered cases of uneasy but formless nocturnal impressions appear here and there, always between March 23 and April 2 – the period of young Wilcox's delirium. Scientific men were little more affected, though four cases of vague description suggest fugitive glimpses of strange landscapes, and in one case there is mentioned a dread of something abnormal.

It was from the artists and poets that the pertinent answers came, and I know that panic would have broken loose had they been able to compare notes. As it was, lacking their original letters, I half suspected the compiler of having asked leading questions, or of having edited the correspon-dence in corroboration of what he had latently resolved to see. That is why I continued to feel that Wilcox, somehow

cognizant of the old data which my uncle had possessed, had
been imposing on the veteran scientist. These responses from
esthetes told a disturbing tale. From February 28 to April 2
a large proportion of them dreamed very bizarre things, the
intensity of the dreams being immeasurably the stronger
during the period of the sculptor's delirium. Over a fourth of
those who reported anything, reported scenes and half-
sounds not unlike those which Wilcox had described; and
some of the dreamers confessed acute fear of the gigantic
nameless thing visible towards the last. One case, which the
note describes with emphasis, was very sad. The subject, a
widely known architect with leanings towards theosophy
and occultism, went violently insane on the date of young
Wilcox's seizure, and expired several months later after
incessant screamings to be saved from some escaped denizen
of hell. Had my uncle referred to these cases by name instead
of merely by number, I should have attempted some corroboration and personal investigation; but as it was, I succeeded in tracing down only a few. All of these, however,
bore out the notes in full. I have often wondered if all the
objects of the professor's questioning felt as puzzled as did
this fraction. It is well that no explanation shall ever reach
them.

The press cuttings, as I have intimated, touch on cases of
panic, mania, and eccentricity during the given period.
Professor Angell must have employed a cutting bureau, for
the number of extracts was tremendous, and the sources
scattered throughout the globe. Here was a nocturnal suicide
in London, where a lone sleeper had leapt from a window
after a shocking cry. Here likewise a rambling letter to the
editor of a paper in South America, where a fanatic deduces
a dire future from visions he has seen. A dispatch from
California describes a theosophist colony as donning white
robes en masse for some 'glorious fulfilment' which never
arrives, whilst items from India speak guardedly of serious
native unrest towards the end of March. Voodoo orgies
multiply in Haiti, and African outposts report ominous
mutterings. American officers in the Philippines find certain

tribes bothersome about this time, and New York policemen
are mobbed by hysterical Levantines on the night of March
22–23. The west of Ireland, too, is full of wild rumour and
legendry, and a fantastic painter named Ardois-Bonnot
hangs a blasphemous *Dream Landscape* in the Paris spring
salon of 1926. And so numerous are the recorded troubles in
insane asylums that only a miracle can have stopped the
medical fraternity from noting strange parallelisms and
drawing mystified conclusions. A weird bunch of cuttings, all
told; and I can at this date scarcely envisage the callous
rationalism with which I set them aside. But I was then
convinced that young Wilcox had known of the older matters
mentioned by the professor.

II. *The tale of Inspector Legrasse*

The older matters which had made the sculptor's dream and
bas-relief so significant to my uncle formed the subject of the
second half of his long manuscript. Once before, it appears,
Professor Angell had seen the hellish outlines of the nameless monstrosity, puzzled over the unknown hieroglyphics,
and heard the ominous syllables which can be rendered only
as '*Cthulhu*'; and all this is so stirring and horrible a
connection that it is small wonder he pursued young Wilcox
with queries and demands for data.

This earlier experience had come in 1908, seventeen years
before, when the American Archaeological Society held its
annual meeting in St Louis. Professor Angell, as befitted one
of his authority and attainments, had had a prominent part
in all the deliberations; and was one of the first to be
approached by the several outsiders who took advantage of
the convocation to offer questions for correct answering and
problems for expert solution.

The chief of these outsiders, and in a short time the focus
of interest for the entire meeting, was a commonplace-
looking middle-aged man who had travelled all the way from
New Orleans for certain special information unobtainable

from any local source. His name was John Raymond
Legrasse, and he was by profession an inspector of police.
With him he bore the subject of his visit, a grotesque,
repulsive, and apparently very ancient stone statuette whose
origin he was at a loss to determine.

It must not be fancied that Inspector Legrasse had the
least interest in archaeology. On the contrary, his wish for
enlightenment was prompted by purely professional considerations. The statuette, idol, fetish, or whatever it was, had
been captured some months before in the wooded swamps of
New Orleans during a raid on a supposed voodoo meeting;
and so singular and hideous were the rites connected with it,
that the police could not but realize that they had stumbled
on a dark cult totally unknown to them, and infinitely more
diabolic than even the blackest of the African voodoo circles.
Of its origin, apart from the erratic and unbelievable tales
extorted from the captured members, absolutely nothing was
to be discovered; hence the anxiety of the police for any
antiquarian lore, which might help them to place the frightful symbol, and through it track down the cult to its
fountainhead.

Inspector Legrasse was scarcely prepared for the sensation
which his offering created. One sight of the thing had been
enough to throw the assembled men of science into a state of
tense excitement, and they lost no time in crowding around
him to gaze at the diminutive figure whose utter strangeness
and air of genuinely abysmal antiquity hinted so potently at
unopened and archaic vistas. No recognized school of sculpture had animated this terrible object, yet centuries and
even thousands of years seemed recorded in its dim and
greenish surface of unplaceable stone.

The figure, which was finally passed around slowly from
man to man for close and careful study, was between seven
and eight inches in height, and of exquisitely artistic workmanship. It represented a monster of vaguely anthropoid
outline, but with an octopuslike head whose face was a mass
of feelers, a scaly, rubbery-looking body, prodigious claws on

hind and fore feet, and long, narrow wings behind. This thing, which seemed instinct with a fearsome and unnatural malignancy, was of a somewhat bloated corpulence, and squatted evilly on a rectangular block or pedestal covered with undecipherable characters. The tips of the wings touched the back edge of the block, the seat occupied the centre, whilst the long, curved claws of the doubled-up, crouching hind legs gripped the front edge and extended a quarter of the way down towards the bottom of the pedestal. The cephalopod head was bent forward, so that the ends of the facial feelers brushed the backs of the huge forepaws which clasped the croucher's elevated knees. The aspect of the whole was abnormally lifelike, and the more subtly fearful because its source was so totally unknown. Its vast, awesome, and incalculable age was unmistakable; yet not one link did it show with any known type of art belonging to civilization's youth – or indeed to any other time.

Totally separate and apart, its very material was a mystery; for the soapy, greenish-black stone with its golden or iridescent flecks and striations resembled nothing familiar to geology or mineralogy. The characters along the base were equally baffling; and no member present, despite a representation of half the world's expert learning in this field, could form the least notion of even their remotest linguistic kinship. They, like the subject and material, belonged to something horribly remote and distinct from mankind as we know it; something frightfully suggestive of old and unhallowed cycles of life in which our world and our conceptions have no part.

And yet, as the members severally shook their heads and confessed defeat at the inspector's problem, there was one man in that gathering who suspected a touch of bizarre familiarity in the monstrous shape and writing, and who presently told with some diffidence of the odd trifle he knew. This person was the late William Channing Webb, professor of anthropology in Princeton University, and an explorer of no slight note.

Professor Webb had been engaged, forty-eight years before, in a tour of Greenland and Iceland in search of some Runic inscriptions which he failed to unearth; and whilst high up on the West Greenland coast had encountered a singular tribe or cult of degenerate Eskimos whose religion, a curious form of devil-worship, chilled him with its deliberate blood-thirstiness and repulsiveness. It was a faith of which other Eskimos knew little, and which they mentioned only with shudders, saying it had come down from horribly ancient eons before ever the world was made. Besides nameless rites and human sacrifices there were certain queer hereditary rituals addressed to a supreme elder devil or *tornasuk*; and of this Professor Webb had taken a careful phonetic copy from an aged *angekok* or wizard-priest, expressing the sounds in Roman letters as best he knew how. But just now of prime significance was the fetish which this cult had cherished, and around which they danced when the aurora leapt high over the ice cliffs. It was, the professor stated, a very crude bas-relief of stone, comprising a hideous picture and some cryptic writing. And as far as he could tell, it was a rough parallel in all essential features of the bestial thing now lying before the meeting.

These data, received with suspense and astonishment by the assembled members, proved doubly exciting to Inspector Legrasse; and he began at once to ply his informant with questions. Having noted and copied an oral ritual among the swamp cult-worshippers his men had arrested, he besought the professor to remember as best he might the syllables taken down among the diabolist Eskimos. There then followed an exhaustive comparison of details, and a moment of really awed silence when both detective and scientist agreed on the virtual identity of the phrase common to two hellish rituals so many worlds of distance apart. What, in substance, both the Eskimo wizards and the Louisiana swamp-priests had chanted to their kindred idols was something very like this – the word-divisions being guessed at from traditional breaks in the phrase as chanted aloud:

'*Ph'nglui mglw'nafh Cthulhu R'lyeh wgah'nagl fhtagn.*'

Legrasse had one point in advance of Professor Webb, for several among his mongrel prisoners had repeated to him what older celebrants had told them the words meant. This text, as given, ran something like this

'In his house at R'lyeh dead Cthulhu waits dreaming.'

And now, in response to a general urgent demand, Inspector Legrasse related as fully as possible his experience with the swamp worshippers; telling a story to which I could see my uncle attached profound significance. It savoured of the wildest dreams of mythmaker and theosophist, and disclosed an astonishing degree of cosmic imagination among such half-castes and pariahs as might be least expected to possess it.

On November 1, 1907, there had come to New Orleans police a frantic summons from the swamp and lagoon country to the south. The squatters there, mostly primitive but goodnatured descendants of Lafitte's men, were in the grip of stark terror from an unknown thing which had stolen upon them in the night. It was voodoo, apparently, but voodoo of a more terrible sort than they had ever known; and some of their women and children had disappeared since the malevolent tom-tom had begun its incessant beating far within the black haunted woods where no dweller ventured. There were insane shouts and harrowing screams, soul-chilling chants, and dancing devil-flames; and, the frightened messenger added, the people could stand it no more.

So a body of twenty police, filling two carriages and an automobile, had set out in the late afternoon with the shivering squatter as a guide. At the end of the passable road they alighted, and for miles splashed on in silence through the terrible cypress woods where day never came. Ugly roots and malignant hanging nooses of Spanish moss beset them, and now and then a pile of dank stones or fragments of a rotting wall intensified by its hint of morbid habitation a depression which every malformed tree and every fungous islet combined to create. At length the squat-

ter settlement, a miserable huddle of huts, hove in sight; and
hysterical dwellers ran out to cluster around the group of
bobbing lanterns. The muffled beat of tom-toms was now
faintly audible far, far ahead; and a curdling shriek came at
infrequent intervals when the wind shifted. A reddish glare,
too, seemed to filter through the pale undergrowth beyond
endless avenues of forest night. Reluctant even to be left
alone again, each one of the cowed squatters refused point-
blank to advance another inch towards the scene of unholy
worship, so Inspector Legrasse and his nineteen colleagues
plunged on unguided into black arcades of horror that none
of them had ever trod before.

The region now entered by the police was one of tradition-
ally evil repute, substantially unknown and untraversed by
white men. There were legends of a hidden lake unglimpsed
by mortal sight, in which dwelt a huge, formless white
polypous thing with luminous eyes; and squatters whispered
that bat-winged devils flew up out of caverns in inner earth
to worship it at midnight. They said it had been there before
D'Iberville, before La Salle, before the Indians, and before
even the wholesome beasts and birds of the woods. It was
nightmare itself, and to see it was to die. But it made men
dream, and so they knew enough to keep away. The present
voodoo orgy, was, indeed, on the merest fringe of this
abhorred area, but that location was bad enough; hence
perhaps the very place of the worship had terrified the
squatters more than the shocking sounds and incidents.

Only poetry or madness could do justice to the noises heard
by Legrasse's men as they ploughed on through the black
morass towards the red glare and the muffled tom-toms.
There are vocal qualities peculiar to men, and vocal qualities
peculiar to beasts; and it is terrible to hear the one when the
source should yield the other. Animal fury and orgiastic
licence here whipped themselves to demoniac heights by
howls and squawking ecstasies that tore and reverberated
through those nighted woods like pestilential tempests from
the gulfs of hell. Now and then the less organized ululations

would cease, and from what seemed a well-drilled chorus of hoarse voices would rise in sing-song chant that hideous phrase or ritual.

'*Ph'nglui mglw'nafh Cthulhu R'lyeh wgah'nagl fhtagn.*'

Then the men, having reached a spot where the trees were thinner, came suddenly in sight of the spectacle itself. Four of them reeled, one fainted, and two were shaken into frantic cry which the mad cacophony of the orgy fortunately deadened. Legrasse dashed swamp water on the face of the fainting man, and all stood trembling and nearly hypnotized with horror.

In a natural glade of the swamp stood a grassy island of perhaps an acre's extent, clear of trees and tolerably dry. On this now leapt and twisted a more indescribable horde of human abnormality than any but a Sime or an Angarola could paint. Void of clothing, this hybrid spawn were braying, bellowing, and writhing about a monstrous ringshaped bonfire; in the centre of which, revealed by occasional rifts in the curtain of flame, stood a great granite monolith some eight feet in height; on top of which, incongruous in its diminutiveness, rested the noxious carven statuette. From a wide circle of ten scaffolds set up at regular intervals with the flame-girt monolith as a centre hung, head downwards, the oddly marred bodies of the helpless squatters who had disappeared. It was inside this circle that the ring of worshippers jumped and roared, the general direction of the mass motion being from left to right in endless bacchanale between the ring of bodies and the ring of fire.

It may have been only imagination and it may have been only echoes which induced one of the men, an excitable Spaniard, to fancy he heard antiphonal responses to the ritual from some far and unillumined spot deeper within the wood of ancient legendry and horror. This man, Joseph D. Galvez, I later met and questioned; and he proved distractingly imaginative. He indeed went so far as to hint the faint beating of great wings, and of a glimpse of shining eyes and mountainous white bulk beyond the remotest trees – but I suppose he had been hearing too much native superstition.

Actually, the horrified pause of the men was of comparatively brief duration. Duty came first; and although there must have been nearly a hundred mongrel celebrants in the throng, the police relied on their firearms and plunged determinedly into the nauseous rout. For five minutes the resultant din and chaos were beyond description. Wild blows were struck, shots were fired, and escapes were made; but in the end Legrasse was able to count some forty-seven sullen prisoners, whom he forced to dress in haste and fall into line between two rows of policemen. Five of the worshippers lay dead, and two severely wounded ones were carried away on improvised stretchers by their fellow-prisoners. The image on the monolith, of course, was carefully removed and carried back by Legrasse.

Examined at headquarters after a trip of intense strain and weariness, the prisoners all proved to be men of a very low, mixed-blooded, and mentally aberrant type. Most were seamen, and a sprinkling of Negroes and mulattos, largely West Indians or Brava Portuguese from the Cape Verde Islands, gave a colouring of voodooism to the heterogeneous cult. But before many questions were asked, it became manifest that something far deeper and older than Negro fetishism was involved. Degraded and ignorant as they were, the creatures held with surprising consistency to the central idea of their loathsome faith.

They worshipped, so they said, the Great Old Ones who lived ages before there were any men, and who came to the young world out of the sky. These Old Ones were gone now, inside the earth and under the sea; but their dead bodies had told their secrets in dreams to the first man, who formed a cult which had never died. This was that cult, and the prisoners said it had always existed and always would exist, hidden in distant wastes and dark places all over the world until the time when the great priest Cthulhu, from his dark house in the mighty city of R'lyeh under the waters, should rise and bring the earth again beneath his sway. Some day he would call, when the stars were ready, and the secret cult would always be waiting to liberate him.

Meanwhile no more must be told. There was a secret which even torture could not extract. Mankind was not absolutely alone among the conscious things of earth, for shapes came out of the dark to visit the faithful few. But these were not the Great Old Ones. No man had ever seen the Old Ones. The carven idol was great Cthulhu, but none might say whether or not the others were precisely like him. No one could read the old writing now, but things were told by word of mouth. The chanted ritual was not the secret – that was never spoken aloud, only whispered. The chant meant only this: 'In his house at R'lyeh dead Cthulhu waits dreaming.'

Only two of the prisoners were found sane enough to be hanged, and the rest were committed to various institutions. All denied a part in the ritual murders, and averred that the killing had been done by Black-winged Ones which had come to them from their immemorial meeting-place in the haunted wood. But of those mysterious allies no coherent account could ever be gained. What the police did extract came mainly from an immensely aged mestizo named Castro, who claimed to have sailed to strange ports and talked with undying leaders of the cult in the mountains of China.

Old Castro remembered bits of hideous legend that paled the speculations of theosophists and made man and the world seem recent and transient indeed. There had been eons when other Things ruled on the earth, and They had had great cities. Remains of Them, he said the deathless Chinamen had told him, were still to be found as Cyclopean stones on islands in the Pacific. They all died vast epochs of time before man came, but there were arts which could revive Them when the stars had come round again to the right positions in the cycle of eternity. They had, indeed, come themselves from the stars, and brought Their images with Them.

These Great Old Ones, Castro continued, were not composed altogether of flesh and blood. They had shape – for did not this star-fashioned image prove it? – but that shape was not made of matter. When the stars were right, They could plunge from world to world through the sky; but when the stars were wrong, They could not live. But although They no longer lived, They would never really die. They all lay in stone houses in Their great city of R'lyeh, preserved by the spells of mighty Cthulhu for a glorious resurrection when the stars and the earth might once more by ready for Them. But at that time some force from outside must serve to liberate Their bodies. The spells that preserved them intact likewise prevented Them from making an initial move, and They could only lie awake in the dark and think whilst uncounted millions of years rolled by. They knew all that was occurring in the universe, for Their mode of speech was transmitted thought. Even now They talked in Their tombs. When, after infinities of chaos, the first men came, the Great Old Ones spoke to the sensitive among them by moulding their dreams; for only thus could Their language reach the fleshy minds of mammals.

Then, whispered Castro, those first men formed the cult around small idols which the Great Ones showed them; idols brought in dim eras from dark stars. That cult would never die till the stars came right again, and the secret priests would take great Cthulhu from His tomb to revive His subjects and resume His rule of earth. The time would be easy to know, for then mankind would have become as the Great Old Ones; free and wild and beyond good and evil, with laws and morals thrown aside and all men shouting and killing and revelling in joy. Then the liberated Old Ones would teach them new ways to shout and kill and revel and enjoy themselves, and all the earth would flame with a holocaust of ecstasy and freedom. Meanwhile the cult, by appropriate rites, must keep alive the memory of those ancient ways and shadow forth the prophecy of their return.

In the elder time chosen men had talked with the entombed Old Ones in dreams, but then something had happened. The great stone city R'lyeh, with its monoliths and sepulchres, had sunk beneath the waves; and the deep

waters, full of the one primal mystery through which not
even thought can pass, had cut off the spectral intercourse.
But memory never died, and high priests said that the city
would rise again when the stars were right. Then came out
of the earth the black spirits of earth, mouldy and shadowy,
and full of dim rumours picked up in caverns beneath
forgotten sea-bottoms. But of them old Castro dared not
speak much. He cut himself off hurriedly, and no amount of
persuasion or subtlety could elicit more in this direction. The
size of the Old Ones, too, he curiously declined to mention.
Of the cult, he said that he thought the centre lay amid the
pathless deserts of Arabia, where Irem, the City of Pillars,
dreams hidden and untouched. It was not allied to the
European witch-cult, and was virtually unknown beyond its
members. No book had ever really hinted of it, though the
deathless Chinamen said that there were double meanings
in the *Necronomicon* of the mad Arab Abdul Alhazred which
the initiated might read as they chose, especially the much-
discussed couplet

> That is not dead which can eternal lie,
> And with strange eons even death may die.

Legrasse, deeply impressed and not a little bewildered,
had inquired in vain concerning the historic affiliation of the
cult. Castro, apparently, had told the truth when he said
that it was wholly secret. The authorities at Tulane University could shed no light upon either cult or image, and now
the detective had come to the highest authorities in the
country and met with no more than the Greenland tale of
Professor Webb.

The feverish interest aroused at the meeting by Legrasse's
tale, corroborated as it was by the statuette, is echoed in the
subsequent correspondence of those who attended; although
scant mention occurs in the formal publication of the society.
Caution is the first care of those accustomed to face occasional charlatanry and imposture. Legrasse for some time

lent the image to Professor Webb, but at the latter's death it was returned to him and remains in his possession, where I viewed it not long ago. It is truly a terrible thing, and unmistakably akin to the dream-sculpture of young Wilcox.

That my uncle was excited by the tale of the sculptor I did not wonder, for what thoughts must arise upon hearing, after a knowledge of what Legrasse had learned of the cult, of a sensitive young man who had *dreamed* not only the figure and exact hieroglyphics of the swamp-found image and the Greenland devil tablet, but had come *in his dreams* upon at least three of the precise words of the formula uttered alike by Eskimo diabolists and mongrel Louisianans? Professor Angell's instant start on an investigation of the utmost thoroughness was eminently natural; though privately I suspected young Wilcox of having heard of the cult in some indirect way, and of having invented a series of dreams to heighten and continue the mystery at my uncle's expense. The dream-narratives and cuttings collected by the professor were, of course, strong corroboration; but the rationalism of my mind and the extravagance of the whole subject led me to adopt what I thought the most sensible conclusions. So, after thoroughly studying the manuscript again and correlating the theosophical and anthropological notes with the cult narrative of Legrasse, I made a trip to Providence to see the sculptor and give him the rebuke I thought proper for so boldly imposing upon a learned and aged man.

Wilcox still lived alone in the Fleur-de-Lys Building in Thomas Street, a hideous Victorian imitation of seventeenth-century Breton architecture which flaunts its stuccoed front amidst the lovely Colonial houses on the ancient hill, and under the very shadow of the finest Georgian steeple in America. I found him at work in his rooms, and at once conceded from the specimens scattered about that his genius is indeed profound and authentic. He will, I believe, be heard from sometime as one of the great decadents; for he has crystallized in clay and will one day mirror in marble those nightmares and fantasies which Arthur Machen evokes in prose, and Clark Ashton Smith makes visible in verse and in painting.

Dark, frail, and somewhat unkempt in aspect, he turned languidly at my knock and asked me my business without rising. When I told him who I was, he displayed some interest; for my uncle had excited his curiosity in probing his strange dreams, yet had never explained the reason for the study. I did not enlarge his knowledge in this regard, but sought with some subtlety to draw him out.

In a short time I became convinced of his absolute sincerity for he spoke of the dreams in a manner none could mistake. They and their subconscious residuum had influenced his art profoundly, and he showed me a morbid statue whose contours almost made me shake with the potency of its black suggestion. He could not recall having seen the original of this thing except in his own dream bas-relief, but the outlines had formed themselves insensibly under his hands. It was, no doubt, the giant shape he had raved of in delirium. That he really knew nothing of the hidden cult, save from what my uncle's relentless catechism had let fall, he soon made clear; and again I strove to think of some way in which he could possibly have received the weird impressions.

He talked of his dreams in a strangely poetic fashion; making me see with terrible vividness the damp Cyclopean city of slimy green stone – whose *geometry*, he oddly said, was *all wrong* – and hear with frightened expectancy the ceaseless, half-mental calling from underground 'Cthulhu fhtagn', 'Cthulhu fhtagn'.

These words had formed part of that dread ritual which told of dead Cthulhu's dream-vigil in his stone vault at R'lyeh, and I felt deeply moved despite my rational beliefs. Wilcox, I was sure, had heard of the cult in some casual way, and had soon forgotten it amidst the mass of his equally weird reading and imagining. Later, by virtue of its sheer impressiveness, it had found subconscious expression in dreams, in the bas-relief, and in the terrible statue I now beheld; so that his imposture upon my uncle had been a very innocent one. The youth was of a type, at once slightly affected and slightly ill-mannered, which I could never like; but I was willing enough now to admit both his genius and his honesty. I took leave of him amicably, and wished him all the success his talent promised.

The matter of the cult still remained to fascinate me, and at times I had visions of personal fame from researches into its origin and connections. I visited New Orleans, talked with Legrasse and others of that old-time raiding-party, saw the frightful image, and even questioned such of the mongrel prisoners as still survived. Old Castro, unfortunately, had been dead for some years. What I now heard so graphically at first hand, though it was really no more than detailed confirmation of what my uncle had written, excited me afresh; for I felt sure that I was on the track of a very real, very secret, and very ancient religion whose discovery would make me an anthropologist of note. My attitude was still one of absolute materialism *as I wish it still were*, and I discounted with a most inexplicable perversity the coincidence of the dream notes and odd cuttings collected by Professor Angell.

One thing which I began to suspect, and which I now fear I *know*, is that my uncle's death was far from natural. He fell on a narrow hill street leading up from an ancient waterfront swarming with foreign mongrels, after a careless push from a Negro sailor. I did not forget the mixed blood and marine pursuits of the cult-members in Louisiana, and would not be surprised to learn of secret methods and poison needles as ruthless and as anciently known as the cryptic rites and beliefs. Legrasse and his men, it is true, have been let alone; but in Norway a certain seaman who saw things is dead. Might not the deeper inquiries of my uncle after encountering the sculptor's data have come to sinister ears? I think Professor Angell died because he knew too much, or because he was likely to learn too much. Whether I shall go as he did remains to be seen, for I have learned much now.

III. *The madness from the sea*

If heaven ever wishes to grant me a boon, it will be a total
effacing of the results of a mere chance which fixed my eye
on a certain stray piece of shelf-paper. It was nothing on
which I would naturally have stumbled in the course of my
daily round, for it was an old number of an Australian
journal, *Sydney Bulletin*, for April 18, 1925. It had escaped
even the cutting bureau which had at the time of its issuance
been avidly collecting material for my uncle's research.

I had largely given over my inquiries into what Professor
Angell called the 'Cthulhu Cult', and was visiting a learned
friend in Paterson, New Jersey; the curator of a local
museum and a mineralogist of note. Examining one day the
reserve specimens roughly set on the storage shelves in a
rear room of the museum, my eye was caught by an odd
picture in one of the old papers spread beneath the stones. It
was the *Sydney Bulletin* I have mentioned, for my friend has
wide affiliations in all conceivable foreign parts; and the
picture was a half-tone cut of a hideous stone image almost
identical with that which Legrasse had found in the swamp.

Eagerly clearing the sheet of its precious contents, I
scanned the item in detail; and was disappointed to find it of
only moderate length. What it suggested, however, was of
portentous significance to my flagging quest; and I carefully
tore it out for immediate action. It read as follows:

MYSTERY DERELICT FOUND AT SEA
Vigilant Arrives with Helpless Armed New Zealand Yacht in
Tow. One Survivor and Dead Man Found Aboard. Tale of
Desperate Battle and Deaths at Sea. Rescued Seaman Refuses
Particulars of Strange Experience. Odd Idol Found in His Pos-
session. Inquiry to Follow.

The Morrison Co.'s freighter *Vigilant*, bound from Valparaiso,
arrived this morning at its wharf in Darling Harbour, having in
tow the battled and disabled but heavily armed steam yacht
Alert of Dunedin, N.Z., which was sighted April 12th in S.
Latitude 34°21', W. Longitude 152°17', with one living and one
dead man aboard.

The *Vigilant* left Valparaiso March 25th, and on April 2nd was driven considerably south of her course by exceptionally heavy storms and monster waves. On April 12th the derelict was sighted; and though apparently deserted, was found upon boarding to contain one survivor in a half-delirious condition and one man who had evidently been dead for more than a week.

The living man was clutching a horrible stone idol of unknown origin, about a foot in height, regarding whose nature authorities at Sydney University, the Royal Society, and the Museum in College Street all profess complete bafflement, and which the survivor says he found in the cabin of the yacht, in a small carved shrine of common pattern.

This man, after recovering his senses, told an exceedingly strange story of piracy and slaughter. He is Gustaf Johansen, a Norwegian of some intelligence, and had been second mate of the two-masted schooner *Emma* of Auckland, which sailed for Callao February 20th, with a complement of eleven men.

The *Emma*, he says, was delayed and thrown widely south of her course by the great storm of March 1st, and on March 22nd, in S. Latitude 49°51', W. Longitude 128°34', encountered the *Alert*, manned by a queer and evil-looking crew of Kanakas and half-castes. Being ordered peremptorily to turn back, Capt. Collins refused; whereupon the strange crew began to fire savagely and without warning upon the schooner with a peculiarly heavy battery of brass cannon forming part of the yacht's equipment.

The *Emma*'s men showed fight, says the survivor, and though the schooner began to sink from shots beneath the waterline they managed to heave alongside their enemy and board her, grappling with the savage crew on the yacht's deck, and being forced to kill them all, the number being slightly superior, because of their particularly abhorrent and desperate though rather clumsy mode of fighting.

Three of the *Emma*'s men, including Capt. Collins and First Mate Green, were killed; and the remaining eight under Second Mate Johansen proceeded to navigate the captured yacht, going ahead in their original direction to see if any reason for their ordering back had existed.

The next day, it appears, they raised and landed on a small island, although none is known to exist in that part of the ocean; and six of the men somehow died ashore, though Johansen is queerly reticent about this part of his story and speaks only of their falling into a rock chasm.

Later, it seems, he and one companion boarded the yacht and tried to manage her, but were beaten about by the storm of April 2nd.

From that time till his rescue on the 12th, the man remembers little, and he does not even recall when William Briden, his companion, died. Briden's death reveals no apparent cause, and was probably due to excitement or exposure.

Cable advices from Dunedin report that the *Alert* was well known there as an island trader, and bore an evil reputation along the waterfront. It was owned by a curious group of half-castes whose frequent meetings and night trips to the woods attracted no little curiosity; and it had set sail in great haste just after the storm and earth tremors of March 1st.

Our Auckland correspondent gives the *Emma* and her crew an excellent reputation, and Johansen is described as a sober and worthy man.

The admiralty will institute an inquiry on the whole matter beginning tomorrow, at which every effort will be made to induce Johansen to speak more freely than he has done hitherto.

This was all, together with the picture of the hellish image; but what a train of ideas it started in my mind! Here were new treasuries of data on the Cthulhu Cult, and evidence that it had strange interests at sea as well as on land. What motive prompted the hybrid crew to order back the *Emma* as they sailed about with their hideous idol? What was the unknown island on which six of the *Emma*'s crew had died, and about which the mate Johansen was so secretive? What had the vice-admiralty's investigation brought out, and what was known of the noxious cult in Dunedin? And most marvellous of all, what deep and more than natural linkage of dates was this which gave a malign and now undeniable significance to the various turns of event so carefully noted by my uncle?

March 1st – our February 28th according to the International Date Line – the earthquake and storm had come. From Dunedin the *Alert* and her noisome crew had darted eagerly forth as if imperiously summoned, and on the other side of the earth poets and artists had begun to dream of a strange, dark Cyclopean city whilst a young sculptor had

moulded in his sleep the form of the dreaded Cthulhu. March
23rd the crew of the *Emma* landed on an unknown island
and left six men dead; and on that date the dreams of
sensitive men assumed a heightened vividness and darkened
with dread of a giant monster's malign pursuit, whilst an
architect had gone mad and a sculptor had lapsed suddenly
into delirium! And what of this storm of April 2nd – the date
on which all dreams of the dank city ceased, and Wilcox
emerged unharmed from the bondage of strange fever? What
of all this – and of those hints of old Castro about the sunken,
starborn Old Ones and their coming reign; their faithful cult
and their mastery of dreams? Was I tottering on the brink of
cosmic horrors beyond man's power to bear? If so, they must
be horrors of the mind alone, for in some way the second of
April had put a stop to whatever monstrous menace had
begun its siege of mankind's soul.

. That evening, after a day of hurried cabling and arranging,
I bade my host adieu and took a train for San Francisco. In
less than a month I was in Dunedin: where, however, I found
that little was known of the strange cult-members who had
lingered in the old sea taverns. Waterfront scum was far too
common for special mention; though there was vague talk
about one inland trip these mongrels had made, during
which faint drumming and red flame were noted on the
distant hills.

In Auckland I learned that Johansen had returned *with
yellow hair turned white* after a perfunctory and inconclusive
questioning at Sydney, and had thereafter sold his cottage in
West Street and sailed with his wife to his old home in Oslo.
Of his stirring experience he would tell his friends no more
than he had told the admiralty officials, and all they could
do was to give me his Oslo address.

After that I went to Sydney and talked profitlessly with
seamen and members of the vice-admiralty court. I saw the
Alert, now sold and in commercial use, at Circular Quay in
Sydney Cove, but gained nothing from its non-committal
bulk. The crouching image with its cuttlefish head, dragon

body, scaly wings, and hieroglyphed pedestal, was preserved in the Museum at Hyde Park; and I studied it long and well, finding it a thing of balefully exquisite workmanship, and with the same utter mystery, terrible antiquity, and unearthly strangeness of material which I had noted in Legrasse's smaller specimen. Geologists, the curator told me, had found it a monstrous puzzle; for they vowed that the world held no rock like it. Then I thought with a shudder of what old Castro had told Legrasse about the primal Great Ones: 'They had come from the stars, and had brought Their images with Them.'

Shaken with such a mental revolution as I had never before known, I now resolved to visit Mate Johansen in Oslo. Sailing for London, I re-embarked at once for the Norwegian capital; and one autumn day landed at the trim wharves in the shadow of the Egeberg.

Johansen's address, I discovered, lay in the Old Town of King Harold Haardrada, which kept alive the name of Oslo during all the centuries that the greater city masqueraded as 'Christiania'. I made the brief trip by taxi-cab, and knocked with palpitant heart at the door of a neat and ancient building with plastered front. A sad-faced woman in black answered my summons, and I was stung with disappointment when she told me in halting English that Gustaf Johansen was no more.

He had not long survived his return, said his wife, for the doings at sea in 1925 had broken him. He had told her no more than he had told the public, but had left a long manuscript – of 'technical matters' as he said – written in English, evidently in order to safeguard her from the peril of casual perusal. During a walk through a narrow lane near the Gothenberg dock, a bundle of papers falling from an attic window had knocked him down. Two Lascar sailors at once helped him to his feet, but before the ambulance could reach him he was dead. Physicians found no adequate cause for the end, and laid it to heart trouble and a weakened constitution.

I now felt gnawing at my vitals that dark terror which will

never leave me till I, too, am at rest; 'accidentally' or
otherwise. Persuading the widow that my connection with
her husband's 'technical matters' was sufficient to entitle me
to his manuscript, I bore the document away and began to
read it on the London boat.

It was a simple, rambling thing – a naïve sailor's effort at
a post-facto diary – and strove to recall day by day that last
awful voyage. I can not attempt to transcribe it verbatim in
all its cloudiness and redundance, but I will tell its gist
enough to show why the sound of the water against the
vessel's sides became so unendurable to me that I stopped
my ears with cotton.

Johansen, thank God, did not know quite all, even though
he saw the city and the Thing, but I shall never sleep calmly
again when I think of the horrors that lurk ceaselessly
behind life in time and in space, and of those unhallowed
blasphemies from elder stars which dream beneath the sea,
known and favoured by a nightmare cult ready and eager to
loose them on the world whenever another earthquake shall
heave their monstrous stone city again to the sun and air.

Johansen's voyage had begun just as he told it to the vice-
admiralty. The *Emma*, in ballast, had cleared Auckland on
February 20th, and had felt the full force of that earthquake-
born tempest which must have heaved up from the sea-
bottom the horrors that filled men's dreams. Once more
under control, the ship was making good progress when held
up by the *Alert* on March 22nd, and I could feel the mate's
regret as he wrote of her bombardment and sinking. Of the
swarthy cult-fiends on the *Alert* he speaks with significant
horror. There was some peculiarly abominable quality about
them which made their destruction seem almost a duty, and
Johansen shows ingenuous wonder at the charge of ruthless-
ness brought against his party during the proceedings of the
court of inquiry. Then, driven ahead by curiosity in their
captured yacht under Johansen's command, the men sight a
great stone pillar sticking out of the sea, and in S. Latitude
47°9′, W. Longitude 126°43′, come upon a coastline of min-

gled mud, ooze, and weedy Cyclopean masonry which can be nothing less than the tangible substance of earth's supreme terror – the nightmare corpse-city of R'lyeh, that was built in measureless eons behind history by the vast, loathsome shapes that seeped down from the dark stars. There lay great Cthulhu and his hordes, hidden in green slimy vaults and sending out at last, after cycles incalculable, the thoughts that spread fear to the dreams of the sensitive and called imperiously to the faithful to come on a pilgrimage of liberation and restoration. All this Johansen did not suspect, but God knows he soon saw enough!

I suppose that only a single mountain-top, the hideous monolith-crowned citadel whereon great Cthulhu was buried, actually emerged from the waters. When I think of the *extent* of all that may be brooding down there I almost wish to kill myself forthwith. Johansen and his men were awed by the cosmic majesty of this dripping Babylon of elder demons, and must have guessed without guidance that it was nothing of this or of any sane planet. Awe at the unbelievable size of the greenish stone blocks, at the dizzying height of the great carven monolith, and at the stupefying identity of the colossal statues and bas-reliefs with the queer image found in the shrine on the *Alert*, is poignantly visible in every line of the mate's frightened description.

Without knowing what futurism is like, Johansen achieved something very close to it when he spoke of the city; for instead of describing any definite structure or building, he dwells only on the broad impressions of vast angles and stone surfaces – surfaces too great to belong to any thing right or proper for this earth, and impious with horrible images and hieroglyphs. I mention his talk about *angles* because it suggests something Wilcox had told me of his awful dreams. He had said that the *geometry* of the dream-place he saw was abnormal, non-Euclidean, and loathsomely redolent of spheres and dimensions apart from ours. Now an unlettered seaman felt the same thing whilst gazing at the terrible reality.

Johansen and his men landed at a sloping mud-bank on this monstrous acropolis, and clambered slipperily up over titan oozy blocks which could have been no mortal staircase. The very sun of heaven seemed distorted when viewed through the polarizing miasma welling out from this sea-soaked perversion, and twisted menace and suspense lurked leeringly in those crazily elusive angles of carven rock where a second glance showed concavity after the first showed convexity.

Something very like fright had come over all the explorers before anything more definite than rock and ooze and weed was seen. Each would have fled had he not feared the scorn of the others, and it was only half-heartedly that they searched – vainly, as it proved – for some portable souvenir to bear away.

It was Rodriguez the Portuguese who climbed up the foot of the monolith and shouted of what he had found. The rest followed him, and looked curiously at the immense carved door with the now familiar squid-dragon bas-relief. It was, Johansen said, like a great barn-door; and they all felt that it was a door because of the ornate lintel, threshold, and jambs around it, though they could not decide whether it lay flat like a trap door or slantwise like an outside cellar-door. As Wilcox would have said, the geometry of the place was all wrong. One could not be sure that the sea and the ground were horizontal, hence the relative position of everything else seemed fantasmally variable.

Briden pushed at the stone in several places without result. Then Donovan felt over it delicately around the edge, pressing each point separately as he went. He climbed interminably along the grotesque stone moulding – that is, one would call it climbing if the thing was not after all horizontal – and the men wondered how any door in the universe could be so vast. Then, very softly and slowly, the acre-great panel began to give inward at the top; and they saw that it was balanced.

Donovan slid or somehow propelled himself down or along

the jamb and rejoined his fellows, and everyone watched the queer recession of the monstrously carven portal. In this fantasy of prismatic distortion it moved anomalously in a diagonal way, so that all the rules of matter and perspective seemed upset.

The aperture was black with a darkness almost material. That tenebrousness was indeed a *positive quality*; for it obscured such parts of the inner walls as ought to have been revealed, and actually burst forth like smoke from its eon-long imprisonment, visibly darkening the sun as it slunk away into the shrunken and gibbous sky on flapping membranous wings. The odour arising from the newly opened depths was intolerable, and at length the quick-eared Hawkins thought he heard a nasty, slopping sound down there. Everyone listened, and everyone was listening still when It lumbered slobberingly into sight and gropingly squeezed Its gelatinous green immensity through the black doorway into the tainted outside air of that poison city of madness.

Poor Johansen's handwriting almost gave out when he wrote of this. Of the six men who never reached the ship, he thinks two perished of pure fright in that accursed instant. The Thing can not be described – there is no language for such abysms of shrieking and immemorial lunacy, such eldritch contradictions of all matter, force, and cosmic order. A mountain walked or stumbled. God! What wonder that across the earth a great architect went mad, and poor Wilcox raved with fever in that telepathic instant? The Thing of the idols, the green, sticky spawn of the stars, had awaked to claim his own. The stars were right again, and what an age-old cult had failed to do by design, a band of innocent sailors had done by accident. After vigintillions of years great Cthulhu was loose again, and ravening for delight.

Three men were swept up by the flabby claws before anybody turned. God rest them, if there be any rest in the universe. They were Donovan, Guerrera, and Angstrom. Parker slipped as the other three were plunging frenziedly

over endless vistas of green-crusted rock to the boat, and
Johansen swears he was swallowed up by an angle of
masonry which shouldn't have been there; an angle which
was acute, but behaved as if it were obtuse. So only Briden
and Johansen reached the boat, and pulled desperately for
the *Alert* as the mountainous monstrosity flopped down the
slimy stones and hesitated, floundering at the edge of the
water.

Steam had not been suffered to go down entirely, despite
the departure of all hands for the shore; and it was the work
of only a few moments of feverish rushing up and down
between wheels and engines to get the *Alert* under way.
Slowly, amidst the distorted horrors of that indescribable
scene, she began to churn the lethal waters; whilst on the
masonry of that charnel shore that was not of earth the titan
Thing from the stars slavered and gibbered like Polypheme
cursing the fleeing ship of Odysseus. Then, bolder than the
storied Cyclops, great Cthulhu slid greasily into the water
and began to pursue with vast wave-raising strokes of cosmic
potency. Briden looked back and went mad, laughing at
intervals till death found him one night in the cabin whilst
Johansen was wandering deliriously.

But Johansen had not given out yet. Knowing that the
Thing could surely overtake the *Alert* until steam was fully
up, he resolved on a desperate chance; and setting the engine
for full speed, ran lightning-like on deck and reversed the
wheel. There was a mighty eddying and foaming in the
noisome brine, and as the steam mounted higher and higher
the brave Norwegian drove his vessel head on against the
pursuing jelly which rose above the unclean froth like the
stern of a demon galleon. The awful squid-head with writhing feelers came nearly up to the bowsprit of the sturdy
yacht, but Johansen drove on relentlessly.

There was bursting as of an exploding bladder, a slushy
nastiness as of a cloven sunfish, a stench as of a thousand
opened graves, and a sound that the chronicler would not
put on paper. For an instant the ship was befouled by an

acrid and blinding green cloud, and then there was only a venomous seething astern; where – God in heaven! – the scattered plasticity of that nameless sky-spawn was nebulously *recombining* in its hateful original form, whilst its distance widened every second as the *Alert* gained impetus from its mounting steam.

That was all. After that Johansen only brooded over the idol in the cabin and attended to a few matters of food for himself and the laughing maniac by his side. He did not try to navigate after the first bold flight; for the reaction had taken something out of his soul. Then came the storm of April 2nd, and a gathering of the clouds about his consciousness. There is a sense of spectral whirling through liquid gulfs of infinity, of dizzying rides through reeling universes on a comet's tail, and of hysterical plunges from the pit to the moon and from the moon back again to the pit, all livened by a cachinnating chorus of the distorted, hilarious elder gods and the green bat-winged mocking imps of Tartarus.

Out of that dream came rescue – the *Vigilant*, the vice-admiralty court, the streets of Dunedin, and the long voyage back home to the old house by the Egeberg. He could not tell – they would think him mad. He would write of what he knew before death came, but his wife must not guess. Death would be a boon if only it could blot out the memories.

That was the document I read, and now I have placed it in the tin box beside the bas-relief and the papers of Professor Angell. With it shall go this record of mine – this test of my own sanity, wherein is pieced together that which I hope may never be pieced together again. I have looked upon all that the universe has to hold of horror, and even the skies of spring and the flowers of summer must ever afterwards be poison to me. But I do not think my life will be long. As my uncle went, as poor Johansen went, so I shall go. I know too much, and the cult still lives.

Cthulhu still lives, too, I suppose, again in that chasm of stone which has shielded him since the sun was young. His

accursed city is sunken once more, for the *Vigilant* sailed
over the spot after the April storm; but his ministers on
earth still bellow and prance and slay around idol-capped
monoliths in lonely places. He must have been trapped by
the sinking whilst within his black abyss, or else the world
would by now be screaming with fright and frenzy. Who
knows the end? What has risen may sink, and what has sunk
may rise. Loathsomeness waits and dreams in the deep, and
decay spreads over the tottering cities of men. A time will
come – but I must not and can not think! Let me pray that,
if I do not survive this manuscript, my executors may put
caution before audacity and see that it meets no other eye.

The Return of the Sorcerer

CLARK ASHTON SMITH

I had been out of work for several months, and my savings were perilously near the vanishing point. Therefore I was naturally elated when I received from John Carnby a favour-able answer inviting me to present my qualifications in person. Carnby had advertised for a secretary, stipulating that all applicants must offer a preliminary statement of their capacities by letter, and I had written in response to the advertisement.

Carnby, no doubt, was a scholarly recluse who felt averse to contact with a long waiting-list of strangers; and he had chosen this manner of weeding out beforehand many, if not all, of those who were ineligible. He had specified his require-ments fully and succinctly, and these were of such nature as to bar even the average well-educated person. A knowledge of Arabic was necessary, among other things; and luckily I had acquired a certain degree of scholarship in this unusual tongue.

I found the address, of whose location I had formed only a vague idea, at the end of a hilltop avenue in the suburbs of Oakland. It was a large, two-storey house, over-shaded by ancient oaks and dark with a mantling of unchecked ivy, among hedges of unpruned privet and shrubbery that had gone wild for many years. It was separated from its neigh-bours by a vacant, weed-grown lot on one side and a tangle of vines and trees on the other, surrounding the black ruins of a burnt mansion.

Even apart from its air of long neglect, there was some-

thing drear and dismal about the place – something that
inhered in the ivy-blurred outlines of the house, in the
furtive, shadowy windows, and the very forms of the misshapen oaks and oddly sprawling shrubbery. Somehow, my
elation became a trifle less exuberant, as I entered the
grounds and followed an unswept path to the front door.

When I found myself in the presence of John Carnby, my
jubilation was still somewhat further diminished; though I
could not have given a tangible reason for the premonitory
chill, the dull, sombre feeling of alarm that I experienced,
and the leaden sinking of my spirits. Perhaps it was the dark
library in which he received me as much as the man himself
– a room whose musty shadows could never have been wholly
dissipated by sun or lamplight. Indeed, it must have been
this; for John Carnby himself was very much the sort of
person I had pictured him to be.

He had all the earmarks of the lonely scholar who has
devoted patient years to some line of erudite research. He
was thin and bent, with a massive forehead and a mane of
grizzled hair; and the pallor of the library was on his hollow
clean-shaven cheeks. But coupled with this, there was a
nerve-shattered air, a fearful shrinking that was more than
the normal shyness of a recluse, and an unceasing apprehen-
siveness that betrayed itself in every glance of his dark-
ringed, feverish eyes and every movement of his bony hands.
In all likelihood his health had been seriously impaired by
overapplication; and I could not help but wonder at the
nature of the studies that had made him a tremulous wreck.
But there was something about him – perhaps the width of
his bowed shoulders and the bold aquilinity of his facial
outlines – which gave the impression of great former
strength and a vigour not yet wholly exhausted.

His voice was unexpectedly deep and sonorous.

'I think you will do, Mr Ogden,' he said, after a few formal
questions, most of which related to my linguistic knowledge,
and in particular my mastery of Arabic. 'Your labours will
not be very heavy; but I want someone who can be on hand

at any time required. Therefore you must live with me. I can
give you a comfortable room, and I guarantee that my
cooking will not poison you. I often work at night; and I hope
you will not find the irregular hours too disagreeable.'

No doubt I should have been overjoyed at this assurance
that the secretarial position was to be mine. Instead, I was
aware of a dim, unreasoning reluctance and an obscure
forewarning of evil as I thanked John Carnby and told him
that I was ready to move in whenever he desired.

He appeared to be greatly pleased; and the queer appre-
hensiveness went out of his manner for a moment.

'Come immediately – this very afternoon, if you can,' he
said. 'I shall be very glad to have you, and the sooner the
better. I have been living entirely alone for some time; and I
must confess that the solitude is beginning to pall upon me.
Also, I have been retarded in my labours for lack of the
proper help. My brother used to live with me and assist me,
but he has gone away on a long trip.'

I returned to my downtown lodgings, paid my rent with
the last few dollars that remained to me, packed my belongings, and in less than an hour was back at my new employer's
home. He assigned me a room on the second floor, which,
though unaired and dusty, was more than luxurious in
comparison with the hall-bedroom that failing funds had
compelled me to inhabit for some time past. Then he took me
to his own study, which was on the same floor, at the further
end of the hall. Here, he explained to me, most of my future
work would be done.

I could hardly restrain an exclamation of surprise as I
viewed the interior of this chamber. It was very much as I
should have imagined the den of some old sorcerer to be.
There were tables strewn with archaic instruments of doubtful use, with astrological charts, with skulls and alembics
and crystals, with censers such as are used in the Catholic
Church, and volumes bound in worm-eaten leather with
verdigris-mottled clasps. In one corner stood the skeleton of

a large ape; in another, a human skeleton; and overhead a stuffed crocodile was suspended.

There were cases overpiled with books, and even a cursory glance at the titles showed me that they formed a singularly comprehensive collection of ancient and modern works on demonology and the black arts. There were some weird paintings and etchings on the walls, dealing with kindred themes; and the whole atmosphere of the room exhaled a medley of half-forgotten superstitions. Ordinarily I would have smiled if confronted with such things; but somehow, in this lonely dismal house, beside the neurotic, hag-ridden Carnby, it was difficult for me to repress an actual shudder.

On one of the tables, contrasting incongruously with this melange of medievalism and Satanism, there stood a type-writer, surrounded with piles of disorderly manuscript. At one end of the room there was a small, curtained alcove with a bed in which Carnby slept. At the end opposite the alcove, between the human and simian skeletons, I perceived a locked cupboard that was set in the wall.

Carnby had noted my surprise, and was watching me with a keen, analytic expression which I found impossible to fathom. He began to speak, in explanatory tones.

'I have made a life-study of demonism and sorcery,' he declared. 'It is a fascinating field, and one that is singularly neglected. I am now preparing a monograph, in which I am trying to correlate the magical practices and demon-worship of every known age and people. Your labours, at least for a while, will consist in typing and arranging the voluminous preliminary notes which I have made, and in helping me to track down other references and correspondences. Your knowledge of Arabic will be invaluable to me, for I am none too well-grounded in this language myself, and I am depending for certain essential data on a copy of the *Necronomicon* in the original Arabic text. I have reason to think that there are certain omissions and erroneous renderings in the Latin version of Olaus Wormius.'

I had heard of this rare, well-nigh fabulous volume, but

had never seen it. The book was supposed to contain the ultimate secrets of evil and forbidden knowledge; and, moreover, the original text, written by the mad Arab, Abdul Alhazred, was said to be unprocurable. I wondered how it had come into Carnby's possession.

'I'll show you the volume after dinner,' Carnby went on. 'You will doubtless be able to elucidate one or two passages that have long puzzled me.'

The evening meal, cooked and served by my employer himself, was a welcome change from cheap restaurant fare. Carnby seemed to have lost a good deal of his nervousness. He was very talkative, and even began to exhibit a certain scholarly gaiety after we had shared a bottle of mellow Sauternes. Still, with no manifest reason, I was troubled by intimations and forebodings which I could neither analyse nor trace to their rightful source.

We returned to the study, and Carnby brought out from a locked drawer the volume of which he had spoken. It was enormously old, and was bound in ebony covers arabesqued with silver and set with darkly glowing garnets. When I opened the yellowing pages, I drew back with involuntary revulsion at the odour which arose from them – an odour that was more than suggestive of physical decay, as if the book had lain among corpses in some forgotten graveyard and had taken on the taint of dissolution.

Carnby's eyes were burning with a fevered light as he took the old manuscript from my hands and turned to a page near the middle. He indicated a certain passage with his lean forefinger.

'Tell me what you make of this,' he said, in a tense, excited whisper.

I deciphered the paragraph, slowly and with some difficulty, and wrote down a rough English version with the pad and pencil which Carnby offered me. Then, at his request, I read it aloud:

'It is verily known by few, but is nevertheless an attestable fact, that the will of a dead sorcerer hath power upon his

own body and can raise it up from the tomb and perform
therewith whatever action was unfulfilled in life. And such
resurrections are invariably for the doing of malevolent
deeds and for the detriment of others. Most readily can the
corpse be animated if all its members have remained intact;
and yet there are cases in which the excelling will of the
wizard hath reared up from death the sundered pieces of a
body hewn in many fragments, and hath caused them to
serve his end, either separately or in a temporary reunion.
But in every instance, after the action hath been completed,
the body lapseth into its former state.'

Of course, all this was errant gibberish. Probably it was
the strange, unhealthy look of utter absorption with which
my employer listened, more than that damnable passage
from the *Necronomicon*, which caused my nervousness and
made me start violently when, towards the end of my
reading, I heard an indescribable slithering noise in the hall
outside. But when I finished the paragraph and looked up at
Carnby, I was more than startled by the expression of stark,
staring fear which his features had assumed – an expression
as of one who is haunted by some hellish phantom. Somehow,
I got the feeling that he was listening to that odd noise in
the hallway rather than to my translation of Abdul Alhazred.

'The house is full of rats,' he explained, as he caught my
inquiring glance. 'I have never been able to get rid of them,
with all my efforts.'

The noise, which still continued, was that which a rat
might make in dragging some object slowly along the floor.
It seemed to draw closer, to approach the door of Carnby's
room, and then, after an intermission, it began to move again
and receded. My employer's agitation was marked; he listened with fearful intentness and seemed to follow the
progress of the sound with a terror that mounted as it drew
near and decreased a little with its recession.

'I am very nervous,' he said. 'I have worked too hard lately,
and this is the result. Even a little noise upsets me.'

The sound had now died away somewhere in the house. Carnby appeared to recover himself in a measure.

'Will you please re-read your translation?' he requested. 'I want to follow it very carefully, word by word.'

I obeyed. He listened with the same look of unholy absorption as before, and this time we were not interrupted by any noises in the hallway. Carnby's face grew paler, as if the last remnant of blood had been drained from it, when I read the final sentences; and the fire in his hollow eyes was like phosphorescence in a deep vault.

'That is a most remarkable passage,' he commented. 'I was doubtful about its meaning, with my imperfect Arabic; and I have found that the passage is wholly omitted in the Latin of Olaus Wormius. Thank you for your scholarly rendering. You have certainly cleared it up for me.'

His tone was dry and formal, as if he were repressing himself and holding back a world of unsurmisable thoughts and emotions. Somehow I felt that Carnby was more nervous and upset than ever, and also that my reading from the *Necronomicon* had in some mysterious manner contributed to his perturbation. He wore a ghastly brooding expression, as if his mind were busy with some unwelcome and forbidden theme.

However, seeming to collect himself, he asked me to translate another passage. This turned out to be a singular incantatory formula for the exorcism of the dead, with a ritual that involved the use of rare Arabian spices and the proper intoning of at least a hundred names of ghouls and demons. I copied it all out for Carnby, who studied it for a long time with a rapt eagerness that was more than scholarly.

'That, too,' he observed, 'is not in Olaus Wormius.' After perusing it again, he folded the paper carefully and put it away in the same drawer from which he had taken the *Necronomicon*.

That evening was one of the strangest I have ever spent. As we sat for hour after hour discussing renditions from that unhallowed volume, I came to know more and more definitely that my employer was mortally afraid of something; that he dreaded being alone and was keeping me with him on this account rather than for any other reason. Always he seemed to be waiting and listening with a painful, tortured expectation, and I saw that he gave only a mechanical awareness to much that was said. Among the weird appurtenances of the room, in that atmosphere of unmanifested evil, or untold horror, the rational part of my mind began to succumb slowly to a recrudescence of the dark ancestral fears. A scorner of such things in my normal moments, I was now ready to believe in the most baleful creations of superstitious fancy. No doubt, by some process of mental contagion, I had caught the hidden terror from which Carnby suffered.

By no word or syllable, however, did the man admit the actual feelings that were evident in his demeanour, but he spoke repeatedly of a nervous ailment. More than once, during our discussion, he sought to imply that his interest in the supernatural and the Satanic was wholly intellectual, that he, like myself, was without personal belief in such things. Yet I knew infallibly that his implications were false; that he was driven and obsessed by a real faith in all that he pretended to view with scientific detachment, and had doubtless fallen a victim to some imaginary horror entailed by his occult researches. But my intuition afforded me no clue to the actual nature of this horror.

There was no repetition of the sounds that had been so disturbing to my employer. We must have sat till after midnight with the writings of the mad Arab open before us. At last Carnby seemed to realize the lateness of the hour.

'I fear I have kept you up too long,' he said apologetically. 'You must go and get some sleep. I am selfish, and I forget that such hours are not habitual to others, as they are to me.'

I made the formal denial of his self-impeachment which courtesy required, said good-night, and sought my own chamber with a feeling of intense relief. It seemed to me that

I would leave behind me in Carnby's room all the shadowy fear and oppression to which I had been subjected.

Only one light was burning in the long passage. It was near Carnby's door; and my own door at the further end, close to the stair-head, was in deep shadow. As I groped for the knob, I heard a noise behind me, and turned to see in the gloom a small, indistinct body that sprang from the hall-landing to the top stair, disappearing from view. I was horribly startled; for even in that vague, fleeting glimpse, the thing was much too pale for a rat and its form was not at all suggestive of an animal. I could not have sworn what it was, but the outlines had seemed unmentionably monstrous. I stood trembling violently in every limb, and heard on the stairs a singular bumping sound like the fall of an object rolling downward from step to step. The sound was repeated at regular intervals, and finally ceased.

If the safety of the soul and body depended upon it, I could not have turned on the stair-light; nor could I have gone to the top steps to ascertain the agency of that unnatural bumping. Anyone else, it might seem, would have done this. Instead, after a moment of virtual petrification, I entered my room, locked the door, and went to bed in a turmoil of unresolved doubt and equivocal terror. I left the light burning; and I lay awake for hours, expecting momentarily a recurrence of that abominable sound. But the house was as silent as a morgue, and I heard nothing. At length, in spite of my anticipations to the contrary, I fell asleep and did not awaken till after many sodden, dreamless hours.

It was ten o'clock, as my watch informed me. I wondered whether my employer had left me undisturbed through thoughtfulness, or had not arisen himself. I dressed and went downstairs, to find him waiting at the breakfast table. He was paler and more tremulous than ever, as if he had slept badly.

'I hope the rats didn't annoy you too much,' he remarked, after a preliminary greeting. 'Something really must be done about them.'

'I didn't notice them at all,' I replied. Somehow, it was utterly impossible for me to mention the queer, ambiguous thing which I had seen and heard on retiring the night before. Doubtless I had been mistaken; doubtless it had been merely a rat after all, dragging something down the stairs. I tried to forget the hideously repeated noise and the momentary flash of unthinkable outlines in the gloom.

My employer eyed me with uncanny sharpness, as if he sought to penetrate my inmost mind. Breakfast was a dismal affair; and the day that followed was no less dreary. Carnby isolated himself till the middle of the afternoon, and I was left to my own devices in the well-supplied but conventional library downstairs. What Carnby was doing alone in his room I could not surmise; but I thought more than once that I heard the faint, monotonous intonations of a solemn voice. Horror-breeding hints and noisome intuitions invaded my brain. More and more the atmosphere of that house enveloped and stifled me with poisonous, miasmal mystery; and I felt everywhere the invisible brooding of malignant incubi.

It was almost a relief when my employer summoned me to his study. Entering, I noticed that the air was full of a pungent, aromatic smell and was touched by the vanishing coils of a blue vapour, as if from the burning of Oriental gums and spices in the church censers. An Ispahan rug had been moved from its position near the wall to the centre of the room, but was not sufficient to cover entirely a curving violet mark that suggested the drawing of a magic circle on the floor. No doubt Carnby had been performing some sort of incantation; and I thought of the awesome formula I had translated at his request.

However, he did not offer any explanation of what he had been doing. His manner had changed remarkably and was more controlled and confident than at any former time. In a fashion almost business-like he laid before me a pile of manuscript which he wanted me to type for him. The familiar click of the keys aided me somewhat in dismissing my apprehensions of vague evil, and I could almost smile at the recherché and terrific information comprised in my employer's notes, which dealt mainly with formulae for the acquisition of unlawful power. But still, beneath my reassurance, there was a vague, lingering disquietude.

Evening came; and after our meal we returned again to the study. There was a tenseness in Carnby's manner now, as if he were eagerly awaiting the result of some hidden test. I went on with my work; but some of his emotion communicated itself to me, and ever and anon I caught myself in an attitude of strained listening.

At last, above the click of the keys, I heard the peculiar slithering in the hall. Carnby had heard it, too, and his confident look had utterly vanished, giving place to the most pitiable fear.

The sound drew nearer and was followed by a dull, dragging noise, and then by more sounds of an unidentifiable slithering and scuttling nature that varied in loudness. The hall was seemingly full of them, as if a whole army of rats were hauling some carrion booty along the floor. And yet no rodent or number of rodents could have made such sounds, or could have moved anything so heavy as the object which came behind the rest. There was something in the character of those noises, something without name or definition, which caused a slowly creeping chill to invade my spine.

'Good Lord! What is all that racket?' I cried.

'The rats! I tell you it is only rats!' Carnby's voice was a high, hysterical shriek.

A moment later, there came an unmistakable knocking on the door, near the sill. At the same time I heard a heavy thudding in the locked cupboard at the further end of the room. Carnby had been standing erect, but now he sank limply into a chair. His features were ashen, and his look was almost maniacal with fright.

The nightmare doubt and tension became unbearable and I ran to the door and flung it open, in spite of a frantic remonstrance from my employer. I had no idea what I should find as I stepped across the sill into the dim-lit hall.

When I looked down and saw the thing on which I had almost trodden, my feeling was one of sick amazement and actual nausea. It was a human hand which had been severed at the wrist – a bony, bluish hand like that of a week-old corpse, with garden-mould on the fingers and under the long nails. *The damnable thing had moved*! It had drawn back to avoid me, and was crawling along the passage somewhat in the manner of a crab! And following it with my gaze, I saw that there were other things beyond it, one of which I recognized as a man's foot and another as a forearm. I dared not look at the rest. All were moving slowly, hideously away in a charnel procession, and I cannot describe the fashion in which they moved. Their individual vitality was horrifying beyond endurance. It was more than the vitality of life, yet the air was laden with a carrion taint. I averted my eyes and stepped back into Carnby's room, closing the door behind me with a shaking hand. Carnby was at my side with the key, which he turned in the lock with palsy-stricken fingers that had become as feeble as those of an old man.

'You saw them?' he asked in a dry, quavering whisper.

'In God's name, what does it all mean?' I cried.

Carnby went back to his chair, tottering a little with weakness. His lineaments were agonized by the gnawing of some inward horror, and he shook visibly like an ague patient. I sat down in a chair beside him, and he began to stammer forth his unbelievable confession, half incoherently, with inconsequential mouthings and many breaks and pauses:

'He is stronger than I am – even in death, even with his body dismembered by the surgeon's knife and saw that I used. I thought he could not return after that – after I had buried the portions in a dozen different places, in the cellar, beneath the shrubs, at the foot of the ivy-vines. But the *Necronomicon* is right . . . and Helman Carnby knew it. He warned me before I killed him, he told me he could return – *even in that condition.*

'But I did not believe him. I hated Helman, and he hated me, too. He had attained to higher power and knowledge and was more favoured by the Dark Ones than I. That was why I killed him – my own twin-brother, and my brother in the service of Satan and of Those who were before Satan. We had studied together for many years. We had celebrated the Black Mass together and we were attended by the same familiars. But Helman Carnby had gone deeper into the occult, into the forbidden, where I could not follow him. I feared him, and I could not endure his supremacy.

'It is more than a week – it is ten days since I did the deed. But Helman – or some part of him – has returned every night . . . God! His accursed hands crawling on the floor! His feet, his arms, the segments of his legs, climbing the stairs in some unmentionable way to haunt me! . . . Christ! His awful, bloody torso lying in wait! I tell you, his hands have come even by day to tap and fumble at my door . . . and I have stumbled over his arms in the dark.

'Oh God! I shall go mad with the awfulness of it. But he wants me to go mad, he wants to torture me till my brain gives way. That is why he haunts me in this piece-meal fashion. He could end it all at any time, with the demoniacal power that is his. He could re-knit his sundered limbs and body and slay me as I slew him.

'How carefully I buried the parts, with what infinite forethought! And how useless it was! I buried the saw and the knife, too, at the farther end of the garden, as far away as possible from his evil, itching hands. But I did not bury the head with the other pieces – I kept it in that cupboard at the end of my room. Sometimes I have heard it moving there, as you heard it a while ago . . . But he does not need the head, his will is elsewhere, and can work intelligently through all his members.

'Of course, I locked all the doors and windows at night when I found that he was coming back . . . But it made no difference. And I have tried to exorcize him with the appropriate incantations – with all those that I knew. Today I

tried that sovereign formula from the *Necronomicon* which
you translated for me. I got you here to translate it. Also, I
could no longer bear to be alone and I thought that it might
help if there were someone else in the house. That formula
was my last hope. I thought it would hold him – it is a most
ancient and most dreadful incantation. But, as you have
seen, it is useless . . .'

His voice trailed off in a broken mumble, and he sat
staring before him with sightless, intolerable eyes in which
I saw the beginning flare of madness. I could say nothing –
the confession he had made was so ineffably atrocious. The
moral shock, and the ghastly supernatural horror, had
almost stupefied me. My sensibilities were stunned; and it
was not till I had begun to recover myself that I felt the
irresistible surge of a flood of loathing for the man beside
me.

I rose to my feet. The house had grown very silent, as if
the macabre and charnel army of beleaguerment had now
retired to its various graves. Carnby had left the key in the
lock; and I went to the door and turned it quickly.

'Are you leaving? Don't go,' Carnby begged in a voice that
was tremulous with alarm, as I stood with my hand on the
doorknob.

'Yes, I am going,' I said coldly. 'I am resigning my position
right now; and I intend to pack my belongings and leave
your house with as little delay as possible.'

I opened the door and went out, refusing to listen to the
arguments and pleadings and protestations he had begun to
babble. For the nonce, I preferred to face whatever might
lurk in the gloomy passage, no matter how loathsome and
terrifying, rather than endure any longer the society of John
Carnby.

The hall was empty; but I shuddered with repulsion at the
memory of what I had seen, as I hastened to my room. I
think I should have screamed aloud at the least sound or
movement in the shadows.

I began to pack my valise with a feeling of the most frantic urgency and compulsion. It seemed to me that I could not escape soon enough from that house of abominable secrets, over which hung an atmosphere of smothering menace. I made mistakes in my haste, I stumbled over chairs, and my brain and my fingers grew numb with a paralysing dread.

I had almost finished my task, when I heard the sound of slow measured footsteps coming up the stairs. I knew that it was not Carnby, for he had locked himself immediately in his room when I had left; and I felt sure that nothing could have tempted him to emerge. Anyway, he could hardly have gone downstairs without my hearing him.

The footsteps came to the top landing and went past my door along the hall, with that same dead monotonous repetition, regular as the movement of a machine. Certainly it was not the soft, nervous tread of John Carnby.

Who, then, could it be? My blood stood still in my veins; I dared not finish the speculation that arose in my mind.

The steps paused; and I knew that they had reached the door of Carnby's room. There followed an interval in which I could scarcely breathe; and then I heard an awful crashing and shattering noise, and above it the soaring scream of a man in the uttermost extremity of fear.

I was powerless to move, as if an unseen iron hand had reached forth to restrain me; and I have no idea how long I waited and listened. The scream had fallen away in a swift silence; and I heard nothing now, except a low, peculiar, recurrent sound which my brain refused to identify.

It was not my own volition, but a stronger will than mine, which drew me forth at last and impelled me down the hall to Carnby's study. I felt the presence of that will as an overpowering, superhuman thing – a demoniac force, a malign mesmerism.

The door of the study had been broken in and was hanging by one hinge. It was splintered as by the impact of more than mortal strength. A light was still burning in the room, and the unmentionable sound I had been hearing ceased as I neared the threshold. It was followed by an evil, utter stillness.

Again I paused, and could go no further. But, this time, it was something other than the hellish, all-pervading magnetism that petrified my limbs and arrested me before the sill. Peering into the room, in the narrow space that was framed by the doorway and lit by an unseen lamp, I saw one end of the Oriental rug, and the gruesome outlines of a monstrous, unmoving shadow that fell beyond it on the floor. Huge, elongated, misshapen, the shadow was seemingly cast by the arms and torso of a naked man who stooped forward with a surgeon's saw in his hand. Its monstrosity lay in this: though the shoulders, chest, abdomen and arms were all clearly distinguishable, the shadow was headless and appeared to terminate in an abruptly severed neck. It was impossible, considering the relative position, for the head to have been concealed from sight through any manner of foreshortening.

I waited, powerless to enter or withdraw. The blood had flowed back upon my heart in an ice-thick tide, and thought was frozen in my brain. An interval of termless horror, and then, from the hidden end of Carnby's room, from the direction of the locked cupboard, there came a fearsome and violent crash, and the sound of splintering wood and whining hinges, followed by the sinister, dismal thud of an unknown object striking the floor.

Again there was silence – a silence as of consummated Evil brooding above its unnamable triumph. The shadow had not stirred. There was a hideous contemplation in its attitude, and the saw was still held in its poised hand, as if above a completed task.

Another interval, and then, without warning, I witnessed the awful and unexplainable *disintegration* of the shadow, which seemed to break gently and easily into many different shadows ere it faded from view. I hesitate to describe the manner, or specify the places, in which this singular disruption, this manifold cleavage, occurred. Simultaneously, I heard the muffled clatter of a metallic implement on the

Persian rug, and a sound that was not of a single body but of many bodies falling.

Once more there was silence – a silence as of some nocturnal cemetery, when grave-diggers and ghouls are done with their macabre toil, and the dead alone remain.

Drawn by the baleful mesmerism, like a somnambulist led by an unseen demon, I entered the room. I knew with a loathly prescience the sight that awaited me beyond the sill – the *double* heap of human segments, some of them fresh and bloody, and others already blue with beginning putrefaction and marked with earthstains, that were mingled in abhorrent confusion on the rug.

A reddened knife and saw were protruding from the pile; and a little to one side, between the rug and the open cupboard with its shattered door, there reposed a human head that was fronting the other remnants in an upright posture. It was in the same condition of incipient decay as the body to which it belonged; but I swear that I saw the fading of a malignant exultation from its features as I entered. Even with the marks of corruption upon them, the lineaments bore a manifest likeness to those of John Carnby, and plainly they could belong only to a twin brother.

The frightful inferences that smothered my brain with their black and clammy cloud are not to be written here. The horror which I beheld – and the greater horror which I surmised – would have put to shame hell's foulest enormities in their frozen pits. There was but one mitigation and one mercy: I was compelled to gaze only for a few instants on that intolerable scene. Then, all at once, I felt that something had withdrawn from the room; the malign spell was broken, the overpowering volition that had held me captive was gone. It had released me now, even as it had released the dismembered corpse of Helman Carnby. I was free to go; and I fled from the ghastly chamber and ran headlong through an unlit house and into the outer darkness of the night.

Ubbo-Sathla

CLARK ASHTON SMITH

... For Ubbo-Sathla is the source and the end. Before the coming of Zhothaqquah or Yok-Zothoth or Kthulhut from the stars, Ubbo-Sathla dwelt in the steaming fens of the new-made Earth: a mass without head or members, spawning the grey, formless efts of the prime and the grisly prototypes of terrene life ... And all earthly life, it is told, shall go back at last through the great circle of time to Ubbo-Sathla.

– The Book of Eibon

Paul Tregardis found the milky crystal in a litter of oddments from many lands and eras. He had entered the shop of the curio-dealer through an aimless impulse, with no object in mind, other than the idle distraction of eyeing and fingering a miscellany of far-gathered things. Looking desultorily about, his attention had been drawn by a dull glimmering on one of the tables; and he had extricated the queer orb-like stone from its shadowy, crowded position between an ugly little Aztec idol, the fossil egg of a dinornis, and an obscene fetish of black wood from the Niger.

The thing was about the size of a small orange and was slightly flattened at the ends, like a planet at its poles. It puzzled Tregardis, for it was not like an ordinary crystal, being cloudy and changeable with an intermittent glowing in its heart, as if it were alternately illumed and darkened from within. Holding it to the wintry window, he studied it for a while without being able to determine the secret of this singular and regular alternation. His puzzlement was soon complicated by a dawning sense of vague and irrecognizable familiarity, as if he had seen the thing before under circumstances that were now wholly forgotten.

He appealed to the curio-dealer, a dwarfish Hebrew with an air of dusty antiquity, who gave the impression of being lost to commercial considerations in some web of cabalistic reverie.

'Can you tell me anything about this?'

The dealer gave an indescribable, simultaneous shrug of his shoulders and his eyebrows.

'It is very old – palagean, one might say. I cannot tell you much, for little is known. A geologist found it in Greenland, beneath glacial ice, in the Miocene strata. Who knows? It may have belonged to some sorcerer of primeval Thule. Greenland was a warm, fertile region beneath the sun of Miocene times. No doubt it is a magic crystal; and a man might behold strange visions in its heart, if he looked long enough.'

Tregardis was quite startled; for the dealer's apparently fantastic suggestion had brought to mind his own delvings in a branch of obscure lore; and, in particular, had recalled *The Book of Eibon*, that strangest and rarest of occult forgotten volumes, which is said to have come down through a series of manifold translations from a prehistoric original written in the lost language of Hyperborea. Tregardis, with much difficulty, had obtained the medieval French version – a copy that had been owned by many generations of sorcerers and Satanists – but had never been able to find the Greek manuscript from which the version was derived.

The remote, fabulous original was supposed to have been the work of a great Hyperborean wizard, from whom it had taken its name. It was a collection of dark and baleful myths, of liturgies, rituals and incantations both evil and esoteric. Not without shudders, in the course of studies that the average person would have considered more than singular, Tregardis had collated the French volume with the frightful *Necronomicon* of the mad Arab, Abdul Alhazred. He had found many correspondences of the blackest and most appalling significance, together with much forbidden data that was either unknown to the Arab or omitted by him . . . or by his translators.

Was this what he had been trying to recall, Tregardis wondered – the brief, casual reference, in *The Book of Eibon*, to a cloudy crystal that had been owned by the Wizard Zon Mezzamalech, in Mhu Thulan? Of course, it was all too fantastic, too hypothetic, too incredible – but Mhu Thulan, that northern portion of ancient Hyperborea, was supposed to have corresponded roughly with modern Greenland, which had formerly been joined as a peninsula to the main continent. Could the stone in his hand, by some fabulous fortuity, be the crystal of Zon Mezzamalech?

Tregardis smiled at himself with inward irony for even conceiving the absurd notion. Such things did not occur – at least not in present-day London; and in all likelihood, *The Book of Eibon* was sheer superstitious fantasy, anyway. Nevertheless, there was something about the crystal that continued to tease and inveigle him. He ended by purchasing it, at a fairly moderate price. The sum was named by the seller and paid by the buyer without bargaining.

With the crystal in his pocket, Paul Tregardis hastened back to his lodgings instead of resuming his leisurely saunter. He installed the milky globe on his writing-table, where it stood firmly enough on one of its oblate ends. Then, still smiling at his own absurdity, he took down the yellow parchment manuscript of *The Book of Eibon* from its place in a somewhat inclusive collection of recherché literature. He opened the vermiculated leather cover with hasps of tarnished steel, and read over to himself, translating from the archaic French as he read, the paragraph that referred to Zon Mezzamalech:

'*This wizard, who was mighty among sorcerers, had found a cloudy stone, orb-like and somewhat flattened at the ends, in which he could behold many visions of the terrene past, even to the Earth's beginning, when Ubbo-Sathla, the unbegotten source, lay vast and swollen and yeasty amid the vapouring slime . . . But of that which he beheld, Zon Mezza-malech left little record; and people say that he vanished presently, in a way that is not known; and after him the cloudy crystal was lost.'*

Paul Tregardis laid the manuscript aside. Again there was something that tantalized and beguiled him, like a lost dream or a memory forfeit to oblivion. Impelled by a feeling which he did not scrutinize or question, he sat down before the table and began to stare intently into the cold, nebulous orb. He felt an expectation which, somehow, was so familiar, so permeative a part of his consciousness, that he did not even name it to himself.

Minute by minute he sat, and watched the alternate glimmering and fading of the mysterious light in the heart of the crystal. By imperceptible degrees, there stole upon him a sense of dream-like duality, both in respect to his person and his surroundings. He was still Paul Tregardis – and yet he was someone else; the room was his London apartment – and chamber in some foreign but well-known place. And in both milieus he peered steadfastly into the same crystal.

After an interim, without surprise on the part of Tregardis, the process of re-identification became complete. He knew that he was Zon Mezzamalech, a sorcerer of Mhu Thulan, and a student of all lore anterior to his own epoch. Wise with dreadful secrets that were not known to Paul Tregardis, amateur of anthropology and the occult sciences in latterday London, he sought by means of the milky crystal to attain an even older and more fearful knowledge.

He had acquired the stone in dubitable ways, from a more than sinister source. It was unique and without fellow in any land or time. In its depths, all former years, all things that had ever been, were supposedly mirrored, and would reveal themselves to the patient visionary. And through the crystal, Zon Mezzamalech had dreamt to recover the wisdom of the gods who died before the Earth was born. They had passed to the lightless void, leaving their lore inscribed upon tablets of ultrastellar stone; and the tablets were guarded in the primal mire by the formless, idiotic demiurge, Ubbo-Sathla. Only by means of the crystal could he hope to find and read the tablets.

For the first time, he was making trial of the globe's reputed virtues. About him an ivory-panelled chamber, filled with his magic books and paraphernalia, was fading slowly from his consciousness. Before him, on a table of some dark Hyperborean wood that had been graven with grotesque ciphers, the crystal appeared to swell and deepen, and in its filmy depth he beheld a swift and broken swirling of dim scenes, fleeting like the bubbles of a millrace. As if he looked upon an actual world, cities, forests, mountains, seas and meadows flowed beneath him, lightening and darkening as with the passage of days and nights in some weirdly accelerated stream of time.

Zon Mezzamalech had forgotten Paul Tregardis – had lost remembrance of his own entity and his own surroundings in Mhu Thulan. Moment by moment, the flowing vision in the crystal became more definite and distinct, and the orb itself deepened till he grew giddy, as if he were peering from an insecure height into some never-fathomed abyss. He knew that time was racing backwards in the crystal, was unrolling for him the pageant of all past days; but a strange alarm had seized him, and he feared to gaze longer. Like one who has nearly fallen from a precipice, he caught himself with a violent start and drew back from the mystic orb.

Again, to his gaze, the enormous whirling world into which he had peered was a small and cloudy crystal on his rune-wrought table in Mhu Thulan. Then, by degrees, it seemed that the great room with sculptured panels of mammoth ivory was narrowing to another and dingier place; and Zon Mezzamalech, losing his preternatural wisdom and sorcerous power, went back by a weird regression into Paul Tregardis.

And yet not wholly, it seemed, was he able to return. Tregardis, dazed and wondering, found himself before the writing-table on which he had set the oblate sphere. He felt

the confusion of one who has dreamt and has not yet fully
awakened from the dream. The room puzzled him vaguely,
as if something were wrong with its size and furnishings;
and his remembrance of purchasing the crystal from a curio-
dealer was oddly and discrepantly mingled with an impression that he had acquired it in a very different manner.

He felt that something very strange had happened to him
when he peered into the crystal; but just what it was he
could not seem to recollect. It had left him in the sort of
psychic muddlement that follows a debauch of hashish. He
assured himself that he was Paul Tregardis, that he lived on
a certain street in London, that the year was 1933; but such
commonplace verities had somehow lost their meaning and
their validity; and everything about him was shadow-like
and insubstantial. The very walls seemed to wave like
smoke; the people in the streets were phantoms of phantoms;
and he himself was a lost shadow, a wandering echo of
something long forgot.

He resolved that he would not repeat his experiment of
crystal-gazing. The effects were too unpleasant and equivocal. But the very next day, by an unreasoning impulse to
which he yielded almost mechanically, without reluctation,
he found himself seated before the misty orb. Again he
became the sorcerer Zon Mezzamalech in Mhu Thulan; again
he dreamt to retrieve the wisdom of the antemundane gods;
again he drew back from the deepening crystal with the
terror of one who fears to fall; and once more – but doubtfully
and dimly, like a failing wraith – he was Paul Tregardis.

Three times did Tregardis repeat the experience on succes-
sive days; and each time his own person and the world about
him became more tenuous and confused than before. His
sensations were those of a dreamer who is on the verge of
waking; and London itself was unreal as the lands that slip
from the dreamer's ken, receding in filmy mist and cloudy
light. Beyond it all, he felt the looming and crowding of vast
imageries, alien but half familiar. It was as if the fantasma-

goria of time and space were dissolving about him, to reveal
some veritable reality – or another dream of space and time.

There came, at last, the day when he sat down before the
crystal – and did not return as Paul Tregardis. It was the
day when Zon Mezzamalech, boldly disregarding certain evil
and portentous warnings, resolved to overcome his curious
fear of falling bodily into the visionary world that he beheld –
a fear that had hitherto prevented him from following the
backward stream of time for any distance. He must, he
assured himself, conquer his fear if he were ever to see and
read the last tablets of the gods. He had beheld nothing more
than a few fragments of the years of Mhu Thulan immediately posterior to the present – the years of his own lifetime;
and there were inestimable cycles between these years and
the Beginning.

Again, to his gaze, the crystal deepened immeasurably,
with scenes and happenings that flowed in a retrograde
stream. Again the magic ciphers of the dark table faded from
his ken, and the sorcerously carven walls of his chamber
melted into less than dream. Once more he grew giddy with
an awful vertigo as he bent above the swirling and milling
of the terrible gulfs of time in the world-like orb. Fearfully,
in spite of his resolution, he would have drawn away; but he
had looked and leaned too long. There was a sense of abysmal
falling, a suction as of ineluctable winds, of maelstroms that
bore him down through fleet unstable visions of his own past
life into antenatal years and dimensions. He seemed to
endure the pangs of an inverse dissolution; and then he was
no longer Zon Mezzamalech, the wise and learned watcher of
the crystal, but an actual part of the weirdly racing stream
that ran back to reattain the Beginning.

He seemed to live unnumbered lives, to die myriad deaths,
forgetting each time the death and life that had gone before.
He fought as a warrior in half-legendary battles; he was a
child playing in the ruins of some olden city of Mhu Thulan;
he was the king who had reigned when the city was in its
prime, the prophet who had foretold its building and its

doom. A woman, he wept for the bygone dead in necropoli
long-crumbled; an antique wizard, he muttered the rude
spells of earlier sorcery; a priest of some pre-human god, he
wielded the sacrificial knife in cave-temples of pillared
basalt. Life by life, era by era, he retraced the long and
groping cycles through which Hyperborea had risen from
savagery to a high civilization.

He became a barbarian of some trogloditic tribe, fleeing
from the slow, turreted ice of a former glacial age into lands
illumed by the ruddy flare of perpetual volcanoes. Then, after
incomputable years, he was no longer man but a man-like
beast, roving in forests of giant fern and calamite, or building
an uncouth nest in the boughs of mighty cycads.

Through eons of anterior sensation, of crude lust and
hunger, of aboriginal terror and madness, there was someone
– or something – that went ever backward in time. Death
became birth, and birth was death. In a slow vision of reverse
change, the earth appeared to melt away, to slough off the
hills and mountains of its latter strata. Always the sun grew
larger and hotter above the fuming swamps that teemed
with a crasser life, with a more fulsome vegetation. And the
thing that had been Paul Tregardis, that had been Zon
Mezzamalech, was a part of all the monstrous devolution. It
flew with the claw-tipped wings of a pterodactyl, it swam in
tepid seas with the vast, winding bulk of an ichthyosaurus,
it bellowed uncouthly with the armoured throat of some
forgotten behemoth to the huge moon that burned through
Liassic mists.

At length, after aeons of immemorial brutehood, it became
one of the lost serpent-men who reared their cities of black
gneiss and fought their venomous wars in the world's first
continent. It walked undulously in ante-human streets, in
strange crooked vaults; it peered at primeval stars from
high, Babelian towers; it bowed with hissing litanies to great
serpent-idols. Through years and ages of the ophidian era it
returned, and was a thing that crawled in the ooze, that had
not yet learned to think and dream and build. And the time

came when there was no longer a continent, but only a vast, chaotic marsh, a sea of slime, without limit or horizon, that seethed with a blind writhing of amorphous vapours.

There, in the grey beginning of earth, the formless mass that was Ubbo-Sathla reposed amid the slime and the vapours. Headless, without organs or members, it sloughed from its oozy sides, in a slow, ceaseless wave, the amoebic forms that were the archetypes of earthly life. Horrible it was, if there had been aught to apprehend the horror; and loathsome, if there had been any to feel loathing. About it, prone or tilted in the mire, there lay the mighty tablets of star-quarried stone that were writ with the inconceivable wisdom of the premundane gods.

And there, to the goal of a forgotten search, was drawn the thing that had been – or would sometime be – Paul Tregardis and Zon Mezzamalech. Becoming a shapeless eft of the prime, it crawled sluggishly and obliviously across the fallen tablets of the gods, and fought and ravened blindly with the other spawn of Ubbo-Sathla.

Of Zon Mezzamalech and his vanishing, there is no mention anywhere, save the brief passage in *The Book of Eibon*. Concerning Paul Tregardis, who also disappeared, there was a curt notice in several London papers. No one seems to have known anything about him: he is gone as if he had never been; and the crystal, presumably, is gone too. At least, no one has found it.

The Black Stone

ROBERT E. HOWARD

'They say foul beings of Old Times still lurk
In dark forgotten corners of the world,
And Gates still gape to loose, on certain nights,
Shapes pent in Hell.'

JUSTIN GEOFFREY

I read of it first in the strange book of Von Junzt, the German
eccentric who lived so curiously and died in such grisly and
mysterious fashion. It was my fortune to have access to his
Nameless Cults in the original edition, the so-called Black
Book, published in Düsseldorf in 1839, shortly before a
hounding doom overtook the author. Collectors of rare literature are familiar with *Nameless Cults* mainly through the
cheap and faulty translation which was pirated in London
by Bridewall in 1845, and the carefully expurgated edition
put out by the Golden Goblin Press of New York in 1909.
But the volume I stumbled upon was one of the unexpurgated
German copies, with heavy leather covers and rusty iron
hasps. I doubt if there are more than half a dozen such
volumes in the entire world today, for the quantity issued
was not great, and when the manner of the author's demise
was bruited about, many possessors of the book burned their
volumes in panic.

Von Junzt spent his entire life (1795–1840) delving into
forbidden subjects; he travelled in all parts of the world,
gained entrance into innumerable secret societies, and read
countless little-known and esoteric books and manuscripts
in the original; and in the chapters of the Black Book, which

range from startling clarity of exposition to murky ambiguity, there are statements and hints to freeze the blood of a thinking man. Reading what Von Junzt *dared* put in print arouses uneasy speculations as to what it was that he dared *not* tell. What dark matters, for instance, were contained in those closely written pages that formed the unpublished manuscript on which he worked unceasingly for months before his death, and which lay torn and scattered all over the floor of the locked and bolted chamber in which Von Junzt was found dead with the marks of taloned fingers on his throat? It will never be known, for the author's closest friend, the Frenchman Alexis Ladeau, after having spent a whole night piecing the fragments together and reading what was written, burnt them to ashes and cut his own throat with a razor.

But the contents of the published matter are shuddersome enough, even if one accepts the general view that they but represent the ravings of a madman. There among many strange things I found mention of the Black Stone, that curious, sinister monolith that broods among the mountains of Hungary, and about which so many dark legends cluster. Von Junzt did not devote much space to it – the bulk of his grim work concerns cults and objects of dark worship which he maintained existed in his day, and it would seem that the Black Stone represents some order or being lost and forgotten centuries ago. But he spoke of it as one of the *keys* – a phrase used many times by him, in various relations, and constituting one of the obscurities of his work. And he hinted briefly at curious sights to be seen about the monolith on Midsummer Night. He mentioned Otto Dostmann's theory that this monolith was a remnant of the Hunnish invasion and had been erected to commemorate a victory of Attila over the Goths. Von Junzt contradicted this assertion without giving any refutory facts, merely remarking that to attribute the origin of the Black Stone to the Huns was as logical as assuming that William the Conqueror reared Stonehenge.

This implication of enormous antiquity piqued my interest

immensely and after some difficulty I succeeded in locating
a rat-eaten and mouldering copy of Dostmann's *Remnants of
Lost Empires* (Berlin, 1809, 'Der Drachenhaus' Press). I was
disappointed to find that Dostmann referred to the Black
Stone even more briefly than had Von Junzt, dismissing it
with a few lines as an artefact comparatively modern in
contrast with the Greco-Roman ruins of Asia Minor which
was his pet theme. He admitted his inability to make out the
defaced characters on the monolith but pronounced them
unmistakably Mongoloid. However, little as I learned from
Dostmann, he did mention the name of the village adjacent
to the Black Stone – Stregoicavar – an ominous name,
meaning something like Witch-Town.

A close scrutiny of guide-books and travel articles gave me
no further information – Stregoicavar, not on any map that
I could find, lay in a wild, little-frequented region, out of the
path of casual tourists. But I did find subject for thought in
Dornly's *Magyar Folklore*. In his chapter on *Dream Myths* he
mentions the Black Stone and tells of some curious
superstitions regarding it – especially the belief that if
anyone sleeps in the vicinity of the monolith, that person
will be haunted by monstrous nightmares for ever after; and
he cited tales of the peasants regarding too-curious people
who ventured to visit the Stone on Midsummer Night and
who died raving mad because of *something* they saw there.

That was all I could glean from Dornly, but my interest
was even more intensely aroused as I sensed a distinctly
sinister aura about the Stone. The suggestion of dark antiquity, the recurrent hint of unnatural events on Midsummer
Night, touched some slumbering instinct in my being, as one
senses, rather than hears, the flowing of some dark subter-
raneous river in the night.

And I suddenly saw a connection between this Stone and a
certain weird and fantastic poem written by the mad poet,
Justin Geoffrey: *The People of the Monolith*. Inquiries led to
the information that Geoffrey had indeed written that poem
while travelling in Hungary, and I could not doubt that the

Black Stone was the very monolith to which he referred in his strange verse. Reading his stanzas again, I felt once more the strange dim stirrings of subconscious promptings that I had noticed when first reading of the Stone.

I had been casting about for a place to spend a short vacation and I made up my mind. I went to Stregoicavar. A train of obsolete style carried me from Temesvar to within striking distance, at least, of my objective, and a three days' ride in a jouncing coach brought me to the little village which lay in a fertile valley high up in the fir-clad mountains. The journey itself was uneventful, but during the first day we passed the old battlefield of Schomvaal where the brave Polish-Hungarian knight, Count Boris Vladinoff, made his gallant and futile stand against the victorious hosts of Suleiman the Magnificent, when the Grand Turk swept over eastern Europe in 1526.

The driver of the coach pointed out to me a great heap of crumbling stones on a hill near by, under which he said, the bones of the brave Count lay. I remembered a passage from Larson's *Turkish Wars*: 'After the skirmish' (in which the Count with his small army had beaten back the Turkish advanceguard) 'the Count was standing beneath the half-ruined walls of the old castle on the hill, giving orders as to the disposition of his forces, when an aide brought to him a small lacquered case which had been taken from the body of the famous Turkish scribe and historian, Selim Bahadur, who had fallen in the fight. The Count took therefrom a roll of parchment and began to read, but he had not read far before he turned very pale and without saying a word, replaced the parchment in the case and thrust the case into his cloak. At that very instant a hidden Turkish battery suddenly opened fire, and the balls striking the old castle, the Hungarians were horrified to see the walls crash down in ruin, completely covering the brave Count. Without a leader the gallant little army was cut to pieces, and in the war-swept years that followed, the bones of the nobleman were never recovered. Today the natives point out a huge and mouldering pile of ruins near Schomvaal beneath which, they say, still rests all that the centuries have left of Count Boris Vladinoff.'

I found the village of Stregoicavar a dreamy, drowsy little village that apparently belied its sinister cognomen – a forgotten back-eddy that Progress had passed by. The quaint houses and the quainter dress and manners of the people were those of an earlier century. They were friendly, mildly curious but not inquisitive, though visitors from the outside world were extremely rare.

'Ten years ago another American came here and stayed a few days in the village,' said the owner of the tavern where I had put up, 'a young fellow and queer-acting – mumbled to himself – a poet, I think.'

I knew he must mean Justin Geoffrey.

'Yes, he was a poet,' I answered, 'and he wrote a poem about a bit of scenery near this very village.'

'Indeed?' Mine host's interest was aroused. 'Then, since all great poets are strange in their speech and actions, he must have achieved great fame, for his actions and conversations were the strangest of any man I ever knew.'

'As is usual with artists,' I answered, 'most of his recognition has come since his death.'

'He is dead, then?'

'He died screaming in a madhouse five years ago.'

'Too bad, too bad,' sighed mine host sympathetically. 'Poor lad – he looked too long at the Black Stone.'

My heart gave a leap, but I masked my keen interest and said casually: 'I have heard something of this Black Stone; somewhere near this village, is it not?'

'Nearer than Christian folk wish,' he responded. 'Look!' He drew me to a latticed window and pointed up at the fir-clad slopes of the brooding blue mountains. 'There beyond where you see the bare face of that jutting cliff stands that accursed Stone. Would that it were ground to powder and the powder flung into the Danube to be carried to the deepest ocean! Once men tried to destroy the thing, but each man who laid hammer or maul against it came to an evil end. So now the people shun it.'

'What is there so evil about it?' I asked curiously.

'It is a demon-haunted thing,' he answered uneasily and with a suggestion of a shudder. 'In my childhood I knew a young man who came up from below and laughed at our traditions – in his foolhardiness he went to the Stone one Midsummer Night and at dawn stumbled into the village again, stricken dumb and mad. Something had shattered his brain and sealed his lips, for until the day of his death, which came soon after, he spoke only to utter terrible blasphemies or to slaver gibberish.

'My own nephew when very small was lost in the mountains and slept in the woods near the Stone, and now in his manhood he is tortured by foul dreams, so that at times he makes the night hideous with his screams and wakes with cold sweat upon him.

'But let us talk of something else, *Herr*; it is not good to dwell upon such things.'

I remarked on the evident age of the tavern and he answered with pride: 'The foundations are more than four hundred years old; the original house was the only one in the village which was not burned to the ground when Suleiman's devils swept through the mountains. Here, in the house that then stood on these same foundations, it is said, the scribe Selim Bahadur had his headquarters while ravaging the country hereabouts.'

I learned that the present inhabitants of Stregoicavar are not descendants of the people who dwelt there before the Turkish raid of 1526. The victorious Moslems left no living human in the village or the vicinity hereabouts when they passed over. Men, women, and children they wiped out in one red holocaust of murder, leaving a vast stretch of country silent and utterly deserted. The present people of Stregoicavar are descended from hardy settlers from the lower valleys who came into the upper levels and rebuilt the ruined village after the Turk was thrust back.

Mine host did not speak of the extermination of the original inhabitants with any great resentment and I learned that his ancestors in the lower levels had looked on the mountaineers with even more hatred and aversion than they regarded the Turks. He was rather vague regarding the causes of this feud, but said that the original inhabitants of Stregoicavar had been in the habit of making stealthy raids on the lowlands and stealing girls and children. Moreover, he said that they were not exactly of the same blood as his own people; the sturdy, original Magyar-Slavic stock had mixed and intermarried with a degraded aboriginal race until the breeds had blended, producing an unsavoury amalgamation. Who these aborigines were, he had not the slightest idea, but maintained that they were 'pagans' and had dwelt in the mountains since time immemorial, before the coming of the conquering peoples.

I attached little importance to this tale; seeing in it merely a parallel to the amalgamation of Celtic tribes with Mediterranean aborigines in the Galloway hills, with the resultant mixed race which, as Picts, has such an extensive part in Scotch legendry. Time has a curiously foreshortening effect on folklore, and just as tales of the Picts became intertwined with legends of an older Mongoloid race, so eventually to the Picts was ascribed the repulsive appearance of the squat primitives, whose individuality merged, in the telling, into Pictish tales, and was forgotten; so, I felt, the supposed inhuman attributes of the first villagers of Stregoicavar could be traced to older, outworn myths with invading Huns and Mongols.

The morning after my arrival I received directions from my host, who gave them worriedly, and set out to find the Black Stone. A few hours' tramp up the fir-covered slopes brought me to the face of the rugged, solid stone cliff which jutted boldly from the mountainside. A narrow trail wound up it, and mounting this, I looked out over the peaceful valley of Stregoicavar, which seemed to drowse, guarded on either hand by the great blue mountains. No huts or any

sign of human tenancy showed between the cliffs whereon I
stood and the village. I saw numbers of scattered farms in
the valley but all lay on the other side of Stregoicavar, which
itself seemed to shrink from the brooding slopes which
masked the Black Stone.

The summit of the cliffs proved to be a sort of thickly
wooded plateau. I made my way through the dense growth
for a short distance and came into a wide glade; and in the
centre of the glade reared a gaunt figure of black stone.

It was octagonal in shape, some sixteen feet in height and
about a foot and half thick. It had once evidently been highly
polished, but now the surface was thickly dinted as if savage
efforts had been made to demolish it; but the hammers had
done little more than to flake off small bits of stone and
mutilate the characters which once had evidently marched
in a spiralling line round and round the shaft to the top. Up
to ten feet from the base these characters were almost
completely blotted out, so that it was very difficult to trace
their direction. Higher up they were plainer, and I managed
to squirm part of the way up the shaft and scan them at close
range. All were more or less defaced, but I was positive that
they symbolized no language now remembered on the face of
the earth. I am fairly familiar with all hieroglyphics known
to researchers and philologists and I can say with certainty
that those characters were like nothing of which I have ever
read or heard. The nearest approach to them that I ever saw
were some crude scratches on a gigantic and strangely
symmetrical rock in the lost valley of Yucatan. I remember
that when I pointed out these marks to the archaeologist
who was my companion, he maintained that they either
represented natural weathering or the idle scratching of
some Indian. To my theory that the rock was really the base
of a long-vanished column, he merely laughed, calling my
attention to the dimensions of it, which suggested, if it were
built with any natural rules of architectural symmetry, a
column a thousand feet high. But I was not convinced.

I will not say that the characters on the Black Stone were

similar to those on the colossal rock in Yucatan; but one suggested the other. As to the substance of the monolith, again I was baffled. The stone of which it was composed was a dully gleaming black, whose surface, where it was not dinted and roughened, created a curious illusion of semi-transparency.

I spent most of the morning there and came away baffled. No connection of the Stone with any other artefact in the world suggested itself to me. It was as if the monolith had been reared by alien hands, in an age distant and apart from human ken.

I returned to the village with my interest in no way abated. Now that I had seen the curious thing, my desire was still more keenly whetted to investigate the matter further and seek to learn by what strange hands and for what strange purpose the Black Stone had been reared in the long ago.

I sought out the tavern-keeper's nephew and questioned him in regard to his dreams, but he was vague, though willing to oblige. He did not mind discussing them, but was unable to describe them with any clarity. Though he dreamed the same dreams repeatedly, and though they were hideously vivid at the time, they left no distinct impression on his waking mind. He remembered them only as chaotic nightmares through which huge whirling fires shot lurid tongues of flame and a black drum bellowed incessantly. One thing only he clearly remembered – in one dream he had seen the Black Stone, not on a mountain slope but set like a spire on a colossal black castle.

As for the rest of the villagers I found them not inclined to talk about the Stone, with the exception of the schoolmaster, a man of surprising education, who spent much more of his time out in the world than any of the rest.

He was much interested in what I told him of Von Junzt's remarks about the Stone, and warmly agreed with the German author on the alleged age of the monolith. He believed that a coven had once existed in the vicinity and that possibly all of the original villagers had been members of that fertility cult which once threatened to undermine European civilization and gave rise to the tales of witchcraft. He cited the very name of the village to prove his point; it had not been originally named Stregoicavar, he said; according to legends the builders had called it Xuthltan, which was the aboriginal name of the site on which the village had been built many centuries ago.

This fact roused again an indescribable feeling of uneasiness. The barbarous name did not suggest connections with any Scythic, Slavic or Mongolian race to which an aboriginal people of these mountains would, under natural circumstances, have belonged.

That the Magyars and Slavs of the lower valleys believed the original inhabitants of the village to be members of the witchcraft cult was evident, the schoolmaster said, by the name they gave it, which name continued to be used even after the older settlers had been massacred by the Turks, and the village rebuilt by a cleaner and more wholesome breed.

He did not believe that the members of the cult erected the monolith but he did believe that they used it as a centre of their activities, and repeating vague legends which had been handed down since before the Turkish invasion, he advanced the theory that the degenerate villagers had used it as a sort of altar on which they offered human sacrifices, using as victims the girls and babies stolen from his own ancestors in the lower valleys.

He discounted the myths of weird events on Midsummer Night, as well as a curious legend of a strange deity which the witch-people of Xuthltan were said to have invoked with chants and wild rituals of flagellation and slaughter.

He had never visited the Stone on Midsummer Night, he said, but he would not fear to do so; whatever *had* existed or taken place there in the past, had been long engulfed in the mists of time and oblivion. The Black Stone had lost its meaning save as a link to a dead and dusty past.

It was while returning from a visit with this schoolmaster one night about a week after my arrival at Stregoicavar that a sudden recollection struck me – it was Midsummer Night! The very time that the legends linked with grisly implications to the Black Stone. I turned away from the tavern and strode swiftly through the village. Stregoicavar lay silent; the villagers retired early. I saw no one as I passed rapidly out of the village and up into the firs which masked the mountain slopes in a weird light and etched the shadows blackly. No wind blew through the firs, but a mysterious, intangible rustling and whispering was abroad. Surely on such nights in past centuries, my whimsical imagination told me, naked witches astride magic broomsticks had flown across this valley, pursued by jeering demoniac familiars.

I came to the cliffs and was somewhat disquieted to note that the illusive moonlight lent them a subtle appearance I had not noticed before – in the weird light they appeared less like natural cliffs and more like the ruins of cyclopean and Titan-reared battlements jutting from the mountainslope.

Shaking off this hallucination with difficulty I came upon the plateau and hesitated a moment before I plunged into the brooding darkness of the woods. A sort of breathless tenseness hung over the shadows, like an unseen monster holding its breath lest it scare away its prey.

I shook off the sensation – a natural one, considering the eeriness of the place and its evil reputation – and made my way through the wood, experiencing a most unpleasant sensation that I was being followed, and halting once, sure that something clammy and unstable had brushed against my face in the darkness.

I came out into the glade and saw the tall monolith rearing its gaunt height above the sward. At the edge of the woods on the side towards the cliff was a stone which formed a sort of natural seat. I sat down, reflecting that it was probably while there that the mad poet, Justin Geoffrey, had written his fantastic *People of the Monolith*. Mine host thought that it was the Stone which had caused Geoffrey's insanity, but the seeds of madness had been sown in the poet's brain long before he ever came to Stregoicavar.

A glance at my watch showed that the hour of midnight was close at hand. I leaned back, awaiting whatever ghostly demonstration might appear. A thin night wind started up among the branches of the firs, with an uncanny suggestion of faint, unseen pipes whispering an eery and evil tune. The monotony of the sound and my steady gazing at the monolith produced a sort of self-hypnosis upon me; I grew drowsy. I fought this feeling, but sleep stole on me in spite of myself; the monolith seemed to sway and dance, strangely distorted to my gaze, and then I slept.

I opened my eyes and sought to rise, but lay still, as if an icy hand gripped me helpless. Cold terror stole over me. The glade was no longer deserted. It was thronged by a silent crowd of strange people, and my distended eyes took in strange barbaric details of costume which my reason told me were archaic and forgotten even in this backward land. Surely, I thought, these are villagers who have come here to hold some fantastic conclave – but another glance told me that these people were not of the folk of Stregoicavar. They were a shorter, more squat race, whose brows were lower, whose faces were broader and duller. Some had Slavic or Magyar features, but those features were degraded as from a mixture of some baser, alien strain I could not classify. Many wore the hides of wild beasts, and their whole appearance, both men and women, was one of sensual brutishness. They terrified and repelled me, but they gave me no heed. They formed in a vast half-circle in front of the monolith and began a sort of chant, flinging their arms in unison and weaving their bodies rhythmically from the waist upward. All eyes were fixed on the top of the Stone which they seemed to be invoking. But the strangest of all was the dimness of their voices; not fifty yards from me hundreds of men and women were unmistakably lifting their voices in a wild

chant, yet those voices came to me as a faint indistinguisha-
ble murmur as if from across vast leagues of Space – or *time*.

Before the monolith stood a sort of brazier from which a
vile, nauseous yellow smoke billowed upward, curling curiously in an undulating spiral around the black shaft, like a
vast unstable serpent.

On one side of this brazier lay two figures – a young girl,
stark naked and bound hand and foot, and an infant, apparently only a few months old. On the other side of the brazier
squatted a hideous old hag with a queer sort of black drum
on her lap; this drum she beat with slow, light blows of her
open palms, but I could not hear the sound.

The rhythm of the swaying bodies grew faster and into the
space between the people and the monolith sprang a naked
young woman, her eyes blazing, her long black hair flying
loose. Spinning dizzily on her toes, she whirled across the
open space and fell prostrate before the Stone, where she lay
motionless. The next instant a fantastic figure followed her –
a man from whose waist hung a goatskin, and whose features
were entirely hidden by a sort of mask made from a huge
wolf's head, so that he looked like a monstrous, nightmare
being, horribly compounded of elements both human and
bestial. In his hand he held a bunch of long fir switches
bound together at the larger ends, and the moonlight glinted
on a chain of heavy gold looped about his neck. A smaller
chain depending from it suggested a pendant of some sort,
but this was missing.

The people tossed their arms violently and seemed to
redouble their shouts as this grotesque creature loped across
the open space with many a fantastic leap and caper. Coming
to the woman who lay before the monolith, he began to lash
her with the switches he bore, and she leapt up and spun
into the wild mazes of the most incredible dance I have ever
seen. And her tormentor danced with her, keeping the wild
rhythm, matching her every whirl and bound, while incessantly raining cruel blows on her naked body. And at every
blow he shouted a single word, over and over, and all the

people shouted it back. I could see the working of their lips,
and now the faint far-off murmur of their voices merged and
blended into one distant shout, repeated over and over with
slobbering ecstasy. But what that one word was, I could not
make out.

In dizzy whirls spun the wild dancers, while the lookers-
on, standing still in their tracks, followed the rhythm of
their dance with swaying bodies and weaving arms. Madness
grew in the eyes of the capering votaress and was reflected
in the eyes of the watchers. Wilder and more extravagant
grew the whirling frenzy of that mad dance – it became a
bestial and obscene thing, while the old hag howled and
battered the drum like a crazy woman, and the switches
cracked out a devil's tune.

Blood trickled down the dancer's limbs but she seemed not
to feel the lashing save as a stimulus for further enormities
of outrageous motion; bounding into the midst of the yellow
smoke which now spread out tenuous tentacles to embrace
both flying figures, she seemed to merge with that foul fog
and veil herself with it. Then emerging into plain view,
closely followed by the beast-thing that flogged her, she shot
into an indescribable, explosive burst of dynamic mad
motion, and on the very crest of that mad wave, she dropped
suddenly to the sward, quivering and panting as if completely overcome by her frenzied exertions. The lashing
continued with unabated violence and intensity and she
began to wriggle towards the monolith on her belly. The
priest – or such I will call him – followed, lashing her
unprotected body with all the power of his arm as she writhed
along, leaving a heavy track of blood on the trampled earth.
She reached the monolith, and gasping and panting, flung
both arms about it and covered the cold stone with fierce hot
kisses, as in frenzied and unholy adoration.

The fantastic priest bounded high in the air, flinging away
the red-dabbled switches, and the worshippers, howling and
foaming at the mouth, turned on each other with tooth and
nail, rending one another's garments and flesh in a blind

passion of bestiality. The priest swept up the infant with a long arm, and shouting again that Name, whirled the wailing babe high in the air and dashed its brains out against the monolith, leaving a ghastly stain on the black surface. Cold with horror I saw him rip the tiny body open with his bare brutish fingers and fling handfuls of blood on the shaft, then toss the red and torn shape into the brazier, extinguishing flame and smoke in a crimson rain, while the maddened brutes behind him howled over and over that Name. Then suddenly they all fell prostrate, writhing like snakes, while the priest flung wide his gory hands as in triumph. I opened my mouth to scream my horror and loathing, but only a dry rattle sounded; a huge monstrous toad-like *thing* squatted on the top of the monolith!

I saw its bloated, repulsive and unstable outline against the moonlight, and set in what would have been the face of a natural creature, its huge, blinking eyes which reflected all the lust, abysmal greed, obscene cruelty and monstrous evil that has stalked the sons of men since their ancestors moved blind and hairless in the tree-tops. In those grisly eyes mirrored all the unholy things and vile secrets that sleep in the cities under the sea, and that skulk from the light of day in the blackness of primordial caverns. And so that ghastly thing that the unhallowed ritual of cruelty and sadism and blood had evoked from the silence of the hills, leered and blinked down on its bestial worshippers, who grovelled in abhorrent abasement before it.

Now the beast-masked priest lifted the bound and weakly writhing girl in his brutish hands and held her up towards that horror on the monolith. And as that monstrosity sucked in its breath, lustfully and slobberingly, something snapped in my brain and I fell into a merciful faint.

I opened my eyes on a still white dawn. All the events of the night rushed back on me and I sprang up, then stared about me in amazement. The monolith brooded gaunt and silent above the sward which waved, green and untrampled, in the morning breeze. A few quick strides took me across the glade; here had the dancers leapt and bounded until the ground should have been trampled bare, and here had the votaress wriggled her painful way to the Stone, streaming blood on the earth. But no drop of crimson showed on the uncrushed sward. I looked, shudderingly, at the side of the monolith against which the bestial priest had brained the stolen baby – but no dark stain or grisly clot showed there.

A dream! It had been a wild nightmare – or else – I shrugged my shoulders. What vivid clarity for a dream!

I returned quietly to the village and entered the inn without being seen. And there I sat meditating over the strange events of the night. More and more was I prone to discard the dream-theory. That what I had seen was illusion and without material substance was evident. But I believed that I had looked on the mirrored shadow of a deed perpetrated in ghastly actuality in bygone days. But how was I to know? What proof to show that my vision had been a gathering of foul spectres rather than a mere nightmare originating in my own brain?

As if for answer a name flashed in my mind – Selim Bahadur! According to legend this man, who had been a soldier as well as a scribe, had commanded that part of Suleiman's army which had devastated Stregoicavar; it seemed logical enough; and if so, he had gone straight from the blotted-out countryside to the bloody field of Schomvaal, and his doom. I sprang up with a sudden shout – that manuscript which was taken from the Turk's body, and which Count Boris shuddered over – might it not contain some narration of what the conquering Turks found in Stregoicavar? What else could have shaken the iron nerves of the Polish adventurer? And since the bones of the Count had never been recovered, what more certain than that lacquered case, with its mysterious contents, still lay hidden beneath the ruins that covered Boris Vladinoff? I began packing my bag with fierce haste.

Three days later found me ensconced in a little village a few miles from the old battlefield, and when the moon rose I was working with savage intensity on the great pile of crumbling stone that crowned the hill. It was back-breaking toil – looking back now I cannot see how I accomplished it, though I laboured without a pause from moonrise to dawn. Just as the sun was coming up I tore aside the last tangle of stones and looked on all that was mortal of Count Boris Vladinoff – only a few pitiful fragments of crumbling bone – and among them, crushed out of all original shape, lay a case whose lacquered surface had kept it from complete decay through the centuries.

I seized it with frenzied eagerness, and piling back some of the stones on the bones I hurried away; for I did not care to be discovered by the suspicious peasants in an act of apparent desecration.

Back in my tavern chamber I opened the case and found the parchment comparatively intact; and there was something else in the case – a small squat object wrapped in silk. I was wild to plumb the secrets of those yellowed pages, but weariness forbade me. Since leaving Stregoicavar I had hardly slept at all, and the terrific exertions of the previous night combined to overcome me. In spite of myself I was forced to stretch myself down on my bed, nor did I awake until sundown.

I snatched a hasty supper, and then in the light of a flickering candle, I set myself to read the neat Turkish characters that covered the parchment. It was difficult work, for I am not deeply versed in the language and the archaic style of the narrative baffled me. But as I toiled through it a word or phrase here and there leapt at me and a dimly growing horror shook me in its grip. I bent my energies fiercely to the task, and as the tale grew clearer and took more tangible form my blood chilled in my veins, my hair stood up and my tongue clove to my mouth. All external things partook of the grisly madness of that infernal manuscript until the night sounds of insects and creatures in the woods took the form of ghastly murmurings and stealthy treadings of ghoulish horrors and the sighing of the night wind changed to tittering obscene gloating of evil over the souls of men.

At last when grey dawn was stealing through the latticed window, I laid down the manuscript and took up and unwrapped the thing in the bit of silk. Staring at it with haggard eyes I knew the truth of the matter was clinched, even had it been possible to doubt the veracity of that terrible manuscript.

And I replaced both obscene things in the case, nor did I rest or sleep or eat until that case containing them had been weighted with stones and flung into the deepest current of the Danube which, God grant, carried them back into the Hell from which they came.

It was no dream I dreamed on Midsummer Midnight in the hills above Stregoicavar. Well for Justin Geoffrey that he tarried there only in the sunlight and went his way, for had he gazed upon that ghastly conclave, his mad brain would have snapped before it did. How my own reason held, I do not know.

No – it was no dream – I gazed upon a foul rite of votaries long dead, come up from Hell to worship as of old; ghosts that bowed before a ghost. For Hell has long claimed their hideous god. Long, long he dwelt among the hills, a brain-shattering vestige of an outworn age, but no longer his obscene talons clutch for the souls of living men, and his kingdom is a dead kingdom, peopled only by the ghosts of those who served him in his lifetime and theirs.

By what foul alchemy or godless sorcery the Gates of Hell are opened on that one eery night I do not know, but mine own eyes have seen. And I know I looked on no living thing that night, for the manuscript written in the careful hand of Selim Bahadur narrated at length what he and his raiders found in the valley of Stregoicavar; and I read, set down in detail, the blasphemous obscenities that torture wrung from the lips of screaming worshippers; and I read, too, of the lost, grim black cavern high in the hills where the horrified Turks hemmed a monstrous, bloated, wallowing toad-like being and slew it with flame and ancient steel blessed in old times by Muhammad, and with incantations that were old when Arabia was young. And even staunch old Selim's hand shook as he recorded the cataclysmic, earth-shaking, death-howls of the monstrosity which died not alone; for a half-score of his slayers perished with him, in ways that Selim would not or could not describe.

And that squat idol carved of gold and wrapped in silk was an image of *himself*, and Selim tore it from the golden chain that looped the neck of the slain high priest of the mask.

Well that the Turks swept that foul valley with torch and cleanly steel! Such sights as those brooding mountains have looked on belong to the darkness and abysses of lost eons. No – it is not fear of the toad-thing that makes me shudder in the night. He is made fast in Hell with his nauseous horde, freed only for an hour on the most weird night of the year, as I have seen. And of his worshippers, none remains.

But it is the realization that such things once crouched beast-like above the souls of men which brings cold sweat to my brow; and I fear to peer again into the leaves of Von Junzt's abomination. For now I understand his repeated phrase of *keys*! – age! Keys to Outer Doors – links with an abhorrent past and – who knows? – of abhorrent spheres of the *present*. And I understand why the cliffs look like battlements in the moonlight and why the tavern-keeper's nightmare-haunted nephew saw in his dream the Black Stone like a spire on a cyclopean black castle. If men ever excavate among those mountains they may find incredible things below those masking slopes. For the cave wherein the Turks trapped the – *thing* – was not truly a cavern, and I shudder to contemplate the gigantic gulf of eons which must stretch between this age and the time when the earth shook herself and reared up, like a wave, those blue mountains that, rising, enveloped unthinkable things. May no man ever seek to uproot that ghastly spire men call the Black Stone!

A Key! Aye, it is a Key, a symbol of a forgotten horror. That horror had faded into the limbo from which it crawled, loathsomely, in the black dawn of the earth. But what of the other fiendish possibilities hinted at by Von Junzt – what of the monstrous hand which strangled out his life? Since reading what Selim Bahadur wrote, I can no longer doubt anything in the Black Book. Man was not always master of the earth – *and is he now?*

And the thought recurs to me – if such a monstrous entity as the Master of the Monolith somehow survived its own unspeakably distant epoch so long – *what nameless shapes may even now lurk in the dark places of the world?*

The Hounds of Tindalos

FRANK BELKNAP LONG

'I'm glad you came,' said Chalmers. He was sitting by the window and his face was very pale. Two tall candles guttered at his elbow and cast a sickly amber light over his long nose and slightly receding chin. Chalmers would have nothing modern about his apartment. He had the soul of a medieval ascetic, and he preferred illuminated manuscripts to auto-mobiles, and leering stone gargoyles to radios and adding-machines.

As I crossed the room to the settee he had cleared for me I glanced at his desk and was surprised to discover that he had been studying the mathematical formulae of a celebrated contemporary physicist, and that he had covered many sheets of thin yellow paper with curious geometric designs.

'Einstein and John Dee are strange bedfellows,' I said as my gaze wandered from his mathematical charts to the sixty or seventy quaint books that comprised his strange little library. Plotinus and Emanuel Moscopulus, St Thomas Aquinas and Frenicle de Bessy stood elbow to elbow in the sombre ebony bookcase, and chairs, table, and desk were littered with pamphlets about medieval sorcery and witch-craft and black magic, and all of the valiant glamorous things that the modern world has repudiated.

Chalmers smiled engagingly, and passed me a Russian cigarette on a curiously carved tray. 'We are just discovering now,' he said, 'that the old alchemists and sorcerers were two-thirds *right*, and that your modern biologist and materialist is nine-tenths *wrong*.'

'You have always scoffed at modern science,' I said, a little impatiently.

'Only at scientific dogmatism,' he replied. 'I have always been a rebel, a champion of originality and lost causes; that is why I have chosen to repudiate the conclusions of contemporary biologists.'

'And Einstein?' I asked.

'A priest of transcendental mathematics!' he murmured reverently. 'A profound mystic and explorer of the great *suspected.*'

'Then you do not entirely despise science.'

'Of course not,' he affirmed. 'I merely distrust the scientific positivism of the past fifty years, the positivism of Haeckel and Darwin and of Mr Bertrand Russell. I believe that biology has failed pitifully to explain the mystery of man's origin and destiny.'

'Give them time,' I retorted.

Chalmers' eyes glowed. 'My friend,' he murmured, 'your pun is sublime. Give them *time*. That is precisely what I would do. But your modern biologist scoffs at time. He has the key but he refuses to use it. What do we know of time, really? Einstein believes that it is relative, that it can be interpreted in terms of space, of *curved* space. But must we stop here? When mathematics fails us can we not advance by – insight?'

'You are treading on dangerous ground,' I replied. 'That is a pitfall that your true investigator avoids. That is why modern science has advanced so slowly. It accepts nothing that it cannot demonstrate. But you – '

'I would take hashish, opium, all manner of drugs. I would emulate the sages of the East. And then perhaps I would apprehend – '

'What?'

'The fourth dimension.'

'Theosophical rubbish!'

'Perhaps. But I believe that drugs expand human consciousness. William James agreed with me. And I have discovered a new one.'

'A new drug?'

'It was used centuries ago by Chinese alchemists, but it is virtually unknown in the West. Its occult properties are amazing. With its aid and the aid of my mathematical knowledge I believe that I can *go back through time.*'

'I do not understand.'

'Time is merely our imperfect perception of a new dimension of space. Time and motion are both illusions. Everything that has existed from the beginning of the world *exists now.* Events that occurred centuries ago on this planet continue to exist in another dimension of space. Events that will occur centuries from now *exist already.* We cannot perceive their existence because we cannot enter the dimension of space that contains them. Human beings as we know them are merely fractions, infinitesimally small fractions of one enormous whole. Every human being is linked with *all* the life that has preceded him on this planet. All of his ancestors are parts of him. Only time separates him from his forebears, and time is an illusion and does not exist.'

'I think I understand,' I murmured.

'It will be sufficient for my purpose if you can form a vague idea of what I wish to achieve. I wish to strip from my eyes the veils of illusion that time has thrown over them, and see the *beginning and the end.*'

'And you think this new drug will help you?'

'I am sure that it will. And I want you to help me. I intend to take the drug immediately. I cannot wait. I must *see.*' His eyes glittered strangely. 'I am going back, back through time.'

He rose and strode to the mantel. When he faced me again he was holding a small square box in the palm of his hand. 'I have here five pellets of the drug Liao. It was used by the Chinese philosopher Lao Tze, and while under its influence he visioned Tao. Tao is the most mysterious force in the world; it surrounds and pervades all things; it contains the visible universe and everything that we call reality. He who apprehends the mysteries of Tao sees clearly all that was and will be.'

'Rubbish!' I retorted.

'Tao resembles a great animal, recumbent, motionless, containing in its enormous body all the worlds of our universe, the past, the present and the future. We see portions of this great monster through a slit, which we call time. With the aid of this drug I shall enlarge the slit. I shall behold the great figure of life, the great recumbent beast in its entirety.'

'And what do you wish me to do?'

'Watch, my friend. Watch and take notes. And if I go back too far you must recall me to reality. You can recall me by shaking me violently. If I appear to be suffering acute physical pain you must recall me at once.'

'Chalmers,' I said, 'I wish you wouldn't make this experiment. You are taking dreadful risks. I don't believe that there is any fourth dimension and I emphatically do not believe in Tao. And I don't approve of your experimenting with unknown drugs.'

'I know the properties of this drug,' he replied. 'I know precisely how it affects the human animal and I know its dangers. The risk does not reside in the drug itself. My only fear is that I may become lost in time. You see, I shall assist the drug. Before I swallow this pellet I shall give my undivided attention to the geometric and algebraic symbols that I have traced on this paper.' He raised the mathematical chart that rested on his knee. 'I shall prepare my mind for an excursion into time. I shall approach the fourth dimension with my conscious mind before I take the drug which will enable me to exercise occult powers of perception. Before I enter the dream world of the Eastern mystic I shall acquire all of the mathematical help that modern science can offer. This mathematical knowledge, this conscious approach to an actual apprehension of the fourth dimension of time will supplement the work of the drug. The drug will open up stupendous new vistas – the mathematical preparation will enable me to grasp them intellectually. I have often grasped the fourth dimension in dreams, emotionally, intuitively, but I have never been able to recall, in waking life, the occult splendours that were momentarily revealed to me.

'But with your aid, I believe that I can recall them. You will take down everything that I say while I am under the influence of the drug. No matter how strange or incoherent my speech may become you will omit nothing. When I awake I may be able to supply the key to whatever is mysterious or incredible. I am not sure that I shall succeed, but if I *do* succeed' – his eyes were strangely luminous – '*time will exist for me no longer!*'

He sat down abruptly. 'I shall make the experiment at once. Please stand over there by the window and watch. Have you a fountain pen?'

I nodded gloomily and removed a pale green Waterman from my upper vest pocket.

'And a pad, Frank?'

I groaned and produced a memorandum book. 'I emphatically disapprove of this experiment,' I muttered. 'You're taking a frightful risk.'

'Don't be an asinine old woman!' he admonished. 'Nothing that you can say will induce me to stop now. I entreat you to remain silent while I study these charts.'

He raised the charts and studied them intently. I watched the clock on the mantel as it ticked out the seconds, and a curious dread clutched at my heart so that I choked.

Suddenly the clock stopped ticking, and exactly at that moment Chalmers swallowed the drug.

I rose quickly and moved towards him, but his eyes implored me not to interfere. 'The clock has stopped,' he murmured. 'The forces that control it approve of my experiment. *Time* stopped, and I swallowed the drug. I pray God that I shall not lose my way.'

He closed his eyes and leaned back on the sofa. All of the

blood had left his face and he was breathing heavily. It was clear that the drug was acting with extraordinary rapidity.

'It is beginning to get dark,' he murmured. 'Write that. It is beginning to get dark and the familiar objects in the room are fading out. I can discern them vaguely through my eyelids, but they are fading swiftly.'

I shook my pen to make the ink come and wrote rapidly in shorthand as he continued to dictate.

'I am leaving the room. The walls are vanishing and I can no longer see any of the familiar objects. Your face, though, is still visible to me. I hope that you are writing. I think that I am about to make a great leap – a leap through space. Or perhaps it is through time that I shall make the leap. I cannot tell. Everything is dark, indistinct.'

He sat for a while silent, with his head sunk upon his breast. Then suddenly he stiffened and his eyelids fluttered open. 'God in heaven!' he cried. 'I *see!*'

He was straining forward in his chair, staring at the opposite wall. But I knew that he was looking beyond the wall and that the objects in the room no longer existed for him. 'Chalmers,' I cried, 'Chalmers, shall I wake you?'

'Do not!' he shrieked. 'I *see everything*. All of the billions of lives that preceded me on this planet are before me at this moment. I see men of all ages, all races, all colours. They are fighting, killing, building, dancing, singing. They are sitting about rude fires on lonely grey deserts, and flying through the air in monoplanes. They are riding the seas in bark canoes and enormous steamships; they are painting bison and mammoths on the walls of dismal caves and covering huge canvases with queer futuristic designs. I watch the migrations from Atlantis. I watch the migrations from Lemuria. I see the elder races – a strange horde of black dwarfs overwhelming Asia, and the Neandertalers with lowered heads and bent knees ranging obscenely across Europe. I watch the Achaeans streaming into the Greek islands, and the crude beginnings of Hellenic culture. I am in Athens and Pericles is young. I am standing on the soil of

Italy. I assist in the rape of the Sabines; I march with the Imperial Legions. I tremble with awe and wonder as the enormous standards go by and the ground shakes with the tread of the victorious *hastati*. A thousand naked slaves grovel before me as I pass in a litter of gold and ivory drawn by night-black oxen from Thebes, and the flowergirls scream "*Ave Caesar*" as I nod and smile. I am myself a slave on a Moorish galley. I watch the erection of a great cathedral. Stone by stone it rises, and through months and years I stand and watch each stone as it falls into place. I am burned on a cross head downward in the thyme-scented gardens of Nero, and I watch with amusement and scorn the torturers at work in the chambers of the Inquisition.

'I walk in the holiest sanctuaries; I enter the temples of Venus. I kneel in adoration before the Magna Mater, and I throw coins on the bare knees of the sacred courtesans who sit with veiled faces in the groves of Babylon. I creep into an Elizabethan theatre and with the stinking rabble about me I applaud *The Merchant of Venice*. I walk with Dante through the narrow streets of Florence. I meet the young Beatrice, and the hem of her garment brushes my sandals as I stare enraptured. I am a priest of Isis, and my magic astounds the nations. Simon Magus kneels before me, imploring my assistance, and Pharaoh trembles when I approach. In India I talk with the Masters and run screaming from their presence, for their revelations are as salt on wounds that bleed.

'I perceive everything *simultaneously*. I perceive everything from all sides; I am a part of all the teeming billions about me. I exist in all men and all men exist in me. I perceive the whole of human history in a single instant, the past and the present.

'By simply *straining* I can see farther and farther back. Now I am going back through strange curves and angles. Angles and curves multiply about me. I perceive great segments of time through *curves*. There is *curved time*, and *angular time*. The beings that exist in angular time cannot enter curved time. It is very strange.

'I am going back and back. Man has disappeared from the earth. Gigantic reptiles crouch beneath enormous palms and swim through the loathly black waters of dismal lakes. Now the reptiles have disappeared. No animals remain upon the land, but beneath the waters, plainly visible to me, dark forms move slowly over the rotting vegetation.

'The forms are becoming simpler and simpler. Now they are single cells. All about me there are angles – strange angles that have no counterparts on the earth. I am desperately afraid.

'There is an abyss of being which man has never fathomed.'

I stared. Chalmers had risen to his feet and he was gesticulating helplessly with his arms. 'I am passing through unearthly angles; I am approaching – oh, the burning horror of it.'

'Chalmers!' I cried. 'Do you wish me to interfere?'

He brought his right hand quickly before his face, as though to shut out a vision unspeakable. 'Not yet!' he cried; 'I will go on. I will see – what – lies – beyond – '

A cold sweat streamed from his forehead and his shoulders jerked spasmodically. 'Beyond life there are' – his face grew ashen with terror – '*things* that I cannot distinguish. They move slowly through angles. They have no bodies, and they move slowly through outrageous angles.'

It was then that I became aware of the odour in the room. It was a pungent, indescribable odour, so nauseous that I could scarcely endure it. I stepped quickly to the window and threw it open. When I returned to Chalmers and looked into his eyes I nearly fainted.

'I think they have scented me!' he shrieked. 'They are slowly turning towards me.'

He was trembling horribly. For a moment he clawed at the air with his hands. Then his legs gave way beneath him and he fell forward on his face, slobbering and moaning.

I watched him in silence as he dragged himself across the

floor. He was no longer a man. His teeth were bared and saliva dripped from the corners of his mouth.

'Chalmers,' I cried. 'Chalmers, stop it! Stop it, do you hear?'

As if in reply to my appeal he commenced to utter hoarse convulsive sounds which resembled nothing so much as the barking of a dog, and began a sort of hideous writhing in a circle about the room. I bent and seized him by the shoulders. Violently, desperately, I shook him. He turned his head and snapped at my wrist. I was sick with horror, but I dared not release him for fear that he would destroy himself in a paroxysm of rage.

'Chalmers,' I muttered, 'you must stop that. There is nothing in this room that can harm you. Do you understand?'

I continued to shake and admonish him, and gradually the madness died out of his face. Shivering convulsively, he crumpled into a grotesque heap on the Chinese rug.

I carried him to the sofa and deposited him upon it. His features were twisted in pain, and I knew that he was still struggling dumbly to escape from abominable memories.

'Whisky,' he muttered. 'You'll find a flask in the cabinet by the window – upper left-hand drawer.'

When I handed him the flask his fingers tightened about it until the knuckles showed blue. 'They nearly got me,' he gasped. He drained the stimulant in immoderate gulps, and gradually the colour crept back into his face.

'That drug was the very devil!' I murmured.

'It wasn't the drug,' he moaned.

His eyes no longer glared insanely, but he still wore the look of a lost soul.

'They scented me in time,' he moaned. 'I went too far.'

'What were *they* like?' I said, to humour him.

He leaned forward and gripped my arm. He was shivering horribly. 'No words in our language can describe them!' He spoke in a hoarse whisper. 'They are symbolized vaguely in the myth of the Fall, and in an obscene form which is occasionally found engraved on ancient tablets. The Greeks had a name for them, which veiled their essential foulness.

The tree, the snake, and the apple – these are the vague symbols of a most awful mystery.'

His voice had risen to a scream. 'Frank, Frank, a terrible and unspeakable *deed* was done in the beginning. Before time, the *deed*, and from the deed – '

He had risen and was hysterically pacing the room. 'The deeds of the dead move through angles in dim recesses of time. They are hungry and athirst!'

'Chalmers,' I pleaded to quiet him. 'We are living in the third decade of the twentieth century.'

'They are lean and athirst!' he shrieked. '*The Hounds of Tindalos!*'

'Chalmers, shall I phone for a physician?'

'A physician cannot help me now. They are horrors of the soul, and yet' – he hid his face in his hands and groaned – 'they are real, Frank. I saw them for a ghastly moment. For a moment I stood on the *other side*. I stood on the pale grey shores beyond time and space. In an awful light that was not light, in a silence that shrieked, I saw *them*.

'All the evil in the universe was concentrated in their lean, hungry bodies. Or had they bodies? I saw them only for a moment; I cannot be certain. *But I heard them breathe.* Indescribably for a moment I felt their breath upon my face. They turned towards me and I fled screaming. In a single moment I fled screaming through time. I fled down quintillions of years.

'But they scented me. Men awake in them cosmic hungers. We have escaped, momentarily, from the foulness that rings them round. They thirst for that in us which is clean, which emerged from the deed without stain. There is a part of us which did not partake in the deed, and that they hate. But do not imagine that they are literally, prosaically evil. They are beyond good and evil as we know it. They are that which in the beginning fell away from cleanliness. Through the deed they became bodies of death, receptacles of all foulness. But they are not evil in *our* sense because in the spheres through which they move there is no thought, no moral, no right or wrong as we understand it. There is merely the pure and the foul. The foul expresses itself through angle; the pure through curves. Man, the pure part of him, is descended from a curve. Do not laugh. I mean that literally.'

I rose and searched for my hat. 'I'm dreadfully sorry for you, Chalmers,' I said, as I walked towards the door. 'But I don't intend to stay and listen to such gibberish. I'll send my physician to see you. He's an elderly, kindly chap and he won't be offended if you tell him to go to the devil. But I hope you'll respect his advice. A week's rest in a good sanitarium should benefit you immeasurably.'

I heard him laughing as I descended the stairs, but his laughter was so utterly mirthless that it moved me to tears.

2

When Chalmers phoned the following morning my first impulse was to hang up the receiver immediately. His request was so unusual and his voice was so wildly hysterical that I feared any further association with him would result in the impairment of my own sanity. But I could not doubt the genuineness of his misery, and when he broke down completely and I heard him sobbing over the wire I decided to comply with his request.

'Very well,' I said. 'I will come over immediately and bring the plaster.'

En route to Chalmers' home I stopped at a hardware store and purchased twenty pounds of plaster of Paris. When I entered my friend's room he was crouching by the window watching the opposite wall out of eyes that were feverish with fright. When he saw me he rose and seized the parcel containing the plaster with an avidity that amazed and horrified me. He had extruded all of the furniture and the room presented a desolate appearance.

'It is just conceivable that we can thwart them!' he

exclaimed. 'But we must work rapidly. Frank, there is a
stepladder in the hall. Bring it here immediately. And then
fetch a pail of water.'

'What for?' I murmured.

He turned sharply and there was a flush on his face. 'To
mix the plaster, you fool!' he cried. 'To mix the plaster that
will save our bodies and souls from a contamination unmentionable. To mix the plaster that will save the world from –
Frank, *they must be kept out*!'

'Who?' I murmured.

'The Hounds of Tindalos!' he muttered. 'They can only
reach us through angles. We must eliminate all angles from
this room. I shall plaster up all of the corners, all of the
crevices. We must make this room resemble the interior of a
sphere.'

I knew that it would have been useless to argue with him.
I fetched the stepladder, Chalmers mixed the plaster, and for
three hours we laboured. We filled in the four corners of the
wall and the intersections of the floor and wall and the wall
and ceiling, and we rounded the sharp angles of the
windowseat.

'I shall remain in this room until they return in time,' he
affirmed when our task was completed. 'When they discover
that the scent leads through curves they will return. They
will return ravenous and snarling and unsatisfied to the
foulness that was in the beginning, before time, beyond
space.'

He nodded graciously and lit a cigarette. 'It was good of
you to help,' he said.

'Will you not see a physician, Chalmers?' I pleaded.

'Perhaps – tomorrow,' he murmured. 'But now I must
watch and wait.'

'Wait for what?' I urged.

Chalmers smiled wanly. 'I know that you think me insane,'
he said. 'You have a shrewd but prosaic mind, and you
cannot conceive of an entity that does not depend for its
existence on force and matter. But did it ever occur to you,

my friend, that force and matter are merely the barriers to perception imposed by time and space? When one knows, as I do, that time and space are identical and that they are both deceptive because they are merely imperfect manifestations of a higher reality, one no longer seeks in the visible world for an explanation of the mystery and terror of being.'

I rose and walked towards the door.

'Forgive me,' he cried. 'I did not mean to offend you. You have a superlative intellect, but I – I have a *superhuman* one. It is only natural that I should be aware of your limitations.'

'Phone if you need me,' I said, and descended the stairs two steps at a time. 'I'll send my physician over at once,' I muttered, to myself. 'He's a hopeless maniac, and heaven knows what will happen if someone doesn't take charge of him immediately.'

3

The following is a condensation of two announcements which appeared in the Partridgeville Gazette *for July 3, 1928:*

EARTHQUAKE SHAKES FINANCIAL DISTRICT

At 2 o'clock this morning an earth tremor of unusual severity broke several plate-glass windows in Central Square and completely disorganized the electric and street railway systems. The tremor was felt in the outlying districts and the steeple of the First Baptist Church on Angell Hill (designed by Christopher Wren in 1717) was entirely demolished. Firemen are now attempting to put out a blaze which threatens to destroy the Partridgeville Glue Works. An investigation is promised by the mayor and an immediate attempt will be made to fix responsibility for this disastrous occurrence.

OCCULT WRITER MURDERED BY UNKNOWN GUEST

HORRIBLE CRIME IN CENTRAL SQUARE

Mystery Surrounds Death of Halpin Chalmers

At 9 A.M. today the body of Halpin Chalmers, author and journalist, was found in an empty room above the jewellery store of Smithwick and Isaacs, 24 Central Square. The coroner's investigation revealed that the room had been rented furnished to Mr Chalmers on May 1, and that he had himself disposed of the furniture a fortnight ago. Chalmers was the author of several recondite books on occult themes, and a member of the Bibliographic Guild. He formerly resided in Brooklyn, New York.

At 7 A.M. Mr L. E. Hancock, who occupies the apartment opposite Chalmers' room in the Smithwick and Isaacs establishment, smelt a peculiar odour when he opened his door to take in his cat and the morning edition of the *Partridgeville Gazette*. The odour he describes as extremely acrid and nauseous, and he affirms that it was so strong in the vicinity of Chalmers' room that he was obliged to hold his nose when he approached that section of the hall.

He was about to return to his own apartment when it occurred to him that Chalmers might have accidentally forgotten to turn off the gas in his kitchenette. Becoming considerably alarmed at the thought, he decided to investigate, and when repeated tappings on Chalmers' door brought no response he notified the superintendent. The latter opened the door by means of a pass key, and the two men quickly made their way into Chalmers' room. The room was utterly destitute of furniture, and Hancock asserts that when he first glanced at the floor his heart went cold within him, and that the superintendent, without saying a word, walked to the open window and stared at the building opposite for fully five minutes.

Chalmers lay stretched upon his back in the centre of the room. He was starkly nude, and his chest and arms were covered with a peculiar bluish pus or ichor. His head lay grotesquely upon his chest. It had been completely severed from his body, and the features were twisted and torn and horribly mangled. Nowhere was there a trace of blood.

The room presented a most astonishing appearance. The intersections of the walls, ceiling and floor had been thickly smeared with plaster of Paris, but at intervals fragments had cracked and fallen off, and someone had grouped these upon the floor about the murdered man so as to form a perfect triangle.

Beside the body were several sheets of charred yellow paper. These bore fantastic geometric designs and symbols and several hastily scrawled sentences. The sentences were almost illegible and so absurd in content that they furnished no possible clue to the perpetrator of the crime. 'I am waiting and watching,' Chalmers wrote. 'I sit by the window and watch walls and ceiling. I do not believe they can reach me, but I must beware of the Doels. Perhaps *they* can help them break through. The satyrs will help, and they can advance through the scarlet circles. The Greeks knew a way of preventing that. It is a great pity that we have forgotten so much.'

On another sheet of paper, the most badly charred of the seven or eight fragments found by Detective Sergeant Douglas (of the Partridge Reserve), was scrawled the following:

'Good God, the plaster is falling! A terrific shock has loosened the plaster and it is falling. An earthquake perhaps! I never could have anticipated this. It is growing dark in the room. I must phone Frank. But can he get here in time? I will try. I will recite the Einstein formula. I will – God, they are breaking through! They are breaking through! Smoke is pouring from the corners of the walls. Their tongues – ahhhh –'

In the opinion of Detective Sergeant Douglas, Chalmers
was poisoned by some obscure chemical. He has sent specimens of the strange blue slime found on Chalmers' body to
the Partridgeville Chemical Laboratories; and he expects the
report will shed new light on one of the most mysterious
crimes of recent years. That Chalmers entertained a guest
on the evening preceding the earthquake is certain, for his
neighbour distinctly heard a low murmur of conversation in
the former's room as he passed it on his way to the stairs.
Suspicion points strongly to this unknown visitor and the
police are diligently endeavouring to discover his identity.

4

Report of James Morton, chemist and bacteriologist:
My dear Mr Douglas:
The fluid sent to me for analysis is the most peculiar that
I have ever examined. It resembles living protoplasm, but it
lacks the peculiar substances known as enzymes. Enzymes
catalyse the chemical reactions occurring in living cells, and
when the cell dies they cause it to disintegrate by hydroly-
sation. Without enyzmes protoplasm should possess enduring
vitality, i.e., immortality. Enzymes are the negative compo-
nents, so to speak, of unicellular organism, which is the basis
of all life. That living matter can exist without enzymes
biologists emphatically deny. And yet the substance that you
have sent me is alive and it lacks these 'indispensable'
bodies. Good God, sir, do you realize what astounding new
vistas this opens up?

5

Excerpt from The Secret Watcher *by the late Halpin Chalmers:*

What if, parallel to the life we know, there is another life that does not die, which lacks the elements that destroy *our* life? Perhaps in another dimension there is a *different* force from that which generates our life. Perhaps this force emits energy, or something similar to energy, which passes from the unknown dimension where *it* is and creates a new form of cell life in our dimension. No one knows that such new cell life does exist in our dimension. Ah, but I have seen *its* manifestations. I have *talked* with them. In my room at night I have talked with the Doels. And in dreams I have seen their maker. I have stood on the dim shore beyond time and matter and seen *it*. It moves through strange curves and outrageous angles. Some day I shall travel in time and meet *it* face to face.

The Space Eaters

FRANK BELKNAP LONG

1

The horror came to Partridgeville in a blind fog.

All that afternoon thick vapours from the sea had swirled and eddied from the farm, and the room in which we sat swam with moisture. The fog ascended in spirals from beneath the door, and its long, moist fingers caressed my hair until it dripped. The square-paned windows were coated with a thick, dewlike moisture; the air was heavy and dank and unbelievably cold.

I stared gloomily at my friend. He had turned his back to the window and was writing furiously. He was a tall, slim man with a slight stoop and abnormally broad shoulders. In profile his face was impressive. He had an extremely broad forehead, long nose and slightly protuberant chin – a strong, sensitive face which suggested a wildly imaginative nature held in restraint by a sceptical and truly extraordinary intellect.

My friend wrote short stories. He wrote to please himself, in defiance of contemporary taste, and his tales were un-usual. They would have delighted Poe; they would have delighted Hawthorne, or Ambrose Bierce, or Villiers de l'Isle Adam. They were studies of abnormal men, abnormal beasts, abnormal plants. He wrote of remote realms of imagination and horror, and the colours, sounds and odours which he dared to evoke were never seen, heard or smelt on the familiar side of the moon. He projected his creations against mind-chilling backgrounds. They stalked through tall and lonely forests, over ragged mountains, and slithered down the stairs of ancient houses, and between the piles of rotting black wharves.

One of his tales, *The House of the Worm*, had induced a young student at a Midwestern University to seek refuge in an enormous red-brick building where everyone approved of his sitting on the floor and shouting at the top of his voice: 'Lo, my beloved is fairer than all the lilies among the lilies in the lily garden.' Another, *The Defilers*, had brought him precisely one hundred and ten letters of indignation from local readers when it appeared in the *Partridgeville Gazette*.

As I continued to stare at him he suddenly stopped writing and shook his head. 'I can't do it,' he said. 'I should have to invent a new language. And yet I can comprehend the thing emotionally, intuitively, if you will. If I could only convey it in a sentence somehow – the strange crawling of its fleshless spirit!'

'Is it some new horror?' I asked.

He shook his head. 'It is not new to me. I have known and felt it for years – a horror utterly beyond anything your prosaic brain can conceive.'

'Thank you,' I said.

'All human brains are prosaic,' he elaborated. 'I meant no offence. It is the shadowy terrors that lurk behind and above them that are mysterious and awful. Our little brains – what can they know of vampire-like entities which may lurk in dimensions higher than our own, or beyond the universe of stars? I think sometimes they lodge in our heads, and our brains feel them, but when they stretch out tentacles to probe and explore us, we go screaming mad.' He was staring at me steadily now.

'But you can't honestly believe in such nonsense!' I exclaimed.

'Of course not!' He shook his head and laughed. 'You know damn well I'm too profoundly sceptical to believe in anything. I have merely outlined a poet's reactions to the universe. If a man wishes to write ghostly stories and actually convey a sensation of horror, he must believe in everything – and *anything*. By *anything* I mean the horror that transcends *everything*, that is more terrible and impossible than *everything*. He must believe that there are things from outer space that can reach down and fasten themselves on us with a malevolence that can destroy us utterly – our bodies as well as our minds.'

'But this thing from outer space – how can he describe it if he doesn't know its shape – or size or colour?'

'It is virtually impossible to describe it. That is what I have sought to do – and failed. Perhaps some day – but then, I doubt if it can ever be accomplished. But your artist can hint, suggest . . .'

'Suggest what?' I asked, a little puzzled.

'Suggest a horror that is utterly unearthly; that makes itself felt in terms that have no counterparts on Earth.'

I was still puzzled. He smiled wearily and elaborated his theory.

'There is something prosaic,' he said, 'about even the best of the classic tales of mystery and terror. Old Mrs Radcliffe, with her hidden vaults and bleeding ghosts; Maturin, with his allegorical Faustlike hero-villains, and his fiery flames from the mouth of hell; Edgar Poe, with his blood-clotted corpses, and black cats, his telltale hearts and disintegrating Valdemars; Hawthorne, with his amusing preoccupation with the problems and horrors arising from mere human sin (as though human sins were of any significance to a coldly malign intelligence from beyond the stars). Then we have modern masters – Algernon Blackwood, who invites us to a feast of the high gods and shows us an old woman with a harelip sitting before a ouija board fingering soiled cards, or an absurd nimbus of ectoplasm emanating from some clairvoyant ninny; Bram Stoker with his vampires and werewolves, mere conventional myths, the tag-ends of medieval folklore; Wells with his pseudo-scientific bogies, fish-men at the bottom of the sea, ladies in the moon, and the hundred

and one idiots who are constantly writing ghost stories for
the magazines – what have they contributed to the literature
of the unholy?

'Are we not made of flesh and blood? It is but natural that
we should be revolted and horrified when we are shown that
flesh and blood in a state of corruption and decay, with the
worms passing over and under it. It is but natural that a
story about a corpse should thrill us, fill us with fear and
horror and loathing. Any fool can awake these emotions in
us – Poe really accomplished very little with his Lady
Ushers, and liquescent Valdemars. He appealed to simple,
natural, understandable emotions, and it was inevitable that
his readers should respond.

'Are we not the descendants of barbarians? Did we not
once dwell in tall and sinister forests, at the mercy of beasts
that rend and tear? It is but inevitable that we should shiver
and cringe when we meet in literature dark shadows from
our own past. Harpies and vampires and werewolves – what
are they but magnifications, distortions of the great birds
and bats and ferocious dogs that harassed and tortured our
ancestors? It is easy enough to arouse fear by such means. It
is easy enough to frighten men with the flames at the mouth
of hell, because they are hot and shrivel and burn the flesh –
and who does not understand and dread a fire? Blows that
kill, fires that burn, shadows that horrify because their
substances lurk evilly in the black corridors of our inherited
memories – I am weary of the writers who would terrify us
by such pathetically obvious and trite unpleasantness.'

Real indignation blazed in his eyes.

'Suppose there were a greater horror? Suppose evil things
from some other universe should decide to invade this one?
Suppose we couldn't see them? Suppose we couldn't feel
them? Suppose they were of a colour unknown on Earth, or
rather, of an *appearance* that was without colour?

'Suppose they had shape unknown on Earth? Suppose they
were four-dimensional, five-dimensional, six-dimensional?

Suppose they were a hundred-dimensional? Suppose they had no dimensions at all and yet existed? What could we do?

'They would not exist for us? They would exist for us if they gave us pain. Suppose it was not the pain of heat or cold or any of the pains we know, but a new pain? Suppose they touched something besides our nerves – reached our brains in a new and terrible way? Suppose they made themselves felt in a new and strange and unspeakable way? What could we do? Our hands would be tied. You cannot oppose what you cannot see or feel. You cannot oppose the thousand-dimensional. *Suppose they should eat their way to us through space!*'

He was speaking now with an intensity of emotion which belied his avowed scepticism of a moment before.

'That is what I have tried to write about. I wanted to make my readers feel and see that thing from another universe, from beyond space. I could easily enough hint at it or suggest it – any fool can do that – but I wanted actually to describe it. To describe a colour that is not a colour! a form that is formless!

'A mathematician could perhaps slightly more than suggest it. There would be strange curves and angles that an inspired mathematician in a wild frenzy of calculation might glimpse vaguely. It is absurd to say that mathematicians have not discovered the fourth dimension. They have often glimpsed it, often approached it, often apprehended it, but they are unable to demonstrate it. I know a mathematician who swears that he once saw the sixth dimension in a wild flight into the sublime skies of the differential calculus.

'Unfortunately I am not a mathematician. I am only a poor fool of a creative artist, and the thing from outer space utterly eludes me.'

Someone was pounding loudly on the door. I crossed the room and drew back the latch. 'What do you want?' I asked. 'What is the matter?'

'Sorry to disturb you, Frank,' said a familiar voice, 'but I've got to talk to someone.'

I recognized the lean white face of my nearest neighbour, and stepped instantly to one side. 'Come in,' I said. 'Come in, by all means. Howard and I have been discussing ghosts, and the things we've conjured up aren't pleasant company. Perhaps you can argue them away.'

I called Howard's horrors ghosts because I didn't want to shock my commonplace neighbour. Henry Wells was immensely big and tall, and as he strode into the room he seemed to bring a part of the night with him.

He collapsed on a sofa and surveyed us with frightened eyes. Howard laid down the story he had been reading, removed and wiped his glasses, and frowned. He was more or less tolerant of my bucolic visitors. We waited for perhaps a minute, and then the three of us spoke almost simultaneously. 'A horrible night!' 'Beastly, isn't it?' 'Wretched.'

Henry Wells frowned. 'Tonight,' he said, 'I – I met with a funny accident. I was driving Hortense through Mulligan Wood . . .'

'Hortense?' Howard interrupted.

'His horse,' I explained impatiently. 'You were returning from Brewster, weren't you, Harry?'

'From Brewster, yes,' he replied. 'I was driving between the trees, keeping a sharp lookout for cars with their lights on too bright, coming right at me out of the murk, and listening to the foghorns in the bay wheezing and moaning, when something wet landed on my head. "Rain," I thought. "I hope the supplies keep dry."

'I turned round to make sure that the butter and flour were covered up, and something soft like a sponge rose up from the bottom of the wagon and hit me in the face. I snatched at it and caught it between my fingers.

'In my hands it felt like jelly. I squeezed it, and moisture ran out of it down my wrists. It wasn't so dark that I couldn't see it, either. Funny how you can see in fogs – they seem to make night lighter. There was a sort of brightness in the air. I dunno, maybe it wasn't the fog, either. The trees seemed to stand out. You could see them sharp and clear. As I was

saying, I looked at the thing, and what do you think it looked
like? Like a piece of raw liver. Or like a calf's brain. There
were grooves in it, and you don't find many grooves in liver.
Liver's usually as smooth as glass.

'It was an awful moment for me. "There's someone up in
one of those trees," I thought. "He's some tramp or crazy man
or fool and he's been eating liver. My wagon frightened him
and he dropped it – a piece of it. I can't be wrong. There was
no liver in my wagon when I left Brewster."

'I looked up. You know how tall all of the trees are in
Mulligan Wood. You can't see the tops of some of them from
the wagon-road on a clear day. And you know how crooked
and queer-looking some of the trees are.

'It's funny, but I've always thought of them as old men –
tall old men, you understand, tall and crooked and very evil.
I've always thought of them as wanting to work mischief.
There's something unwholesome about trees that grow very
close together and grow crooked.

'I looked up.

'At first I didn't see anything but the tall trees, all white
and glistening with the fog, and above them a thick white
mist that hid the stars. And then something long and white
ran quickly down the trunk of one of the trees.

'It ran so quickly down the tree that I couldn't see it
clearly. And it was so thin anyway that there wasn't much
to see. But it was like an arm. It was like a long, white and
very thin arm. But of course it wasn't an arm. Who ever
heard of an arm as tall as a tree? I don't know what made
me compare it to an arm, because it was really nothing but a
thin line – like a wire, a string. I'm not sure that I saw it at
all. Maybe I imagined it. I'm not even sure that it was as
wide as a string. But it had a hand. Or didn't it? When I
think of it my brain gets dizzy. You see, it moved so quickly
I couldn't see it clearly at all.

'But it gave me the impression that it was looking for
something that it had dropped. For a minute the hand
seemed to spread out over the road, and then it left the tree

and came towards the wagon. It was like a huge white hand walking on its fingers with a terribly long arm fastened to it that went up and up until it touched the fog, or perhaps until it touched the stars.

'I screamed and slashed Hortense with the reins, but the horse didn't need any urging. She was up and off before I could throw the liver, or calf's brain, or whatever it was, into the road. She raced so fast she almost upset the wagon, but I didn't draw in the reins. I'd rather lie in a ditch with a broken rib than have a long white hand squeezing the breath out of my throat.

'We had almost cleared the wood and I was just beginning to breathe again when my brain went cold. I can't describe what happened in any other way. My brain got as cold as ice inside my head. I can tell you I was frightened.

'Don't imagine I couldn't think clearly. I was conscious of everything that was going on about me, but my brain was so cold I screamed with the pain. Have you ever held a piece of ice in the palm of your hand for as long as two or three minutes? It burnt, didn't it? Ice burns worse than fire. Well, my brain felt as though it had lain on ice for hours and hours. There was a furnace inside my head, but it was a cold furnace. It was roaring with raging cold.

'Perhaps I should have been thankful that the pain didn't last. It wore off in about ten minutes, and when I got home I didn't think I was any the worse for my experience. I'm sure I didn't think I was any the worse until I looked at myself in the glass. Then I saw the hole in my head.'

Henry Wells leaned forward and brushed back the hair from his right temple.

'Here is the wound,' he said. 'What do you make of it?' He tapped with his fingers a small round opening in the side of his head. 'It's like a bullet-wound,' he elaborated, 'but there was no blood and you can look in pretty far. It seems to go right into the centre of my head. I shouldn't be alive.'

Howard had risen and was staring at my neighbour with angry and accusing eyes.

'Why have you lied to us?' he shouted. 'Why have you told us this absurd story? A long hand! You were drunk, man. Drunk – and yet you've succeeded in doing what I'd have sweated blood to accomplish. If I could have made my readers feel that horror, know it for a moment, that horror that you described in the woods, I should be with the immortals – I should be greater than Poe, greater than Hawthorne. And you – a clumsy drunken liar . . .'

I was on my feet with a furious protest.

'He's not lying,' I said. 'He's been shot – someone has shot him in the head. Look at this wound. My God, man, you have no call to insult him!'

Howard's wrath died and the fire went out of his eyes. 'Forgive me,' he said. 'You can't imagine how badly I've wanted to capture that ultimate horror, to put it on paper, and he did it so easily. If he had warned me that he was going to describe something like that I would have taken notes. But of course he doesn't know he's an artist. It was an accidental *tour de force* that he accomplished; he couldn't do it again, I'm sure. I'm sorry I went up in the air – I apologize. Do you want me to go for a doctor? That *is* a bad wound.'

My neighbour shook his head. 'I don't want a doctor,' he said. 'I've seen a doctor. There's no bullet in my head – that hole was not made by a bullet. When the doctor couldn't explain it I laughed at him. I hate doctors; and I haven't much use for fools that think I'm in the habit of lying. I haven't much use for people who won't believe me when I tell 'em I saw the long, white thing come sliding down the tree as clear as day.'

But Howard was examining the wound in defiance of my neighbour's indignation. 'It was made by something round and sharp,' he said. 'It's curious, but the flesh isn't torn. A knife or bullet would have torn the flesh, left a ragged edge.'

I nodded, and was bending to study the wound when Wells shrieked, and clapped his hands to his head. 'Ah-h-h!' he choked. 'It's come back – the terrible, terrible cold.'

Howard stared. 'Don't expect me to believe such nonsense!' he exclaimed disgustedly.

But Wells was holding on to his head and dancing about the room in a delirium of agony. 'I can't stand it!' he shrieked. 'It's freezing up my brain. It's not like ordinary cold. It isn't. Oh God! It's like nothing you've ever felt. It bites, it scorches, it tears. It's like acid.'

I laid my hand upon his shoulder and tried to quiet him, but he pushed me aside and made for the door.

'I've got to get out of here,' he screamed. 'The thing wants room. My head won't hold it. It wants the night – the vast night. It wants to wallow in the night.'

He threw back the door and disappeared into the fog. Howard wiped his forehead with the sleeve of his coat and collapsed into a chair.

'Mad,' he muttered. 'A tragic case of manic-depressive psychosis. Who would have suspected it? The story he told us wasn't conscious art at all. It was simply a nightmare-fungus conceived by the brain of a lunatic.'

'Yes,' I said, 'but how do you account for the hole in his head?'

'Oh, that!' Howard shrugged. 'He probably always had it – probably was born with it.'

'Nonsense,' I said. 'The man never had a hole in his head before. Personally, I think he's been shot. Something ought to be done. He needs medical attention. I think I'll phone Dr Smith.'

'It is useless to interfere,' said Howard. 'That hole was *not* made by a bullet. I advise you to forget him until tomorrow. His insanity may be temporary; it may wear off; and then he'd blame us for interfering. If he's still emotionally disturbed tomorrow, if he comes here again and tries to make trouble, you can notify the proper authorities. Has he ever acted queerly before?'

'No,' I said. 'He was always quite sane. I think I'll take your advice and wait. But I wish I could explain the hole in his head.'

'The story he told interests me more,' said Howard. 'I'm going to write it out before I forget it. Of course I shan't be able to make the horror as real as he did, but perhaps I can catch a bit of the strangeness and glamour.'

He unscrewed his fountain pen and began to cover a sheet of paper with curious phrases.

I shivered and closed the door.

For several minutes there was no sound in the room save the scratching of his pen as it moved across the paper. For several minutes there was silence – and then the shrieks commenced. Or were they wails?

We heard them through the closed door, heard them above the moaning of the foghorns and the wash of the waves on Mulligan's Beach. We heard them above the million sounds of night that had horrified and depressed us as we sat and talked in that fog-enshrouded and lonely house. We heard them so clearly that for a moment we thought they came from just outside the house. It was not until they came again and again – long, piercing wails – that we discovered in them a quality of remoteness. Slowly we became aware that the wails came from far away, as far away, perhaps, as Mulligan Wood.

'A soul in torture,' muttered Howard. 'A poor, damned soul in the grip of the horror I've been telling you about – the horror I've known and felt for years.'

He rose unsteadily to his feet. His eyes were shining and he was breathing heavily.

I seized his shoulders and shook him. 'You shouldn't project yourself into your stories that way,' I exclaimed. 'Some poor chap is in distress. I don't know what's happened. Perhaps a ship foundered. I'm going to put on a slicker and find out what it's all about. I have an idea we may be needed.'

'We *may* be needed,' repeated Howard slowly. 'We may be needed indeed. It will not be satisfied with a single victim. Think of that great journey through space, the thirst and dreadful hungers it must have known! It is preposterous to imagine that it will be content with a single victim!'

Then, suddenly, a change came over him. The light went out of his eyes and his voice lost its quaver. He shivered.

'Forgive me,' he said. 'I'm afraid you'll think I'm as mad as the yokel who was here a few minutes ago. But I can't help identifying myself with my characters when I write. I'd described something very evil, and those yells – well, they are exactly like the yells a man would make if – if . . .'

'I understand,' I interrupted, 'but we've no time to discuss that now. There's a poor chap out there' – I pointed vaguely towards the door – 'with his back against the wall. He's fighting off something – I don't know what. We've got to help him.'

'Of course, of course,' he agreed, and followed me into the kitchen.

Without a word I took down a slicker and handed it to him. I also handed him an enormous rubber hat.

'Get into these as quickly as you can,' I said. 'The chap's desperately in need of us.'

I had got my own slicker down from the rack and was forcing my arms through its sticky sleeves. In a moment we were both pushing our way through the fog.

The fog was like a living thing. Its long fingers reached up and slapped us relentlessly on the face. It curled about our bodies and ascended in great, greyish spirals from the tops of our heads. It retreated before us, and as suddenly closed in and enveloped us.

Dimly ahead of us we saw the lights of a few lonely farms. Behind us the sea drummed, and the foghorns sent out a continuous, mournful ululation. The collar of Howard's slicker was turned up over his ears, and from his long nose moisture dripped. There was a grim decision in his eyes, and his jaw was set.

For many minutes we plodded on in silence, and it was not until we approached Mulligan Wood that he spoke.

'If necessary,' he said, 'we shall enter the wood.'

I nodded. 'There is no reason why we should not enter the wood,' I said. 'It isn't a large wood.'

'One could get out quickly?'

'One could get out very quickly indeed. My God, did you hear that?'

The shrieks had grown horribly loud.

'He is suffering,' said Howard. 'He is suffering terribly. Do you suppose – do you suppose it's your crazy friend?'

He had voiced a question which I had been asking myself for some time.

'It's conceivable,' I said. 'But we'll have to interfere if he's as mad as that. I wish I'd brought some of the neighbours with me.'

'Why in heaven's name didn't you?' Howard shouted. 'It may take a dozen men to handle him.' He was staring at the tall trees that towered before us, and I didn't think he really gave Henry Wells so much as a thought.

'That's Mulligan Wood,' I said. I swallowed nervously. 'It isn't a big wood,' I added idiotically.

'Oh my God!' Out of the fog came the sound of a voice in the last extremity of pain. 'They're eating up my brain. Oh my God!'

I was at that moment in deadly fear that I might become as mad as the man in the woods. I clutched Howard's arm.

'Let's go back,' I shouted. 'Let's go back at once. We were fools to come. There is nothing here but madness and suffering and perhaps death.'

'That may be,' said Howard, 'but we're going on.'

His face was ashen beneath his dripping hat, and his eyes were thin blue slits.

'Very well,' I said grimly. 'We'll go on.'

Slowly we moved among the trees. They towered above us, and the thick fog so distorted them and merged them together that they seemed to move forward with us. From their twisted branches the fog hung in ribbons. Ribbons, did I say? Rather were they snakes of fog – writhing snakes with venomous tongues and leering eyes. Through swirling clouds of fog we saw the scaly, gnarled boles of the trees, and every bole resembled the twisted body of an evil old man. Only the small oblong of light cast by my electric torch protected us against their malevolence.

Through great banks of fog we moved, and every moment the screams grew louder. Soon we were catching fragments of sentences, hysterical shoutings that merged into prolonged wails. 'Colder and colder and colder . . . they are eating up my brain. Colder! Ah-h-h!'

Howard gripped my arm. 'We'll find him,' he said. 'We can't turn back now.'

When we found him he was lying on his side. His hands were clasped about his head, and his body was bent double, and knees drawn up so tightly that they almost touched his chest. He was silent. We bent and shook him, but he made no sound.

'Is he dead?' I choked out. I wanted desperately to turn and run. The trees were very close to us.

'I don't know,' said Howard. 'I don't know. I hope that he is dead.'

I saw him kneel and slide his hand under the poor devil's shirt. For a moment his face was a mask. Then he got up quickly and shook his head.

'He is alive,' he said. 'We must get him into some dry clothes as quickly as possible.'

I helped him. Together we lifted the bent figure from the ground and carried it forward between the trees. Twice we stumbled and nearly fell, and the creepers tore at our clothes. The creepers were little malicious hands grasping and tearing under the malevolent guidance of the great trees. Without a star to guide us, without a light except the little pocket lamp which was growing dim, we fought our way out of Mulligan Wood.

The droning did not commence until we had left the wood. At first we scarcely heard it, it was so low, like the purring of gigantic engines far down in the earth. But slowly, as we stumbled forward with our burden, it grew so loud that we could not ignore it.

'What is that?' muttered Howard, and through the wraiths of fog I saw that his face had a greenish tinge.

'I don't know,' I mumbled. 'It's something horrible. I never heard anything like it. Can't you walk faster?'

So far we had been fighting familiar horrors, but the droning and humming that rose behind us was like nothing that I had ever heard on Earth. In excruciating fright, I shrieked aloud. 'Faster, Howard, faster! For God's sake, let's get out of this!'

As I spoke, the body that we were carrying squirmed, and from its cracked lips issued a torrent of gibberish: 'I was walking between the trees looking up. I couldn't see their tops. I was looking up, and then suddenly I looked down and the thing landed on my shoulders. It was all legs – all long, crawling legs. It went right into my head. I wanted to get away from the trees, but I couldn't. I was alone in the forest with the thing on my back, in my head, and when I tried to run, the trees reached out and tripped me. It made a hole so it could get in. It's my brain it wants. Today it made a hole, and now it's crawled in and sucking and sucking and sucking. It's as cold as ice and it makes a noise like a great big fly. But it isn't a fly. And it isn't a hand. I was wrong when I called it a hand. You can't see it. I wouldn't have seen it or felt it if it hadn't made a hole and got in. You almost see it, you almost feel it, and that means that it's getting ready to go in.'

'Can you walk, Wells? Can you walk?'

Howard had dropped Wells' legs and I could hear the harsh intake of his breath as he struggled to rid himself of his slicker.

'I think so,' Wells sobbed. 'But it doesn't matter. It's got me now. Put me down and save yourselves.'

'We've got to run!' I yelled.

'It's our one chance,' cried Howard. 'Wells, you follow us. Follow us, do you understand? They'll burn up your brain if they catch you. We're going to run, lad. Follow us!'

He was off through the fog. Wells shook himself free, and

followed like a man in a trance. I felt a horror more terrible than death. The noise was dreadfully loud; it was right in my ears, and yet for a moment I couldn't move. The wall of fog was growing thicker.

'Frank will be lost!' It was the voice of Wells, raised in a despairing shout.

'We'll go back!' It was Howard shouting now. 'It's death, or worse, but we can't leave him.'

'Keep on,' I called out. 'They won't get me. Save yourselves!'

In my anxiety to prevent them from sacrificing themselves I plunged wildly forward. In a moment I had joined Howard and was clutching at his arm.

'What is it?' I cried. 'What have we to fear?'

The droning was all about us now, but no louder.

'Come quickly or we'll be lost!' he urged frantically. 'They've broken down all barriers. That buzzing is a warning. We're sensitives – we've been warned, but if it gets louder we're lost. They're strong near Mulligan Wood, and it's here they've made themselves felt. They're experimenting now – feeling their way. Later, when they've learned, they'll spread out. If we can only reach the farm . . .'

'We'll reach the farm!' I shouted as I clawed my way through the fog.

'Heaven help us if we don't!' moaned Howard.

He had thrown off his slicker, and his seeping wet shirt clung tragically to his lean body. He moved through the blackness with long, furious strides. Far ahead we heard the shrieks of Henry Wells. Ceaselessly the foghorns moaned; ceaselessly the fog swirled and eddied about us.

And the droning continued. It seemed incredible that we should ever have found a way to the farm in the blackness. But find the farm we did, and into it we stumbled with glad cries.

'Shut the door!' shouted Howard.

I shut the door.

'We are safe here, I think,' he said. 'They haven't reached the farm yet.'

'What has happened to Wells?' I gasped, and then I saw the wet tracks leading into the kitchen.

Howard saw them too. His eyes flashed with momentary relief.

'I'm glad he's safe,' he muttered. 'I feared for him.'

Then his face darkened. The kitchen was unlighted and no sound came from it.

Without a word Howard walked across the room and into the darkness beyond. I sank into a chair, flicked the moisture from my eyes and brushed back my hair, which had fallen in soggy strands across my face. For a moment I sat, breathing heavily, and when the door creaked, I shivered. But I remembered Howard's assurance: 'They haven't reached the farm yet. We're safe here.'

Somehow, I had confidence in Howard. He realized that we were threatened by a new and unknown horror, and in some occult way he had grasped its limitations.

I confess, though, that when I heard the screams that came from the kitchen, my faith in my friend was slightly shaken. There were low growls, such as I could not believe came from any human throat, and the voice of Howard raised in wild expostulation. 'Let go, I say! Are you quite mad? Man, man, we have saved you! Don't, I say – let go of my leg. Ah-hh!'

As Howard staggered into the room I sprang forward and caught him in my arms. He was covered with blood from head to foot and his face was ashen.

'He's gone raving mad,' he moaned. 'He was running about on his hands and knees like a dog. He sprang at me, and almost killed me. I fought him off, but I'm badly bitten. I hit him in the face – knocked him unconscious. I may have killed him. He's an animal – I had to protect myself.'

I laid Howard on the sofa and knelt beside him, but he scorned my aid.

'Don't bother with me!' he commanded. 'Get a rope,

quickly, and tie him up. If he comes to, we'll have to fight for our lives.'

What followed was a nightmare. I remember vaguely that I went into the kitchen with a rope and tied poor Wells to a chair; then I bathed and dressed Howard's wounds, and lit a fire in the grate. I remember also that I telephoned for a doctor. But the incidents are confused in my memory, and I have no clear recollection of anything until the arrival of a tall, grave man with kindly and sympathetic eyes and a presence that was as soothing as an opiate.

He examined Howard, nodded, and explained that the wounds were not serious. He examined Wells, and did not nod. He explained slowly, 'His pupils don't respond to light,' he said. 'An immediate operation will be necessary. I tell you frankly, I don't think we can save him.'

'That wound in his head, Doctor,' I said. 'Was it made by a bullet?'

The doctor frowned. 'It puzzles me,' he said. 'Of course it was made by a bullet, but it should have partially closed up. It goes right into the brain. You say you know nothing about it. I believe you, but I think the authorities should be notified at once. Someone will be wanted for manslaughter, unless' – he paused – 'unless the wound was self-inflicted. What you tell me is curious. That he should have been able to walk about for hours seems incredible. The wound has obviously been dressed, too. There is no clotted blood at all.'

He paced slowly back and forth. 'We must operate here – at once. There is a slight chance. Luckily, I brought some instruments. We must clear this table and – do you think you could hold a lamp for me?'

I nodded. 'I'll try,' I said.

'Good!'

The doctor busied himself with preparations while I debated whether or not I should phone the police.

'I'm convinced,' I said at last, 'that the wound was self-inflicted. Wells acted very strangely. If you are willing, Doctor . . .'

'Yes?'

'We will remain silent about this matter until after the operation. If Wells lives, there would be no need of involving the poor chap in a police investigation.'

The doctor nodded. 'Very well,' he said. 'We will operate first and decide afterwards.'

Howard was laughing silently from his couch. 'The police,' he snickered. 'Of what use would they be against the things in Mulligan Wood?'

There was an ironic and ominous quality about his mirth that disturbed me. The horrors that we had known in the fog seemed absurd and impossible in the cool, scientific presence of Dr Smith, and I didn't want to be reminded of them.

The doctor turned from his instruments and whispered into my ear. 'Your friend has a slight fever, and apparently it has made him delirious. If you will bring me a glass of water I will mix him a sedative.'

I raced to secure a glass, and in a moment we had Howard sleeping soundly.

'Now then,' said the doctor as he handed me the lamp. 'You must hold this steady and move it as I direct.'

The white, unconscious form of Henry Wells lay upon the table that the doctor and I had cleared, and I trembled all over when I thought of what lay before me.

I should be obliged to stand and gaze into the living brain of my poor friend as the doctor relentlessly laid it bare.

With swift, experienced fingers the doctor administered an anaesthetic. I was oppressed by a dreadful feeling that we were committing a crime, that Henry Wells would have violently disapproved, that he would have preferred to die. It is a dreadful thing to mutilate a man's brain. And yet I knew that the doctor's conduct was above reproach, and that the ethics of his profession demanded that he operate.

'We are ready,' said Dr Smith. 'Lower the lamp. Carefully now!'

I saw the knife moving in his competent, swift fingers. For a moment I stared, and then I turned my head away. What I had seen in that brief glance made me sick and faint. It may have been fancy, but as I stared at the wall I had the impression that the doctor was on the verge of collapse. He made no sound, but I was almost certain that he had made some horrible discovery.

'Lower the lamp,' he said. His voice was hoarse and seemed to come from far down within his throat.

I lowered the lamp an inch without turning my head. I waited for him to reproach me, to swear at me perhaps, but he was as silent as the man on the table. I knew, though, that his fingers were still at work, for I could hear them as they moved about. I could hear his swift, agile fingers moving about the head of Henry Wells.

I suddenly became conscious that my hand was trembling. I wanted to lay down the lamp; I felt that I could no longer hold it.

'Are you nearly through?' I gasped in desperation.

'Hold that lamp steady!' The doctor screamed the command. 'If you move that lamp again – I – I won't sew him up. I don't care if they hang me! I'm not a healer of devils!'

I knew not what to do. I could scarcely hold the lamp, and the doctor's threat horrified me.

'Do everything you can,' I urged hysterically. 'Give him a chance to fight his way back. He was kind and good – once!'

For a moment there was silence, and I feared that he would not need me. I momentarily expected him to throw down his scalpel and sponge, and dash across the room and out into the fog. It was not until I heard his fingers moving about again that I knew he had decided to give even the damned a chance.

It was after midnight when the doctor told me that I could lay down the lamp. I turned with a cry of relief and encountered a face that I shall never forget. In three quarters of an hour the doctor had aged ten years. There were dark hollows beneath his eyes, and his mouth twitched convulsively.

'He'll not live,' he said. 'He'll be dead in an hour. I did not touch his brain. I could do nothing. When I saw – how things were – I – I – sewed him up immediately.'

'What did you see?' I half-whispered.

A look of unutterable fear came into the doctor's eyes. 'I saw – I saw . . .' His voice broke and his whole body quivered. 'I saw . . . oh, the burning shame of it . . . evil that is without shape, that is formless . . .'

Suddenly he straightened and looked wildly about him.

'They will come here and claim him!' he cried. 'They have laid their mark upon him and they will come for him. You must not stay here. This house is marked for destruction!'

I watched him helplessly as he seized his hat and bag and crossed to the door. With white, shaking fingers he drew back the latch, and in a moment his lean figure was silhouetted against a square of swirling vapour.

'Remember that I warned you!' he shouted back; and then the fog swallowed him.

Howard was sitting up and rubbing his eyes.

'A malicious trick, that!' he was muttering. 'To deliberately drug me! Had I known that glass of water . . .'

'How do you feel?' I asked as I shook him violently by the shoulders. 'Do you think you can walk?'

'You drug me, and then ask me to walk! Frank, you're as unreasonable as an artist. What is the matter now?'

I pointed to the silent figure on the table. 'Mulligan Wood is safer,' I said. 'He belongs to them now!'

Howard sprang to his feet and shook me by the arm.

'What do you mean?' he cried. 'How do you know?'

'The doctor saw his brain,' I explained. 'And he also saw something that he would not – could not describe. But he told me that they would come for him, and I believe him.'

'We must leave here at once!' cried Howard. 'Your doctor was right. We are in deadly danger. Even Mulligan Wood – but we need not return to the wood. There is your launch!'

'There is the launch!' I echoed, faint hope rising in my mind.

'The fog will be a most deadly menace,' said Howard grimly. 'But even death at sea is preferable to *this* horror.'

It was not far from the house to the dock, and in less than a minute Howard was seated in the stern of the launch and I was working furiously on the engine. The foghorns still moaned, but there were no lights visible anywhere in the harbour. We could not see two feet before our faces. The white wraiths of the fog were dimly visible in the darkness, but beyond them stretched endless night, lightless and full of terror.

Howard was speaking. 'Somehow I feel that there is death out there,' he said.

'There is more death here,' I said as I started the engine. 'I think I can avoid the rocks. There is very little wind and I know the harbour.'

'And of course we shall have the foghorns to guide us,' muttered Howard. 'I think we had better make for the open sea.'

I agreed.

'The launch wouldn't survive a storm,' I said, 'but I've no desire to remain in the harbour. If we reach the sea we'll probably be picked up by some ship. It would be sheer folly to remain where they can reach us.'

'How do we know how far they can reach?' groaned Howard. 'What are the distances of Earth to things that have travelled through space? They will over-run Earth. They will destroy us all utterly.'

'We'll discuss that later,' I cried as the engine roared into life. 'We're going to get as far away from them as possible. Perhaps they haven't *learned* yet! While there's still limitations we may be able to escape.'

We moved slowly into the channel, and the sound of the water splashing against the sides of the launch soothed us strangely. At a suggestion from me, Howard had taken the wheel and was slowly bringing her about.

'Keep her steady,' I shouted. 'There isn't any danger until we get into the Narrows!'

For several minutes I crouched above the engine while Howard steered in silence. Then, suddenly, he turned to me with a gesture of elation.

'I think the fog's lifting,' he said.

I stared into the darkness before me. Certainly it seemed less oppressive, and the white spirals of mist that had been continually ascending through it were fading into insubstantial wisps. 'Keep her head on,' I shouted. 'We're in luck. If the fog clears we'll be able to see the Narrows. Keep a sharp lookout for Mulligan Light.'

There is no describing the joy that filled us when we saw the light. Yellow and bright it streamed over the water and illuminated sharply the outlines of the great rocks that rose on both sides of the Narrows.

'Let me have the wheel,' I shouted as I stepped quickly forward. 'This is a ticklish passage, but we'll come through now with colours flying.'

In our excitement and elation we almost forgot the horror that we had left behind us. I stood at the wheel and smiled confidently as we raced over the dark water. Quickly the rocks drew nearer until their vast bulk towered above us.

'We shall certainly make it!' I cried.

But no response came from Howard. I heard him choke and gasp.

'What is the matter?' I asked suddenly and, turning, saw that he was crouching in terror above the engine. His back was turned towards me, but I knew instinctively in which direction he was gazing.

The dim shore that we had left shone like a flaming sunset. Mulligan Wood was burning. Great flames shot up from the highest of the tall trees, and a thick curtain of black smoke rolled slowly eastward, blotting out the few remaining lights in the harbour.

But it was not the flames that caused me to cry out in fear and horror. It was the shape that towered above the trees, the vast, formless shape that moved slowly to and fro across the sky.

God knows I tried to believe that I saw nothing. I tried to believe that the shape was a mere shadow cast by the flames, and I remember that I gripped Howard's arm reassuringly.

'The wood will be destroyed completely,' I cried, 'and those ghastly things with us will be destroyed with it.'

But when Howard turned and shook his head, I knew that the dim, formless thing that towered above the trees was more than a shadow.

'If we see it clearly, we are lost!' he warned, his voice vibrant with terror. 'Pray that it remains without form!'

It is older than the world, I thought, *older than all religion. Before the dawn of civilization men knelt in adoration before it. It is present in all mythologies. It is the primal symbol. Perhaps, in the dim past, thousands and thousands of years ago, it was used to – repel the invaders. I shall fight the shape with a high and terrible mystery.*

I became suddenly curiously calm. I knew that I had hardly a minute to act, that more than our lives were threatened, but I did not tremble. I reached calmly beneath the engine and drew out a quantity of cotton waste.

'Howard,' I said, 'light a match. It is our only hope. You must strike a match at once.'

For what seemed eternities Howard stared at me uncomprehendingly. Then the night was clamorous with his laughter.

'A match!' he shrieked. 'A match to warm our little brains! Yes, we shall need a match.'

'Trust me!' I entreated. 'You must – it is our one hope. Strike a match quickly.'

'I do not understand!' Howard was sober now, but his voice quivered.

'I have thought of something that may save us,' I said. 'Please light this waste for me.'

Slowly he nodded. I had told him nothing, but I knew he guessed what I intended to do. Often his insight was uncanny. With fumbling fingers he drew out a match and struck it.

'Be bold,' he said. 'Show them that you are unafraid. Make the sign boldly.'

As the waste caught fire, the form above the trees stood out with a frightful clarity.

I raised the flaming cotton and passed it quickly before my body in a straight line from my left to my right shoulder. Then I raised it to my forehead and lowered it to my knees.

In an instant Howard had snatched the brand and was repeating the sign. He made two crosses, one against his body and one against the darkness with the torch held at arm's length.

For a moment I shut my eyes, but I could still see the shape above the trees. Then slowly its form became less distinct, became vast and chaotic – and when I opened my eyes it had vanished. I saw nothing but the flaming forest and the shadows cast by the tall trees.

The horror had passed, but I did not move. I stood like an image of stone staring over the black water. Then something seemed to burst in my head. My brain spun dizzily, and I tottered against the rail.

I would have fallen, but Howard caught me about the shoulders. 'We're saved!' he shouted. 'We've won through.'

'I'm glad,' I said. But I was too utterly exhausted to really rejoice. My legs gave way beneath me and my head fell forward. All the sights and sounds of Earth were swallowed up in a merciful blackness.

2

Howard was writing when I entered the room.

'How is the story going?' I asked.

For a moment he ignored my question. Then he slowly turned and faced me. He was hollow-eyed, and his pallor was alarming.

'It's not going well,' he said at last. 'It doesn't satisfy me.

There are problems that still elude me. I haven't been able to capture *all* of the horror of the thing in Mulligan Wood.'

I sat down and lit a cigarette.

'I want you to explain that horror to me,' I said. 'For three weeks I have waited for you to speak. I know that you have some knowledge which you are concealing from me. What was the damp, spongy thing that landed on Wells' head in the woods? Why did we hear a droning as we fled in the fog? What was the meaning of the shape that we saw above the trees? And why, in heaven's name, didn't the horror spread as we feared it might? What stopped it? Howard, what do you think really happened to Wells' brain? Did his body burn with the farm, or did they – *claim* it? And the other body that was found in Mulligan Wood – that lean, blackened horror with riddled head – how did you explain that?'

(Two days after the fire a skeleton had been found in Mulligan Wood. A few fragments of burnt flesh still adhered to the bones, and the skullcap was missing.)

It was a long time before Howard spoke again. He sat with bowed head fingering his notebook, and his body trembled all over. At last he raised his eyes. They shone with a wild light and his lips were ashen.

'Yes,' he said. 'We will discuss the horror together. Last week I did not want to speak of it. It seemed too awful to put into words. But I shall never rest in peace until I have woven it into a story, until I have made my readers feel and see that dreadful, unspeakable thing. And I cannot write of it until I am convinced beyond the shadow of a doubt that I understand it myself. It may help me to talk about it.

'You have asked me what the damp thing was that fell on Wells' head. I believe that it was a human brain – the essence of a human brain drawn out through a hole, or holes, in a human head. I believe the brain was drawn out by imperceptible degrees, and reconstructed again by the horror. I believe that for some purposes of its own it used human brains – perhaps to learn from them. Or perhaps it merely played with them. The blackened, riddled body in

Mulligan Wood? That was the body of the first victim, some
poor fool who got lost between the tall trees. I rather suspect
the trees helped. I think the horror endowed them with a
strange life. Anyhow, the poor chap lost his brain. The horror
took it, and played with it, and then accidentally dropped it.
It dropped it on Wells' head. Wells said that the long, thin
and very white arm he saw was looking for something that
it had dropped. Of course Wells didn't really see the arm
objectively, but the horror that is without form or colour had
already entered his brain and clothed itself in human
thought.

'As for the droning that we heard and the shape we thought
we saw above the burning forest – that was the horror
seeking to make itself felt, seeking to break down barriers,
seeking to enter our brains and clothe itself with our
thoughts. It almost got us. If we had seen the white arm we
should have been lost.'

Howard walked to the window. He drew back the curtains
and gazed for a moment at the crowded harbour and the tall,
white buildings that towered against the moon. He was
staring at the skyline of lower Manhattan. Sheer beneath
him the cliffs of Brooklyn Heights loomed darkly.

'Why didn't they conquer?' he cried. 'They could have
destroyed us utterly. They could have wiped us from Earth –
all our wealth and power would have gone down before
them.'

I shivered. 'Yes . . . why didn't the horror spread?' I asked.

Howard shrugged his shoulders. 'I do not know. Perhaps
they discovered that human brains were too trivial and
absurd to bother with. Perhaps we ceased to amuse them.
Perhaps they grew tired of us. But it is conceivable that the
sign destroyed them – or sent them back through space. I
think they came millions of years ago, and were frightened
away by the sign. When they discovered that we had not
forgotten the use of the sign they may have fled in terror.
Certainly there has been no manifestation for three weeks. I
think that they are gone.'

'And Henry Wells?' I asked.

'Well, his body was not found. I imagine they came for him.'

'And you honestly intend to put this – this obscenity into a story? Oh my God! The whole thing is so incredible, so unheard of, that I can't believe it. Did we not dream it all? Were we ever really in Partridgeville? Did we sit in an ancient house and discuss frightful things while the fog curled about us? Did we walk through that unholy wood? Were the trees really alive, and did Henry Wells run about on his hands and knees like a wolf?'

Howard sat down quietly and rolled up his sleeve. He thrust his thin arm towards me.

'Can you argue away that scar?' he said. 'There are the marks of the beast that attacked me – the man-beast that was Henry Wells. A dream? I would cut off this arm immediately at the elbow if you could convince me that it was a dream.'

I walked to the window and remained for a long time staring at Manhattan. *There*, I thought, *is something substantial. It is absurd to imagine that anything could destroy it. It is absurd to imagine that the horror was really as terrible as it seemed to us in Partridgeville. I must persuade Howard not to write about it. We must both try to forget it.*

I returned to where he sat and laid my hand on his shoulder.

'You'll give up the idea of putting it into a story?' I urged gently.

'Never!' He was on his feet, and his eyes were blazing. 'Do you think I would give up now when I've almost captured it? I shall write a story that will penetrate to the inmost core of a horror that is without form and substance, but more terrible than a plague-stricken city when the cadences of a tolling bell sound an end to all hope. I shall surpass Poe. I shall surpass all the masters.'

'Surpass them and be damned then,' I said angrily. 'That

way madness lies, but it is useless to argue with you. Your
egoism is too colossal.'

I turned and walked swiftly out of the room. It occurred to
me as I descended the stairs that I made an idiot of myself
with my fears, but even as I went down I looked fearfully
back over my shoulder, as though I expected a great stone
weight to descend from above and crush me to the earth. *He
should forget the horror*, I thought. *He should wipe it from
his mind. He will go mad if he writes about it.*

Three days passed before I saw Howard again.

'Come in,' he said in a curiously hoarse voice when I
knocked on his door.

I found him in dressing-gown and slippers, and I knew as
soon as I saw him that he was terribly exultant.

'I have triumphed, Frank!' he cried. 'I have reproduced the
form that is formless, the burning shame that man has not
looked upon, the crawling, fleshless obscenity that sucks at
our brains!'

Before I could so much as gasp he placed the bulky
manuscript in my hands.

'Read it, Frank,' he commanded. 'Sit down at once and
read it!'

I crossed to the window and sat down on the lounge. I sat
there oblivious to everything but the typewritten sheets
before me. I confess that I was consumed with curiosity. I
had never questioned Howard's power. With words he
wrought miracles; breaths from the unknown blew always
over his pages, and things that had passed beyond Earth
returned at his bidding. But could he even suggest the horror
that we had known? – could he even so much as hint at the
loathsome, crawling thing that had claimed the brain of
Henry Wells?

I read the story through. I read it slowly, and clutched at
the pillows beside me in a frenzy of loathing. As soon as I
had finished it Howard snatched it from me. He evidently
suspected that I desired to tear it to shreds.

'What do you think of it?' he cried exultantly.

'It is indescribably foul!' I exclaimed. 'It violates privacies of the mind that should never be laid bare.'

'But you will concede that I have made the horror convincing?'

I nodded and reached for my hat. 'You have made it so convincing that I cannot remain and discuss it with you. I intend to walk until morning. I intend to walk until I am too weary to care, or think, or remember.'

'It is a very great story!' he shouted at me, but I passed down the stair and out of the house without replying.

3

It was past midnight when the telephone rang. I laid down the book I was reading and lowered the receiver.

'Hello. Who is there?' I asked.

'Frank, this is Howard!' The voice was strangely high-pitched. 'Come as quickly as you can. *They've come back!* And Frank, the sign is powerless. I've tried the sign, but the droning is getting louder, and a dim shape . . .' Howard's voice trailed off disastrously.

I fairly screamed into the receiver. 'Courage, man! Do not let them suspect that you are afraid. Make the sign again and again. I will come at once.'

Howard's voice came again, more hoarsely this time. 'The shape is growing clearer and clearer. And there is nothing I can do! Frank, I have lost the power to make the sign. I have forfeited all right to the protection of the sign. I've become a priest of the Devil. That story – I should never have written that story.'

'Show them that you are unafraid!' I cried.

'I'll try! I'll try! Ah, my God! The shape is . . .'

I did not wait to hear more. Frantically seizing my hat and coat I dashed down the stairs and out into the street. As I reached the kerb a dizziness seized me. I clung to a lamp post to keep from falling, and waved my hand madly at a fleeting taxi. Luckily the driver saw me. The car stopped and I staggered out into the street and climbed into it.

'Quick!' I shouted. 'Take me to Ten Brooklyn Heights!'

'Yes, sir. Cold night, ain't it?'

'Cold!' I shouted. 'It will be cold indeed when they get in. It will be cold indeed when they start to . . .'

The driver stared at me in amazement. 'That's all right, sir,' he said. 'We'll get you home all right, sir. Brooklyn Heights, did you say, sir?'

'Brooklyn Heights,' I groaned, and collapsed against the cushions.

As the car raced forward I tried not to think of the horror that awaited me. I clutched desperately at straws. *It is conceivable*, I thought, *that Howard has gone temporarily insane. How could the horror have found him among so many millions of people? It cannot be that* they *have deliberately sought him out. It cannot be that they would deliberately choose him from among such multitudes. He is too insignificant – all human beings are too insignificant. They would never deliberately angle for human beings. They would never deliberately trawl for human beings – but they did seek Henry Wells. And what did Howard say? 'I have become a priest of the Devil.' Why not* their *priest? What if Howard has become their priest on Earth? What if his story has made him their priest?*

The thought was a nightmare to me, and I put it furiously from me. *He will have courage to resist them*, I thought. *He will show them that he is not afraid.*

'Here we are, sir. Shall I help you in, sir?'

The car had stopped, and I groaned as I realized that I was about to enter what might prove to be my tomb. I descended to the sidewalk and handed the driver all the change that I possessed. He stared at me in amazement.

'You've given me too much,' he said. 'Here, sir . . .'

But I waved him aside and dashed up the stoop of the house before me. As I fitted a key into the door I could hear him muttering: 'Craziest drunk I ever seen! He gives me four bucks to drive him ten blocks, and doesn't want no thanks or nothin' . . .'

The lower hall was unlighted. I stood at the foot of the stairs and shouted, 'I'm here, Howard! Can you come down?'

There was no answer. I waited for perhaps ten seconds, but not a sound came from the room above.

'I'm coming up!' I shouted in desperation, and started to climb the stairs. I was trembling all over. *They've got him,* I thought. *I'm too late. Perhaps I had better not – great God, what was that?*

I was unbelievably terrified. There was no mistaking the sounds in the room above, someone was volubly pleading and crying aloud in agony. Was it Howard's voice that I heard? I caught a few words indistinctly. 'Crawling – ugh! Crawling – ugh! Oh, have pity! Cold and clee-ar. Crawling – ugh! God in heaven!'

I had reached the landing, and when the pleadings rose to hoarse shrieks I fell to my knees, and made against my body, and upon the wall beside me, and in the air – the sign. I made the primal sign that had saved us in Mulligan Wood, but this time I made it crudely, not with fire, but with fingers that trembled and caught at my clothes, and I made it without courage or hope, made it darkly, with a conviction that nothing could save me.

And then I got up quickly and went on up the stairs. My prayer was that they would take me quickly, that my sufferings should be brief under the stars.

The door of Howard's room was ajar. By a tremendous effort I stretched out my hand and grasped the knob. Slowly I swung it inward.

For a moment I saw nothing but the motionless form of Howard lying upon the floor. He was lying upon his back. His knees were drawn up and he had raised his hand before his face, palms outward, as if to blot out a vision unspeakable.

Upon entering the room I had deliberately, by lowering my eyes, narrowed my range of vision. I saw only the floor and the lower section of the room. I did not want to raise my eyes. I had lowered them in self-protection because I dreaded what the room held.

I did not want to raise my eyes, but there were forces, powers at work in the room which I could not resist. I knew that if I looked up, the horror might destroy me, but I had no choice.

Slowly, painfully, I raised my eyes and stared across the room. It would have been better, I think, if I had rushed forward immediately and surrendered to the thing that towered there. The vision of that terrible, darkly shrouded shape will come between me and the pleasures of the world as long as I remain in the world.

From the ceiling to the floor it towered, and it threw off blinding light. And pierced by the shafts, whirling around and around, were the pages of Howard's story.

In the centre of the room, between the ceiling and the floor, the pages whirled about, and the light burned through the sheets, and descending in spiralling shafts entered the brain of my poor friend. Into his head, the light was pouring in a continuous stream, and above, the Master of the light moved with a slow swaying of its entire bulk. I screamed and covered my eyes with my hands, but still the Master moved – back and forth, back and forth. And still the light poured into the brain of my friend.

And then there came from the mouth of the Master a most awful sound ... I had forgotten the sign that I had made three times below in the darkness. I had forgotten the high and terrible mystery before which all the invaders were powerless. But when I saw it forming itself in the room, forming itself immaculately, with a terrible integrity above the downstreaming light, I knew that I was saved.

I sobbed and fell upon my knees. The light dwindled, and the Master shrivelled before my eyes.

And then from the walls, from the ceiling, from the floor, there leapt flame – a white and cleansing flame that consumed, that devoured and destroyed for ever.

But my friend was dead.

The Dweller in Darkness

AUGUST DERLETH

Searchers after horror haunt strange, far places. For them are
the catacombs of Ptolemais, and the carven mausolea of the
nightmare countries. They climb to the moonlit towers of ruined
Rhine castles, and falter down black cobwebbed steps beneath
the scattered stones of forgotten cities in Asia. The haunted
wood and the desolate mountain are their shrines and they
linger around the sinister monoliths of uninhabited islands. But
the true epicure in the terrible, to whom a new thrill of
unutterable ghastliness is the chief end and justification of
existence, esteems most of all the ancient, lonely farmhouses of
backwoods regions; for there the dark elements of strength,
solitude, grotesqueness and ignorance combine to form the
perfection of the hideous.

– H. P. LOVECRAFT

Until recently, if a traveller in north central Wisconsin took
the left fork at the junction of the Brule River highway and
the Chequamegon pike on the way to Pashepaho, he would
find himself in country so primitive that it would seem
remote from all human contact. If he drove on along the
little-used road, he might in time pass a few tumble-down
shacks where presumably people had once lived and which
have long ago been taken back by the encroaching forest; it
is not desolate country, but an area thick with growth, and
over all its expanse there persists an intangible aura of the
sinister, a kind of ominous oppression of the spirit quickly
manifest to even the most casual traveller, for the road he
has taken becomes ever more and more difficult to travel,
and is eventually lost just short of a deserted lodge built on

the edge of a clear blue lake around which century-old trees brood eternally, a country where the only sounds are the cries of the owls, the whippoor-wills, and the eerie loons at night, and the wind's voice in the trees, and – but is it always the wind's voice in the trees? And who can say whether the snapped twig is the sign of an animal passing – or of something more, some other creature beyond man's ken?

For the forest surrounding the abandoned lodge at Rick's Lake had a curious reputation long before I myself knew it, a reputation which transcended similar stories about similar primeval places. There were odd rumours about something that dwelt in the depths of the forest's darkness – by no means the conventional wild whisperings of ghosts – of something half-animal, half-man, fearsomely spoken of by such natives as inhabited the edges of that region, and referred to only by stubborn head-shakings among the Indians who occasionally came out of that country and made their way south. The forest had an evil reputation; it was nothing short of that; and already, before the turn of the century, it had a history that gave pause even to the most intrepid adventurer.

The first record of it was left in the writings of a missionary on his way through that country to come to the aid of a tribe of Indians reported to the post at Chequamegon Bay in the north to be starving. Fr. Piregard vanished, but the Indians later brought in his effects: a sandal, his rosary, and a prayerbook in which he had written certain curious words which had been carefully preserved: 'I have the conviction that some creature is following me. I thought at first it was a bear, but I am now compelled to believe that it is something incredibly more monstrous than anything on this earth. Darkness is falling, and I believe I have developed a slight delirium, for I persist in hearing strange music and other curious sounds which can surely not derive from any natural source. There is also a disturbing illusion as of great footsteps which actually shake the earth, and I have several times encountered a very large footprint which varies in shape . . .'

The second record is far more sinister. When Big Bob Hiller, one of the most rapacious lumber barons of the entire midwest, began to encroach upon the Rick's Lake country in the middle of the last century, he could not fail to be impressed by the stand of pine in the area near the lake, and, though he did not own it, he followed the usual custom of the lumber barons and sent his men in from an adjoining piece he did own, under the intended explanation that he did not know where his line ran. Thirteen men failed to return from that first day's work on the edge of the forest area surrounding Rick's Lake; two of their bodies were never recovered; four were found – inconceivably – in the lake, several miles from where they had been cutting timber; the others were discovered at various places in the forest. Hiller thought he had a lumber war on his hands, laid his men off to mislead his unknown opponent, and then suddenly ordered them back to work in the forbidden region. After he had lost five more men, Hiller pulled out, and no hand since his time touched the forest, save for one or two individuals who took up land and moved into the area.

One and all, these individuals moved out within a short time, saying little, but hinting much. Yet, the nature of their whispered hints was such that they were soon forced to abandon any explanation; so incredible were the tales they told, with overtones of something too horrible for description, of age-old evil which preceded anything dreamed of by even the most learned archaeologist. Only one of them vanished, and no trace of him was ever found. The others came back out of the forest and in the course of time were lost somewhere among other people in the United States – all save a half-breed known as Old Peter, who was obsessed with the idea that there were mineral deposits in the vicinity of the wood, and occasionally went to camp on its edge, being careful not to venture in.

It was inevitable that the Rick's Lake legends would ultimately reach the attention of Professor Upton Gardner of the State university; he had completed collections of Paul

Bunyan, Whiskey Jack and Hodag tales, and was engaged
upon a compilation of place legends when he first encountered the curious half-forgotten tales that emanated from
the region of Rick's Lake. I discovered later that his first
reaction to them was one of casual interest; legends abound
in out-of-the-way places, and there was nothing to indicate
that these were of any more import than others. True, there
was no similarity in the strictest sense of the word to the
more familiar tales; for, while the usual legends concerned
themselves with ghostly appearances of men and animals,
lost treasure, tribal beliefs, and the like, those of Rick's Lake
were curiously unusual in their insistence upon utterly outré
creatures – or 'a creature' – since no one had ever reported
seeing more than one even vaguely in the forest's darkness,
half-man, half-beast, with always the hint that this description was inadequate in that it did injustice to the narrator's
concept of what it was that lurked there in the vicinity of the
lake. Nevertheless, Professor Gardner would in all probability have done little more than add the legends as he heard
them to his collection, if it had not been for the reports –
seemingly unconnected – of two curious facts, and the accidental discovery of a third.

The two facts were both newspaper accounts carried by
Wisconsin papers within a week of each other. The first was
a terse, half-comic report headed: *Sea Serpent in Wisconsin
Lake?*, and read: 'Pilot Joseph X. Castleton, on test flight
over northern Wisconsin yesterday, reported seeing a large
animal of some kind bathing by night in a forest lake in the
vicinity of Chequamegon. Castleton was caught in a thunder-
shower and was flying low at the time, when, in an effort to
ascertain his whereabouts, he looked down when lightning
flashed, and saw what appeared to be a very large animal
rising from the waters of a lake below him, and vanish into
the forest. The pilot added no details to his story, but asserts
that the creature he saw was not the Loch Ness monster.'
The second story was the utterly fantastic tale of the discovery of the body of Fr. Piregard, well-preserved, in the hollow

trunk of a tree along the Brule River. At first called a lost member of the Marquette-Joliet Expedition, Fr. Piregard was quickly identified. To this report was appended a frigid statement by the President of the State Historical Society dismissing the discovery as a hoax.

The discovery Professor Gardner made was simply that an old friend was actually the owner of the abandoned lodge and most of the shore of Rick's Lake.

The sequence of events was thus clearly inevitable. Professor Gardner instantly associated both newspaper accounts with the Rick's Lake legends; this might not have been enough to stir him to drop his researches into the general mass of legends abounding in Wisconsin for specific research of quite another kind, but the occurrence of something even more astonishing sent him posthaste to the owner of the abandoned lodge for permission to take the place over in the interests of science. What spurred him to take this action was nothing less than a request from the curator of the state museum to visit his office late one night and view a new exhibit which had arrived. He went there in the company of Laird Dorgan, and it was Laird who came to me.

But that was after Professor Gardner vanished.

For he did vanish; after sporadic reports from Rick's Lake over a period of three months, all word from the lodge ceased entirely, and nothing further was heard of Professor Upton Gardner.

Laird came to my room at the University Club late one night in October; his frank blue eyes were clouded, his lips tense, his brow furrowed, and there was everything to show that he was in a state of moderate excitation which did not derive from liquor. I assumed that he was working too hard; the first period tests in his University of Wisconsin classes were just over; and Laird habitually took tests seriously – even as a student he had done so, and now as an instructor, he was doubly conscientious.

But it was not that. Professor Gardner had been missing almost a month now, and it was this which preyed on his mind. He said as much in so many words, adding, 'Jack, I've got to go up there and see what I can do.'

'Man, if the sheriff and the posse haven't discovered anything, what can you do?' I asked.

'For one thing, I know more than they do.'

'If so, why didn't you tell them?'

'Because it's not the sort of thing they'd pay any attention to.'

'Legends?'

'No.'

He was looking at me speculatively, as if wondering whether he could trust me. I was suddenly conscious of the conviction that he *did* know something which he, at least, regarded with the gravest concern; and at the same time I had the most curious sensation of premonition and warning that I have ever experienced. In that instant the entire room seemed tense, the air electrified.

'If I go up there – do you think you could go along?'

'I guess I could manage.'

'Good.' He took a turn or two about the room, his eyes brooding, looking at me from time to time, still betraying uncertainty and an inability to make up his mind.

'Look, Laird – sit down and take it easy. That caged lion stuff isn't good for your nerves.'

He took my advice; he sat down, covered his face with his hands, and shuddered. For a moment I was alarmed; but he snapped out of it in a few seconds, leaned back, and lit a cigarette.

'You know those legends about Rick's Lake, Jack?'

I assured him that I knew them and the history of the place from the beginning – as much as had been recorded.

'And those stories in the papers I mentioned to you . . . ?'

The stories, too. I remembered them since Laird had discussed with me their effect on his employer.

'That second one, about Fr. Piregard,' he began, hesitated, stopped. But then, taking a deep breath, he began again.

'You know, Gardner and I went over to the curator's office one night last spring.'

'Yes, I was east at the time.'

'Of course. Well, we went over there. The curator had something to show us. What do you think it was?'

'No idea. What was it?'

'That body in the tree!'

'No!'

'Gave us quite a jolt. There it was, hollow trunk and all, just the way it had been found. It had been shipped down to the museum for the exhibition. But it was never exhibited, of course – for a very good reason. When Gardner saw it, he thought it was a waxwork. But it wasn't.'

'You don't mean that it was the real thing?'

Laird nodded. 'I know it's incredible.'

'It's just not possible.'

'Well, yes, I suppose it's impossible. But it was so. That's why it wasn't exhibited – just taken out and buried.'

'I don't quite follow that.'

He leaned forward and said very earnestly, 'Because when it came in it had all the appearance of being completely preserved, as if by some natural embalming process. It wasn't. It was frozen. It began to thaw out that night. And there were certain things about it that indicated that Fr. Piregard hadn't been dead the three centuries history said he had. The body began to go to pieces in a dozen ways – but no crumbling into dust, nothing like that. Gardner estimated that he hadn't been dead over five years. Where had he been in the meantime?'

He was quite sincere. I would not at first have believed it. But there was a certain disquieting earnestness about Laird that forbade any levity on my part. If I had treated his story as a joke, as I had the impulse to do, he would have shut up like a clam, and walked out of my room to brood about this thing in secret, with Lord knows what harm to himself. For a little while I said absolutely nothing.

'You don't believe it.'

'I haven't said so.'

'I can feel it.'

'No. It's hard to take. Let's say I believe in your sincerity.'

'That's fair enough,' he said grimly. 'Do you believe in me sufficiently to go along up to the lodge and find out what may have happened there?'

'Yes, I do.'

'But I think you'd better read these excerpts from Gardner's letters first.' He put them down on my desk like a challenge. He had copied them off on to a single sheet of paper, and as I took this up he went on, talking rapidly, explaining that the letters had been those written by Gardner from the lodge. When he finished, I turned to the excerpts and read.

I cannot deny that there is about the lodge, the lake, even the forest an aura of evil, of impending danger – it is more than that, Laird, if I could explain it, but archaeology is my forte, and not fiction. For it would take fiction, I think, to do justice to this thing I feel ... Yes, there are times when I have the distinct feeling that *someone* or *something* is watching me out of the forest or from the lake – there does not seem to be a distinction as I would like to understand it, and while it does not make me uneasy, nevertheless it is enough to give me pause. I managed the other day to make contact with Old Peter, the half-breed. He was at the moment a little the worse for firewater, but when I mentioned the lodge and the forest to him, he drew into himself like a clam. But he did put words to it: he called it the Wendigo – you are familiar with this legend, which properly belongs to the French-Canadian country.

That was the first letter, written about a week after Gardner had reached the abandoned lodge on Rick's Lake. The second was extremely terse, and had been sent by special delivery.

Will you wire Miskatonic University at Arkham, Massachusetts to ascertain if there is available for study a photostatic copy of a book known as the *Necronomicon*, by an Arabian writer who signs himself Abdul Alhazred? Make inquiry also for the *Pnakotic Manuscripts* and the *Book of Eibon*, and determine whether it is possible to purchase through one of the local bookstores a copy of *The Outsider and Others*, by H. P. Lovecraft, published by Arkham House last year. I believe that these books individually and collectively may be helpful in determining just what it is that haunts this place. For there *is* something; make no mistake about that; I am convinced of it, and when I tell you that I believe it has lived here not for years, but for centuries – perhaps even before the time of man – you will understand that I may be on the threshold of great discoveries.

Startling as this letter was, the third was even more so. For an interval of a fortnight went by between the second and third letters, and it was apparent that something had happened to threaten Professor Gardner's composure, for his third letter was even in this selected excerpt marked by extreme perturbation.

Everything evil here . . . I don't know whether it is the Black Goat With a Thousand Young or the Faceless One and/or something more that rides the wind. For God's sake . . . those accursed fragments! . . . Something in the lake, too, and at night the sounds! How still, and then suddenly those horrible flutes, those watery ululations! Not a bird, not an animal then – only those ghastly sounds. And the voices! . . . Or is it but dream? Is it my own voice I hear in the darkness? . . .

I found myself increasingly shaken as I read those excerpts. Certain implications and hints lodged between the lines of what Professor Gardner had written were suggestive of terrible, ageless evil, and I felt that there was opening up before Laird Dorgan and myself an adventure so incredible, so bizarre, and so unbelievably dangerous that we might well not return to tell it. Yet even then there was a lurking doubt in my mind that we would say anything about what we found at Rick's Lake.

'What do you say?' asked Laird impatiently.

'I'm going.'

'Good! Everything's ready. I've even got a dictaphone and batteries enough to run it. I've arranged for the sheriff of the county at Pashepaho to replace Gardner's notes, and leave everything just the way it was.'

'A dictaphone,' I broke in. 'What for?'

'Those sounds he wrote about – we can settle that for once and all. If they're there to be heard, the dictaphone will record them; if they're just imagination, it won't.' He paused, his eyes very grave. 'You know, Jack, we may not come out of this thing.'

'I know.'

I did not say so, because I knew that Laird, too, felt the same way I did that we were going like two dwarfed Davids to face an adversary greater than any Goliath, an adversary invisible and unknown, who bore no name and was shrouded in legend and fear, a dweller not only of the darkness of the wood but in that greater darkness which the mind of man has sought to explore since his dawn.

2

Sheriff Cowan was at the lodge when we arrived. Old Peter was with him. The sheriff was a tall, saturnine individual clearly of Yankee stock; though representing the fourth generation of his family in the area, he spoke with a twang which doubtless had persisted from generation to generation. The half-breed was a dark-skinned, ill-kempt fellow; he had a way of saying little, and from time to time grinned or snickered as at some secret joke.

'I brung up express that come some time past for the professor,' said the sheriff. 'From some place in Massachusetts was one of 'em, and the other from down near Madison. Didn't seem t' me 'twas worth sendin' back. So I took and brung 'em with the keys. Don't know that you fellers 'll git anyw'eres. My posse and me went through the hull woods, didn't see a thing.'

'You ain't tellin' 'em everything,' put in the half-breed, grinning.

'Ain't no more to tell.'

'What about that carvin'?'

The sheriff shrugged irritably. 'Damn it, Peter, that ain't got nothin' to do with the professor's disappearance.'

'He made a drawin' of it, didn't he?'

So pressed, the sheriff confided that two members of his posse had stumbled upon a great slab of rock in the centre of the wood; it was mossy and overgrown, but there was upon it an odd drawing, plainly as old as the forest – probably the work of one of the primitive Indian tribes once known to inhabit northern Wisconsin before the Dacotah Sioux and the Winnebago –

Old Peter grunted with contempt. 'No Indian drawing.'

The sheriff shook this off and went on. The drawing represented some kind of creature, but no one could tell what it was; it was certainly not a man, but on the other hand, it did not seem to be hairy, like a beast. Moreover, the unknown artist had forgotten to put in a face.

''N beside it there wuz two things,' said the half-breed.

'Don't pay no attention to him,' said the sheriff then.

'What two things?' demanded Laird.

'Jest things,' replied the half-breed, snickering. 'Heh, heh! Ain't no other way to tell it – warn't human, warn't animal, jest things.'

Cowan was irritated. He became suddenly brusque; he ordered the half-breed to keep still, and went on to say that if we needed him, he would be at his office in Pashepaho. He did not explain how we were to make contact with him, since there was no telephone at the lodge, but plainly he had no high regard for the legends abounding about the area into which we had ventured with such determination. The half-breed regarded us with an almost stolid indifference, broken only by his sly grin from time to time, and his dark eyes examined our luggage with keen speculation and interest. Laird met his gaze occasionally, and each time Old Peter indolently shifted his eyes. The sheriff went on talking; the notes and drawings the missing man had made were on the desk he had used in the big room which made up almost the entire ground floor of the lodge, just where he had found them; they were the property of the State of Wisconsin and were to be returned to the sheriff's office when we had finished with them. At the threshold he turned for a parting shot to say he hoped we would not be staying too long, because 'While I ain't givin' in to any of them crazy ideas — it jest ain't been so healthy for some of the people who came here.'

'The half-breed knows or suspects something,' said Laird at once. 'We'll have to get in touch with him sometime when the sheriff's not around.'

'Didn't Gardner write that he was pretty close-mouthed when it came to concrete data?'

'Yes, but he indicated the way out. Firewater.'

We went to work and settled ourselves, storing our food supplies, setting up the dictaphone, getting things into readiness for a stay of at least a fortnight; our supplies were sufficient for this length of time, and if we had to remain longer, we could always go into Pashepaho for more food. Moreover, Laird had brought fully two dozen dictaphone cylinders, so that we had plenty of them for an indefinite time, particularly since we did not intend to use them except when we slept — and this would not be often, for we had agreed that one of us would watch while the other took his rest, an arrangement we were not sanguine enough to believe would hold good without fail, hence the machine. It was not until after we had settled our belongings that we turned to the things the sheriff had brought and, meanwhile, we had ample opportunity to become aware of the very definite aura of the place.

For it was not imagination that there was a strange aura about the lodge and the grounds. It was not alone the brooding, almost sinister stillness, not alone the tall pines encroaching upon the lodge, not alone the blue-black waters of the lake, but something more than that: a hushed, almost menacing air of waiting, a kind of aloof assurance that was ominous — as one might imagine a hawk might feel leisurely

cruising above prey it knows will not escape its talons. Nor
was this a fleeting impression, for it was obvious almost at
once, and it grew with sure steadiness throughout the hour
or so that we worked there; moreover, it was so plainly to be
felt, that Laird commented upon it as if he had long ago
accepted it, and knew that I too had done so! Yet there was
nothing primary to which this could be attributed. There are
thousands of lakes like Rick's in northern Wisconsin and
Minnesota, and while many of them are not in forest areas,
those which are do not differ greatly in their physical aspects
from Rick's; so there was nothing in the appearance of the
place which at all contributed to the brooding sense of horror
which seemed to invade us from outside. Indeed, the setting
was rather the opposite; under the afternoon sunlight, the
old lodge, the lake, the high forest all around had a pleasant
air of seclusion – an air which made the contrast with the
intangible aura of evil all the more pointed and fearsome.
The fragrance of the pines, together with the freshness of the
water served, too, to emphasize the intangible mood of
menace.

We turned at last to the material left on Professor Gardner's
desk. The express packages contained, as expected, a copy of
The Outsider and Others, by H. P. Lovecraft, shipped by the
publishers, and photostatic copies of manuscript and printed
pages taken from the *R'lyeh Text* and Ludvig Prinn's *De
Vermis Mysteriis* – apparently sent for to supplement the
earlier data dispatched to the professor by the librarian of
Miskatonic University, for we found among the material
brought back by the sheriff certain pages from the *Necronomicon*, in the translation by Olaus Wormius, and likewise
from the *Pnakotic Manuscripts*. But it was not these pages,
which for the most part were unintelligible to us, which held
our attention. It was the fragmentary notes left by Professor
Gardner.

It was quite evident that he had not had time to do more
than put down such questions and thoughts as had occurred
to him, and, while there was little assimilation manifest, yet

there was about what he had written a certain terrible suggestiveness which grew to colossal proportions as everything he had not put down became obvious.

'Is the slab a) only an ancient ruin, b) a marker similar to a tomb, c) or a focal point for Him? If the latter, from outside? Or from beneath? (NB: Nothing to show that the thing has been disturbed.)

'Cthulhu or Kthulhut. In Rick's Lake? Subterrene passage to Superior and the sea via the St Lawrence? (NB: Except for the aviator's story, nothing to show that the Thing has anything to do with the water. Probably not one of the water beings.)

'Hastur. But manifestations do not seem to have been of air beings either.

'Yog-Sothoth. Of earth certainly – but he is not the Dweller in Darkness.' (NB: The Thing, whatever it is, must be of the earth deities, even though it travels in time and space. It could possibly be more than one, of which only the earth being is occasionally visible. Ithaqua, perhaps?)

'"Dweller in Darkness." Could He be the same as the Blind, Faceless One? He could be truly said to be dwelling in darkness. Nyarlathotep? Or Shub-Niggurath?

'What of fire? There must be a deity here, too. But no mention. (NB: Presumably, if the Earth and Water Beings oppose those of Air, then they must oppose those of Fire as well. Yet there is evidence here and there to show that there is more constant struggle between Air and Water Beings than between those of Earth and Air. Abdul Alhazred is damnably obscure in places. There is no clue as to the identity of Cthugha in that terrible footnote.

'Partier says I am on the wrong track. I'm not convinced. Whoever it is that plays the music in the night is a master of hellish cadence and rhythm. And, yes, of cacophony. (Cf. Bierce and Chambers.)'

That was all.

'What incredible gibberish!' I exclaimed.

And yet – and yet I knew instinctively it was not gibberish.

Strange things had happened here, things which demanded an explanation which was not terrestrial; and here, in Gardner's handwriting, was evidence to show that he had not only arrived at the same conclusion, but passed it. However it might sound, Gardner had written it in all seriousness, and clearly for his own use alone, since only the vaguest and most suggestive outline seemed apparent. Moreover, the notes had a startling effect on Laird; he had gone quite pale, and now stood looking down as if he could not believe what he had seen.

'What is it?' I asked.

'Jack – he was in contact with Partier.'

'It doesn't register,' I answered, but even as I spoke I remembered the hush-hush that had attended the severing of old Professor Partier's connection with the University of Wisconsin. It had been given out to the press that the old man had been somewhat too liberal in his lectures in anthropology – that is, he had 'Communistic leanings!' – which everyone who knew Partier realized was far from the facts. But he had said strange things in his lectures, he had talked of horrible, forbidden matters, and it had been thought best to let him out quietly. Unfortunately, Partier went out trumpeting in his contemptuous manner, and it had been difficult to hush the matter up satisfactorily.

'He's living down in Wausau now,' said Laird.

'Do you suppose he could translate all this?' I asked and knew that I had echoed the thought in Laird's mind.

'He's three hours away by car. We'll copy these notes, and if nothing happens – if we can't discover anything, we'll go to see him.'

If nothing happened – !

If the lodge by day had seemed brooding in an air of ominousness, by night it seemed surcharged with menace. Moreover, events began to take place with disarming and insidious suddenness, beginning in mid-evening, when Laird and I were sitting over those curious photostats sent out by Miskatonic University in lieu of the books and manuscripts themselves, which were far too valuable to permit out of their haven. The first manifestation was so simple that for some time neither of us noticed its strangeness. It was simply the sound in the trees as of rising wind, the growing song among the pines. The night was warm, and all the windows of the lodge stood open. Laird commented on the wind, and went on giving voice to his perplexity regarding the fragments before us. Not until half an hour had gone by and the sound of the wind had risen to the proportions of a gale did it occur to Laird that something was wrong, and he looked up, his eyes going from one open window to another in growing apprehension. Then I, too, became aware.

Despite the tumult of the wind, no draught of air had circulated in the room, not one of the light curtains at the windows was so much as trembling!

With one simultaneous movement, both of us stepped out upon the broad verandah of the lodge.

There was no wind, no breath of air stirring to touch our hands and faces. There was only the sound in the forest. And both of us looked up to where the pines were silhouetted against the starswept heavens, expecting their tops would be bending before a high gale; but there was no movement whatever; the pines stood still, motionless; and the sound as of wind continued all around us. We stood on the verandah for half an hour, vainly attempting to determine the source of the sound – and then, as unobtrusively as it had begun, it stopped!

The hour was now approaching midnight, and Laird prepared for bed; he had slept little the previous night, and we had agreed that I was to take the first watch until four in the morning. Neither of us said much about the sound in the pines, but what was said indicated a desire to believe that there was a natural explanation for the phenomenon, if we could establish a point of contact for understanding. It was inevitable, I suppose, that even in the face of all the curious facts which had come to our attention, there should still be an earnest wish to find a natural explanation. Certainly the

oldest fear and the greatest fear to which man is prey is fear
of the unknown; anything capable of rationalization and
explanation cannot be feared; but it was growing hourly
more patent that we were facing something which defied all
known rationales and credos, but hinged upon a system of
belief that ante-dated even primitive man, and indeed, as
scattered hints within the photostat pages from Miskatonic
University suggested, ante-dated even earth itself. And there
was always that brooding terror, the ominous suggestion of
menace from something far beyond the grasp of such a puny
intelligence as man's.

Thus it was with some trepidation that I prepared for my
vigil. After Laird had gone to his room, which was at the
head of the stairs, with a door opening upon a railed-in
balcony looking down into the lodge room where I sat with
the book by Lovecraft, reading here and there in its pages, I
settled down to a kind of apprehensive waiting. It was not
that I was afraid of what might take place, but rather that I
was afraid that what took place might be beyond my understanding. However, as the minutes ticked past, I became
engrossed in *The Outsider and Others*, with its hellish
suggestions of aeon-old evil, of entities coexistent with all
time and conterminous with all space, and began to understand, however vaguely, a relation between the writings of
this fantasiste and the curious notes Professor Gardner had
made. The most disturbing factor in this cognizance was the
knowledge that Professor Gardner had made his notes independent of the book I now read, since it had arrived after his
disappearance. Moreover, though there were certain keys to
what Gardner had written in the first material he had
received from Miskatonic University, there was growing now
a mass of evidence to indicate that the professor had had
access to some other source of information.

What was that source? Could he have learned something
from Old Peter? Hardly likely. Could he have gone to
Partier? It was not impossible that he had done so, though
he had not imparted this information to Laird. Yet it was

not to be ruled out that he had made contact with still another source of which there was no hint among his notes.

It was while I was engaged in this engrossing speculation that I became conscious of the music. It may actually have been sounding for some time before I heard it, but I do not think so. It was a curious melody that was being played, beginning as something lulling and harmonious, and then subtly becoming cacophonous and demoniac, rising in tempo, though all the time coming as from a great distance. I listened to it with growing astonishment; I was not at first aware of the sense of evil which fell upon me the moment I stepped outside and became cognizant that the music emanated from the depths of the dark forest. There, too, I was sharply conscious of its weirdness; the melody was unearthly, utterly bizarre and foreign, and the instruments which were being used seemed to be flutes, or certainly some variation of flutes.

Up to that moment there was no really alarming manifestation. That is, there was nothing but the suggestiveness of the two events which had taken place to inspire fear. There was, in short, always a good possibility that there might be a natural explanation about the sound as of wind and that of music.

But now, suddenly, there occurred something so utterly horrible, something so fraught with terror, that I was at once made prey to the most terrible fear known to man, a surging primitive horror of the unknown, of something from outside – for if I had had doubts about the things suggested by Gardner's notes and the material accompanying them, I knew instinctively that they were unfounded, for the sound that succeeded the strains of that unearthly music was of such a nature that it defied description, and defies it even now. It was simply a ghastly ululation, made by no beast known to man, and certainly by no man. It rose to an awful crescendo and fell away into a silence that was the more terrible for this soul-searing crying. It began with a two-note call, twice repeated, a frightful sound 'Ygnaiih! Ygnaiih!'

and then became a triumphant wailing cry that ululated out of the forest and into the dark night like the hideous voice of the pit itself: '*Eh-ya-ya-ya-yahaaahaaahaaahaaa-ah-ah-ah-ngh'aaa-ngh'aaa-ya-ya-ya . . .*'

I stood for a minute absolutely frozen to the verandah. I could not have uttered a sound if it had been necessary to save my life. The voice had ceased, but the trees still seemed to echo its frightful syllables. I heard Laird tumble from his bed, I heard him running down the stairs calling my name, but I could not answer. He came out on the verandah and caught hold of my arm.

'Good God! What was that?'

'Did you hear it?'

'I heard enough.'

We stood waiting for it to sound again, but there was no repetition of it. Nor was there a repetition of the music. We returned to the sitting room and waited there, neither of us able to sleep.

But there was not another manifestation of any kind throughout the remainder of that night!

3

The occurrences of that first night more than anything else decided our direction on the following day. For, realizing that we were too ill-informed to cope with any understanding with what was taking place, Laird set the dictaphone for that second night, and we started out for Wausau and Professor Partier, planning to return on the following day. With forethought, Laird carried with him our copy of the notes Gardner had left, skeletal as they were.

Professor Partier, at first reluctant to see us, admitted us finally to his study in the heart of the Wisconsin city, and cleared books and papers from two chairs, so that we could sit down. Though he had the appearance of an old man, wore a long white beard, and a fringe of white hair straggled from under his black skull cap, he was as agile as a young man; he was thin, his fingers were bony, his face gaunt, with deep, black eyes, and his features were set in an expression that was one of profound cynicism, disdainful, almost contemptuous, and he made no effort to make us comfortable, beyond providing places for us to sit. He recognized Laird as Professor Gardner's secretary, said brusquely that he was a busy man preparing what would doubtless be his last book for his publishers, and he would be obliged to us if we would state the object of our visit as concisely as possible.

'What do you know of Cthulhu?' asked Laird bluntly.

The professor's reaction was astonishing. From an old man whose entire attitude had been one of superiority and aloof disdain, he became instantly wary and alert; with exaggerated care he put down the pencil he had been holding, his eyes never once left Laird's face, and he leaned forward a little over his desk.

'So,' he said, 'you come to me.' He laughed then, a laugh which was like the cackling of some centenarian. 'You come to me to ask about Cthulhu. Why?'

Laird explained curtly that we were bent upon discovering what had happened to Professor Gardner. He told as much as he thought necessary, while the old man closed his eyes, picked up his pencil once more and, tapping gently with it, listened with marked care, prompting Laird from time to time. When he had finished, Professor Partier opened his eyes slowly and looked from one to the other of us with an expression that was not unlike one of pity mixed with pain.

'So he mentioned me, did he? But I had no contact with him other than one telephone call.' He pursed his lips. 'He had more reference to an earlier controversy than to his discoveries at Rick's Lake. I would like now to give you a little advice.'

'That's what we came for.'

'Go away from that place, and forget all about it.'

Laird shook his head in determination.

Partier estimated him, his dark eyes challenging his decision; but Laird did not falter. He had embarked upon this venture, and he meant to see it through.

'These are not forces with which common men have been accustomed to deal,' said the old man then. 'We are frankly not equipped to do so.' He began then, without other preamble, to talk of matters so far removed from the mundane as to be almost beyond conception. Indeed, it was some time before I began to comprehend what he was hinting at, for his concept was so broad and breathtaking that it was difficult for anyone accustomed to so prosaic an existence as mine to grasp. Perhaps it was because Partier began obliquely by suggesting that it was not Cthulhu or his minions who haunted Rick's Lake, but clearly another; the existence of the slab and what was carved upon it clearly indicated the nature of the being who dwelled there from time to time. Professor Gardner had in final analysis got on to the right path, despite thinking that Partier did not believe it. Who was the Blind, Faceless One but Nyarlathotep? Certainly not Shub-Niggurath, the Black Goat of a Thousand Young.

Here Laird interrupted him to press for something more understandable, and then at last, realizing that we knew nothing, the professor went on, still in that vaguely irritable oblique manner, to expound mythology – a mythology of pre-human life not only on the earth, but on the stars of all the universe. 'We know nothing,' he repeated from time to time. 'We know nothing at all. But there are certain signs, certain shunned places. Rick's Lake is one of them.' He spoke of beings whose very names were awesome – of the Elder Gods who live on Betelgeuse, remote in time and space, who had cast out into space the Great Old Ones, led by Azathoth and Yog-Sothoth, and numbering among them the primal spawn of the amphibious Cthulhu, the bat-like followers of Hastur the Unspeakable, of Lloigor, Zhar, and Ithaqua, who walked the winds and interstellar space, the earth beings. Nyarlathotep and Shub-Niggurath – the evil beings who sought always to triumph once more over the Elder Gods, who had shut them out or imprisoned them – as Cthulhu long ago slept in the ocean realm of R'lyeh, as Hastur was imprisoned upon a black star near Aldebaran in the Hyades. Long before human beings walked the earth, the conflict between the Elder Gods and the Great Old Ones had taken place; and from time to time the Old Ones had made a resurgence towards power, sometimes to be stopped by direct interference by the Elder Gods, but more often by the agency of human or non-human beings serving to bring about a conflict among the beings of the elements, for, as Gardner's notes indicated, the evil Old Ones were elemental forces. And every time there had been a resurgence, the mark of it had been left deep upon man's memory – though every attempt was made to eliminate the evidence and quiet survivors.

'What happened at Innsmouth, Massachusetts, for instance?' he asked tensely. 'What took place at Dunwich? In the wilds of Vermont? At the old Tuttle house on the Aylesbury Pike? What of the mysterious cult of Cthulhu, and the utterly strange voyage of exploration to the Mountains of Madness? What beings dwelt on the hidden and shunned Plateau of Leng? And what of Kadath in the Cold Waste? Lovecraft knew! Gardner and many another have sought to discover those secrets, to link the incredible happenings which have taken place here and there on the face of the planet – but it is not desired by the Old Ones that mere man shall know too much. Be warned!'

He took up Gardner's notes without giving either of us a chance to say anything, and studied them, putting on a pair of gold-rimmed spectacles which made him look more ancient than ever, and going on talking, more to himself than to us, saying that it was held that the Old Ones had achieved a higher degree of development in some aspects of science than was hitherto believed possible, but that, of course, nothing was *known*. The way in which he consistently emphasized this indicated very clearly that only a fool or an idiot would disbelieve, proof or no proof. But in the next sentence, he admitted that there was certain proof – the revolting and bestial plaque bearing a representation of a hellish monstrosity walking on the winds above the earth found in the hand of Josiah Alwyn when his body was discovered on a small Pacific island months after his incredible disappearance from his home in Wisconsin; the drawings made by Professor Gardner – and, even more than anything else, that curious slab of carven stones in the forest at Rick's Lake.

'Cthugha,' he murmured then, wonderingly. 'I've not read the footnote to which he makes reference. And there's nothing in Lovecraft.' He shook his head. 'No, I don't know.' He looked up. 'Can you frighten something out of the half-breed?'

'We've thought of that,' admitted Laird.

'Well, now, I advise a try. It seems evident that he knows something – it may be nothing but an exaggeration to which his more or less primitive mind has lent itself; but on the other hand – who can say?'

More than this Professor Partier could not or would not tell us. Moreover, Laird was reluctant to ask, for there was obviously a damnably disturbing connection between what he had revealed, however incredible it might be, and what Professor Gardner had written.

Our visit, however, despite its inconclusiveness – or perhaps because of it – had a curious effect on us. The very indefiniteness of the professor's summary and comments, coupled with such fragmentary and disjointed evidence which had come to us independently of Partier, sobered us and increased Laird's determination to get to the bottom of the mystery surrounding Gardner's disappearance, a mystery which had now become enlarged to encompass the greater mystery of Rick's Lake and the forest around it.

On the following day we returned to Pashepaho, and, as luck would have it, we passed Old Peter on the road leading from town. Laird slowed down, backed up, and leaned out to meet the old fellow's speculative gaze.

'Lift?'

'Reckon so.'

Old Peter got in and sat on the edge of the seat until Laird unceremoniously produced a flask and offered it to him; then his eyes lit up; he took it eagerly and drank deeply, while Laird made small talk about life in the north woods and encouraged the half-breed to talk about the mineral deposits he thought he could find in the vicinity of Rick's Lake. In this way some distance was covered, and during this time, the half-breed retained the flask, handing it back at last when it was almost empty. He was not intoxicated in the strictest sense of the word, but he was uninhibited, and he made no protest when we took the lake road without stopping to let him out, though when he saw the lodge and knew where he was, he said thickly that he was off his route, and had to be getting back before dark.

He would have started back immediately, but Laird persuaded him to come in with the promise that he would mix him a drink.

He did. He mixed him as stiff a drink as he could, and Peter downed it.

Not until he had begun to feel its effects did Laird turn to the subject of what Peter knew about the mystery of the Rick's Lake country, and instantly then the half-breed became close-mouthed, mumbling that he would say nothing, he had seen nothing, it was all a mistake, his eyes shifting from one to the other of us. But Laird persisted. He had seen the slab of carven stone, hadn't he? Yes – reluctantly. Would he take us to it? Peter shook his head violently. Not now. It was nearly dark, it might be dark before they could return.

But Laird was adamant, and finally the half-breed, convinced by Laird's insistence that they could return to the lodge and even to Pashepaho, if Peter liked, before darkness fell, consented to lead us to the slab. Then, despite his unsteadiness, he set off swiftly into the woods along a lane that could hardly be called a trail, so faint it was, and loped along steadily for almost a mile before he drew up short and, standing behind a tree, as if he were afraid of being seen, pointed shakily to a little open spot surrounded by high trees at enough of a distance that ample sky was visible overhead.

'There – that's it.'

The slab was only partly visible, for moss had grown over much of it. Laird, however, was at the moment only second-arily interested in it; it was manifest that the half-breed stood in mortal terror of the spot and wished only to escape.

'How would you like to spend the night here, Peter?' asked Laird.

The half-breed shot a frightened glance at him. 'Me? Gawd, no!'

Suddenly Laird's voice steeled. 'Unless you tell us what it was you saw here, that's what you're going to do.'

The half-breed was not so much the worse for liquor that he could not foresee events – the possibility that Laird and I might overcome him and tie him to a tree at the edge of this open space. Plainly, he considered a bolt for it, but he knew that in his condition, he could not out-run us.

'Don't make me tell,' he said. 'It ain't supposed to be told. I ain't never told no one – not even the professor.'

'We want to know, Peter,' said Laird with no less menace.

The half-breed began to shake; he turned and looked at the slab as if he thought at any moment an inimical being might rise from it and advance upon him with lethal intent. 'I can't, I can't,' he muttered, and then, forcing his bloodshot eyes to meet Laird's once more, he said in a low voice, 'I don't know what it was. Gawd! it was awful. It was a Thing – didn't have no face, hollered there till I thought my eardrums 'd bust, and them things that was with it – Gawd!' He shuddered and backed away from the tree, towards us. 'Honest t' Gawd, I seen it there one night. It jist come, seems like, out of the air and there it was a-singin' and a-wailin' and them things playin' that damn' music. I guess I was crazy for a while afore I got away.' His voice broke, his vivid memory recreated what he had seen; he turned, shouting harshly, 'Let's git outa here!' and ran back the way we had come, weaving among the trees.

Laird and I ran after him, catching up easily, Laird reassuring him that we would take him out of the woods in the car, and he would be well away from the forest's edge before darkness overtook him. He was as convinced as I that there was nothing imagined about the half-breed's account, that he had indeed told us all he knew; and he was silent all the way back from the highway to which we took Old Peter, pressing five dollars upon him so that he could forget what he had seen in liquor if he were so inclined.

'What do you think?' asked Laird when we reached the lodge once more.

I shook my head.

'That wailing night before last,' said Laird. 'The sounds Professor Gardner heard – and now this. It ties up – damnably, horribly.' He turned on me with intense and fixed urgency. 'Jack, are you game to visit that slab tonight?'

'Certainly.'

'We'll do it.'

It was not until we were inside the lodge that we thought of the dictaphone, and then Laird prepared at once to play whatever had been recorded back to us. Here at least, he reflected, was nothing dependent in any way upon anyone's imagination; here was the product of the machine, pure and simple, and everyone of intelligence knew full well that machines were far more dependable than men, having neither nerves nor imagination, knowing neither fear nor hope. I think that at most we counted upon hearing a repetition of the sounds of the previous night; not in our wildest dreams did we look forward to what we did actually hear, for the record mounted from the prosaic to the incredible, from the incredible to the horrible, and at last to a cataclysmic revelation that left us completely cut away from every credo of normal existence.

It began with the occasional singing of loons and owls, followed by a period of silence. Then there was once more that familiar rushing sound, as of wind in the trees, and this was followed by the curious cacophonous piping of flutes.

Then there was recorded a series of sounds, which I put down here exactly as we heard them in that unforgettable evening hour:

Ygnaiih! Ygnaiih! EEE-ya-ya-ya-Yahaahaaahaaa-ah-ah-ah-ngh'aaa-ngh'aaa-ya-yayaaa! (In a voice that was neither human nor bestial, but yet of both.)

(An increased tempo in the music, becoming more wild and demoniac.)

Mighty Messenger – Nyarlathotep ... from the world of Seven Suns to his earth place, the Wood of N'gai, whither may come Him Who Is Not to be Named ... There shall be abundance of those from the Black Goat of the Woods, the Goat With the Thousand Young ... (In a voice that was curiously human.)

(A succession of odd sounds, as if audience-response: a buzzing and humming, as of telegraph wires.)

Iä! Iä! Shub-Niggurath! Ygnaiih! Ygnaiih! EEE-yaa-yaa-haa-haaa-haaaa! (In the original voice neither human nor beast, yet both.)

Ithaqua shall serve thee, Father of the million favoured ones, and Zhar shall be summoned from Arcturus, by the command of 'Umr At-Tcwil, Guardian of the Gate ... Ye shall unite in praise of Azathoth, of Great Cthulhu, of Tsath-oggua ... (The human voice again.)

Go forth in his form or in whatever form chosen in the guise of man, and destroy that which may lead them to us ... (The half-bestial, half-human voice once more.)

(An interlude of furious piping accompanied once again by a sound as of the flapping of great wings.)

Ygnaiih! Y'bthnk ... h'ehye-n'grkdl'lh ... Iä! Iä! Iä! (Like a chorus.)

These sounds had been spaced in such a way that it seemed as if the beings giving rise to them were moving about within or around the lodge, and the last choral chanting faded away, as if the creatures were departing. Indeed, there followed such an interval of silence that Laird had actually moved to shut off the machine when once again a voice came

from it. But the voice that now emanated from the dictaphone was one which, simply because of its nature, brought
to a climax all the horror so cumulative in what had gone
before it; for whatever had been inferred by the half-bestial
bellowings and chants, the horribly suggestive conversation
in accented English, that which now came from the dictaphone was unutterably terrible.

Dorgan! Laird Dorgan! Can you hear me?

A hoarse, urgent whisper calling out to my companion,
who sat white-faced now, staring at the machine above which
his hand was still poised. Our eyes met. It was not the
appeal, it was not everything that had gone before, it was
the identity of that voice — *for it was the voice of Professor
Upton Gardner!* But we had no time to ponder this, for the
dictaphone went mechanically on.

'Listen to me! Leave this place. Forget. But before you go,
summon Cthugha. For centuries this has been the place
where evil beings from outermost cosmos have touched upon
Earth. I know. I am theirs. They have taken me, as they took
Piregard and many others — all who came unwarily within
their wood and whom they did not at once destroy. It is His
wood — the Wood of N'gai, the terrestrial abode of the Blind,
Faceless One, the Howler in the Night, the Dweller in
Darkness, Nyarlathotep, who fears only Cthugha. I have
been with him in the star spaces. I have been on the shunned
Plateau of Leng — to Kadath in the Cold Waste, beyond the
Gates of the Silver Key, even to Kythamil near Arcturus and
Mnar, to N'kai and the Lake of Hali, to K'n-yan and fabled
Carcosa, to Yaddith and Y'ha-nthlei near Innsmouth, to
Yoth and Yuggoth, and from far off I have looked upon
Zothique, from the eye of Algod. When Fomalhaut has topped
the trees, call forth to Cthugha in these words, thrice
repeated: *Ph'nglui mglw'nafh Cthugha Fomalhaut n'gha-
ghaa naf'l thagn. Iä! Cthugha!* When He has come, go
swiftly, lest you too be destroyed. For it is fitting that this
accursed spot be blasted so that Nyarlathotep comes no more

out of interstellar space. Do you hear me, Dorgan? Do you
hear me? Dorgan! Laird Dorgan!'

There was a sudden sound of sharp protest, followed by a
scuffling and tearing noise, as if Gardner had been forcibly
removed, and then silence, utter and complete!

For a few moments longer Laird let the record run, but
there was nothing more and finally he started it over, saying
tensely, 'I think we'd better copy that as best we can. You
take every other speech, and let's both copy that formula
from Gardner.'

'Was it . . . ?'

'I'd know his voice anywhere,' he said shortly.

'He's alive then?'

He looked at me, his eyes narrowed. 'We don't know that.'

'But his voice!'

He shook his head, for the sounds were coming forth once
more, and both of us had to bend to the task of copying,
which was easier than it promised to be for the spaces
between speeches were great enough to enable us to copy
without undue haste. The language of the chants and the
words to Cthugha enunciated by Gardner's voice offered
extreme difficulty, but by means of repeated playings, we
managed to put down the approximate equivalent of the
sounds. When finally we had finished, Laird shut the dictaphone off and looked at me with quizzical and troubled eyes,
grave with concern and uncertainty. I said nothing; what we
had just heard, added to everything that had gone before,
left us no alternative. There was room for doubt about
legends, beliefs, and the like – but the infallible record of the
dictaphone was conclusive even if it did no more than verify
half-heard credos – for it was true, there was still nothing
definite; it was as if the whole were so completely beyond the
comprehension of man that only in the oblique suggestion of
its individual parts could something like understanding be
achieved, as if the entirety were too unspeakably soul-
searing for the mind of man to withstand.

'Fomalhaut rises almost at sunset – a little before, I think,' mused Laird – clearly, like myself, he had accepted what we had heard without challenge other than the mystery surrounding its meaning. 'It should be above the trees – presumably twenty to thirty degrees above the horizon, because it doesn't pass near enough to the zenith in this latitude to appear above these pines – at approximately an hour after darkness falls. Say nine-thirty or so.'

'You aren't thinking of trying it tonight?' I asked. 'After all – what does it mean? Who or what is Cthugha?'

'I don't know any more than you. And I'm not trying it tonight. You've forgotten the slab. Are you still game to go out there – after this?'

I nodded. I did not trust myself to speak, but I was not consumed by any eagerness whatever to dare the darkness that lingered like a living entity within the forest surrounding Rick's Lake.

Laird looked at his watch, and then at me, his eyes burning now with a kind of feverish determination, as if he were forcing himself to take this final step to face the unknown being whose manifestations had made the woods its own. If he expected me to hesitate, he was disappointed; however beset by fear I might be, I would not show it. I got up and went out of the lodge at his side.

4

There are aspects of hidden life, exterior as well as of the depths of the mind, that are better kept secret and away from the awareness of common man; for there lurk in dark places of the earth terrible desiderata, horrible revenants belonging to a stratum of the subconscious which is mercifully beyond the apprehension of common man – indeed, there are aspects of creation so grotesquely shuddersome that the very sight of them would blast the sanity of the beholder. Fortunately, it is not possible even to bring back in anything but suggestion what we saw on the slab in the forest at Rick's Lake that night in October, for the thing was so unbelievable, transcending all known laws of science, that adequate words for its description have no existence in the language.

We arrived at the belt of trees around the slab while afterglow yet lingered in the western heavens, and by the illumination of a flashlight Laird carried, we examined the face of the slab itself, and the carving on it of a vast, amorphous creature, drawn by an artist who evidently lacked sufficient imagination to etch the creature's face, for it had none, bearing only a curious, cone-like head which even in stone seemed to have a fluidity which was unnerving; moreover, the creature was depicted as having both tentacle-like appendages and hands – or growths similar to hands, not only two, but several; so that it seemed both human and non-human in its structure. Beside it had been carved two squat squid-like figures from a part of which – presumably the heads, though no outline was definitive – projected what must certainly have been instruments of some kind, for the strange repugnant attendants appeared to be playing them.

Our examination was necessarily hurried, for we did not want to risk being seen here by whatever might come, and it may be that in the circumstances, imagination got the better of us. But I do not think so. It is difficult to maintain that consistently, sitting here at my desk, removed in space and time from what happened there; but I maintain it. Despite the quickened awareness and irrational fear of the unknown which obsessed both of us, we kept a determined open-mindedness about every aspect of the problem we had chosen to solve. If anything, I have erred in this account on the side of science over that of imagination. In the plain light of reason, the carvings on that stone slab were not only obscene, but bestial and frightening beyond measure, particularly in the light of what Partier had hinted, and what Gardner's notes and the material from Miskatonic University had vaguely outlined, and even if time had permitted, it is doubtful if we could have looked long upon them.

We retreated to a spot comparatively near the way we must take to return to the lodge, and yet not too far from the open place where the slab lay, so that we might see clearly and still remain hidden in a place easy of access to the return path. There we took our stand and waited in that chilling hush of an October evening, while stygian darkness encompassed us, and only one or two stars twinkled high overhead, miraculously visible among the towering treetops.

According to Laird's watch, we waited exactly an hour and ten minutes before the sound as of wind began, and at once there was a manifestation which had about it all the trappings of the supernatural; for no sooner had the rushing sound begun, than the slab we had so quickly quitted began to glow – at first so indistinguishably that it seemed an illusion, and then with a phosphorescence of increasing brilliance, until it gave off such a glow that it was as if a pillar of light extended upward into the heavens. This was the second curious circumstance – the light followed the outlines of the slab, and flowed upward; it was not diffused and dispersed around the glade and into the woods, but shone heavenward with the insistence of a directed beam. Simultaneously, the very air seemed charged with evil; all around us lay thickly such an aura of fearsomeness that it rapidly became impossible to remain free of it. It was apparent that by some means unknown to us the rushing sound as of wind which now filled the air was not only associated with the broad beam of light flowing upward, *but was caused by it*; moreover, as we watched, the intensity and colour of the light varied constantly, changing from a blinding white to a lambent green, from green to a kind of lavender; occasionally it was so intensely brilliant that it was necessary to avert our eyes, but for the most part it could be looked at without hurt to our eyes.

As suddenly as it had begun, the rushing sound stopped, the light became diffuse and dim; and almost immediately the weird piping as of flutes smote upon our ears. It came not from around us, but from *above*, and with one accord, both of us turned to look as far into heaven as the now fading light would permit.

Just what took place then before our eyes I cannot explain. Was it actually something that came hurtling down, streaming down, rather? – for the masses were shapeless – or was it the product of imagination that proved singularly uniform when later Laird and I found opportunity to compare notes? The illusion of great black things streaking down in the path of that light was so great that we glanced back at the slab.

What we saw there sent us screaming voicelessly from that hellish spot.

For, where but a moment before there had been nothing, there was now a gigantic protoplasmic mass, a colossal being who towered upward towards the stars, and whose actual physical being was in constant flux; and flanking it on either side were two lesser beings, equally amorphous, holding pipes or flutes in appendages and making that demoniac music which echoed and reechoed in the enclosing forest. But the thing on the slab, the Dweller in Darkness, was the ultimate in horror; for from its mass of amorphous flesh there grew at will before our eyes tentacles, claws, hands, and withdrew again; the mass itself diminished and swelled effortlessly, and where its head was and the features should have been there was only a blank facelessness all the more horrible because even as we looked there rose from its blind mass a low ululation in that half-bestial, half-human voice so familiar to us from the record made in the night!

We fled, I say, so shaken that it was only by a supreme effort of will that we were able to take flight in the right direction. And behind us the voice rose, the blasphemous voice of Nyarlathotep, the Blind, Faceless One, the Mighty Messenger, even while there rang in the channels of memory the frightened words of the half-breed, Old Peter – *It was a Thing – didn't have no face, hollered there till I thought my eardrums'd bust, and them things that was with it – Gawd! –*

echoed there while the voice of that Being from outermost space shrieked and gibbered to the hellish music of the hideous attending flute players, rising to ululate through the forest and leave its mark forever in memory!

Yghaiih! Yghaiih! EEE-yayayayayaaa-haaahaaahaaa-haaa-ngh'aaa-ngh'aaa-ya-ya-yaaa!

Then all was still.

And yet, incredible as it may seem, the ultimate horror awaited us.

For we had gone but half way to the lodge when we were simultaneously aware of something following; behind us rose a hideous, horribly suggestive *sloshing* sound, as if the amorphous entity had left the slab which in some remote time must have been erected by its worshippers, and were pursuing us. Obsessed by abysmal fright, we ran as neither of us has ever run before, and we were almost upon the lodge before we were aware that the sloshing sound, the trembling and shuddering of the earth – as if some gigantic being walked upon it – had ceased, and in their stead came only the calm, unhurried tread of footsteps.

But the footsteps were not our own. And in the aura of unreality, the fearsome outsideness in which we walked and breathed, the suggestiveness of those footsteps was almost maddening!

We reached the lodge, lit a lamp and sank into chairs to await whatever it was that was coming so steadily, unhurriedly on, mounting the verandah steps, putting its hand on the knob of the door, swinging the door open . . .

It was Professor Gardner who stood there!

Then Laird sprang up, crying, 'Professor Gardner!'

The professor smiled reservedly and put one hand up to shade his eyes. 'If you don't mind, I'd like the light dimmed. I've been in the dark so long . . .'

Laird turned to do his bidding without question, and he came forward into the room, walking with the ease and poise of a man who is as sure of himself as if he had never vanished from the face of the earth more than three months before, as if he had not made a frantic appeal to us during the night just past, as if . . .

I glanced at Laird; his hand was still at the lamp, but his fingers were no longer turning down the wick, simply holding to it, while he gazed down unseeing. I looked over at Professor Gardner; he sat with his head turned from the lights, his eyes closed, a little smile playing about his lips; at that moment he looked precisely as I had often seen him look at the University Club in Madison, and it was as if everything that had taken place here at the lodge were but an evil dream.

But it was not a dream!

'You were gone last night?' asked the professor.

'Yes. But, of course, we had the dictaphone.'

'Ah. You heard something then?'

'Would you like to hear the record, sir?'

'Yes, I would.'

Laird went over and put it on the machine to play it again, and we sat in silence, listening to everything upon it, no one saying anything until it had been completed. Then the professor slowly turned his head.

'What do you make of it?'

'I don't know what to make of it, sir,' answered Laird. 'The speeches are too disjointed – except for yours. There seems to be some coherence there.'

Suddenly, without warning, the room was surcharged with menace; it was but a momentary impression, but Laird felt it as keenly as I did, for he started noticeably. He was taking the record from the machine when the professor spoke again.

'It doesn't occur to you that you may be the victim of a hoax?'

'No.'

'And if I told you that I had found it possible to make every sound that was registered on that record?'

Laird looked at him for a full minute before replying in a low voice that of course, Professor Gardner had been investigating the phenomena of Rick's Lake woods for a far longer time than we had, and if he said so . . .

A harsh laugh escaped the professor. 'Entirely natural phenomena, my boy! There's a mineral deposit under that grotesque slab in the woods; it gives off light and also a miasma that is productive of hallucinations. It's as simple as that. As for the various disappearances – sheer folly, human failing, nothing more, but with the air of coincidence. I came here with high hopes of verifying some of the nonsense to which old Partier lent himself long ago – but – ' He smiled disdainfully, shook his head, and extended his hand. 'Let me have the record, Laird.'

Without question, Laird gave Professor Gardner the record. The older man took it and was bringing it up before his eyes when he jogged his elbow and, with a sharp cry of pain, dropped it. It broke into dozens of pieces on the floor of the lodge.

'Oh!' cried the professor. 'I'm sorry.' He turned his eyes on Laird. 'But then – since I can duplicate it any time for you from what I've learned about the lore of this place, by way of Partier's mouthings – ' He shrugged.

'It doesn't matter,' said Laird quietly.

'Do you mean to say that everything on that record was just your imagination, Professor?' I broke in. 'Even that chant for the summoning of Cthugha?'

The older man turned on me; his smile was sardonic. 'Cthugha? What do you suppose he or that is but the figment of someone's imagination? And the inference – my dear boy, use your head. You have before you the clear inference that Cthugha has his abode on Fomalhaut which is twenty-seven light years away, and that, if this chant is thrice repeated when Fomalhaut has risen, Cthugha will appear to somehow render this place no longer habitable by man or outside entity. How do you suppose that could be accomplished?'

'Why, by something akin to thought-transference,' replied Laird doggedly. 'It's not unreasonable to suppose that if we

were to direct thoughts towards Fomalhaut something there
might receive them – granting that there might be life there.
Thought is instant. And that they in turn may be so highly
developed that dematerialization and rematerialization
might be as swift as thought.'

'My boy – are you serious?' The older man's voice revealed
his contempt.

'You asked.'

'Well, then, as the hypothetic answer to a theoretical
problem, I can overlook that.'

'Frankly,' I said again, disregarding a curious negative
shaking of Laird's head, 'I don't think that what we saw in
the forest tonight was just hallucination – caused by a
miasma rising out of the earth or otherwise.'

The effect of this statement was extraordinary. Visibly,
the professor made every effort to control himself; his reactions were precisely those of a savant challenged by a cretin
in one of his classes. After a few moments he controlled
himself and said only, 'You've been there then. I suppose it's
too late to make you believe otherwise . . .'

'I've always been open to conviction, sir, and I lean to the
scientific method,' said Laird.

Professor Gardner put his hand over his eyes and said, 'I'm
tired. I noticed last night when I was here that you're in my
old room, Laird – so I'll take the room next to you, opposite
Jack's.'

He went up the stairs as if nothing had happened between
the last time he had occupied the lodge and this.

5

The rest of the story – and the culmination of that apocalyp-
tic night – are soon told.

I could not have been asleep for more than an hour – the
time was one in the morning – when I was awakened by
Laird. He stood beside my bed fully dressed and in a tense

voice ordered me to get up and dress, to pack whatever
essentials I had brought, and be ready for anything. Nor
would he permit me to put on a light to do so, though he
carried a small pocket-flash, and used it sparingly. To all my
questions, he cautioned me to wait.

When I had finished, he led the way out of the room with a
whispered, 'Come.'

He went directly to the room into which Professor Gardner
had disappeared. By the light of his flash, it was evident that
the bed had not been touched; moreover, in the faint film of
dust that lay on the floor, it was clear that Professor Gardner
had walked into the room, over to a chair beside the window,
and out again.

'Never touched the bed, you see,' whispered Laird.

'But why?'

Laird gripped my arm, hard. 'Do you remember what
Partier hinted – what we saw in the woods – the protoplasmic, amorphousness of the thing? And what the record
said?'

'But Gardner told us – ' I protested.

Without a further word, he turned. I followed him downstairs, where he paused at the table where we had worked
and flashed the light upon it. I was surprised into making a
startled exclamation which Laird hushed instantly. For the
table was bare of everything but the copy of *The Outsider
and Others* and three copies of *Weird Tales*, a magazine
containing stories supplementing those in the book by the
eccentric Providence genius, Lovecraft. All Gardner's notes,
all our own notations, the photostats from Miskatonic University – everything gone!

'He took them,' said Laird. 'No one else could have done
so.'

'Where did he go?'

'Back to the place from which he came.' He turned on me,
his eyes gleaming in the reflected glow of the flashlight. 'Do
you understand what that means, Jack?'

I shook my head.

'*They* know we've been there, *they* know we've seen and learned too much . . .'

'But how?'

'You told them.'

'I? Good God, man, are you mad? How could I have told them.'

'Here, in this lodge, tonight – you yourself gave the show away, and I hate to think of what might happen now. We've got to get away.'

For one moment all the events of the past few days seemed to fuse into an unintelligible mass; Laird's urgency was unmistakable, and yet the thing he suggested was so utterly unbelievable that its contemplation even for so fleeting a moment threw my thoughts into the extremest confusion.

Laird was talking now, quickly. 'Don't you think it odd – how he came back? How he came out of the woods *after* that hellish thing we saw there – not before? And the questions he asked – the drift of those questions. And how he managed to break the record – our one scientific proof of something? And now, the disappearance of all the notes – of everything that might point to substantiation of what he called "Partier's nonsense"?'

'But if we are to believe what he told us . . .'

He broke in before I could finish. 'One of them was right. Either the voice on the record calling to me – or the man who was here tonight.'

'The man . . .'

But whatever I wanted to say was stilled by Laird's harsh, '*Listen!*'

From outside, from the depths of the horror-haunted dark, the earth-haven of the dweller in darkness, came once more, for the second time that night, the weirdly beautiful, yet cacophonous strains of flute-like music, rising and falling, accompanied by a kind of chanted ululation, and by the sound as of great wings flapping.

'Yes, I heard,' I whispered.

'*Listen closely!*'

Even as he spoke, I understood. There was something more – the sounds from the forest were not only rising and falling – *they were approaching!*

'Now do you believe me?' demanded Laird. *'They're coming for us!'* He turned on me. 'The chant!'

'What chant?' I fumbled stupidly.

'The Cthugha chant – do you remember it?'

'I took it down. I've got it here.'

For an instant I was afraid that this, too, might have been taken from us, but it was not; it was in my pocket where I had left it. With shaking hands, Laird tore the paper from my grasp.

'Ph'nglui mglw'nafh Cthugha Fomalhaut n'gha-ghaa naf'l thagn! Iä! Cthugha!' he said, running to the verandah, myself at his heels.

Out of the woods came the bestial voice of the dweller in the dark, *'Ee-ya-ya-haa-haahaaa! Ygnaiih! Ygnaiih!'*

'Ph-nglui mglw'nafh Cthugha Fomalhaut n'gha-ghaa naf'l thagn! Iä! Cthugha!' repeated Laird for the second time.

Still the ghastly mêlée of sounds from the woods came on, in no way diminished, rising now to supreme heights of terror-fraught fury, with the bestial voice of the thing from the slab added to the wild, mad music of the pipes, and the sound as of wings.

And then, once more, Laird repeated the primal words of the chant.

On the instant that the final guttural sound had left his lips, there began a sequence of events no human eye was ever destined to witness. For suddenly the darkness was gone, giving way to a fearsome amber glow; simultaneously the flute-like music ceased, and in its place rose cries of rage and terror. Then, there appeared thousands of tiny points of light – not only on and among the trees, but on the earth itself, on the lodge and the car standing before it. For still a further moment we were rooted to the spot, and then it was borne in upon us that the myriad points of light were *living entities of flame!* For wherever they touched, fire sprang up,

seeing which, Laird rushed into the lodge for such of our
things as he could carry forth before the holocaust made it
impossible for us to escape Rick's Lake.

He came running out – our bags had been taken downstairs – gasping that it was too late to take the dictaphone or
anything else, and together we dashed towards the car,
shielding our eyes a little from the blinding light all around.
But even though we had shielded our eyes, it was impossible
not to see the great amorphous shapes streaming skyward
from this accursed place, nor the equally great being hover-
ing like a cloud of living fire above the trees. So much we
saw, before the frightful struggle to escape the burning
woods forced us to forget mercifully the other details of that
terrible, maddened flight.

Horrible as were the things that took place in the darkness
of the forest at Rick's Lake, there was something more
cataclysmic still, something so blasphemously conclusive
that even now I shudder and tremble uncontrollably to think
of it. For in that brief dash to the car, I saw something that
explained Laird's doubt, I saw what had made him take heed
of the voice on the record and not of the thing that came to
us as Professor Gardner. The keys were there before, but I
did not understand; even Laird had not fully believed. Yet it
was given to us – we did not know. 'It is not desired by the
Old Ones that mere man shall know too much,' Partier had
said. And that terrible voice on the record had hinted even
more clearly: *Go forth in his form or in whatever form chosen
in the guise of man, and destroy that which may lead them to
us* ... Destroy that which may lead them to us! Our record,
the notes, the photostats from Miskatonic University, yes,
and even Laird and myself! And the thing had gone forth,
for it was Nyarlathotep, the Night Messenger, the Dweller
in Darkness who had gone forth and who had returned into
the forest to send his minions back to us. It was he who had
come from interstellar space even as Cthugha, the fire-being,
had come from Fomalhaut upon the utterance of the command that woke him from his eon-long sleep under that

amber star, the command that Gardner, the living-dead captive of the terrible Nyarlathotep, had discovered in those fantastic travellings in space and time; and it was he who returned whence he had come, with his earth-haven now forever rendered useless for him with its destruction by the minions of Cthugha!

I know, and Laird knows. We never speak of it.

If we had had any doubt, despite everything that had gone before, we could not forget that final, soul-searing discovery, the thing we saw when we shielded our eyes from the flames all around and looked away from those beings in the heavens, the line of footprints that led away from the lodge in the direction of that hellish slab deep in the black forest, *the footprints that began in the soft soil beyond the verandah in the shape of a man's footprints, and changed with each step into a hideously suggestive imprint made by a creature of incredible shape and weight, with variations of outline and size so grotesque as to have been incomprehensible to anyone who had not seen the thing on the slab — and beside them, torn and rent as if by an expanding force, the clothing that once belonged to Professor Gardner, left piece by piece along the trail back into the woods, the trail taken by the hellish monstrosity that had come out of the night, the Dweller in Darkness who had visited us in the shape and guise of Professor Gardner!*

Beyond the Threshold

AUGUST DERLETH

The story is really my grandfather's.

In a manner of speaking, however, it belongs to the entire
family, and beyond them, to the world; and there is no longer
any reason for suppressing the singularly terrible details of
what happened in that lonely house deep in the forest places
of northern Wisconsin.

The roots of the story go back into the mists of early time,
far beyond the beginnings of the Alwyn family line, but of
this I knew nothing at the time of my visit to Wisconsin in
response to my cousin's letter about our grandfather's
strange decline in health. Josiah Alwyn had always seemed
somehow immortal to me even as a child, and he had not
appeared to change throughout the years from a barrel-
chested old man, with a heavy, full face, decorated with a
closely-clipped moustache and a small beard to soften the
hard line of his square jaw. His eyes were dark, not over-
large, and his brows were shaggy; he wore his hair long, so
that his head had a leonine appearance. Though I saw little
of him when I was very young, still he left an indelible
impression on me in the brief visits he paid when he stopped
at the ancestral country home near Arkham, in Massachusetts – those short calls he made on his way to and from
remote corners of the world: Tibet, Mongolia, the Arctic
regions, and certain little-known islands in the Pacific.

I had not seen him for years when the letter came from my
cousin Frolin, who lived with him in the old house grandfather owned in the heart of the forest and lake country of

northern Wisconsin. 'I wish you could uproot yourself from
Massachusetts long enough to come out here. A great deal of
water has passed under various bridges, and the wind has
blown about many changes since last you were here.
Frankly, I think it most urgent that you come. In present
circumstances, I don't know to whom to turn, grandfather
being not himself, and I need someone who can be trusted.'
There was nothing obviously urgent about the letter, and yet
there was a queer constraint, there was something between
the lines that stood out invisibly, intangibly to make possible
only one answer to Frolin's letter – something in his phrase
about the wind, something in the way he had written
grandfather being not himself, something in the need he had
expressed for *someone who can be trusted*.

I could easily take leave of absence from my position as
assistant librarian at Miskatonic University in Arkham and
go west that September; so I went. I went, harassed by an
almost uncanny conviction that the need for haste was great:
from Boston by plane to Chicago, and from there by train to
the village of Harmon, deep in the forest country of Wisconsin – a place of great natural beauty, not far from the shores
of Lake Superior, so that it was possible on days of wind and
weather to hear the water's sound.

Frolin met me at the station. My cousin was in his late
thirties then, but he had the look of someone ten years
younger, with hot, intense brown eyes, and a soft, sensitive
mouth that belied his inner hardness. He was singularly
sober, though he had always alternated between gravity and
a kind of infectious wildness – 'the Irish in him,' as grandfather had once said. I met his eyes when I shook his hand,
probing for some clue to his withheld distress, but I saw only
that he was indeed troubled, for his eyes betrayed him, even
as the roiled waters of a pond reveal disturbances below,
though the surface may be as glass.

'What is it?' I asked, when I sat at his side in the coupe,
riding into the country of the tall pines. 'Is the old man
abed?'

He shook his head. 'Oh, no, nothing like that, Tony.' He shot me a queer, restrained glance. 'You'll see. You wait and see.'

'What is it then?' I pressed him. 'Your letter had the damndest sound.'

'I hoped it would,' he said gravely.

'And yet there was nothing I could put my finger on,' I admitted. 'But it was there, nevertheless.'

He smiled. 'Yes, I knew you'd understand. I tell you, it's been difficult – extremely difficult. I thought of you a good many times before I sat down and wrote that letter, believe me!'

'But if he's not ill ... ? I thought you said he wasn't himself.'

'Yes, yes, so I did. You wait now, Tony; don't be so impatient; you'll see for yourself. It's his mind, I think.'

'His mind!' I felt a distinct wave of regret and shock at the suggestion that grandfather's mind had given way; the thought that that magnificent brain had retreated from sanity was intolerable, and I was loath to entertain it. 'Surely not!' I cried. 'Frolin – what the devil is it?'

He turned his troubled eyes on me once more. 'I don't know. But I think it's something terrible. If it were only grandfather. But there's the music – and then there are all the other things, the sounds and smells and – ' He caught my amazed stare and turned away, almost with physical effort pausing in his talk. 'But I'm forgetting. Don't ask me anything more. Just wait. You'll see for yourself.' He laughed shortly, a forced laugh. 'Perhaps it's not the old man who's losing his mind. I've thought of that sometimes, too – with reason.'

I said nothing more, but there was beginning to mushroom up inside me now a kind of tense fear, and for some time I sat by his side, thinking only of Frolin and old Josiah Alwyn living together in that old house, unaware of the towering pines all around, and the wind's sound, and the fragrant pungence of leaf-fire smoke riding the wind out of the northwest. Evening came early to this country, caught in the dark pines, and, though afterglow still lingered in the west, fanning upward in a great wave of saffron and amethyst, darkness already possessed the forest through which we rode. Out of the darkness came the cries of the great horned owls and their lesser cousins, the screech owls, making an eerie magic in the stillness broken otherwise only by the wind's voice and the noise of the car passing along the comparatively little-used road to the Alwyn house.

'We're almost there,' said Frolin.

The lights of the car passed over a jagged pine, lightning-struck years ago, and standing still with two gaunt limbs arched like gnarled arms towards the road: an old landmark to which Frolin's words called my attention, since he knew I would remember it but half a mile from the house.

'If grandfather should ask,' he said then, 'I'd rather you said nothing about my sending for you. I don't know that he'd like it. You can tell him you were in the midwest and came up for a visit.'

I was curious anew, but forbore to press Frolin further. 'He does know I'm coming, then?'

'Yes. I said I had word from you and was going down to meet your train.'

I could understand that if the old man thought Frolin had sent for me about his health, he would be annoyed and perhaps angry; and yet more than this was implied in Frolin's request, more than just the simple salving of grandfather's pride. Once more that odd, intangible alarm rose up within me, that sudden, inexplicable feeling of fear.

The house looked forth suddenly in a clearing among the pines. It had been built by an uncle of grandfather's in Wisconsin's pioneering days, back in the 1850s: by one of the seafaring Alwyns of Innsmouth, that strange, dark town on the Massachusetts coast. It was an unusually unattractive structure, snug against the hillside like a crusty old woman in furbelows. It defied many architectural standards without, however, seeming ever fully free of most of the superficial

facets of architecture circa 1850 making for the most grotesque and pompous appearance of structures of that day. It
suffered a wide verandah, one side of which led directly into
the stables where, in former days, horses, surreys, and
buggies had been kept, and where now two cars were housed
– the only corner of the building which gave any evidence at
all of having been remodelled since it was built. The house
rose two and one-half storeys above a cellar floor; presumably, for darkness made it impossible to ascertain, it was
still painted the same hideous brown; and, judging by what
light shone forth from the curtained windows, grandfather
had not yet taken the trouble to install electricity, a contin-
gency for which I had come well prepared by carrying a
flashlight and an electric candle, with extra batteries for
both.

Frolin drove into the garage, left the car and, carrying
some of my baggage, led the way down the verandah to the
front door, a large, thick-panelled oak piece, decorated with
a ridiculously large iron knocker. The hall was dark, save
for a partly open door at the far end, out of which came a
faint light which was yet enough to illumine spectrally the
broad stairs leading to the upper floor.

'I'll take you to your room first,' said Frolin, leading the
way up the stairs, surefooted with habitual walking there.
'There's a flashlight on the newel post at the landing,' he
added. 'If you need it. You know the old man.'

I found the light and lit it, making only enough delay so
that when I caught up with Frolin, he was standing at the
door of my room, which, I noticed, was almost directly over
the front entrance and thus faced west, as did the house
itself.

'He's forbidden us to use any of the rooms east of the hall
up here,' said Frolin, fixing me with his eyes, as much as to
say: You see how queer he's got! He waited for me to say
something, but since I did not, he went on. 'So I have the
room next to yours, and Hough is on the other side of me, in
the southwest corner. Right now, as you might have noticed,
Hough's getting something to eat.'

'And grandfather?'

'Very likely in his study. You'll remember that room.'

I did indeed remember that curious windowless room, built under explicit directions by great-uncle Leander, a room that occupied the majority of the rear of the house, the entire northwest corner and all the west width save for a small corner at the southwest, where the kitchen was, the kitchen from which a light had streamed into the lower hall at our entrance. The study had been pushed part way back into the hill slope, so that the east wall could not have windows, but there was no reason save uncle Leander's eccentricity for the windowless north wall. Squarely in the centre of the east wall, indeed, built into the wall, was an enormous painting, reaching from the floor to the ceiling and occupying a width of over six feet. If this painting, apparently executed by some unknown friend of uncle Leander's, if not by my great-uncle himself, had had about it any mark of genius or even of unusual talent, this display might have been overlooked, but it did not, it was a perfectly prosaic representation of a north country scene, showing a hillside, with a rocky cave opening out into the centre of the picture, a scarcely defined path leading to the cave, an impressionistic beast which was evidently meant to resemble a bear, once common in this country, walking towards it, and overhead something that looked like an unhappy cloud lost among the pines rising darkly all around. This dubious work of art completely and absolutely dominated the study, despite the shelves of books that occupied almost every available niche in what remained of the walls in that room, despite the absurd collection of oddities strewn everywhere – bits of curiously carven stone and wood, strange mementoes of great-uncle's sea-faring life. The study had all the lifelessness of a museum and yet, oddly, it responded to my grandfather like something alive; even the painting on the wall seeming to take on an added freshness whenever he entered.

'I don't think anyone who ever stepped into that room could forget it,' I said with a grim smile.

'He spends most of his time there. Hardly goes out at all,
and I suppose, with winter coming on, he'll come out only for
his meals. He's moved his bed, too.'

I shuddered. 'I can't imagine sleeping in that room.'

'No, nor I. But you know, he's working on something, and
I sincerely believe his mind has been affected.'

'Another book on his travels, perhaps?'

He shook his head. 'No, a translation, I think. Something
different. He found some old papers of Leander's one day,
and ever since then he seems to have got progressively
worse.' He raised his eyebrows and shrugged. 'Come on.
Hough will have supper ready by this time, and you'll see for
yourself.'

Frolin's cryptic remarks had led me to expect an emaciated
old man. After all, grandfather was in his early seventies,
and even he could not be expected to live forever. But he had
not changed physically at all, as far as I could see. There he
sat at his supper table – still the same hardy old man, his
moustache and beard not yet white, but only iron grey, and
still with plenty of black in them; his face was no less heavy,
his colour no less ruddy. At the moment of my entrance he
was eating heartily from the drumstick of a turkey. Seeing
me, he raised his eyebrows a little, took the drumstick from
his lips and greeted me with no more excitement than if I
had been away from him but half an hour.

'You're looking well,' he said.

'And you,' I said. 'An old war horse.'

He grinned. 'My boy, I'm on the trail of something new –
some unexplored country apart from Africa, Asia, and the
Arctic regions.'

I flashed a glance at Frolin. Clearly, this was news to him;
whatever hints grandfather might have dropped of his activities, they had not included this.

He asked then about my trip west, and the rest of the
supper hour was taken up with small talk of other relatives.
I observed that the old man returned insistently to long-
forgotten relatives in Innsmouth: what had become of them?

Had I ever seen them? What did they look like? Since I knew practically nothing of the relatives in Innsmouth, and had the firm conviction that all had died in a strange catastrophe which had washed many inhabitants of that shunned city out to sea, I was not helpful. But the tenor of these innocuous questions puzzled me no little. In my capacity as librarian at Miskatonic University, I had heard strange and disturbing hints of the business in Innsmouth, I knew something of the appearance of Federal men there, and stories of foreign agents had never had about them that essential ring of truth which made a plausible explanation for the terrible events which had taken place in that city. He wanted to know at last whether I had ever seen pictures of them, and when I said I had not, he was quite patently disappointed.

'Do you know,' he said dejectedly, 'there does not exist even a likeness of uncle Leander, but the oldtimers around Harmon told me years ago that he was a very homely man, that he reminded them of a *frog*.' Abruptly, he seemed more animated, he began to talk a little faster. 'Do you have any conception of what that meant, my boy? But no, you wouldn't have. It's too much to expect . . .'

He sat for a while in silence, drinking his coffee, drumming on the table with his fingers and staring into space with a curiously preoccupied air until suddenly he rose and left the room, inviting us to come to the study when we had finished.

'What do you make of that?' asked Frolin, when the sound of the study door closing came to us.

'Curious,' I said. 'But I see nothing abnormal there, Frolin. I'm afraid . . .'

He smiled grimly. 'Wait. Don't judge yet; you've been here scarcely two hours.'

We went to the study after supper, leaving the dishes to Hough and his wife, who had served my grandfather for twenty years in this house. The study was unchanged, save for the addition of the old double bed, pushed up against the wall which separated the room from the kitchen. Grandfather was clearly waiting for us, or rather for me, and, if I had had occasion to think cousin Frolin cryptic, there is no word adequate to describe my grandfather's subsequent conversation.

'Have you ever heard of the Wendigo?' he asked.

I admitted that I had come upon it among other north country Indian legends: the belief in a monstrous, supernatural being, horrible to look upon, the haunter of the great forest silences.

He wanted to know whether I had ever thought of there being a possible connection between this legend of the Wendigo and the air elements, and, upon my replying in the affirmative, he expressed a curiosity about how I had come to know the Indian legend in the first place, taking pains to explain that the Wendigo had nothing whatever to do with his question.

'In my capacity as a librarian, I have occasion to run across a good many out of the way things,' I answered.

'Ah!' he exclaimed, reaching for a book next to his chair. 'Then doubtless you may be familiar with this volume.'

I looked at the heavy black-bound volume whose title was stamped only on its backbone in goldleaf. *The Outsider and Others*, by H. P. Lovecraft.

I nodded. 'This book is on our shelves.'

'You've read it, then?'

'Oh, yes. Most interesting.'

'Then you'll have read what he has to say about Innsmouth in his strange story, 'The Shadow Over Innsmouth'. What do you make of that?'

I reflected hurriedly, thinking back to the story, and presently it came to me: a fantastic tale of horrible sea-beings, spawn of Cthulhu, beast of primordial origin, living deep in the sea.

'The man had a good imagination,' I said.

'Had! Is he dead, then?'

'Yes, three years ago.'

'Alas! I had thought to learn from him . . .'

'But, surely, this fiction . . .' I began.

He stopped me. 'Since you have offered no explanation of what took place in Innsmouth, how can you be so sure that this narrative is fiction?'

I admitted that I could not, but it seemed that the old man had already lost interest. Now he drew forth a bulky envelope bearing many of the familiar three-cent 1869 stamps so dear to collectors, and from this took out various papers, which, he said, uncle Leander had left with instructions for their consignment to the flames. His wish, however, had not been carried out, explained grandfather, and he had come into possession of them. He handed a few sheets to me, and requested my opinion of them, watching me shrewdly all the while.

The sheets were obviously from a long letter, written in a crabbed hand, and with some of the most awkward sentences imaginable. Moreover, many of the sentences did not seem to me to make sense, and the sheet at which I looked longest was filled with allusions strange to me. My eyes caught words like *Ithaqua*, *Lloigor*, *Hastur*; it was not until I handed the sheets back to my grandfather that it occurred to me that I had seen those words elsewhere, not too long ago. But I said nothing. I explained that I could not help feeling that uncle Leander wrote with needless obfuscation.

Grandfather chuckled. 'I should have thought that the first thing which would have occurred to you would have been similar to my own reaction, but no, you failed me! Surely it's obvious that the whole business is a code!'

'Of course! That would explain the awkwardness of his lines.'

My grandfather smirked. 'A fairly simple code, but adequate – entirely adequate. I have not yet finished with it.' He tapped the envelope with one index finger. 'It seems to concern this house, and there is in it a repeated warning that one must be careful, and not pass beyond the threshold, for fear of dire consequences. My boy, I've crossed and recrossed every threshold in this house scores of times, and there have been no consequences. So therefore, somewhere there must exist a threshold I have not yet crossed.'

I could not help smiling at his animation. 'If uncle Leander's mind was wandering, you've been off on a pretty chase,' I said.

Abruptly grandfather's well-known impatience boiled to the surface. With one hand he swept my uncle's papers away; with the other he dismissed us both, and it was plain to see that Frolin and I had on the instant ceased to exist for him.

We rose, made our excuses, and left the room.

In the half-dark of the hall beyond, Frolin looked at me, saying nothing, only permitting his hot eyes to dwell upon mine for a long minute before he turned and led the way upstairs, where we parted, each to go to his own room for the night.

2

The nocturnal activity of the subconscious mind has always been of deep interest to me, since it has seemed to me that unlimited opportunities are opened up before every alert individual. I have repeatedly gone to bed with some problem vexing me, only to find it solved insofar as I am capable of solving it, upon waking. Of those other, more devious activities of the night mind, I have less knowledge. I know that I retired that night with the question of where I had encountered my uncle Leander's strange words before strong and foremost in mind, and I know that I went to sleep at last with that question unanswered.

Yet, when I awoke in the darkness some hours later, I knew at once that I had seen those words, those strange proper names in the book by H. P. Lovecraft which I had read at Miskatonic and it was only secondarily that I was aware of someone tapping at my door, and calling out in a hushed voice,

'It's Frolin. Are you awake? I'm coming in.'

I got up, slipped on my dressing gown, and lit my electric

candle. By this time Frolin was in the room, his thin body trembling a little, possibly from the cold, for the September night air flowing through my window was no longer of summer.

'What's the matter?' I asked.

He came over to me, a strange light in his eyes, and put a hand on my arm. 'Can't you hear it?' he asked. 'God, perhaps it *is* my mind . . .'

'No, wait!' I exclaimed.

From somewhere outside, it seemed, came the sound of weirdly beautiful music: flutes, I thought.

'Grandfather's at the radio,' I said. 'Does he often listen so late?'

The expression on his face halted my words. 'I own the only radio in the house. It's in my room, and it's not playing. The battery's run down, in any case. Besides, did you ever hear *such* music on the radio?'

I listened with renewed interest. The music seemed strangely muffled, and yet it came through. I observed also that it had no definite direction; while before it had seemed to come from outside, it now seemed to come from underneath the house – a curious, chant-like playing of reeds and pipes.

'A flute orchestra,' I said.

'Or Pan pipes,' said Frolin.

'They don't play them any more,' I said absently.

'Not on the radio,' answered Frolin.

I looked up at him sharply; he returned my gaze as steadily. It occurred to me that his unnatural gravity had a reason for being, whether or not he wished to put that reason into words. I caught hold of his arms.

'Frolin – what is it? I can tell you're alarmed.'

He swallowed hard. 'Tony, that music doesn't come from anything in the house. It's from outside.'

'But who would be outside?' I demanded.

'Nothing – no one human.'

It had come at last. Almost with relief I faced this issue I

had been afraid to admit to myself must be faced. *Nothing –
no one human.*

'Then – what agency?' I asked.

'I think grandfather knows,' he said. 'Come with me, Tony.
Leave the light; we can make our way in the dark.'

Out in the hall, I was stopped once more by his hand tense
on my arm. 'Do you notice?' he whispered sibilantly. 'Do you
notice this, too?'

'The smell,' I said. The vague, elusive smell of water, of
fish and frogs and the inhabitants of water places.

'And now!' he said.

Quite suddenly the smell of water was gone, and instead
came a swift frostiness, flowing through the hall as of
something alive, the indefinable fragrance of snow, the crisp
moistness of snowy air.

'Do you wonder I've been concerned?' asked Frolin.

Giving me no time to reply, he led the way downstairs to
the door of grandfather's study, beneath which there shone
yet a fine line of yellow light. I was conscious in every step
of our descent to the floor below that the music was growing
louder, if no more understandable, and now, before the study
door, it was apparent that the music emanated from within,
and that the strange variety of odours came, too, from that
study. The darkness seemed alive with menace, charged with
an impending, ominous terror, which enclosed us as in a
shell, so that Frolin trembled at my side.

Impulsively I raised my arm and knocked on the door.

There was no answer from within, but on the instant of
my knock, the music stopped, the strange odours vanished
from the air!

'You shouldn't have done that!' whispered Frolin. 'If he . . .'

I tried the door. It yielded to my pressure, and I opened it.

I do not know what I expected to see there in the study,
but certainly not what I did see. No single aspect of the room
had changed, save that grandfather had gone to bed, and the
lamp was burning. I stood for an instant staring, not daring
to believe my eyes, incredible before the prosaic scene I

looked upon. Whence then had come the music I had heard? And the odours and fragrances in the air? Confusion took possession of my thoughts, and I was about to withdraw, disturbed by the repose of my grandfather's features, when he spoke.

'Come in, then,' he said, without opening his eyes. 'So you heard the music, too? I had begun to wonder why no one else heard it. Mongolian, I think. Three nights ago, it was clearly Indian – north country again, Canada and Alaska. I believe there are places where Ithaqua is still worshipped. Yes, yes – and a week ago, notes I last heard played in Tibet, in forbidden Lhasa years ago, decades ago.'

'Who made it?' I cried. 'Where did it come from?'

He opened his eyes and regarded us standing there. 'It came from here, I think,' he said, placing the flat of one hand on the manuscript before him, the sheets written by my great-uncle. 'And Leander's friends made it. Music of the spheres, my boy – do you credit your senses?'

'I heard it. So did Frolin.'

'And what can Hough be thinking?' mused grandfather. He sighed. 'I have nearly got it, I think. It only remains to determine with which of them Leander communicated.'

'Which?' I repeated. 'What do you mean?'

He closed his eyes and the smile came briefly back to his lips. 'I thought at first it was Cthulhu; Leander was, after all, a sea-faring man. But now – I wonder if it might not be one of the creatures of air: Lloigor, perhaps – or Ithaqua, whom I believe certain of the Indians call the Wendigo. There is a legend that Ithaqua carried his victims with him in the far spaces above the earth – but I am forgetting myself again, my mind wanders.' His eyes flashed open, and I found him regarding us with a peculiarly aloof stare. 'It's late,' he said. 'I need sleep.'

'What in God's name was he talking about?' asked Frolin in the hall.

'Come along,' I said.

But, back in my room once more, with Frolin waiting

expectantly to hear what I had to say, I did not know how to
begin. How would I tell him about the weird knowledge
hidden in the forbidden texts at Miskatonic University – the
dread *Book of Eibon*, the obscure *Pnakotic Manuscripts*, the
terrible *R'lyeh Text*, and, most shunned of all, the *Necronomicon* of the mad Arab Abdul Alhazred? How could I say
to him with any conviction at all the things that crowded
into my mind as a result of hearing my grandfather's strange
words, the memories that boiled up from deep within – of
powerful Ancient Ones, elder beings of unbelievable evil, old
gods who once inhabited the earth and all the universe as we
know it now, and perhaps far more – old gods of ancient
good, and forces of ancient evil, of whom the latter were now
in leash, and yet ever breaking forth, becoming manifest
briefly, horribly to the world of men. And their terrible
names came back now, as if before this hour my clue to
remembrance had not been made strong enough, had been
refused in the fastnesses of my inherent prejudices –
Cthulhu, potent leader of the forces of the waters of earth;
Yog-Sothoth and Tsathoggua, dwellers in the depths of earth;
Lloigor, Hastur, and Ithaqua, the Snow-Thing, and Wind-
Walker, who were the elementals of air. It was of these
beings that grandfather had spoken; and the inference he
had made was too plain to be disregarded, or even to be
subject to any other interpretations – that my great-uncle
Leander, whose home, after all, had once been in the shunned
and now deserted city of Innsmouth, had had traffic with at
least one of these beings. And there was a further inference
that he had not made, but only hinted at in something he
had said earlier in the evening – that there was somewhere
in the house a threshold, beyond which a man dared not
walk, and what danger could lurk beyond that threshold but
the path back into time, the way back to that hideous
communication with the elder beings my uncle Leander had
had!

And yet, somehow, the full import of grandfather's words
had not dawned upon me. Though he had said so much, there

was far more he had left unsaid, and I could not blame myself later for not fully realizing that grandfather's activities were clearly bent towards discovering that hidden threshold of which uncle Leander had so cryptically written – *and crossing it!* In the confusion of thought to which I had now come in my preoccupation with the ancient mythology of Cthulhu, Ithaqua and the elder gods, I did not follow the obvious indications to that logical conclusion, possibly because I feared instinctively to go so far.

I turned to Frolin and explained to him as clearly as I could. He listened attentively, asking a few pointed questions from time to time, and, though he paled slightly at certain details I could not refrain from mentioning, he did not seem to be as incredulous as I might have thought. This in itself was evidence of the fact that there was still more to be discovered about my grandfather's activities and the occurrences in the house, though I did not immediately realize this. However, I was shortly to discover more of the underlying reason for Frolin's ready acceptance of my necessarily sketchy outline.

In the middle of a question, he ceased talking abruptly, and there came into his eyes an expression indicating that his attention had passed from me, from the room to somewhere beyond; he sat in an attitude of listening, and, impelled by his own actions, I, too, strained to hear what he heard.

Only the wind's voice in the trees, rising now a little, I thought. A storm coming.

'Do you hear it?' he said in a shaky whisper.

'No,' I said quietly. 'Only the wind.'

'Yes, yes – the wind. I wrote you, remember. Listen.'

'Now, come, Frolin, take hold of yourself. It's only the wind.'

He gave me a pitying glance, and, going to the window, beckoned me after him. I followed, coming to his side. Without a word he pointed into the darkness pressing close to the house. It took me a moment to accustom myself to the

night, but presently I was able to see the line of trees struck
sharply against the starswept heavens. And then, instantly,
I understood.

*Though the sound of the wind roared and thundered about
the house, nothing whatever disturbed the trees before my eyes
– not a leaf, not a treetop, not a twig swayed by so much as a
hair's breadth!*

'Good God!' I exclaimed, and fell back, away from the pane,
as if to shut the sight from my eyes.

'Now, you see,' he said, stepping back from the window,
also. 'I have heard all this before.'

He stood quietly, as if waiting, and I, too, waited. The
sound of the wind continued unabated; it had by this time
reached a frightful intensity, so that it seemed as if the old
house must be torn from the hillside and hurtled into the
valley below. Indeed, a faint trembling made itself manifest
even as I thought this: a strange tremor, as if the house were
shuddering, and the pictures on the walls made a slight,
almost *stealthy* movement, almost imperceptible, and yet
quite unmistakably visible. I glanced at Frolin, but his
features were not disquieted; he continued to stand, listening
and waiting, so that it was patent that the end of this
singular manifestation was not yet. The wind's sound was
now a terrible, demoniac howling, and it was accompanied
by notes of music, which must have been audible for some
time, but were so perfectly blended with the wind's voice
that I was not at first aware of them. The music was similar
to that which had gone before, as of pipes and occasionally
stringed instruments, but was now much wilder, sounding
with a terrifying abandon, with a character of unmentionable evil about it. At the same time, two further manifestations occurred. The first was the sound as of someone
walking, some great being whose footsteps seemed to flow
into the room from the heart of the wind itself; certainly they
did not originate in the house, though there was about them
the unmistakable swelling which betokened their approach

to the house. The second was the sudden change in the temperature.

The night outside was warm for September in upstate Wisconsin, and the house, too, had been reasonably comfortable. Now, abruptly, coincident with the approaching footsteps, the temperature began to drop rapidly, so that in a little while the air in the room was cold, and both Frolin and I had to put on more clothing in order to keep comfortable. Still this did not seem to be the height of the manifestations for which Frolin so obviously waited; he continued to stand, saying nothing, though his eyes, meeting mine from time to time, were eloquent enough to speak his mind. How long we stood there, listening to those frightening sounds from outside before the end came, I do not know.

But suddenly Frolin caught my arm, and in a hoarse whisper, cried, 'There! There they are! Listen!'

The tempo of the weird music had changed abruptly to a diminuendo from its previous wild crescendo; there came into it now a strain of almost unbearable sweetness, with a little of melancholy to it, music as lovely as previously it had been evil, and yet the note of terror was not completely absent. At the same time, there was apparent the sound of voices, raised in a kind of swelling chant, rising from the back of the house somewhere – as if from the study.

'Great God in Heaven!' I cried, seizing Frolin. 'What is it now?'

'It's grandfather's doing,' he said. 'Whether he knows it or not, that thing comes and sings to him.' He shook his head and closed his eyes tightly for an instant before saying bitterly in a low, intense voice, 'If only that accursed paper of Leander's had been burned as it ought to have been!'

'You could almost make out the words,' I said, listening intently.

There *were* words – but not words I have ever heard before: a kind of horrible, primeval mouthing, as if some bestial creature with but half a tongue ululated syllables of meaningless horror. I went over and opened the door; immediately

the sounds seemed clearer, so that it was evident that what
I had mistaken for many voices was but one, which could
nevertheless convey the illusion of many. Words – or perhaps
I had better write *sounds*, bestial sounds – rose from below,
a kind of awe-inspiring ululation.

'*Iä! Iä! Ithaqua! Ithaqua cf'ayak vulgtmm. Iä! Uhg!
Cthulhu fhtagn! Shub-Niggurath! Ithaqua naflfhtagn!*'

Incredibly, the wind's voice rose to howl ever more terribly,
so that I thought at any moment the house would be hurled
into the void, and Frolin and myself torn from its rooms, and
the breath sucked from our helpless bodies. In the confusion
of fear and wonder that held me, I thought at that instant of
grandfather in the study below and, beckoning Frolin, I ran
from the room to the stairs, determined, despite my ghastly
fright, to put myself between the old man and whatever
menaced him. I ran to his door and flung myself upon it –
and once more, as before, all manifestations stopped as if by
the flick of a switch, silence fell like a pall of darkness upon
the house, a silence that was momentarily even more
terrible.

The door gave, and once more I faced grandfather.

He was sitting still as we had left him but a short time
before, though now his eyes were open, his head was cocked
a little to one side, and his gaze was fixed upon the over-
large painting on the east wall.

'In God's name!' I cried. 'What was that?'

'I hope to find out before long,' he answered with great
dignity and gravity.

His utter lack of fear quieted my own alarm to some
degree, and I came a little further into the room, Frolin
following. I leaned over his bed, striving to fix his attention
upon me, but he continued to gaze at the painting with
singular intensity.

'What are you doing?' I demanded. 'Whatever it is, there's
danger in it.'

'An explorer like your grandfather would hardly be content

if there were not, my boy,' he replied crisply, matter-of-factly.

I knew it was true.

'I would rather die with my boots on than here in this bed,' he went on. 'As for what we heard – I don't know how much of it *you* heard – that's something for the moment not yet explicable. But I would call to your attention the strange action of the wind.'

'There was no wind,' I said. 'I looked.'

'Yes, yes,' he said a little impatiently. 'True enough. And yet the wind's sound was there, and all the voices of the wind – just as I have heard it singing in Mongolia, in the great snowy spaces, over the shunned and hidden Plateau of Leng where the Tcho-Tcho people worship strange ancient gods.' He turned to face me suddenly, and I thought his eyes feverish. 'I did tell you, didn't I, about the worship of Ithaqua, sometimes called Wind-Walker, and by some, surely, the Wendigo, by certain Indians in upper Manitoba, and of their beliefs that the Wind-Walker takes human sacrifices and carries them over the far places of the earth before leaving them behind, dead at last? Oh, there are stories, my boy, odd legends – and something more.' He leaned towards me now with a fierce intensity. 'I have myself seen things – things found on a body dropped from the air – just that – things that could not possibly have been got in Manitoba, things belonging to Leng, to the Pacific Isles.' He brushed me away with one arm, and an expression of disgust crossed his face. 'You don't believe me. You think I'm wandering. Go on then, go back to your little sleep, and wait for your last through the eternal misery of monotonous day after day!'

'No! Say it now. I'm in no mood to go.'

'I will talk to you in the morning,' he said tiredly, leaning back.

With that I had to be content; he was adamant, and could not be moved. I bade him good-night once more and retreated into the hall with Frolin, who stood there shaking his head slowly, forbiddingly.

'Every time a little worse,' he whispered. 'Every time the wind blows a little louder, the cold comes more intensely, the voices and the music more clearly — and the sound of those terrible footsteps!'

He turned away and began to retrace the way upstairs, and, after a moment of hesitation, I followed.

In the morning my grandfather looked his usual picture of good health. At the moment of my entrance into the dining room, he was speaking to Hough, evidently in answer to a request, for the old servant stood respectfully bowed, while he heard grandfather tell him that he and Mrs Hough might indeed take a week off, beginning today, if it was necessary for Mrs Hough's health that she go to Wausau to consult a specialist. Frolin met my eyes with a grim smile; his colour had faded a little, leaving him pale and sleepless-looking, but he ate heartily enough. His smile, and the brief indicative glance of his eyes towards Hough's retreating back, said clearly that this necessity which had come upon Hough and his wife was their way of fighting the manifestations which had so disturbed my own first night in the house.

'Well, my boy,' said grandfather quite cheerfully, 'you're not looking nearly as haggard as you did last night. I confess, I felt for you. I daresay also you aren't nearly so sceptical as you were.'

He chuckled, as if this were a subject for joking. I could not, unfortunately, feel the same way about it. I sat down and began to eat a little, glancing at him from time to time, waiting for him to begin his explanation of the strange events of the previous night. Since it became evident shortly that he did not intend to explain, I was impelled to ask for an explanation, and did so with as much dignity as possible.

'I'm sorry if you've been disturbed,' he said. 'The fact of the matter is that that threshold of which Leander wrote must be in that study somewhere, and I felt quite certain I was on to it last night, before you burst into my room the second time. Furthermore, it seems undisputable that at least one member of the family has had traffic with one of those beings – Leander, obviously.'

Frolin leaned forward. 'Do you believe in them?'

Grandfather smiled unpleasantly. 'It must be obvious that, whatever my abilities, the disturbance you heard last night could hardly have been caused by me.'

'Yes, of course,' agreed Frolin. 'But some other agency . . .'

'No, no – it remains to be determined only which one. The water smells are the sign of the spawn of Cthulhu, but the winds might be Lloigor or Ithaqua or Hastur. But the stars aren't right for Hastur,' he went on. 'So we are left with the other two. There they are, then, or one of them, just across that threshold. I want to know what lies beyond that threshold, if I can find it.'

It seemed incredible that my grandfather should be talking so unconcernedly about these ancient beings; his prosaic air was in itself almost as alarming as had been the night's occurrences. The temporary feeling of security I had had at the sight of him eating breakfast was washed away; I began to be conscious again of that slowly growing fear I had known on my way to the house last evening, and I regretted having pushed my inquiry.

If my grandfather was aware of anything of this, he made no sign. He went on talking much in the manner of a lecturer pursuing a scientific inquiry for the benefit of an audience before him. It was obvious, he said, that a connection existed between the happenings at Innsmouth and Leander Alwyn's non-human contact *outside*. Did Leander leave Innsmouth originally because of the cult of Cthulhu that existed there, because he, too, was becoming afflicted with that curious facial change which overtook so many of the inhabitants of accursed Innsmouth? – those strange batrachian lineaments which horrified the Federal investigators who came to examine into the Innsmouth affair? Perhaps this was so. In any event, leaving the Cthulhu cult behind, he had made his way into the wilds of Wisconsin and somehow he had established contact with another of the elder beings, Lloigor or Ithaqua –

all, to be noted, elemental forces of evil. Leander Alwyn was
apparently a wicked man.

'If there is any truth to this,' I cried, 'then surely Leander's
warning ought to be observed. Give up this mad hope of
finding the threshold of which he writes!'

Grandfather gazed at me for a moment with speculative
mildness; but it was plain to see that he was not actually
concerning himself with my outburst. 'Now I've embarked
upon this exploration, I mean to keep to it. After all, Leander
died a natural death.'

'But, following your own theory, he had traffic with these –
these things,' I said. 'You have none. You're to venture out
into unknown space – it comes to that – without regard for
what horrors might lie there.'

'When I went into Mongolia, I encountered horrors, too. I
never thought to escape Leng with my life.' He paused
reflectively, and then rose slowly. 'No, I mean to discover
Leander's threshold. And tonight, no matter what you hear,
try not to interrupt me. It would be a pity, if after so long a
time, I am still further delayed by your impetuosity.'

'And having discovered the threshold,' I cried. 'What then?'

'I'm not sure I'll want to cross it.'

'The choice may not be yours.'

He looked at me for a moment in silence, smiled gently,
and left the room.

3

Of the events of that catastrophic night, I find it difficult
even at this late date to write, so vividly do they return to
mind, despite the prosaic surroundings of Miskatonic University where so many of those dread secrets are hidden in
ancient and little-known texts. And yet, to understand the
widespread occurrences that came after, the events of that
night must be known.

Frolin and I spent most of the day investigating my grandfather's books and papers, in search of verification of certain legends he had hinted at in his conversation, not only with me, but with Frolin even before my arrival. Throughout his work occurred many cryptic allusions, but only one narrative at all relative to our inquiry – a somewhat obscure story, clearly of legendary origin, concerning the disappearance of two residents of Nelson, Manitoba, and a constable of the Royal Northwest Mounted Police, and their subsequent reappearance, as if dropped from the heavens, frozen and either dead or dying, babbling of *Ithaqua*, of the *Wind-Walker*, and of many places on the face of the earth, and carrying with them strange objects, mementoes of far places, which they had never been known to carry in life. The story was incredible, and yet it was related to the mythology so clearly put down in *The Outsider and Others*, and even more horribly narrated in the *Pnakotic Manuscripts*, the *R'lyeh Text*, and the terrible *Necronomicon*.

Apart from this, we found nothing tangible enough to relate to our problem, and we resigned ourselves to waiting for the night.

At luncheon and dinner, prepared by Frolin in the absence of the Houghs, my grandfather carried on as normally he was accustomed to, making no reference to his strange exploration, beyond saying that he now had definite proof that Leander had painted that unattractive landscape on the east wall of the study, and that he hoped soon, as he neared the end of the deciphering of Leander's long, rambling letter, to find the essential clue to that threshold of which he wrote, and to which he now alluded increasingly. When he rose from the dinner table, he solemnly cautioned us once more not to interrupt him in the night, under pain of his extreme displeasure, and so departed into that study out of which he never walked again.

'Do you think you can sleep?' Frolin asked me, when we were alone.

I shook my head. 'Impossible. I'll stay up.'

'I don't think he'd like us to stay downstairs,' said Frolin, a faint frown on his forehead.

'In my room, then,' I replied. 'And you?'

'With you, if you don't mind. He means to see it through, and there's nothing we can do until he needs us. He may call . . .'

I had the uncomfortable conviction that if my grandfather called for us, it would be too late, but I forbore to give voice to my fears.

The events of that evening started as before – with the strains of that weirdly beautiful music welling flute-like from the darkness around the house. Then, in a little while, came the wind, and the cold, and the ululating voice. And then, preceded by an aura of evil so great that it was almost stifling in the room – then came something more, something unspeakably terrible. We had been sitting, Frolin and I, with the light out; I had not bothered to light my electric candle, since no light we could show would illumine the source of these manifestations. I faced the window and, when the wind began to rise, looked once again to the line of trees, thinking that surely, certainly, they must bend before this great onrushing storm of wind; but again there was nothing, no movement in that stillness. And there was no cloud in the heavens; the stars shone brightly, the constellations of summer moving down to the western rim of the earth to make the signature of autumn in the sky. The wind's sound had risen steadily, so that now it had the fury of a gale, and yet nothing, no movement disturbed the line of trees dark upon the night sky.

But suddenly – so suddenly that for a moment I blinked my eyes in an effort to convince myself that a dream had shuttered my sight – in one large area of the sky the stars were gone! I came to my feet and pressed my face to the pane. It was as if a cloud had abruptly reared up into the heavens, to a height almost at the zenith; but no cloud could have come upon the sky so swiftly. On both sides and overhead stars still shone. I opened the window and leaned out, trying to follow the dark outline against the stars. *It was the outline of some great beast, a horrible caricature of man, rising to a semblance of a head* high in the heavens, and there, where its eyes might have been *glowed with a deep carmine fire two stars!* – Or were they stars? At the same instant, the sound of those approaching footsteps grew so loud that the house shook and trembled with their vibrations, and the wind's demoniac fury rose to indescribable heights, and the ululation reached such a pitch that it was maddening to hear.

'Frolin!' I called hoarsely.

I felt him come to my side, and in a moment felt his tight grasp on my arm. So he, too, had seen; it was not hallucination, not dream – this giant thing outlined against the stars, and moving!

'It's moving,' whispered Frolin. 'Oh, God! – it's coming!'

He pulled frantically away from the window, and so did I. But in an instant, the shadow on the sky was gone, the stars shone once more. The wind, however, had not decreased in intensity one iota; indeed, if it were possible, it grew momentarily wilder and more violent; the entire house shuddered and quaked, while those thunderous footsteps echoed and reechoed in the valley before the house. And the cold grew worse, so that breath hung a white vapour in air – a cold as of outer space.

Out of all the turmoil of mind, I thought of the legend in my grandfather's papers – the legend of *Ithaqua*, whose signature lay in the cold and snow of far northern places. Even as I remembered, everything was driven from my mind by a frightful chorus of ululation, the triumphant chanting as of a thousand bestial mouths –

'Iä! Iä! Ithaqua, Ithaqua! Ai! Ai! Ai! Ithaqua cf'ayak vulgtmm vugtlagln vulgtmm. Ithaqua fhatagn! Ugh! Iä! Iä! Ai! Ai! Ai!'

Simultaneously came a thunderous crash, and immediately after, the voice of my grandfather, raised in a terrible cry, a cry that rose into a scream of mortal terror, so that the names he would have uttered – Frolin's and mine – were lost, choked back into his throat by the full force of the horror revealed to him.

And, as abruptly as his voice ceased to sound, all other manifestations came to a stop, leaving again that ghastly, portentous silence to close around us like a cloud of doom.

Frolin reached the door of my room before I did, but I was not far behind. He fell part of the way down the stairs, but recovered in the light of my electric candle, which I had seized on my way out, and together we assaulted the door of the study, calling to the old man inside.

But no voice answered, though the line of yellow under the door was evidence that his lamp burned still.

The door had been locked from the inside, so that it was necessary to break it down before we could enter.

Of my grandfather, there was no trace. But in the east wall yawned a great cavity, where the painting, now prone upon the floor, had been – a rocky opening leading into the depths of earth – and over everything in the room lay the mark of Ithaqua – a fine carpet of snow, whose crystals gleamed as from a million tiny jewels in the yellow light of grandfather's lamp. Save for the painting, only the bed was disturbed – *as if grandfather had been literally torn out of it by stupendous force!*

I looked hurriedly to where the old man had kept uncle Leander's manuscript – but it was gone; nothing of it remained. Frolin cried out suddenly and pointed to the painting uncle Leander had made, and then to the opening yawning before us.

'It was here all the time – the threshold,' he said.

And I saw even as he; as grandfather had seen too late – *for the painting by uncle Leander was but the representation of the site of his home before the house had been erected to conceal that cavernous opening into the earth on the hillside, the hidden threshold against which Leander's manuscript had warned, the threshold beyond which my grandfather had vanished!*

Though there is little more to tell, yet the most damning of all the curious facts remain to be revealed. A thorough search of the cavern was subsequently made by county officials and certain intrepid adventurers from Harmon; it was found to have several openings, and it was plain that anyone or *anything* wishing to reach the house through the cavern would have had to enter through one of the innumerable hidden crevices discovered among the surrounding hills. The nature of uncle Leander's activities was revealed after grandfather's disappearance. Frolin and I were put through a hard grilling by suspicious county officials, but were finally released when the body of my grandfather did not come to light.

But since that night, certain facts came into the open, facts which, in the light of my grandfather's hints, coupled with the horrible legends contained in the shunned books locked away here in the library of Miskatonic University, are damning and damnably inescapable.

The first of them was the series of gigantic footprints found in the earth at that place where on that fatal night the shadow had risen into the starswept heavens – the unbelievable wide and deep depressions, as of some prehistoric monster walking there, steps a half mile apart, steps that led beyond the house and vanished at a crevice leading down into that hidden cavern in tracks identical with those found in the snow in northern Manitoba where those unfortunate travellers and the constable sent to find them had vanished from the face of the earth!

The second was the discovery of my grandfather's notebook, together with a portion of uncle Leander's manuscript, encased in ice, found deep in the forest snows of upper Saskatchewan, and bearing every sign of having been dropped from a great height. The last entry was dated on the day of his disappearance in late September; the notebook was not found until the following April. Neither Frolin nor I dared to make the explanation of its strange appearance which came immediately to mind, and together we burned

that horrible letter and the imperfect translation grandfather had made, the translation which in itself, as it was
written down, with all its warnings against the terror beyond
the threshold, had served to summon from *outside* a creature
so horrible that its description has never been attempted by
even those ancient writers whose terrible narratives are
scattered over the face of the earth!

And last of all, the most conclusive, the most damning
evidence – the discovery seven months later of my grandfather's body on a small Pacific island not far southeast of
Singapore, and the curious report made of his condition;
perfectly preserved, *as if in ice*, so cold that no one could
touch him with bare hands for five days after his discovery,
and the singular fact that he was found half buried in sand,
as if 'he had fallen from an aeroplane!' Neither Frolin nor I
could any longer have any doubt; this was the legend of
Ithaqua, who carried his victims with him into far places of
the earth, in time and space, before leaving them behind.
And the evidence was undeniable that my grandfather had
been alive for part of that incredible journey, for if we had
had any doubt, the things found in his pockets, the mementoes carried from strange hidden places where he had been,
and sent to us, were final and damning testimony – the gold
plaque, with its miniature presentation of a struggle between
ancient beings, and bearing on its surface inscriptions in
cabalistic designs, the plaque which Dr Rackham of Miskatonic University identified as having come from some place
beyond the memory of man; the loathsome book in Burmese
that revealed ghastly legends of that shunned and hidden
Plateau of Leng, the place of the dread Tcho-Tcho people;
and finally, the *revolting and bestial stone miniature of a
hellish monstrosity walking on the winds above the earth!*

The Salem Horror

HENRY KUTTNER

When Carson first noticed the sounds in his cellar, he ascribed them to the rats. Later he began to hear the tales which were whispered by the superstitious Polish mill workers in Derby Street regarding the first occupant of the ancient house, Abigail Prinn. There was none living today who could remember the diabolical old hag, but the morbid legends which thrive in the 'witch district' of Salem like rank weeds on a neglected grave gave disturbing particulars of her activities, and were unpleasantly explicit regarding the detestable sacrifices she was known to have made to a worm-eating, crescent-horned image of dubious origin. The oldsters still muttered of Abbie Prinn and her monstrous boasts that she was high priestess of a fearfully potent god which dwelt deep in the hills. Indeed, it was the old witch's reckless boasting which had led to her abrupt and mysterious death in 1692, about the time of the famous hangings on Gallows Hill. No one liked to talk about it, but occasionally a toothless crone would mumble fearfully that the flames could not burn her, for her whole body had taken on the peculiar anaesthesia of her witch-mark.

Abbie Prinn and her anomalous statue had long since vanished, but it was still difficult to find tenants for her decrepit, gabled house, with its overhanging second storey and curious diamond-paned casement windows. The house's evil notoriety had spread throughout Salem. Nothing had actually happened there of recent years which might give rise to the inexplicable tales, but those who rented the house had a habit of moving out hastily, generally with vague and unsatisfactory explanations connected with the rats.

And it was a rat which led Carson to the Witch Room. The squealing and muffled pattering within the rotting walls had disturbed Carson more than once during the nights of his first week in the house, which he had rented to obtain the solitude that would enable him to complete a novel for which his publishers had been asking – another light romance to add to Carson's long string of popular successes. But it was not until some time later that he began to entertain wildly fantastic surmises regarding the intelligence of the rat that scurried from under his feet in the dark hallway one evening.

The house had been wired for electricity, but the bulb in the hall was small and gave a dim light. The rat was a misshapen, black shadow as it darted a few feet away and paused, apparently watching him.

At another time Carson might have dismissed the animal with a threatening gesture and returned to his work. But the traffic on Derby Street had been unusually noisy, and he had found it difficult to concentrate upon his novel. His nerves, for no apparent reason, were taut; and somehow it seemed that the rat, watching just beyond his reach, was eyeing him with sardonic amusement.

Smiling at the conceit, he took a few steps towards the rat, and it rushed away to the cellar door, which he saw with surprise was ajar. He must have neglected to close it the last time he had been in the cellar, although he generally took care to keep the doors shut, for the ancient house was draughty. The rat waited in the doorway.

Unreasonably annoyed, Carson hurried forward, sending the rat scurrying down the stairway. He switched on the cellar light and observed the rat in a corner. It watched him keenly out of glittering little eyes.

As he descended the stairs he could not help feeling that he was acting like a fool. But his work had been tiring, and subconsciously he welcomed any interruption. He moved across the cellar to the rat, seeing with astonishment that the creature remained unmoving, staring at him. A strange feeling of uneasiness began to grow within him. The rat was acting abnormally, he felt; and the unwinking gaze of its cold shoe-button eyes was somehow disturbing.

Then he laughed to himself, for the rat had suddenly whisked aside and disappeared into a little hole in the cellar wall. Idly he scratched a cross with his toe in the dirt before the burrow, deciding that he would set a trap there in the morning.

The rat's snout and ragged whiskers protruded cautiously. It moved forward and then hesitated, drew back. Then the animal began to act in a singular and unaccountable manner – almost as though it were dancing, Carson thought. It moved tentatively forward, retreated again. It would give a little dart forward and be brought up short, then leap back hastily, as though – the simile flashed into Carson's mind – a snake were coiled before the burrow, alert to prevent the rat's escape. But there was nothing there save the little cross Carson had scratched in the dust.

No doubt it was Carson himself who blocked the rat's escape, for he was standing within a few feet of the burrow. He moved forward, and the animal hurriedly retreated out of sight.

His interest piqued, Carson found a stick and poked it exploringly into the hole. As he did so his eye, close to the wall, detected something strange about the stone slab just above the rat burrow. A quick glance around its edge confirmed his suspicion. The slab was apparently movable.

Carson examined it closely, noticed a depression on its edge which would afford a handhold. His fingers fitted easily into the groove, and he pulled tentatively. The stone moved a trifle and stopped. He pulled harder, and with a sprinkling of dry earth the slab swung away from the wall as though on hinges.

A black rectangle, shoulder-high, gaped in the wall. From its depths a musty, unpleasant stench of dead air welled out, and involuntarily Carson retreated a step. Suddenly he remembered the monstrous tales of Abbie Prinn and the hideous secrets she was supposed to have kept hidden in her house. Had he stumbled upon some hidden retreat of the long-dead witch?

Before entering the dark gap he took the precaution of obtaining a flashlight from upstairs. Then he cautiously bent his head and stepped into the narrow, evil-smelling passage, sending the flashlight's beam probing out before him.

He was in a narrow tunnel, scarcely higher than his head, and walled and paved with stone slabs. It ran straight ahead for perhaps fifteen feet, and then broadened out into a roomy chamber. As Carson stepped into the underground room – no doubt a hidden retreat of Abbie Prinn's, a hiding-place, he thought, which nevertheless could not save her on the day the fright-crazed mob had come raging along Derby Street – he caught his breath in a gasp of amazement. The room was fantastic, astonishing.

It was the floor which held Carson's gaze. The dull grey of the circular wall gave place here to a mosaic of varicoloured stone, in which blues and greens and purples predominated – indeed, there were none of the warmer colours. There must have been thousands of bits of coloured stone making up that pattern, for none was larger than a walnut. And the mosaic seemed to follow some definite pattern, unfamiliar to Carson; there were curves of purple and violet mingled with angled lines of green and blue, intertwining in fantastic arabesques. There were circles, triangles, a pentagram, and other, less familiar, figures. Most of the lines and figures radiated from a definite point: the centre of the chamber, where there was a circular disc of dead black stone perhaps two feet in diameter.

It was very silent. The sounds of the cars that occasionally went past overhead in Derby Street could not be heard. In a shallow alcove in the wall Carson caught a glimpse of markings on the walls, and he moved slowly in that direction, the beam of his light travelling up and down the walls of the niche.

The marks, whatever they were, had been daubed upon the stone long ago, for what was left of the cryptic symbols was indecipherable. Carson saw several partly-effaced hieroglyphics which reminded him of Arabic, but he could not be sure. On the floor of the alcove was a corroded metal disc about eight feet in diameter, and Carson received the distinct impression that it was movable. But there seemed no way to lift it.

He became conscious that he was standing in the exact centre of the chamber, in the circle of black stone where the odd design centred. Again he noticed the utter silence. On an impulse he clicked off the ray of his flashlight. Instantly he was in dead blackness.

At that moment a curious idea entered his mind. He pictured himself at the bottom of a pit, and from above a flood was descending, pouring down the shaft to engulf him. So strong was this impression that he actually fancied he could hear a muffled thundering, the roar of the cataract. Then, oddly shaken, he clicked on the light, glanced around swiftly. The drumming, of course, was the pounding of his blood, made audible by the complete silence – a familiar phenomenon. But, if the place was so still –

The thought leapt into his mind, as though suddenly thrust into his consciousness. This would be an ideal place to work. He could have the place wired for electricity, have a table and chair brought down, use an electric fan if necessary – although the musty odour he had first noticed seemed to have disappeared completely. He moved to the tunnel mouth, and as he stepped from the room he felt an inexplicable relaxation of his muscles, although he had not realized that they had been contracted. He ascribed it to nervousness, and went upstairs to brew black coffee and write to his landlord in Boston about his discovery.

The visitor stared curiously about the hallway after Carson had opened the door, nodding to himself as though with satisfaction. He was a lean, tall figure of a man, with thick steel-grey eyebrows overhanging keen grey eyes. His face, although strongly marked and gaunt, was unwrinkled.

'About the Witch Room, I suppose?' Carson said ungraciously. His landlord had talked, and for the last week he had been unwillingly entertaining antiquaries and occultists anxious to glimpse the secret chamber in which Abbie Prinn had mumbled her spells. Carson's annoyance had grown, and he had considered moving to a quieter place; but his inherent stubbornness had made him stay on, determined to finish his novel in spite of interruptions. Now, eyeing his guest coldly, he said, 'I'm sorry, but it's not on exhibition any more.'

The other looked startled, but almost immediately a gleam of comprehension came into his eyes. He extracted a card and offered it to Carson.

'Michael Leigh . . . occultist, eh?' Carson repeated. He drew in a deep breath. The occultists, he had found, were the worst, with their dark hints of nameless things and their profound interest in the mosaic pattern on the floor of the Witch Room. 'I'm sorry, Mr Leigh, but – I'm really quite busy. You'll excuse me.'

Ungraciously he turned back to the door.

'Just a moment,' Leigh said swiftly.

Before Carson could protest he had caught the writer by the shoulders and was peering closely into his eyes. Startled, Carson drew back, but not before he had seen an extraordinary expression of mingled apprehension and satisfaction appear on Leigh's gaunt face. It was as though the occultist had seen something unpleasant – but not unexpected.

'What's the idea?' Carson asked harshly. 'I'm not accustomed – '

'I'm very sorry,' Leigh said. His voice was deep, pleasant. 'I must apologize. I thought – well, again I apologize. I'm rather excited, I'm afraid. You see, I've come from San Francisco to see this Witch Room of yours. Would you really mind letting me see it? I should be glad to pay any sum.'

Carson made a deprecatory gesture.

'No,' he said, feeling a perverse liking for this man growing within him – his well-modulated, pleasant voice, his power-ful face, his magnetic personality. 'No, I merely want a little peace – you have no idea how I've been bothered,' he went on, vaguely surprised to find himself speaking apologetically. 'It's a frightful nuisance. I almost wish I'd never found the room.'

Leigh leaned forward anxiously. 'May I see it? It means a great deal to me – I'm vitally interested in these things. I promise not to take up more than ten minutes of your time.'

Carson hesitated, then assented. As he led his guest into the cellar he found himself telling the circumstances of his discovery of the Witch Room. Leigh listened intently, occasionally interrupting with questions.

'The rat – did you see what became of it?' he asked.

Carson looked surprised. 'Why, no. I suppose it hid in its burrow. Why?'

'One never knows,' Leigh said cryptically as they came into the Witch Room.

Carson switched on the light. He had had an electrical extension installed, and there were a few chairs and a table, but otherwise the chamber was unchanged. Carson watched the occultist's face, and with surprise saw it become grim, almost angry.

Leigh strode to the centre of the room, staring at the chair that stood on the black circle of stone.

'You work here?' he asked slowly.

'Yes. It's quiet – I found I couldn't work upstairs. Too noisy. But this is ideal – somehow I find it very easy to write here. My mind feels' – he hesitated – 'free; that is, disasso-ciated with other things. It's quite an unusual feeling.'

Leigh nodded as though Carson's words had confirmed some idea in his own mind. He turned towards the alcove and the metal disc in the floor. Carson followed him. The occultist moved close to the wall, tracing out the faded symbols with a long forefinger. He muttered something under his breath – words that sounded like gibberish to Carson.

'*Nyogtha . . . k'yarnak . . .*'

He swung about, his face grim and pale. 'I've seen enough,' he said softly. 'Shall we go?'

Surprised, Carson nodded and led the way back into the cellar.

Upstairs Leigh hesitated, as though finding it difficult to broach his subject. At length he asked, 'Mr Carson – would you mind telling me if you have had any peculiar dreams lately.'

Carson stared at him, mirth dancing in his eyes. 'Dreams?' he repeated. 'Oh – I see. Well, Mr Leigh, I may as well tell you that you can't frighten me. Your compatriots – the other occultists I've entertained – have already tried it.'

Leigh raised his thick eyebrows. 'Yes? Did they ask you whether you'd dreamed?'

'Several did – yes.'

'And you told them?'

'No.' Then as Leigh leaned back in his chair, a puzzled expression on his face, Carson went on slowly, 'Although, really, I'm not quite sure.'

'You mean?'

'I *think* – I have a vague impression – that I have dreamed lately. But I can't be sure. I can't remember anything of the dream, you see. And – oh, very probably your brother occultists put the idea into my mind!'

'Perhaps,' Leigh said non-committally, getting up. He hesitated. 'Mr Carson, I'm going to ask you a rather presumptuous question. Is it necessary for you to live in this house?'

Carson sighed resignedly. 'When I was first asked that question I explained that I wanted a quiet place to work on a novel, and that any quiet place would do. But it isn't easy to find 'em. Now that I have this Witch Room, and I'm turning out my work so easily, I see no reason why I should move and perhaps upset my programme. I'll vacate this house when I finish my novel, and then you occultists can come in and turn it into a museum or do whatever you want with it.

I don't care. But until the novel is finished I intend to stay here.'

Leigh rubbed his chin. 'Indeed. I can understand your point of view. But – is there no other place in the house where you can work?'

He watched Carson's face for a moment, and then went on swiftly.

'I don't expect you to believe me. You are a materialist. Most people are. But there are a few of us who know that above and beyond what men call science there is a greater science that is built on laws and principles which to the average man would be almost incomprehensible. If you have read Machen you will remember that he speaks of the gulf between the world of consciousness and the world of matter. It is possible to bridge that gulf. The Witch Room is such a bridge! Do you know what a whispering-gallery is?'

'Eh?' Carson said, staring. 'But there's no – '

'An analogy – merely an analogy. A man may whisper a word in a gallery – or a cave – and if you are standing in a certain spot a hundred feet away you will hear that whisper, although someone ten feet away will not. It's a simple trick of acoustics – bringing the sound to a focal point. And this principle can be applied to other things besides sound. To any wave impulse – *even to thought*!'

Carson tried to interrupt, but Leigh kept on.

'That black stone in the centre of your Witch Room is one of those focal points. The design on the floor – when you sit on the black circle there you are abnormally sensitive to certain vibrations – certain thought commands – dangerously sensitive! Why do you suppose your mind is so clear when you are working there? A deception, a false feeling of lucidity – for you are merely an instrument, a microphone, tuned to pick up certain malign vibrations the nature of which you could not comprehend!'

Carson's face was a study in amazement and incredulity. 'But – you don't mean you actually *believe* – '

Leigh drew back, the intensity fading from his eyes,

leaving them grim and cold. 'Very well. But I have studied
the history of your Abigail Prinn. She too, understood this
super-science of which I speak. She used it for evil purposes –
the black art, as it is called. I have read that she cursed
Salem in the old days – and a witch's curse can be a frightful
thing. Will you – ' He got up, gnawing at his lip. 'Will you,
at least, allow me to call on you tomorrow?'

Almost involuntarily Carson nodded. 'But I'm afraid you'll
be wasting your time. I don't believe – I mean, I have no – '
He stumbled, at a loss for words.

'I merely wish to assure myself that you – oh, another
thing. If you dream tonight, will you try to remember the
dream? If you attempt to recapture it immediately after
waking, it is often possible to recall it.'

'All right. If I dream – '

That night Carson dreamed. He awoke just before dawn
with his heart racing furiously and a curious feeling of
uneasiness. Within the walls and from below he could hear
the furtive scurryings of the rats. He got out of bed hastily,
shivering in the cold greyness of early morning. A wan moon
still shone faintly in a paling sky.

Then he remembered Leigh's words. He *had* dreamed –
there was no question of that. But the content of his dream –
that was another matter. He absolutely could not recall it to
his mind, much as he tried, although there was a very vague
impression of running frantically in darkness.

He dressed quickly, and because the stillness of early
morning in the old house got on his nerves, went out to buy
a newspaper. It was too early for shops to be open, however,
and in search of a news-boy he set off westward, turning at
the first corner. And as he walked a curious and inexplicable
feeling began to take possession of him: a feeling of –
familiarity! He had walked here before, and there was a dim
and disturbing familiarity about the shapes of the houses,
the outline of the roofs. But – and this was the fantastic part
of it – to his knowledge he had never been on this street
before. He had spent little time walking about this region of

Salem, for he was indolent by nature; yet there was this extraordinary feeling of remembrance, and it grew more vivid as he went on.

He reached a corner, turned unthinkingly to the left. The odd sensation increased. He walked on slowly, pondering.

No doubt he *had* travelled by this way before – and very probably he had done so in a brown study, so that he had not been conscious of his route. Undoubtedly that was the explanation. Yet as Carson turned into Charter Street he felt a nameless unease waking within him. Salem was rousing; with daylight impassive Polish workers began to hurry past him towards the mills. An occasional automobile went by.

Before him a crowd was gathered on the sidewalk. He hastened his steps, conscious of a feeling of impending calamity. With an extraordinary sense of shock he saw that he was passing the Charter Street Burying Ground, the ancient, evilly famous 'Burying Point'. Hastily he pushed his way into the crowd.

Comments in a muffled undertone came to Carson's ears, and a bulky blue-clad back loomed up before him. He peered over the policeman's shoulder and caught his breath in a horrified gasp.

A man leaned against the iron railing that fenced the old graveyard. He wore a cheap, gaudy suit, and he gripped the rusty bars in a clutch that made the muscles stand out in ridges on the hairy back of his hands. He was dead, and on his face, staring up at the sky at a crazy angle, was frozen an expression of abysmal and utterly shocking horror. His eyes, all whites, were bulging hideously; his mouth was a twisted, mirthless grin.

A man at Carson's side turned a white face towards him. 'Looks as if he was scared to death,' he said somewhat hoarsely. 'I'd hate to have seen what he saw. Ugh – look at that face!'

Mechanically Carson backed away, feeling an icy breath of nameless things chill him. He rubbed his hand across his eyes, but still that contorted, dead face swam in his vision. He began to retrace his steps, shaken and trembling a little. Involuntarily his glance moved aside, rested on the tombs and monuments that dotted the old graveyard. No one had been buried there for over a century, and the lichen-stained tombstones, with their winged skulls, fat-cheeked cherubs, and funeral urns, seemed to breathe out an indefinable miasma of antiquity. What had frightened the man to death?

Carson drew a deep breath. True, the corpse had been a frightful spectacle, but he must not allow it to upset his nerves. He could not – his novel would suffer. Besides, he argued grimly to himself, the affair was obvious enough in its explanation. The dead man was apparently a Pole, one of the group of immigrants who dwell about Salem Harbor. Passing by the graveyard at night, a spot about which eldritch legends had clung for nearly three centuries, his drink-befuddled eyes must have given reality to the hazy phantoms of a superstitious mind. These Poles were notoriously unstable emotionally, prone to mob hysteria and wild imaginings. The great Immigrant Panic of 1853, in which three witch-houses had been burned to the ground, had grown from an old woman's confused and hysterical statement that she had seen a mysterious white-clad foreigner 'take off his face'. What else could be expected of such people?, Carson thought.

Nevertheless he remained in a nervous state, and did not return home until nearly noon. When on his arrival he found Leigh, the occultist, waiting, he was glad to see the man, and invited him in with cordiality.

Leigh was very serious. 'Did you hear about your friend Abigail Prinn?' he asked without preamble, and Carson started, pausing in the act of siphoning charged water into a glass. After a long moment he pressed the lever, sent the liquid sizzling and foaming into the whisky. He handed Leigh the drink and took one himself – neat – before answering the question.

'I don't know what you're talking about. Has — what's she been up to?' he asked, with an air of forced levity.

'I've been checking up the records,' Leigh said, 'and I find Abigail Prinn was buried on December 14th, 1690, in the Charter Street Burying Ground — with a stake through her heart. What's the matter?'

'Nothing,' Carson said tonelessly. 'Well?'

'Well — her grave's been opened and robbed, that's all. The stake was found uprooted near by, and there were footprints all around the grave. Shoe-prints. Did you dream last night, Carson?' Leigh snapped out the question, his grey eyes hard.

'I don't know,' Carson said confusedly, rubbing his forehead. 'I can't remember. I was at the Charter Street graveyard this morning.'

'Oh. Then you must have heard something about the man who — '

'I saw him,' Carson interrupted, shuddering. 'It upset me.'

He downed the whisky at a gulp.

Leigh watched him. 'Well,' he said presently, 'are you still determined to stay in this house?'

Carson put down the glass and stood up.

'Why not?' he snapped. 'Is there any reason why I shouldn't? Eh?'

'After what happened last night — '

'After *what* happened? A grave was robbed. A superstitious Pole saw the robbers and died of fright. Well?'

'You're trying to convince yourself,' Leigh said calmly. 'In your heart you know — you must know — the truth. You've become a tool in the hands of tremendous and terrible forces, Carson. For three centuries Abbie Prinn has lain in her grave — *undead* — waiting for someone to fall into her trap — the Witch Room. Perhaps she foresaw the future when she built it, foresaw that some day someone would blunder into that hellish chamber and be caught by the trap of the mosaic pattern. It caught you, Carson — and enabled that undead horror to bridge the gulf between consciousness and matter, to get *en rapport* with you. Hypnotism is child's play to a being with Abigail Prinn's frightful powers. She could very easily force you to go to her grave and uproot the stake that held her captive, and then erase the memory of that act from your mind so that you could not remember it even as a dream!'

Carson was on his feet, his eyes burning with a strange light. 'In God's name, man, do you know what you're saying?'

Leigh laughed harshly. 'God's name! The devil's name, rather – the devil that menaces Salem at this moment; for Salem is in danger, terrible danger. The men and women and children of the town Abbie Prinn cursed when they bound her to the stake – and found they couldn't burn her! I've been going through certain secret archives this morning, and I've come to ask you, for the last time, to leave this house.'

'Are you through?' Carson asked coldly. 'Very well. I shall stay here. You're either insane or drunk, but you can't impress me with your poppycock.'

'Would you leave if I offered you a thousand dollars?' Leigh asked. 'Or more, then – ten thousand? I have a considerable sum at my command.'

'No, damn it!' Carson snapped in a sudden blaze of anger. 'All I want is to be left alone to finish my novel. I can't work anywhere else – I don't want to, I won't – '

'I expected this,' Leigh said, his voice suddenly quiet, and with a strange note of sympathy. 'Man, you can't get away! You're caught in the trap, and it's too late for you to extricate yourself so long as Abbie Prinn's brain controls you through the Witch Room. And the worst part of it is that she can only manifest herself with your aid – she drains your life forces, Carson, feeds on you like a vampire.'

'You're mad,' Carson said dully.

'I'm afraid. That iron disc in the Witch Room – I'm afraid of that, and what's under it. Abbie Prinn served strange gods, Carson – and I read something on the wall of that alcove that gave me a hint. Have you ever heard of Nyogtha?'

Carson shook his head impatiently. Leigh fumbled in a

pocket, drew out a scrap of paper. 'I copied this from a book in the Kester Library,' he said, 'a book called the *Necronomicon*, written by a man who delved so deeply into forbidden secrets that men called him mad. Read this.'

Carson's brows drew together as he read the excerpt:

Men know him as the Dweller in Darkness, that brother of the Old Ones called Nyogtha, the Thing that should not be. He can be summoned to Earth's surface through certain secret caverns and fissures, and sorcerers have seen him in Syria and below the black tower of Leng; from the Thang Grotto of Tartary he has come ravening to bring terror and destruction among the pavilions of the great Khan. Only by the looped cross, by the Vach-Viraj incantation and by the Tikkoun elixir may he be driven back to the nighted caverns of hidden foulness where he dwelleth.

Leigh met Carson's puzzled gaze calmly. 'Do you understand now?'

'Incantations and elixirs!' Carson said, handing back the paper. 'Fiddle-sticks!'

'Far from it. That incantation and that elixir have been known to occultists and adepts for thousands of years. I've had occasion to use them myself in the past on certain – occasions. And if I'm right about this thing – ' He turned to the door, his lips compressed in a bloodless line. 'Such manifestations have been defeated before, but the difficulty lies in obtaining the elixir – it's very hard to get. But I hope . . . I'll be back. Can you stay out of the Witch Room until then?'

'I'll promise nothing,' Carson said. He had a dull headache, which had been steadily growing until it obtruded upon his consciousness, and he felt vaguely nauseated. 'Good-bye.'

He saw Leigh to the door and waited on the steps, with an odd reluctance to return to the house. As he watched the tall occultist hurry down the street, a woman came out of the adjoining house. She caught sight of him, and her huge breasts heaved. She burst into a shrill, angry tirade.

Carson turned, staring at her with astonished eyes. His

head throbbed painfully. The woman was approaching, shaking a fat fist threateningly.

'Why you scare my Sarah?' she cried, her swarthy face flushed. 'Why you scare her wit' your fool tricks, eh?'

Carson moistened his lips.

'I'm sorry,' he said slowly. 'Very sorry. I didn't frighten your Sarah. I haven't been home all day. What frightened her?'

'T'e brown t'ing – it ran in your house, Sarah say – '

The woman paused, and her jaw dropped. Her eyes widened. She made a peculiar sign with her right hand – pointing her index and little fingers at Carson, while her thumb was crossed over the other fingers. 'T'e old witch!'

She returned hastily, muttering in Polish in a frightened voice.

Carson turned, went back into the house. He poured some whisky into a tumbler, considered, and then set it aside untasted. He began to pace the floor, occasionally rubbing his forehead with fingers that felt dry and hot. Vague, confused thoughts raced through his mind. His head was throbbing and feverish.

At length he went down to the Witch Room. He remained there, although he did not work; for his headache was not so oppressive in the dead quiet of the underground chamber. After a time he slept.

How long he slumbered he did not know. He dreamed of Salem, and of a dimly-glimpsed, gelatinous black thing that hurtled with frightful speed through the streets, a thing like an incredibly huge, jet-black amoeba that pursued and engulfed men and women who shrieked and fled vainly. He dreamed of a skull-face peering into his own, a withered and shrunken countenance in which only the eyes seemed alive, and they shone with a hellish and evil light.

He awoke at last, sat up with a start. He was very cold.

It was utterly silent. In the light of the electric bulb the green and purple mosaic seemed to writhe and contract towards him, an illusion which disappeared as his sleep-

fogged vision cleared. He glanced at his wrist-watch. It was
two o'clock. He had slept through the afternoon and the
better part of the night.

He felt oddly weak, and a lassitude held him motionless in
his chair. The strength seemed to have been drained from
him. The piercing cold seemed to strike through to his brain,
but his headache was gone. His mind was very clear –
expectant, as though waiting for something to happen. A
movement near by caught his eye.

A slab of stone in the wall was moving. He heard a gentle
grating sound, and slowly a black cavity widened from a
narrow rectangle to a square. There was something crouching there in the shadow. Stark, blind horror struck through
Carson as the thing moved and crept forward into the light.

It looked like a mummy. For an intolerable, age-long
second the thought pounded frightfully at Carson's brain: *It
looked like a mummy*! It was a skeleton-thin, parchment-
brown corpse, and it looked like a skeleton with the hide of
some great lizard stretched over its bones. It stirred, it crept
forward, and its long nails scratched audibly against the
stone. It crawled out into the Witch Room, its passionless
face pitilessly revealed in the white light, and its eyes were
gleaming with charnel life. He could see the serrated ridge
of its brown, shrunken back . . .

Carson sat motionless. Abysmal horror had robbed him of
the power to move. He seemed to be caught in the fetters of
dream-paralysis, in which the brain, an aloof spectator, is
unable or unwilling to transmit the nerve-impulses to the
muscles. He told himself frantically that he was dreaming,
that he would presently awaken.

The withered horror arose. It stood upright, skeleton-thin,
and moved to the alcove where the iron disc lay embedded in
the floor. Standing with its back to Carson it paused, and a
dry and sere whisper rustled out in the dead stillness. At the
sound Carson would have screamed, but he could not. Still
the dreadful whisper went on, in a language Carson knew

was not of Earth, and as though in response an almost imperceptible quiver shook the iron disc.

It quivered and began to rise, very slowly, and as if in triumph the shrivelled horror lifted its pipestem arms. The disc was nearly a foot thick, but presently as it continued to rise above the level of the floor an insidious odour began to penetrate the room. It was vaguely reptilian, musky and nauseating. The disc lifted inexorably, and a little finger of blackness crept out from beneath its edge. Abruptly Carson remembered his dream of a gelatinous black creature that hurtled through the Salem streets. He tried vainly to break the fetters of paralysis that held him motionless. The chamber was darkening, and a black vertigo was creeping up to engulf him. The room seemed to rock.

Still the iron disc lifted; still the withered horror stood with its skeleton arms raised in blasphemous benediction; still the blackness oozed out in slow amoeboid movement.

There came a sound breaking through the sere whisper of the mummy, the quick patter of racing footsteps. Out of the corner of his eye Carson saw a man come racing into the Witch Room. It was the occultist, Leigh, and his eyes were blazing in a face of deathly pallor. He flung himself past Carson to the alcove where the black horror was surging into view.

The withered thing turned with dreadful slowness. Leigh carried some implement in his left hand, Carson saw, a *crux ansata* of gold and ivory. His right hand was clenched at his side. His voice rolled out, sonorous and commanding. There were little beads of perspiration on his white face.

'*Ya na kadishtu nilgh'ri . . . stell'bsna kn'aa Nyogtha . . . k'yarnak phlegethor . . .*'

The fantastic, unearthly syllables thundered out, echoing from the walls of the vault. Leigh advanced slowly, the *crux ansata* held high. And from beneath the iron disc black horror came surging!

The disc was lifted, flung aside, and a great wave of iridescent blackness, neither liquid nor solid, a frightful gelatinous mass, came pouring straight for Leigh. Without pausing in his advance he made a quick gesture with his right hand, and a little glass tube hurtled at the black thing was engulfed.

The formless horror paused. It hesitated, with a dreadful air of indecision, and then swiftly drew back. A choking stench of burning corruption began to pervade the air, and Carson saw great pieces of the black thing flake off, shrivelling as though destroyed with corroding acid. It fled back in a liquescent rush, hideous black flesh dropping as it retreated.

A pseudopod of blackness elongated itself from the central mass and like a great tentacle clutched the corpse-like being, dragged it back to the pit and over the brink. Another tentacle seized the iron disc, pulled it effortlessly across the floor, and as the horror sank from sight, the disc fell into place with a thunderous crash.

The room swung in wide circles about Carson, and a frightful nausea clutched him. He made a tremendous effort to get to his feet, and then the light faded swiftly and was gone. Darkness took him.

Carson's novel was never finished. He burned it, but continued to write, although none of his later work was ever published. His publishers shook their heads and wondered why such a brilliant writer of popular fiction had suddenly become infatuated with the weird and ghastly.

'It's powerful stuff,' one man told Carson, as he handed back his novel, *Black God of Madness*. 'It's remarkable in its way, but it's morbid and horrible. Nobody would read it. Carson, why don't you write the type of novel you used to do, the kind that made you famous?'

It was then that Carson broke his vow never to speak of the Witch Room, and he poured out the entire story, hoping for understanding and belief. But as he finished, his heart sank as he saw the other's face, sympathetic but sceptical.

'You dreamed it, didn't you?' the man asked, and Carson laughed bitterly.

'Yes – I dreamed it.'

'It must have made a terribly vivid impression on your mind. Some dreams do. But you'll forget about it in time,' he predicted, and Carson nodded.

And because he knew that he would only be arousing doubts of his sanity, he did not mention that thing that was burned indelibly on his brain, the horror he had seen in the Witch Room after wakening from his faint. Before he and Leigh had hurried, white-faced and trembling, from the chamber, Carson had cast a quick glance behind him. The shrivelled and corroded patches that he had seen slough off from that being of insane blasphemy had unaccountably disappeared, although they had left black stains upon the stones. Abbie Prinn, perhaps, had returned to the hell she had served, and her inhuman god had withdrawn to hidden abysses beyond man's comprehension, routed by powerful forces of elder magic which the occultist had commanded. But the witch had left a memento behind her, a hideous thing which Carson, in that last backward glance, had seen protruding from the edge of the iron disc, as though raised in ironic salute – *a withered, claw-like hand!*

The Haunter of the Graveyard

J. VERNON SHEA

New acquaintances always had difficulty in locating Elmer Harrod's address, for, although his street was just off one of the main arteries of the city, a stand of firs partially obscured the entrance. A large sign, DEAD END STREET, further discouraged entry, seemingly contradicted by a tiny arrow that quivered in the wind, bearing the legend: OLD DETHSHILL CEMETERY.

Despite the sign, no entrance way was provided for either car or pedestrian, nor was there a custodian's building. One had to clamber over a low stone fence, for this was the rear of the cemetery. The cemetery itself was long disused, every lot occupied. The last burial there had taken place more than fifty years before.

City officials were uninterested in the maintenance of the cemetery. They had tried to cut a freeway through the grounds twelve years ago, but such a hue and cry had been raised about the desecration of consecrated grounds that they had had to abandon the project. Having won their case, the defenders of the historic cemetery promptly forgot about it. Now its roads were in such a state of disrepair, with Joe Pye weed rustling triumphantly above the cracked concrete, that they were closed to automobile traffic. Even the bridle path that ran outside the cemetery and crossed its roads at several points had been forsaken, for horses there always behaved strangely, skittering and shying at invisible obstacles.

Harrod's street debouched sharply downhill. Harrod had

few neighbours, although a number of mouldering, tumble-down houses, long abandoned, offered hazardous shelter to vagrants. Harrod's home was the last one on the street, close by the stone fence of the cemetery. It was a house straight out of the Victorian era, with a cupola, a widow's walk, gables, and other evidences of gingerbread. Its bravura delighted the pronounced histrionic streak in Harrod, and was the sole reason for his purchase. Had the house not afforded such Gothic touches, Harrod would have found it necessary to have them built in.

Harrod even boasted that the house contained a secret passageway, but he would never show it to his guests 'else it wouldn't be secret any longer'. His guests suspected him of fantasticating in this manner – Harrod always overdid everything – but it was quite true.

Harrod had discovered the passageway in a curious manner. Shortly after he had moved in, he had had a dream, a very disturbing dream, in which he had been summoned in the night for some strange ritual and had gone down into the basement and, as if through long familiarity, had pressed upon the wall in a certain place and had gone through a suddenly revealed opening. The dream had ended at this point, before he could discover where the passageway led or why he had been called. In the morning he had retraced his steps to the basement wall and, feeling rather silly, had looked for a hidden switch – and had found one.

The passageway, he had discovered, was a tunnel hewn out of the earth. It appeared to burrow deep for many miles, a dank and cobwebbed place seemingly without end, and with some undisclosed vents that permitted a little air to circulate. Along the way were fixtures to hold torches, and it was evident from the flooring – not just packed earth, but some finished material – that many feet had trod this way before. Even the beam of his flashlight could not penetrate all the recesses cut out along the way, but they apparently contained nothing of interest, not even the bones and skulls he half-suspected to find. The tunnel was broad and high enough for several people to hasten along here at the same time.

Hasten – for there was a feeling of urgency about the tunnel. The people who had passed here had not dallied. Even Harrod was conscious of a compulsion to reach the tunnel's end.

It ended unexpectedly in a blank wall. No turn veered off it on either side, and though he played the flashlight over its entire expanse again and again, he could discover no sign of a switch or button. It seemed to Harrod that when he pressed his ear against the wall he could hear from behind it a distant roaring, like the pounding of surf; but he knew very well that that couldn't be, for the house was miles away from the sea.

In the days that followed Harrod made many trips to the tunnel, but never managed to get past the wall. However, further exploration revealed that one of the recesses contained an exit that he had overlooked, an extension of the tunnel that led upward, and following its course he was brought outdoors, to a secluded corner behind a mausoleum, in old Dethshill Cemetery.

Perhaps this discovery whetted his interest in the cemetery. Old Dethshill Cemetery had very few visitors. Sometimes Harrod would see from his bay window some oldster laboriously seeking an ancestor's grave, or some antiquarian with camera case slung over strolling along looking for some especially old gravestone, or a youthful art student intent upon making a rubbing of some curious inscription. Lovers came there occasionally for trysts; vagrants for a brief time cooked edibles over little fires; and children new to the neighbourhood enchantedly climbed over the fence, bemused by all those acres to play in. But even in broad daylight children did not tarry there long. They soon withdrew, subtly frightened.

The cemetery had long had a name in the city as a place to be shunned, and its reputation was not helped by Harrod's discovery, during the first year of his occupancy of the house, of the body of a vagrant close by one of the paths. The throat had been freshly torn out by something very sharp. Possibly it was the deed of another vagrant, seeking vengeance, or the work of some large animal. He reported his discovery to the officials; the police came, made but a cursory examination, and hastily had the body carted away.

Trees proliferated in the cemetery, descending into the valley to drink from the meandering creek and marching resolutely up the hillsides. They grew quite fat, elbowing one another for living space, so close together that even at noon the sunlight could not quite penetrate their masses; when Harrod lay under one of the trees, the sun was but a rumour in the sky.

One would think that with such a bounty of trees, the cemetery would be alive with birdsong, but Harrod had never heard or seen a bird there. Yet the cemetery was never still: there were constant faint rustlings or scutterings; but Harrod had yet to encounter any small creatures, not even a muskrat down at the creek or a nervous field mouse. But perhaps he was just not observant enough; when he paused to examine an inscription, he might hear the snapping of twigs behind him, but no matter how swiftly he turned then, nothing would be in sight.

There is something eerie about trees undappled by sun, where a sense of twilight prevails even at high noon; and Harrod found himself returning to the grounds again and again, if only to catch whatever it was that lurked among the trees. But strain his eyes though he might, turn his head unexpectedly, keep his eyes to the ground then suddenly look up, he never could surprise anything in the act of watching him, not even a deer sticking out an inquisitive nose. There was nothing to see but trees and the spaces between them and leaves twisting in the wind.

And the trees had the look of a primeval forest, as this land might have looked before the advent of man. These woods wanted no visitors, and Harrod sensed that he was an intruder.

But intrude he must, for that was in his nature, like the actor who feels compelled to perform upon a darkened stage in an empty theatre. He felt because of the nearness of his house a sense of proprietorship over the cemetery grounds, and was made actively resentful on the rare day when he passed someone strolling along.

Harrod's house was familiar to thousands of TV viewers, for on his show Harrod frequently was pictured before it in some horrendous makeup or other. Or the camera would dwell lovingly upon some architectural oddity or other – the gargoyle on the roof was a favourite subject – and eventually would discover Harrod in his library, in the midst of his tremendous collection of books of fantasy. Harrod would smirk at the viewer, perhaps stroke a phoney beard, and finger some book that might have some relationship to the film about to be shown. In over-rich, fluting tones he would give a history of the vampire or the werewolf or ghoul while the screen credits flashed on.

For Harrod's speciality – and means of livelihood – was the showing of horror films, the older and more rubbishy the better, for television audiences predominantly teenagers. He knew that they turned on his programme – or claimed to – not for vicarious chills, but for the sardonic commentaries with which he frequently laced the proceedings. He would comment scathingly upon the acting and the quality of the script and the obvious phoniness of the backgrounds and he would 'encourage' the actors: 'Come on, Bela, show your fangs now.' 'Better not go in there, little lady.' 'Boo to you, too.' Harrod turned a deaf ear to those horror film buffs who phoned in to suggest he let the films alone. Once it had been released, any film was fair game for his arrows.

Increasingly, as the years went by, the cemetery exerted a fascination for Harrod. It concealed a mystery he was determined to unfathom. For some time he had harboured a suspicion that someone – one of his neighbours, perhaps, or even one of his TV viewing public – was in the habit of playing tricks upon him. Sometimes of an evening he might see flickering lights deep within the cemetery, but whenever he went in to investigate he could find no evidence of another's presence.

Sometimes there were subtle sounds on the wind, like whispering or keening, sounds that were eldritch and infinitely chilling; and whenever he heard them he would feel that his heart had stopped beating, and nothing could drag him into the cemetery then.

Harrod told his acquaintances that the cemetery reminded him of a movie set. When fog collected in the valley, and the gravestones loomed crazily askew, one half-expected Count Dracula to emerge upon a nocturnal errand. Certain areas of the cemetery could pass readily enough for Brontë moors. At first Harrod had delighted in being photographed against such backgrounds – his scrapbook bulged with snaps of him in weird disguises – but after a time he began to realize that it was all very well to have fun in the cemetery, but that he had been overlooking its readily exploitable possibilities.

He devised dramatic little scripts for use on TV films and enlisted the aid of some students from Miskatonic University to enact them. The unaccustomed sounds of camera crews in action were now heard in the cemetery. The actors entered readily into the spirit of things. It was not difficult to register shock or horror in these macabre surroundings, especially when it seemed that the cemetery itself wished to co-operate. When the day's rushes were shown, it seemed to the company that things appeared thereon that they did not remember filming: deep menacing shadows that seemed to reach for the players; just a suggestion of gibbering things on the periphery of the action; clouds of mists that obscured the screen momentarily; skies far more lowering that memory pictured them. And the sound track had recorded far more things than the sound engineers had counted upon – not the things that plague Hollywood crews like the buzzing of insects or the roar of passing planes, but sounds thoroughly in keeping with the mood of the film, a really inspired series of whisperings and rustlings of half-heard scutterings. The sound track, in fact, was so very busy that Harrod decided to dispense with the usual (and costly) electronic background music. Music here would be too much like painting the lily.

These films, shown to the TV studios, impressed the advertising agencies greatly; and the films formed the basis for the spot offered Harrod. After an introductory shot of Harrod picking his way up the grave-strewn hillside, with trees bending so far in the wind that it seemed that they were reaching out to clutch Harrod, the horror film that followed seemed doubly synthetic and Harrod's gibes the more diverting. He suspected – but did not want to know – that some of these presumably genuine shots had been faked by the Miskatonic students when his back was turned, for to think otherwise – that these unrehearsed sights and sounds were quite authentic – was a possibility too chilling to be long entertained.

For his memory would not permit him to rest. He remembered that when the camera crews had gone for the day, and he went for his wonted stroll through the cemetery, he sensed almost immediately a change in the atmosphere. He felt himself under surveillance – and the surveillance was distinctly inimical. It was as if he had betrayed a trust. And when he noticed the ravages left by the company – the cigarette butts mashed into the ground, the litter of paper cups with an inch or two of coffee still in them, the used flashbulbs, the trampled grass, the scuffmarks on gravestones, the treads left by the camera equipment – he realized why the atmosphere was so actively hostile. There was a stillness in the air, as if something were waiting. A branch of a tree he passed under tensed as if about to tear at his throat. Old Dethshill Cemetery employs no caretakers, and he felt just a bit foolish as he began to repair the damage as best he could, gathering up the accumulated litter into one pile and going back to his home for cardboard boxes into which to place it – but he had the definite feeling that his presence would be unwelcome here until he made at least a show of effort on the cemetery's behalf.

It was true that the cemetery did not always wear so forbidding an air, else he would have been reluctant to visit it so frequently. There were bright days in spring and summer when the cemetery seemed in a relaxed mood, like a tiger washing itself in the sun. There were never any flowers upon the graves, of course, but during the warm months nature itself provided bouquets of wild flowers. Even a hillside yellow with dandelions in the sun is a joy to the eye, and in the soft light that sometimes filtered through the trees and dappled the ground the cemetery looked almost benign. And down in the creek the water that gurgled over the rocks pretended to be rapids. Sometimes a big brindle cat would walk for some distance along the stone fence and seem about to venture inside, but at the last moment would think better of it and drop hastily down.

It was on such a day that Harrod first thought of bringing reading material to the cemetery, and thereafter whenever he strolled there a book or magazine always accompanied him. He had to select his reading carefully, for he had found that such favourite writers of his as Jane Austen and Peacock, for instance, clashed immediately with the surroundings. He discovered, conversely, that whenever he stretched out upon a gravestone to read, even the most spurious story in a pulp horror magazine seemed to gain validity thereby. He realized that such behaviour was sheerest bravado, but it gave him a delectable titillation. Once when a child strayed into the cemetery and found him enwrapped in an Inverness cape (part of his Dracula getup) dozing upon a grave, the child screamed and screamed and ran and ran, and the sound of his screams brought chuckles to Harrod in delighted remembrance.

But reading in Old Dethshill Cemetery at night, with a strong flashing light spilling over the pages of Blackwood or Machen, was the greatest thrill of all. He chose usually the finest horror tales for these nocturnal excursions, sometimes almost afraid to turn a page because the sentence he had

been reading had been punctuated by a quite indefinable
sound . . .

It had been warm during the day, but now the sharpness of
the night air presaged the winter to come. Harrod drew the
flaps of his topcoat protectively about his face. It was uncommonly quiet in the cemetery, the only sounds for a moment
being the crackling of the sere leaves underfoot.

With so many leaves fallen, the branches looked unduly
prominent, each contorted shape as eye-arresting as if it had
been newly painted. The trees seemed huddled less in coterie,
their bareness permitting the full moonlight to penetrate the
cemetery grounds.

But the moonlight held no warmth. It was obscured of a
sudden by a passing cloud, causing Harrod to look up. The
sight was so reminiscent of a hundred horror films that
Harrod tittered involuntarily and lifted his head mockingly
and bayed the moon in deft imitation of the Wolf Man.

The mockery was out of place, Harrod suddenly had cause
to feel. He felt a prickling of the skin. The cemetery was
sentiently aware of his presence. He had the disquieting
sensation of being *watched*. He half-expected the tentacle of
some extra-terrestrial monster to come probing out of the
bushes.

The grass along the path had not been cut within memory
and came up past his knees, the blades seeming to cut at him
with serrated teeth. The wind came up strong just then, and
a rippling ran through the high grasses as if to mark the
passage of some small creature.

He stumbled and almost fell over a gravestone that had
been hidden by weeds. He pulled them back and sent a beam
from his flashlight upon the marker. OBEDIAH CARTER
the marker read; the dates had been almost obliterated by
time, but so far as he could decipher they read 179 – 18-7.
There was a number of Carter graves hereabouts, part of a
once flourishing shipbuilding family. Hadn't he known a

Randolph Carter in his youth, one who had a fearsome tale of some cemetery such as this?

Old Dethshill Cemetery no doubt knew many such tales. Harrod had often wondered what the faces of the people who dwelt in cold solitude here had been like. Dour, Puritanical faces, no doubt, or disturbed, mad faces. The faces of nightmare . . .

Obediah Carter's grave was too weed-choked to provide what he was looking for, and so he hastened on. He had come along this way dozens of times, and yet in the moonlight everything looked oddly different, graves appearing before his eyes in places where he hadn't remembered them, and the path meandering in unexpected turns. Before he was quite prepared for it, he came upon the spot he had termed Witches' Hollow, his destination.

It was a place where the trees and the underbrush had been pushed back as if by the hand of a gigantic gardener, a place roughly the shape of a circle, where the earth looked as black and dead as that of a burned-out forest, although no fire had blazed here within anyone's memory. Perhaps, a century or so ago, this had been the meeting place of a coven of witches who had burned sacrificial offerings to their black goat god.

The place was fringed by firs standing like sentries, the tallest trees of the cemetery; and just beyond them oaks and willows and maples crowded in for a look. The gravestones were arranged within the circle to an order lost to history. Harrod suspected that were one to shift the markers of the principal graves a few inches here and there, a perfect pentagram would be formed. And it took little imagination to picture witches and warlocks sitting upon the markers of their graves, watching him; indeed, Harrod had filmed just such a scene here.

He himself had been the sacrificial victim of the film, for with his rather plump body and look of preening self-indulgence, he was marked for the part. He considered that he had given quite a good performance, rolling his eyes in terror and quavering in his speech.

Harrod settled himself as comfortably as he could in his usual position upon the grave of Jeremy Kent and opened his book, directing the beam of his powerful flashlight upon the pages, although the moonlight washed the scene so brightly here that he could almost dispense with the flashlight. The marble of the gravestone was quite cold in the night air, and after a while its chill began to seep into his buttocks even through the thickness of his topcoat. His ungloved fingers grew so stiff and numb that he could scarce turn the pages.

Jeremy Kent. A euphonious, harmless-sounding name. But in local folklore Jeremy Kent was reputed to have been a warlock or wizard, possibly the leader of the coven. The gravestone attested that he had been still in his early thirties when he died, a handsome man with the coldest of blue eyes. The legends concerning Kent were uncommonly interesting, and it had long been Harrod's plan, whenever he could raise the necessary capital, to make a feature-length film about his life. But how would he be able to suggest the scene in which Jeremy Kent tears the living heart out of a child's body?

Jeremy Kent had not died of natural causes. The enflamed townspeople had taken matters into their own hands. But if Harrod acceded to historical accuracy in this matter, the scene would be too much like scenes from *Frankenstein* and a dozen other horror films. Possibly, Harrod thought, he could have Kent visited by celestial vengeance . . .

He kept pondering about Kent, as if loath to continue reading the Lovecraft story at the point at which he had left off last evening. For the Providence recluse had come too uncomfortably close to reality. Old Dethshill Cemetery itself was like a plagiarism from his pages, this clearing which Harrod had termed Witches' Hollow would fit all too easily into a Lovecraftian work, and Jeremy Kent differed very little from one of Lovecraft's villains. It was almost as if

Lovecraft had visited this place himself; and considering his extensive antiquarian wandering in this region, the possibility that he had done so was not unlikely.

The most disturbing thing was the dream. It was well-known that H. P. Lovecraft had had a number of distinctly disturbing dreams, eerie dislocations of time and space, nightmares so complete and well-organized in themselves that frequently he was able to transfer the dreams to the printed page virtually without change. His dreams had none of the random illogic that characterizes the usual dream, but granted their fantastic premise, were quite compellingly real.

The story Harrod had been reading last evening, Harrod suspected, had likewise had its genesis in one of Lovecraft's dreams. It was such a disquieting story that it had filled Harrod's thoughts all last evening; so that it was not really surprising that when at last he fell off to sleep he had found himself re-living Lovecraft's story.

With this difference: that he found that the locale of the story had shifted to Harrod's own house. He was part of a group of cowled figures, with clothes beneath the cowls that were suitable for another century, that was moving swiftly along the secret passageway that he had discovered. They had seized torches from the brackets along the walls and were moving three abreast. When they came to the terminal wall, they did not hesitate long; the leader inserted his fingers into grooves at the base of the wall and lifted; and in a moment the entire wall slid up like a garage door.

From behind the wall came a sudden breath of cold air; and Harrod found himself moving along with the group into a grotto whose immensity staggered his eyes, an ill-illumined cavern whose walls dripped slime. The greenish light revealed water lapping only a few hundred yards from his feet, the water of a cove with apparently an entrance to the sea beyond the rocks far in the distance. The curious part was that Harrod knew himself to be in a dream *at the time*, and tried to struggle awake. There must have been some

elision of time in the dream at this point, for the next thing
he knew he was participating with a group in some kind of
ceremony at the shore of the cove, chanting a gibberish
incantation:

*Iä! Iä! Cthulhu fhtagn! Ph'nglui mglw'nafh Cthulhu R'lyeh
wgah-nagl fhtagn.*

And in the dream, presently, there was an *answer* to the
call. His memory refused to sort out the details of the thing
that rose to the surface then, a thing tremendous in size,
with unbelievably long tentacles . . .

The dream mercifully had come to an end at this point. In
the morning Harrod had been so shaken that his mind balked
at the thought of going down into the passageway to confirm
that the wall would indeed slide up as it had done in the
dream; the thought that he might see the cove again was too
much for his peace of mind.

Fortunately, a call had come later from the studio, and he
had busied himself most of the day preparing a script. But
now, as he read the pages of the Lovecraft story, the monstrous dream kept intruding . . .

A sudden great gust of wind riffled the pages as he read,
almost tearing the book from his hands. It diminished,
moaning. A stillness overtook the clearing. The firs at its
edge, which had been tossing and quivering like a dog
shedding water, stood now monumentally erect.

It was too still. Seized by a sudden impulse, whose origin
he couldn't fathom, Harrod turned back in the Lovecraft
story, going through the pages until he found what he
sought. He drew the topcoat about him, rose as if on cue, and
with great histrionic effect slowly pronounced the words,
pronouncing them as best he could:

*Iä! Iä! Cthulhu fhtagn! Ph'nglui mglw'nafh Cthulhu R'lyeh
wgah-nagl fhtagn.*

The moonlight paled. There was a gathering of shadows
where there had been no shadows, a sudden suspension of
light that blotted out the trees and tall grasses. The shadows
appeared to advance.

Harrod blinked and rubbed his eyelids to clear them of granular roughnesses. No, it wasn't his imagination. The shadows *were* there, somehow more solid than they had been an instant before, an advancing phalanx of darkness.

Icewater coursed down his spine. The shadows were there. They had stopped now, but did not retreat; they stopped, and looked at Harrod, and waited.

The darkness disappeared from the face of the moon, and there was light in the sky once again, a precipitous flow of light at the edge of the clearing, between the flanking firs.

And there were things in the sky there, high above the trees; there were faces on a gigantic scale, faces that were only remotely human, and a tumultuous threshing of non-human parts, with a suggestion of tentacles.

They were up there, with rapacious eyes, but it seemed that their concentration had not yet been engaged upon Harrod; they were searching the ground like a bird looking for insects. Harrod whimpered and sought to hide, heaving himself off the gravestone and scrabbling in the loose gravel with his hands.

Possibly the movement of his feet had triggered some mechanism, for as he cowered beside the marker there was a creaking sound, as of protesting hinges, that set up a reverberating clangour on the night air; and the gravestone he had just vacated slowly began to rise before his eyes.

And now Harrod saw that the gravestone had concealed steps, a flight of stairs that descended subterraneously, and from them came a breath of stale and noisome air.

As he gazed at the steps in terror, he was conscious of a diminution of light just beyond the periphery of his vision, and looking up he saw that the moonlight had quitted the clearing and that the shadows had come very near, surrounding him in an inescapable ring, with little pinpoints of light which might have been eyes.

The pale light could not define their shapes. They were not wraith-like at all, not in the least transparent, but rather concentrations of darkness.

There was the slightest susurration of sound, almost below hearing level, and it gradually grew into a hollow whispering. It came from the subterranean passage.

There was no one, no thing down there, he knew. There couldn't be. And yet he kept looking fearfully down the steps, as if expecting momentarily the appearance of a shrouded figure, possibly one with cold blue eyes . . .

The whispering increased in volume, insistent, urgent. The voice sounded cold and ancient and unspeakably corrupt. And now he began to distinguish its words:

Come down, Harrod. Come down.

Old Dethshill Cemetery is little frequented, and it was a considerable time later that a pair of lovers, cutting off from the main path, almost trod upon a body. It was so badly decomposed that it required a dental checkup to identify it as that of the missing Elmer Harrod.

Had Harrod still been living, he himself would have cut the shot as too horrifying for his TV viewers. For the head had almost been completely torn from the body, adhering to it only by a few shreds of rotting flesh. The mouth was engaged in a perpetual scream, and the eyes, almost popping from their sockets, held too much nightmare horror to contemplate for long. The body was only barely recognizable as human; it had been twisted almost inside out, and something had gnawed upon it for quite a little while.

The Shambler from the Stars

ROBERT BLOCH

I am what I profess to be – a writer of weird fiction. Since earliest childhood I have been enthralled by the cryptic fascination of the unknown and the unguessable. The nameless fears, the grotesque dreams, the queer, half-intuitive fancies that haunt our minds have always exercised for me a potent and inexplicable delight.

In literature I have walked the midnight paths with Poe or crept amidst the shadows with Machen; combed the realms of horrific stars with Baudelaire, or steeped myself with earth's inner madness amidst the tales of ancient lore. A meagre talent for sketching and crayon work led me to attempt crude picturizations involving the outlandish denizens of my nighted thoughts. The same sombre trend of intellect which drew me in my art interested me in obscure realms of musical composition; the symphonic strains of the *Planets Suite* and the like were my favourites. My inner life soon became a ghoulish feast of eldritch, tantalizing horrors.

My outer existence was comparatively dull. As time went on I found myself drifting more and more into the life of a penurious recluse; a tranquil, philosophical existence amidst a world of books and dreams.

A man must live. By nature constitutionally and spiritually unfitted for manual labour, I was at first puzzled about the choice of a suitable vocation. The Depression complicated matters to an almost intolerable degree, and for a time I was close to utter economic disaster. It was then that I decided to write.

I procured a battered typewriter, a ream of cheap paper, and a few carbons. My subject matter did not bother me. What better field than the boundless realms of a colourful imagination? I would write of horror, fear, and the riddle that is Death. At least, in the callowness of my unsophistication, this was my intention.

My first attempts soon convinced me how utterly I had failed. Sadly, miserably, I fell short of my aspired goal. My vivid dreams became on paper merely meaningless jumbles of ponderous adjectives, and I found no ordinary words to express the wondrous terror of the unknown. My first manuscripts were miserable and futile documents; the few magazines using such materials being unanimous in their rejections.

I had to live. Slowly but surely I began to adjust my style to my ideas. Laboriously I experimented with words, phrases, sentence-structure. It was work, and hard work at that. I soon learned to sweat. At last, however, one of my stories met with favour; then a second, a third, a fourth. Soon I had begun to master the more obvious tricks of the trade, and the future looked brighter at last. It was with an easier mind that I returned to my dream-life and my beloved books. My stories afforded me a somewhat meagre livelihood, and for a time this sufficed. But not for long. Ambition, ever an illusion, was the cause of my undoing.

I wanted to write a real story; not the stereotyped, ephemeral sort of tale I turned out for the magazines, but a real work of art. The creation of such a masterpiece became my ideal. I was not a good writer, but that was not entirely due to my errors in mechanical style. It was, I felt, the fault of my subject matter. Vampires, werewolves, ghouls, mythological monsters – these things constituted material of little merit. Commonplace imagery, ordinary adjectival treatment, and a prosaically anthropocentric point of view were the chief detriments to the production of a really good weird tale.

I must have new subject matter, truly unusual plot

material. If only I could conceive of something that was teratologically incredible!

I longed to learn the songs the demons sing as they swoop between the stars, or hear the voices of the olden gods as they whisper their secrets to the echoing void. I yearned to know the terrors of the grave; the kiss of maggots on my tongue, the cold caress of a rotting shroud upon my body. I thirsted for the knowledge that lies in the pits of mummied eyes, and burned for wisdom known only to the worm. Then I could really write, and my hopes be truly realized.

I sought a way. Quietly I began a correspondence with isolated thinkers and dreamers all over the country. There was a hermit in the western hills, a savant in the northern wilds, a mystic dreamer in New England. It was from the latter that I learned of the ancient books that hold strange lore. He quoted guardedly from the legendary *Necronomicon*, and spoke timidly of a certain *Book of Eibon* that was reputed to surpass it in the utter wildness of its blasphemy. He himself had been a student of these volumes of primal dread, but he did not want me to search too far. He had heard many strange things as a boy in witch-haunted Arkham, where the old shadows still leer and creep, and since then he had wisely shunned the blacker knowledge of the forbidden.

At length, after much pressing on my part, he reluctantly consented to furnish me with the names of certain persons he deemed able to aid me in my quest. He was a writer of notable brilliance and wide reputation among the discriminating few, and I knew he was keenly interested in the outcome of the whole affair.

As soon as his precious list came into my possession, I began a widespread postal campaign in order to obtain access to the desired volumes. My letters went out to universities, private libraries, reputed seers, and the leaders of carefully hidden and obscurely designated cults. But I was foredoomed to disappointment.

The replies I received were definitely unfriendly, almost

hostile. Evidently the rumoured possessors of such lore were angered that their secret should be thus unveiled by a prying stranger. I was subsequently the recipient of several anonymous threats through the mails, and I had one very alarming phone-call. This did not bother me nearly so much as the disappointing realization that my endeavours had failed. Denials, evasions, refusals, threats – these would not aid me. I must look elsewhere.

The book stores! Perhaps on some musty and forgotten shelf I might discover what I sought.

Then began an interminable crusade. I learned to bear my numerous disappointments with unflinching calm. Nobody in the common run of shops seemed ever to have heard of the frightful *Necronomicon*, the evil *Book of Eibon*, or the disquieting *Cultes des Goules*.

Persistence brings results. In a little old shop on South Dearborn Street, amidst dusty shelves seemingly forgotten by time, I came to the end of my search. There, securely wedged between two century-old editions of Shakespeare, stood a great black volume with iron facings. Upon it, in hand-engraved lettering, was the inscription *De Vermis Mysteriis*, or 'Mysteries of the Worm'.

The proprietor could not tell how it had come into his possession. Years before, perhaps, it had been included in some second-hand job-lot. He was obviously unaware of its nature, for I purchased it with a dollar bill. He wrapped the ponderous thing for me, well pleased at this unexpected sale, and bade me a very satisfied good-day.

I left hurriedly, the precious prize under my arm. What a find! I had heard of this book before. Ludvig Prinn was its author; he who had perished at the inquisitorial stake in Brussels when the witchcraft trials were at their height. A strange character – alchemist, necromancer, reputed mage – he boasted of having attained a miraculous age when he at last suffered a fiery immolation at the hands of the secular arm. He was said to have proclaimed himself the sole survivor of the ill-fated ninth crusade, exhibiting as proof

certain musty documents of attestation. It is true that a
certain Ludvig Prinn was numbered among the gentlemen
retainers of Montserrat in the olden chronicles, but the
incredulous branded Ludvig as a crack-brained impostor,
though perchance a lineal descendant of the original warrior.

Ludvig attributed his sorcerous learning to the years he
had spent as a captive among the wizards and wonder-
workers of Syria, and glibly he spoke of encounters with the
djinns and efreets of elder Eastern myth. He is known to
have spent some time in Egypt, and there are legends among
the Libyan dervishes concerning the old seer's deeds in
Alexandria.

At any rate, his declining days were spent in the Flemish
lowland country of his birth, where he resided, appropriately
enough, in the ruins of a pre-Roman tomb that stood in the
forest near Brussels. Ludvig was reputed to have dwelt there
amidst a swarm of familiars and fearsomely invoked conjur-
ations. Manuscripts still extant speak of him guardedly as
being attended by 'invisible companions' and 'Star-sent servants'. Peasants shunned the forest by night, for they did not
like certain noises that resounded to the moon, and they
most certainly were not anxious to see what worshipped at
the old pagan altars that stood crumbling in certain of the
darker glens.

Be that as it may, these creatures that he commanded
were never seen after Prinn's capture by the inquisitorial
minions. Searching soldiers found the tomb entirely
deserted, though it was thoroughly ransacked before its
destruction. The supernatural entities, the unusual instruments and compounds – all had most curiously vanished. A
search of the forbidding woods and a timorous examination
of the strange altars did not add to the information. There
were fresh blood-stains on the altars, and fresh blood-stains
on the rack, too, before the questioning of Prinn was finished.
A series of particularly atrocious tortures failed to elicit any
further disclosures from the silent wizard, and at length the

weary interrogators ceased, and cast the aged sorcerer into a dungeon.

It was in prison, while awaiting trial, that he penned the morbid, horror-hinting lines of *De Vermis Mysteriis*, known today as *Mysteries of the Worm*. How it was ever smuggled through the alert guards is a mystery in itself, but a year after his death it saw print in Cologne. It was immediately suppressed, but a few copies had already been privately distributed. These in turn were transcribed, and although there was a later censored and deleted printing, only the Latin original is accepted as genuine. Throughout the centuries a few of the elect have read and pondered on its lore. The secrets of the old archimage are known today only to the initiated, and they discourage all attempts to spread their fame, for certain very definite reasons.

This, in brief, was what I knew of the volume's history at the time it came into my possession. As a collector's item alone the book was a phenomenal find, but on its contents I could pass no judgement. It was in Latin. Since I can speak or translate only a few words of that learned tongue, I was confronted by a barrier as soon as I opened the musty pages. It was maddening to have such a treasure-trove of dark knowledge at my command and yet lack the key to its unearthing.

For a moment I despaired, since I was unwilling to approach any local classical or Latin scholar in connection with so hideous and blasphemous a text. Then came an inspiration. Why not take it east and seek the aid of my friend? He was a student of the classics, and would be less likely to be shocked by the horrors of Prinn's baleful revelations. Accordingly I addressed a hasty letter to him, and shortly thereafter received my reply. He would be glad to assist me – I must by all means come at once.

2

Providence is a lovely town. My friend's house was ancient
and quaintly Georgian. The first floor was a gem of Colonial
atmosphere. The second, beneath antique gables that shadowed the enormous window, served as a workroom for my
host.

It was here that we pondered that grim, eventful night
last April; here beside the open window that overlooked the
azure sea. It was a moonless night; haggard and wan with a
fog that filled the darkness with bat-like shadows. In my
mind's eye I can see it still – the tiny, lamp-lit room with the
big table and the high-backed chairs; the bookcases border-
ing the walls; the manuscripts stacked in special files.

My friend and I sat at the table, the volume of mystery
before us. His lean profile threw a disturbing shadow on the
wall, and his waxen face was furtive in the pale light. There
was an inexplicable air of portentous revelation quite disturbing in its potency; I sensed the presence of secrets
waiting to be revealed.

My companion detected it too. Long years of occult experience had sharpened his intuition to an uncanny degree. It
was not cold that made him tremble as he sat there in his
chair; it was not fever that caused his eyes to flame like
jewel-incarned fires. He knew, even before he opened that
accursed tome, that it was evil. The musty scent that rose
from those antique pages carried with it the reek of the
tomb. The faded leaves were maggoty at the edges, and rats
had gnawed the leather; rats which perchance had a ghastlier food for common fare.

I had told my friend the volume's history that afternoon,
and had unwrapped it in his presence. Then he had seemed
willing and eager to begin an immediate translation. Now
he demurred.

It was not wise, he insisted. This was evil knowledge –
who could say what demon-dreaded lore these pages might
contain, or what ills befall the ignorant one who sought to
tamper with their contents? It is not good to learn too much,
and men had died for exercising the rotted wisdom that these
leaves contained. He begged me to abandon the quest while
the book was still unopened and to seek my inspiration in
saner things.

I was a fool. Hastily I overruled his objections with vain
and empty words. I was not afraid. Let us at least gaze into
the contents of our prize. I began to turn the pages.

The result was disappointing. It was an ordinary-looking
volume after all – yellow, crumbling leaves set with heavy
black-lettered Latin texts. That was all; no illustrations, no
alarming designs.

My friend could no longer resist the allurement of such a
rare bibliophilic treat. In a moment he was peering intently
over my shoulder, occasionally muttering snatches of Latin
phrasing. Enthusiasm mastered him at last. Seizing the
precious tome in both hands, he seated himself near the
window and began reading paragraphs at random, occasionally translating them into English.

His eyes gleamed with a feral light; his cadaverous profile
grew intent as he pored over the mouldering runes. Sentences thundered in fearsome litany, then faded into tones
below a whisper as his voice became as soft as a viper's hiss.
I caught only a few phrases now, for in his introspection he
seemed to have forgotten me. He was reading of spells and
enchantments. I recall allusions to such gods of divination as
Father Yig, dark Han, and serpent-bearded Byatis. I shuddered; for I knew these names of old; but I would have
shuddered more had I known what was yet to come.

It came quickly. Suddenly he turned to me in great
agitation, and his excited voice was shrill. He asked me if I
remembered the legends of Prinn's sorcery, and the tales of
the invisible servants he commanded from the stars. I
assented, little understanding the cause of his sudden frenzy.

Then he told me the reason. Here, under a chapter on familiars, he had found an orison or spell, perhaps the very one Prinn had used to call upon his unseen servitors from beyond the stars! Let me listen while he read.

I sat there dully, like a stupid, uncomprehending fool. Why did I not scream, try to escape, or tear that monstrous manuscript from his hands? Instead I sat there – sat there while my friend, in a voice cracked with unnatural excitement, read in Latin a long and sonorously sinister invocation.

'*Tibi Magnum Innominandum, signa stellarum nigrarum et bufaniformis Sadoquae sigillum . . .*'

The croaking ritual proceeded, then rose on wings of nighted, hideous horror. The words seemed to writhe like flames in the air, burning into my brain. The thundering tones cast an echo into infinity, beyond the farthermost star. They seemed to pass into primal and undimensioned gates, to seek out a listener there, and summon him to earth. Was it all an illusion? I did not pause to ponder.

For that unwitting summons was answered. Scarcely had my companion's voice died away in that little room before the terror came. The room turned cold. A sudden wind shrieked in through the open window; a wind that was not of earth. It bore an evil bleating from afar, and at the sound, my friend's face became a pale white mask of newly awakened fear. Then there was a crunching at the walls, and the window-ledge buckled before my staring eyes. From out of the nothingness beyond that opening came a sudden burst of lubricious laughter – a hysterical cackling born of utter madness. It rose to the grinning quintessence of all horror, without mouth to give it birth.

The rest happened with startling swiftness. All at once my friend began to scream as he stood by the window; scream and claw wildly at empty air. In the lamplight I saw his features contort into a grimace of insane agony. A moment later, his body rose unsupported from the floor, and began to bend outward to a backbreaking degree. A second later came

the sickening grind of broken bones. His form now hung in
midair, the eyes glazed and the hands clutching convulsively
as if at something unseen. Once again there came the sound
of maniacal tittering, but this time it came from *within the
room!*

The stars rocked in red anguish; the cold wind gibbered in
my ears. I crouched in my chair, my eyes riveted on that
astounding scene in the corner.

My friend was shrieking now; his screams blended with
that gleeful, atrocious laughter from the empty air. His
sagging body, dangling in space, bent backward once again
as blood spurted from the torn neck, spraying like a ruby
fountain.

That blood never reached the floor. It stopped in midair as
the laughter ceased, and a loathsome sucking noise took its
place. With a new and accelerated horror, I realized that
that blood was being drained to feed the invisible entity from
beyond! What creature of space had been so suddenly and
unwittingly invoked? What was that vampiric monstrosity I
could not see?

Even now a hideous metamorphosis was taking place. The
body of my companion became shrunken, wizened, lifeless.
At length it dropped to the floor and lay nauseatingly still.
But in midair another and a ghastlier change occurred.

A reddish glow filled the corner by the window – a *bloody*
glow. Slowly but surely the dim outlines of a Presence came
into view; the blood-filled outlines of that unseen shambler
from the stars. It was red and dripping; an immensity of
pulsing, moving jelly; a scarlet blob with myriad tentacular
trunks that waved and waved. There were suckers on the
tips of the appendages, and these were opening and closing
with ghoulish lust . . . The thing was bloated and obscene; a
headless, faceless, eyeless bulk with the ravenous maw and
titanic talons of a starborn monster. The human blood on
which it had fed revealed the hitherto invisible outlines of
the feaster. It was not a sight for sane eyes to see.

Fortunately for my reason, the creature did not linger.

Spurning the dead and flabby corpse-like thing on the floor, it purposely seized the opening. There it disappeared, and I heard its far-off, derisive laughter floating on the wings of the wind as it receded into the gulfs from whence it had come.

That was all. I was left alone in the room with the limp and lifeless body at my feet. The book was gone; but there were bloody prints upon the wall, bloody swaths upon the floor, and the face of my poor friend was a bloody death's head, leering up at the stars.

For a long time I sat alone in silence before I set to fire that room and all it contained. After that I went away, laughing, for I knew that the blaze would eradicate all trace of what remained. I had arrived only that afternoon, and there was none who knew, and none to see me go, for I departed ere the glowing flames were detected. I stumbled for hours through the twisted streets, and quaked with renewed and idiotic laughter as I looked up at the burning, ever-gloating stars that eyed me furtively through wreaths of haunted fog.

After a long while I became calm enough to board a train. I have been calm throughout the long journey home, and calm throughout the penning of this screed. I was even calm when I read of my friend's curious accidental death in the fire that destroyed his dwelling.

It is only at nights, when the stars gleam, that dreams return to drive me into a gigantic maze of frantic fears. Then I take to drugs, in a vain attempt to ban those leering memories from my sleep. But I really do not care, for I shall not be here long.

I have a curious suspicion that I shall again see that shambler from the stars. I think it will return soon without being resummoned, and I know that when it comes it will seek me out and carry me down into the darkness that holds my friend. Sometimes I almost yearn for the advent of that day, for then I shall learn, once and for all, the *Mysteries of the Worm*.

The Haunter of the Dark

H. P. LOVECRAFT

DEDICATED TO ROBERT BLOCH

I have seen the dark universe yawning
  Where the black planets roll without aim –
Where they roll in their horror unheeded,
  Without knowledge or lustre or name.

— NEMESIS

Cautious investigators will hesitate to challenge the common belief that Robert Blake was killed by lightning, or by some profound nervous shock derived from an electrical discharge. It is true that the window he faced was unbroken, but nature has shown herself capable of many freakish performances. The expression on his face may easily have arisen from some obscure muscular source unrelated to anything he saw, while the entries in his diary are clearly the result of a fantastic imagination aroused by certain local superstitions and by certain old matters he had uncovered. As for the anomalous conditions at the deserted church of Federal Hill – the shrewd analyst is not slow in attributing them to some charlatanry, conscious or unconscious, with at least some of which Blake was secretly connected.

For after all, the victim was a writer and painter wholly devoted to the field of myth, dream, terror, and superstition, and avid in his quest for scenes and effects of a bizarre, spectral sort. His earlier stay in the city – a visit to a strange old man as deeply given to occult and forbidden lore as he – had ended amidst death and flame, and it must have been some morbid instinct which drew him back from his home in Milwaukee. He may have known of the old stories despite his statements to the contrary in the diary, and his death may have nipped in the bud some stupendous hoax destined to have a literary reflection.

Among those, however, who have examined and correlated all this evidence, there remain several who cling to less rational and commonplace theories. They are inclined to take much of Blake's diary at its face value, and point significantly to certain facts such as the undoubted genuineness of the old church record, the verified existence of the disliked and unorthodox Starry Wisdom sect prior to 1877, the recorded disappearance of an inquisitive reporter named Edwin M. Lillibridge in 1893, and – above all – the look of monstrous, transfiguring fear on the face of the young writer when he died. It was one of these believers who, moved to fanatical extremes, threw into the bay the curiously angled stone and its strangely adorned metal box found in the old church steeple – the black windowless steeple, and not the tower where Blake's diary said those things originally were. Though widely censured both officially and unofficially, this man – a reputable physician with a taste for odd folklore – averred that he had rid the earth of something too dangerous to rest upon it.

Between these two schools of opinion the reader must judge for himself. The papers have given the tangible details from a sceptical angle, leaving for others the drawing of the picture as Robert Blake saw it – or thought he saw it – or pretended to see it. Now, studying the diary closely, dispassionately, and at leisure, let us summarize the dark chain of events from the expressed point of view of their chief actor.

Young Blake returned to Providence in the winter of 1934–5, taking the upper floor of a venerable dwelling in a grassy court off College Street – on the crest of the great eastward hill near the Brown University campus and behind the marble John Hay Library. It was a cosy and fascinating place, in a little garden oasis of village-like antiquity where huge, friendly cats sunned themselves atop a convenient shed. The square Georgian house had a monitor roof, classic doorway with fan carving, small-paned windows, and all the other earmarks of early 19th-century workmanship. Inside were six-panelled doors, wide floorboards, a curving colonial staircase, white Adam-period mantels, and a rear set of rooms three steps below the general level.

Blake's study, a large southwest chamber, overlooked the front garden on one side, while its west windows – before one of which he had his desk – faced off from the brow of the hill and commanded a splendid view of the lower town's outspread roofs and of the mystical sunsets that flamed behind them. On the far horizon were the open countryside's purple slopes. Against these, some two miles away, rose the spectral hump of Federal Hill, bristling with huddled roofs and steeples whose remote outlines wavered mysteriously, taking fantastic forms as the smoke of the city swirled up and enmeshed them. Blake had a curious sense that he was looking upon some unknown, ethereal world which might or might not vanish in dream if ever he tried to seek it out and enter it in person.

Having sent home for most of his books, Blake bought some antique furniture suitable to his quarters and settled down to write and paint – living alone, and attending to the simple housework himself. His studio was in a north attic room, where the panes of the monitor roof furnished admirable lighting. During that first winter he produced five of his best-known short stories – 'The Burrower Beneath', 'The Stairs in the Crypt', 'Shaggai', 'In the Vale of Pnath', and 'The Feaster from the Stars' – and painted seven canvases; studies of nameless, unhuman monsters, and profoundly alien, non-terrestrial landscapes.

At sunset he would often sit at his desk and gaze dreamily off at the outspread west – the dark towers of Memorial Hall just below, the Georgian courthouse belfry, the lofty pinnacles of the downtown section, and that shimmering, spire-crowned mound in the distance whose unknown streets and labyrinthine gables so potently provoked his fancy. From his few local acquaintances he learned that the far-off slope was a vast Italian quarter, though most of the houses were remnants of older Yankee and Irish days. Now and then he would train his field-glasses on that spectral, unreachable world beyond the curling smoke; picking out individual roofs and chimneys and steeples, and speculating upon the bizarre and curious mysteries they might house. Even with optical aid Federal Hill seemed somehow alien, half fabulous, and linked to the unreal, intangible marvels of Blake's own tales and pictures. The feeling would persist long after the hill had faded into the violet, lamp-starred twilight, and the courthouse floodlights and the red Industrial Trust beacon had blazed up to make the night grotesque.

Of all the distant objects on Federal Hill, a certain huge, dark church most fascinated Blake. It stood out with especial distinctness at certain hours of the day, and at sunset the great tower and tapering steeple loomed blackly against the flaming sky. It seemed to rest on especially high ground; for the grimy façade, and the obliquely seen north side with sloping roof and the tops of great pointed windows, rose boldly above the tangle of surrounding ridgepoles and chimney-pots. Peculiarly grim and austere, it appeared to be built of stone, stained and weathered with the smoke and storms of a century and more. The style, so far as the glass could show, was that earliest experimental form of Gothic revival which preceded the stately Upjohn period and held over some of the outlines and proportions of the Georgian age. Perhaps it was reared around 1810 or 1815.

As months passed, Blake watched the far-off, forbidding structure with an oddly mounting interest. Since the vast windows were never lighted, he knew that it must be vacant. The longer he watched, the more his imagination worked, till at length he began to fancy curious things. He believed that a vague, singular aura of desolation hovered over the place, so that even the pigeons and swallows shunned its smoky eaves. Around other towers and belfries his glass would reveal great flocks of birds, but here they never rested. At least, that is what he thought and set down in his diary. He pointed the place out to several friends, but none of them had even been on Federal Hill or possessed the faintest notion of what the church was or had been.

In the spring a deep restlessness gripped Blake. He had begun his long-planned novel – based on a supposed survival of the witchcult in Maine – but was strangely unable to make progress with it. More and more he would sit at his westward window and gaze at the distant hill and the black, frowning steeple shunned by the birds. When the delicate leaves came out on the garden boughs the world was filled with a new beauty, but Blake's restlessness was merely increased. It was then that he first thought of crossing the city and climbing bodily up that fabulous slope into the smoke-wreathed world of dream.

Late in April, just before the eon-shadowed Walpurgis time, Blake made his first trip into the unknown. Plodding through the endless downtown streets and the bleak, decayed squares beyond, he came finally upon the ascending avenue of century-worn steps, sagging Doric porches, and blear-paned cupolas which he felt must lead up to the long-known, unreachable world beyond the mists. There were dingy blue-and-white street signs which meant nothing to him, and presently he noted the strange, dark faces of the drifting crowds, and the foreign signs over curious shops in brown, decade-weathering buildings. Nowhere could he find any of the objects he had seen from afar; so that once more he half fancied that the Federal Hill of that distant view was a dream world never to be trod by living human feet.

Now and then a battered church façade or crumbling spire came in sight, but never the blackened pile that he sought. When he asked a shopkeeper about a great stone church the man smiled and shook his head, though he spoke English freely. As Blake climbed higher, the region seemed stranger and stranger, with bewildering mazes of brooding brown alleys leading eternally off to the south. He crossed two or

three broad avenues, and once thought he glimpsed a familiar tower. Again he asked a merchant about the massive
church of stone, and this time he could have sworn that the
plea of ignorance was feigned. The dark man's face had a
look of fear which he tried to hide, and Blake saw him make
a curious sign with his right hand.

Then suddenly a black spire stood out against the cloudy
sky on his left, above the tiers of brown roofs lining the
tangled southerly alleys. Blake knew at once what it was,
and plunged towards it through the squalid, unpaved lanes
that climbed from the avenue. Twice he lost his way, but he
somehow dared not ask any of the patriarchs or housewives
who sat on their doorsteps, or any of the children who
shouted and played in the mud of the shadowy lanes.

At last he saw the tower plain against the southwest, and
a huge stone bulk rose darkly at the end of an alley.
Presently he stood in a wind-swept open square, quaintly
cobblestoned, with a high bank wall on the farther side. This
was the end of his quest; for upon the wide, iron-railed, weed-
grown plateau which the wall supported – a separate, lesser
world raised fully six feet above the surrounding streets –
there stood a grim, titan bulk whose identity, despite Blake's
new perspective, was beyond dispute.

The vacant church was in a state of great decrepitude.
Some of the high stone buttresses had fallen, and several
delicate finials lay half lost among the brown, neglected
weeds and grasses. The sooty Gothic windows were largely
unbroken, though many of the stone mullions were missing.
Blake wondered how the obscurely painted panes could have
survived so well, in view of the known habits of small boys
the world over. The massive doors were intact and tightly
closed. Around the top of the bank wall, fully enclosing the
grounds, was a rusty iron fence whose gate – at the head of a
flight of steps from the square – was visibly padlocked. The
path from the gate to the building was completely overgrown.
Desolation and decay hung like a pall above the place, and

in the birdless eaves and black, ivyless walls Blake felt a touch of the dimly sinister beyond his power to define.

There were very few people in the square, but Blake saw a policeman at the northerly end and approached him with questions about the church. He was a great wholesome Irishman, and it seemed odd that he would do little more than make the sign of the cross and mutter that people never spoke of that building. When Blake pressed him he said very hurriedly that the Italian priests warned everybody against it, vowing that a monstrous evil had once dwelt there and left its mark. He himself had heard dark whispers of it from his father, who recalled certain sounds and rumours from his boyhood.

There had been a bad sect there in the old days – an outlaw sect that called up awful things from some unknown gulf of night. It had taken a good priest to exorcize what had come, though there did be those who said that merely the light could do it. If Father O'Malley were alive there would be many the thing he could tell. But now there was nothing to do but let it alone. It hurt nobody now, and those that owned it were dead or far away. They had run away like rats after the threatening talk in '77, when people began to mind the way folks vanished now and then in the neighbourhood. Some day the city would step in and take the property for lack of heirs, but little good would come of anybody's touching it. Better it be left alone for the years to topple, lest things be stirred that ought to rest for ever in their black abyss.

After the policeman had gone Blake stood staring at the sullen steepled pile. It excited him to find that the structure seemed as sinister to others as to him, and he wondered what grain of truth might lie behind the old tales the bluecoat had repeated. Probably they were mere legends evoked by the evil look of the place, but even so, they were like a strange coming to life of one of his own stories.

The afternoon sun came out from behind dispersing clouds, but seemed unable to light up the stained, sooty walls of the

old temple that towered on its high plateau. It was odd that
the green of spring had not touched the brown, withered
growths in the raised, iron-fenced yard. Blake found himself
edging nearer the raised area and examining the bank wall
and rusted fence for possible avenues of ingress. There was a
terrible lure about the blackened fane which was not to be
resisted. The fence had no opening near the steps, but around
on the north side were some missing bars. He could go up
the steps and walk around on the narrow coping outside the
fence till he came to the gap. If the people feared the place so
wildly, he would encounter no interference.

He was on the embankment and almost inside the fence
before anyone noticed him. Then, looking down, he saw the
few people in the square edging away and making the same
sign with their right hands that the shopkeeper in the
avenue had made. Several windows were slammed down,
and a fat woman darted into the street and pulled some
small children inside a rickety, unpainted house. The gap in
the fence was very easy to pass through, and before long
Blake found himself wading amidst the rotting, tangled
growths of the deserted yard. Here and there the worn stump
of a headstone told him that there had once been burials in
this field; but that, he saw, must have been very long ago.
The sheer bulk of the church was oppressive now that he was
close to it, but he conquered his mood and approached to try
the three great doors in the façade. All were securely locked,
so he began a circuit of the Cyclopean building in quest of
some minor and more penetrable opening. Even then he
could not be sure that he wished to enter that haunt of
desertion and shadow, yet the pull of its strangeness dragged
him on automatically.

A yawning and unprotected cellar window in the rear
furnished the needed aperture. Peering in, Blake saw a
subterrene gulf of cobwebs and dust faintly lit by the western
sun's filtered rays. Debris, old barrels, and ruined boxes and
furniture of numerous sorts met his eye, though over every-

thing lay a shroud of dust which softened all sharp outlines.
The rusted remains of a hot-air furnace showed that the
building had been used and kept in shape as late as mid-
Victorian times.

Acting almost without conscious initiative, Blake crawled
through the window and let himself down to the dust-
carpeted and debris-strewn concrete floor. The vaulted cellar
was a vast one, without partitions; and in a corner far to the
right, amid dense shadows, he saw a black archway evidently
leading upstairs. He felt a peculiar sense of oppression at
being actually within the great spectral building, but kept it
in check as he cautiously scouted about – finding a still-
intact barrel amid the dust, and rolling it over to the open
window to provide for his exit. Then, bracing himself, he
crossed the wide, cobweb-festooned space towards the arch.
Half choked with the omnipresent dust, and covered with
ghostly gossamer fibres, he reached and began to climb the
worn stone steps which rose into the darkness. He had no
light, but groped carefully with his hands. After a sharp turn
he felt a closed door ahead, and a little fumbling revealed its
ancient latch. It opened inward, and beyond it he saw a
dimly illumined corridor lined with worm-eaten panelling.

Once on the ground floor, Blake began exploring in a rapid
fashion. All the inner doors were unlocked, so that he freely
passed from room to room. The colossal nave was an almost
eldritch place with its drifts and mountains of dust over box
pews, altar, hour-glass pulpit, and sounding-board, and its
titanic ropes of cobweb stretching among the pointed arches
of the gallery and entwining the clustered Gothic columns.
Over all this hushed desolation played a hideous leaden light
as the declining afternoon sun sents its rays through the
strange, half-blackened panes of the great apsidal windows.

The paintings on those windows were so obscured by soot
that Blake could scarcely decipher what they had represented, but from the little he could make out he did not like
them. The designs were largely conventional, and his knowledge of obscure symbolism told him much concerning some
of the ancient patterns. The few saints depicted bore expres-

sions distinctly open to criticism, while one of the windows seemed to show merely a dark space with spirals of curious luminosity scattered about in it. Turning away from the windows, Blake noticed that the cobwebbed cross above the altar was not of the ordinary kind, but resembled the primordial ankh or crux ansata of shadowy Egypt.

In a rear vestry room beside the apse Blake found a rotting desk and ceiling-high shelves of mildewed, disintegrating books. Here for the first time he received a positive shock of objective horror, for the titles of those books told him much. They were the black, forbidden things which most sane people have never even heard of, or have heard of only in furtive, timorous whispers; the banned and dreaded repositories of equivocal secrets and immemorial formulae which have trickled down the stream of time from the days of man's youth, and the dim, fabulous days before man was. He had himself read many of them — a Latin version of the abhorred *Necronomicon*, the sinister *Liber Ivonis*, the infamous *Cultes des Goules* of Comte d'Erlette, the *Unaussprechlichen Kulten* of von Junzt, the old Ludvig Prinn's hellish *De Vermis Mysteriis*. But there were others he had known merely by reputation or not at all — the *Pnakotic Manuscripts*, the *Book of Dzyan*, and a crumbling volume in wholly unidentifiable characters yet with certain symbols and diagrams shudderingly recognizable to the occult student. Clearly, the lingering local rumours had not lied. This place had once been the seat of an evil older than mankind and wider than the known universe.

In the ruined desk was a small leatherbound record-book filled with entries in some odd cryptographic medium. The manuscript writing consisted of the common traditional symbols used today in astronomy and anciently in alchemy, astrology, and other dubious arts — the devices of the sun, moon, planets, aspects, and zodiacal signs — here massed in solid pages of text, with divisions and paragraphings suggesting that each symbol answered to some alphabetical letter.

In the hope of later solving the cryptogram, Blake bore off this volume in his coat pocket. Many of the great tomes on the shelves fascinated him unutterably, and he felt tempted to borrow them at some later time. He wondered how they could have remained undisturbed so long. Was he the first to conquer the clutching, pervasive fear which had for nearly sixty years protected this deserted place from visitors?

Having now thoroughly explored the ground floor, Blake ploughed again through the dust of the spectral nave to the front vestibule, where he had seen a door and staircase presumably leading up to the blackened tower and steeple – objects so long familiar to him at a distance. The ascent was a choking experience, for dust lay thick, while the spiders had done their worst in this constricted place. The staircase was a spiral with high, narrow wooden treads, and now and then Blake passed a clouded window looking dizzily out over the city. Though he had seen no ropes below, he expected to find a bell or peal of bells in the tower whose narrow, louvre-boarded lancet windows his field-glass had studied so often. Here he was doomed to disappointment; for when he attained the top of the stairs he found the tower chamber vacant of chimes, and clearly devoted to vastly different purposes.

The room, about fifteen feet square, was faintly lighted by four lancet windows, one on each side, which were glazed within their screening of decayed louvre-boards. These had been further fitted with tight, opaque screens, but the latter were now largely rotted away. In the centre of the dust-laden floor rose a curiously angled stone pillar some four feet in height and two in average diameter, covered on each side with bizarre, crudely incised and wholly unrecognizable hieroglyphs. On this pillar rested a metal box of peculiarly asymmetrical form; its hinged lid thrown back, and its interior holding what looked beneath the decade-deep dust to be an egg-shaped or irregularly spherical object some four inches through. Around the pillar in a rough circle were seven high-backed Gothic chairs still largely intact, while behind them, ranging along the dark-panelled walls, were seven colossal images of crumbling black-painted plaster, resembling more than anything else the cryptic carven megaliths of mysterious Easter Island. In one corner of the cobwebbed chamber a ladder was built into the wall, leading up to the closed trap door of the windowless steeple above.

As Blake grew accustomed to the feeble light he noticed odd bas-reliefs on the strange open box of yellowish metal. Approaching, he tried to clear the dust away with his hands and handkerchief, and saw that the figurings were of a monstrous and utterly alien kind; depicting entities which, though seemingly alive, resembled no known life-form ever evolved on this planet. The four-inch seeming sphere turned out to be a nearly black, red-striated polyhedron with many irregular flat surfaces; either a very remarkable crystal of some sort, or an artificial object of carved and highly polished mineral matter. It did not touch the bottom of the box, but was held suspended by means of a metal band around its centre, with seven queerly-designed supports extending horizontally to angles of the box's inner wall near the top. This stone, once exposed, exerted upon Blake an almost alarming fascination. He could scarcely tear his eyes from it, and as he looked at its glistening surfaces he almost fancied it was transparent, with half-formed worlds of wonder within. Into his mind floated pictures of alien orbs with great stone towers, and other orbs with titan mountains and no mark of life, and still remoter spaces where only a stirring in vague blackness told of the presence of consciousness and will.

When he did look away, it was to notice a somewhat singular mound of dust in the far corner near the ladder to the steeple. Just why it took his attention he could not tell, but something in its contours carried a message to his unconscious mind. Ploughing towards it, and brushing aside the hanging cobwebs as he went, he began to discern something grim about it. Hand and handkerchief soon revealed the truth, and Blake gasped with a baffling mixture of emotions. It was a human skeleton, and it must have been there for a very long time. The clothing was in shreds, but some buttons and fragments of cloth bespoke a man's grey suit. There were other bits of evidence – shoes, metal clasps, huge buttons for round cuffs, a stickpin of bygone pattern, a reporter's badge with the name of the old *Providence Telegram*, and a crumbling leather pocketbook. Blake examined the latter with care, finding within it several bills of antiquated issue, a celluloid advertising calendar for 1893, some cards with the name 'Edwin M. Lillibridge', and a paper covered with pencilled memoranda.

This paper held much of a puzzling nature, and Blake read it carefully at the dim westward window. Its disjointed text included such phrases as the following:

'Prof. Enoch Bowen home from Egypt May 1844 – buys old Free-Will Church in July – his archaeological work & studies in occult well known.'

'Dr Drowne of 4th Baptist warns against Starry Wisdom in sermon Dec. 29, 1844.'

'Congregation 97 by end of '45.'

'1846 – 3 disappearances – first mention of Shining Trapezohedron.'

'7 disappearances 1848 – stories of blood sacrifice begin.'

'Investigation 1853 comes to nothing – stories of sounds.'

'Fr O'Malley tells of devil-worship with box found in great Egyptian ruins – says they call up something that can't exist in light. Flees a little light, and banished by strong light. Then has to be summoned again. Probably got this from deathbed confession of Francis X. Feeney, who had joined Starry Wisdom in '49. These people say the Shining Trapezohedron shows them heaven & other worlds, & that the Haunter of the Dark tells them secrets in some way.'

'Story of Orrin B. Eddy 1857. They call it up by gazing at the crystal, & have a secret language of their own.'

'200 or more in cong. 1863, exclusive of men at front.'

'Irish boys mob church in 1869 after Patrick Regan's disappearance.'

'Veiled article in J. March 14, '72, but people don't talk about it.'

'6 disappearances 1876 – secret committee calls on Major Doyle.'

'Action promised Feb. 1877 – church closes in April.'

'Gang – Federal Hill Boys – threaten Dr – and vestrymen in May.'

'181 persons leave city before end of '77 – mention no names.'

'Ghost stories begin around 1880 – try to ascertain truth of report that no human being has entered church since 1877.'

'Ask Lanigan for photography of place taken 1851.' . . .

Restoring the paper to the pocketbook and placing the latter in his coat, Blake turned to look down at the skeleton in the dust. The implications of the notes were clear, and there could be no doubt but that this man had come to the deserted edifice forty-two years before in quest of a newspaper sensation which no one else had been bold enough to attempt. Perhaps no one else had known of his plan – who could tell? But he had never returned to his paper. Had some bravely-suppressed fear risen to overcome him and bring on sudden heart-failure? Blake stooped over the gleaming bones and noticed their peculiar state. Some of them were badly scattered, and a few seemed oddly *dissolved* at the ends. Others were strangely yellowed, with vague suggestions of charring. This charring extended to some of the fragments of clothing. The skull was in a very peculiar state – stained yellow, and with a charred aperture in the top as if some powerful acid had eaten through the solid bone. What had happened to the skeleton during its four decades of silent entombment here Blake could not imagine.

Before he realized it, he was looking at the stone again, and letting its curious influence call up a nebulous pageantry in his mind. He saw processions of robed, hooded figures whose outlines were not human, and looked on endless leagues of desert lined with carved, sky-reaching monoliths. He saw towers and walls in nighted depths under the sea, and vortices of space where wisps of black mist floated before thin shimmerings of cold purple haze. And beyond all else he glimpsed an infinite gulf of darkness, where solid and semi-solid forms were known only by their windy stirrings, and cloudy patterns of force seemed to superimpose order on chaos and hold forth a key to all the paradoxes and arcana of the worlds we know.

Then all at once the spell was broken by an access of gnawing, indeterminate panic fear. Blake choked and turned away from the stone, conscious of some formless alien presence close to him and watching him with horrible intentness. He felt entangled with something – something which was not in the stone, but which had looked through it at him – something which would ceaselessly follow him with a cognition that was not physical sight. Plainly, the place was getting on his nerves – as well it might in view of his gruesome find. The light was waning, too, and since he had no illuminant with him he knew he would have to be leaving soon.

It was then, in the gathering twilight, that he thought he saw a faint trace of luminosity in the crazily angled stone. He had tried to look away from it, but some obscure compulsion drew his eyes back. Was there a subtle phosphorescence of radio-activity about the thing? What was it that the dead man's notes had said concerning a *Shining Trapezohedron*? What, anyway, was this abandoned lair of cosmic evil? What had been done here, and what might still be lurking in the bird-shunned shadows? It seemed now as if an elusive touch of fetor had arisen somewhere close by, though its source was not apparent. Blake seized the cover of the long-open box and snapped it down. It moved easily on its alien hinges, and closed completely over the unmistakably glowing stone.

At the sharp click of that closing a soft stirring sound seemed to come from the steeple's eternal blackness overhead, beyond the trapdoor. Rats, without question – the only living things to reveal their presence in this accursed pile since he had entered it. And yet that stirring in the steeple frightened him horribly, so that he plunged almost wildly down the spiral stairs, across the ghoulish nave, into the vaulted basement, out amidst the gathering dusk of the deserted square, and down through the teeming, fear-haunted alleys and avenues of Federal Hill towards the sane central streets and the home-like brick sidewalks of the college district.

During the days which followed, Blake told no one of his expedition. Instead, he read much in certain books, examined long years of newspaper files downtown, and worked feverishly at the cryptogram in that leather volume from the cobwebbed vestry room. The cipher, he soon saw, was no simple one; and after a long period of endeavour he felt sure that its language could not be English, Latin, Greek, French, Spanish, Italian, or German. Evidently he would have to draw upon the deepest wells of his strange erudition.

Every evening the old impulse to gaze westward returned, and he saw the black steeple as of yore among the bristling roofs of a distant and half-fabulous world. But now it held a fresh note of terror for him. He knew the heritage of evil it masked, and with the knowledge his vision ran riot in queer new ways. The birds of spring were returning, and as he watched their sunset flights he fancied they avoided the gaunt, lone spire as never before. When a flock of them approached it, he thought, they would wheel and scatter in panic confusion – and he could guess at the wild twitterings which failed to reach him across the intervening miles.

It was in June that Blake's diary told of his victory over the cryptogram. The text was, he found, in the dark Aklo language used by certain cults of evil antiquity, and known to him in a halting way through previous researchers. The diary is strangely reticent about what Blake deciphered, but he was patently awed and disconcerted by his results. There are references to a Haunter of the Dark awakened by gazing into the Shining Trapezohedron, and insane conjectures about the black gulfs of chaos from which it was called. The being is spoken of as holding all knowledge, and demanding monstrous sacrifices. Some of Blake's entries show fear lest the thing, which he seemed to regard as summoned, stalk abroad; though he adds that the streetlights form a bulwark which cannot be crossed.

Of the Shining Trapezohedron he speaks often, calling it a

window on all time and space, and tracing its history from the days it was fashioned on dark Yuggoth, before ever the Old Ones brought it to earth. It was treasured and placed in its curious box by the crinoid things of Antarctica, salvaged from their ruins by the serpent-men of Valusia, and peered at eons later in Lemuria by the first human beings. It crossed strange lands and stranger seas, and sank with Atlantis before a Minoan fisher meshed it in his net and sold it to swarthy merchants from nighted Khem. The Pharaoh Nephren-Ka built around it a temple with a windowless crypt, and did that which caused his name to be stricken from all monuments and records. Then it slept in the ruins of that evil fane which the priests and the new Pharaoh destroyed, till the delver's spade once more brought it forth to curse mankind.

Early in July the newspapers oddly supplemented Blake's entries, though in so brief and casual a way that only the diary has called general attention to their contribution. It appears that a new fear had been growing on Federal Hill since a stranger had entered the dreaded church. The Italians whispered of unaccustomed stirrings and bumpings and scrapings in the dark windowless steeple, and called on their priests to banish an entity which haunted their dreams. Something, they said, was constantly watching at a door to see if it were dark enough to venture forth. Press items mentioned the long-standing local superstitions, but failed to shed much light on the earlier background of the horror. It was obvious that the young reporters of today are no antiquarians. In writing of these things in his diary, Blake expresses a curious kind of remorse, and talks of the duty of burying the Shining Trapezohedron and of banishing what he had evoked by letting daylight into the hideous jutting spire. At the same time, however, he displays the dangerous extent of his fascination, and admits a morbid longing – pervading even his dreams – to visit the accursed tower and gaze again into the cosmic secrets of the glowing stone.

Then something in the *Journal* on the morning of July 17

threw the diarist into a veritable fever of horror. It was only a variant of the other half-humorous items about the Federal Hill restlessness, but to Blake it was somehow very terrible indeed. In the night a thunderstorm had put the city's lighting-system out of commission for a full hour, and in that black interval the Italians had nearly gone mad with fright. Those living near the dreaded church had sworn that the thing in the steeple had taken advantage of the street lamps' absence and gone down into the body of the church, flopping and bumping around in a viscous, altogether dreadful way. Towards the last it had bumped up to the tower, where there were the sounds of the shattering of glass. It could go wherever the darkness reached, but light would always send it fleeing.

When the current blazed on again there had been a shocking commotion in the tower, for even the feeble light trickling through the grime-blackened, louvre-boarded windows was too much for the thing. It had bumped and slithered up into its tenebrous steeple just in time – for a long dose of light would have sent it back into the abyss whence the crazy stranger had called it. During the dark hour praying crowds had clustered round the church in the rain with lighted candles and lamps somehow shielded with folded paper and umbrellas – a guard of light to save the city from the nightmare that stalks in darkness. Once, those nearest the church declared, the outer door had rattled hideously.

But even this was not the worst. That evening in the *Bulletin* Blake read of what the reporters had found. Aroused at last to the whimsical news value of the scare, a pair of them had defied the frantic crowds of Italians and crawled into the church through the cellar window after trying the doors in vain. They found the dust of the vestibule and of the spectral nave ploughed up in a singular way, with pits of rotted cushions and satin pew-linings scattered curiously around. There was a bad odour everywhere, and here and there were bits of yellow stain and patches of what looked like charring. Opening the door to the tower, and pausing a moment at the suspicion of a scraping sound above, they found the narrow stairs wiped thoroughly clean.

In the tower itself a similarly half-swept condition existed. They spoke of the heptagonal stone pillar, the overturned Gothic chairs, and the bizarre plaster images; though strangely enough the metal box and the old mutilated skeleton were not mentioned. What disturbed Blake the most – except for the hints of stains and charring and bad odours – was the final detail that explained the crashing glass. Every one of the tower's lancet windows was broken, and two of them had been darkened in a crude and hurried way by the stuffing of satin pew-linings and cushion-horse-hair into the spaces between the slanting exterior louvre-boards. More satin fragments and bunches of horsehair lay scattered around the newly swept floor, as if someone had been interrupted in the act of restoring the tower to the absolute blackness of its tightly curtained days.

Yellowish stains and charred patches were found on the ladder to the windowless spire, but when a reporter climbed up, opened the horizontally-sliding trapdoor and shot a feeble flashlight beam into the black and strangely fetid space, he saw nothing but darkness, and a heterogeneous litter of shapeless fragments near the aperture. The verdict, of course, was charlatanry. Somebody had played a joke on the superstitious hill-dwellers, or else some fanatic had striven to bolster up their fears for their own supposed good. Or perhaps some of the younger and more sophisticated dwellers had staged an elaborate hoax on the outside world. There was an amusing aftermath when the police sent an officer to verify the reports. Three men in succession found ways of evading the assignment, and the fourth went very reluctantly and returned very soon without adding to the account given by the reporters.

From this point onward Blake's diary shows a mounting tide of insidious horror and nervous apprehension. He upbraids himself for not doing something, and speculates wildly on the consequences of another electrical breakdown.

It has been verified that on three occasions – during thunderstorms – he telephoned the electric light company in a frantic vein and asked that desperate precautions against a lapse of power be taken. Now and then his entries show concern over the failure of the reporters to find the metal box and stone, and the strangely marred old skeleton, when they explored the shadowy tower room. He assumed that these things had been removed – whither, and by whom or what, he could only guess. But his worst fears concerned himself, and the kind of unholy rapport he felt to exist between his mind and that lurking horror in the distant steeple – that monstrous thing of night which his rashness had called out of the ultimate black spaces. He seemed to feel a constant tugging at his will, and callers of that period remember how he would sit abstractedly at his desk and stare out of the west window at that far-off spire-bristling mound beyond the swirling smoke of the city. His entries dwell monotonously on certain terrible dreams, and of a strengthening of the unholy rapport in his sleep. There is mention of a night when he awakened to find himself fully dressed, outdoors, and headed automatically down College Hill towards the west. Again and again he dwells on the fact that the thing in the steeple knows where to find him.

The week following July 30 is recalled as the time of Blake's partial breakdown. He did not dress, and ordered all his food by telephone. Visitors remarked the cords he kept near his bed, and he said that sleep-walking had forced him to bind his ankles every night with knots which would probably hold or else waken him with the labour of untying.

In his diary he told of the hideous experience which had brought the collapse. After retiring on the night of the 30th he had suddenly found himself groping about in an almost black space. All he could see were short, faint, horizontal streaks of bluish light, but he could smell an overpowering fetor and hear a curious jumble of soft, furtive sounds above him. Whenever he moved he stumbled over something, and at each noise there would come a sort of answering sound from above — a vague stirring, mixed with the cautious sliding of wood on wood.

Once his groping hands encountered a pillar of stone with a vacant top, whilst later he found himself clutching the rungs of a ladder built into the wall, and fumbling his uncertain way upward towards some region of intenser stench where a hot, searing blast beat down against him. Before his eyes a kaleidoscopic range of fantasmal images played, all of them dissolving at intervals into the picture of a vast, unplumbed abyss of night wherein whirled suns and worlds of an even profounder blackness. He thought of the ancient legends of Ultimate Chaos, at whose centre sprawls the blind idiot god Azathoth, Lord of All Things, encircled by his flopping horde of mindless and amorphous dancers, and lulled by the thin monotonous piping of a demoniac flute held in nameless paws.

Then a sharp report from the outer world broke through his stupor and roused him to the unutterable horror of his position. What it was, he never knew — perhaps it was some belated peal from the fireworks heard all summer on Federal Hill, as the dwellers hail their various patron saints, or the saints of their native villages in Italy. In any event he shrieked aloud, dropping frantically from the ladder, and stumbled blindly across the obstructed floor of the almost lightless chamber that encompassed him.

He knew instantly where he was, and plunged recklessly down the narrow spiral staircase, tripping and bruising himself at every turn. There was a nightmare flight through a vast cobwebbed nave whose ghostly arches reached up to realms of leering shadow, a sightless scramble through a littered basement, a climb to regions of air and street lights outside, and a mad racing down a spectral hill of gibbering gables, across a grim, silent city of tall black towers, and up the steep eastward precipice to his own ancient door.

On regaining consciousness in the morning he found himself lying on his study floor fully dressed. Dirt and

cobwebs covered him, and every inch of his body seemed sore
and bruised. When he faced the mirror he saw that his hair
was badly scorched, while a trace of strange, evil odour
seemed to cling to his upper outer clothing. It was then that
his nerves broke down. Thereafter, lounging exhaustedly
about in a dressing-gown, he did little but stare from his
west window, shiver at the threat of thunder, and make wild
entries in his diary.

The great storm broke just before midnight on August 8.
Lightning struck repeatedly in all parts of the city, and two
remarkable fireballs were reported. The rain was torrential,
while a constant fusillade of thunder brought sleeplessness
to thousands. Blake was utterly frantic in his fear for the
lighting system, and tried to telephone the company around
1 A.M., though by that time service had been temporarily cut
off in the interest of safety. He recorded everything in his
diary – the large, nervous, and often undecipherable hieroglyphs telling their own story of growing frenzy and despair,
and of entries scrawled blindly in the dark.

He had to keep the house dark in order to see out of the
window, and it appears that most of his time was spent at
his desk, peering anxiously through the rain across the
glistening miles of downtown roofs at the constellation of
distant lights marking Federal Hill. Now and then he would
fumblingly make an entry in his diary, so that detached
phrases such as 'The lights must not go'; 'It knows where I
am'; 'I must destroy it'; and 'It is calling to me, but perhaps
it means no injury this time'; are found scattered down two
of the pages.

Then the lights went out all over the city. It happened at
2:12 A.M. according to power-house records, but Blake's diary
gives no indication of the time. The entry is merely, 'Lights
out – God help me.' On Federal Hill there were watchers as
anxious as he, and rain-soaked knots of men paraded the
square and alleys around the evil church with umbrella-
shaded candles, electric flashlights, oil lanterns, crucifixes,

and obscure charms of the many sorts common to southern Italy. They blessed each flash of lightning, and made cryptical signs of fear with their right hands when a turn in the storm caused the flashes to lessen and finally to cease altogether. A rising wind blew out most of the candles, so that the scene grew threateningly dark. Someone roused Father Merluzzo of Spirito Santo Church, and he hastened to the dismal square to pronounce whatever helpful syllables he could. Of the restless and curious sounds in the blackened tower, there could be no doubt whatever.

For what happened at 2:35 we have the testimony of the priest, a young, intelligent, and well-educated person; of Patrolman William J. Monahan of the Central Station, an officer of the highest reliability who had paused at that part of his beat to inspect the crowd; and of most of the seventy-eight men who had gathered around the church's high bank wall – especially those in the square where the east façade was visible. Of course there was nothing which can be proved as being outside the order of nature. The possible cause of such an event are many. No one can speak with certainty of the obscure chemical processes arising in a vast, ancient, ill-aired, and long-deserted building of heterogeneous contents. Mephitic vapours – spontaneous combustion – pressure of gases born of long decay – any one of numberless phenomena might be responsible. And then, of course, the factor of conscious charlatanry can by no means be excluded. The thing was really quite simple in itself, and covered less than three minutes of actual time. Father Merluzzo, always a precise man, looked at his watch repeatedly.

It started with a definite swelling of the dull fumbling sounds inside the black tower. There had for some time been a vague exhalation of strange, evil odours from the church, and this had now become emphatic and offensive. Then at last there was a sound of splintering wood, and a large, heavy object crashed down in the yard beneath the frowning easterly façade. The tower was invisible now that the candles would not burn, but as the object neared the ground the

people knew that it was the smoke-grimed louvre-boarding
of that tower's east window.

Immediately afterwards an utterly unbearable fetor welled
forth from the unseen heights, choking and sickening the
trembling watchers, and almost prostrating those in the
square. At the same time the air trembled with a vibration
as of flapping wings, and a sudden east-blowing wind more
violent than any previous blast snatched off the hats and
wrenched the dripping umbrellas of the crowd. Nothing
definite could be seen in the candleless night, although some
upward-looking spectators thought they glimpsed a great
spreading blur of denser blackness against the inky sky –
something like a formless cloud of smoke that shot with
meteor-speed towards the east.

That was all. The watchers were half numbed with fright,
awe, and discomfort, and scarcely knew what to do, or
whether to do anything at all. Not knowing what had
happened, they did not relax their vigil; and a moment later
they sent up a prayer as a sharp flash of belated lightning,
followed by an earsplitting crash of sound, rent the flooded
heavens. Half an hour later the rain stopped, and in fifteen
minutes more the street lights sprang on again, sending the
weary, bedraggled watchers relievedly back to their homes.

The next day's papers gave these matters minor mention
in connection with the general storm reports. It seems that
the great lightning and deafening explosion which followed
the Federal Hill occurrence were even more tremendous
farther east, where a burst of the singular fetor was likewise
noticed. The phenomenon was most marked over College
Hill, where the crash awakened all the sleeping inhabitants
and led to a bewildered round of speculations. Of those who
were already awake only a few saw the anomalous blaze of
light near the top of the hill, or noticed the inexplicable
upward rush of air which almost stripped the leaves from
the trees and blasted the plants in the gardens. It was agreed
that the lone, sudden lightning-bolt must have struck somewhere in this neighbourhood, though no trace of its striking

could afterwards be found. A youth in the Tau Omega fraternity house thought he saw a grotesque and hideous mass of smoke in the air just as the preliminary flash burst, but his observation has not been verified. All of the few observers, however, agree as to the violent gust from the west and the flood of intolerable stench which preceded the belated stroke; whilst evidence concerning the momentary burned odour after the stroke is equally general.

These points were discussed very carefully because of their probable connection with the death of Robert Blake. Students in the Psi Delta house, whose upper rear windows looked into Blake's study, noticed the blurred white face at the westward window on the morning of the ninth, and wondered what was wrong with the expression. When they saw the same face in the same position that evening, they felt worried, and watched for the lights to come up in his apartment. Later they rang the bell of the darkened flat, and finally had a policeman force the door.

The rigid body sat bolt upright at the desk by the window, and when the intruders saw the glassy, bulging eyes, and the marks of stark, convulsive fright on the twisted features, they turned away in sickened dismay. Shortly afterwards the coroner's physician made an examination, and despite the unbroken window reported electrical shock, or nervous tension induced by electrical discharge, as the cause of death. The hideous expression he ignored altogether, deeming it a not improbable result of the profound shock as experienced by a person of such abnormal imagination and unbalanced emotions. He deduced these latter qualities from the books, paintings, and manuscripts found in the apartment, and from the blindly scrawled entries in the diary on the desk. Blake had prolonged his frenzied jottings to the last, and the broken-pointed pencil was found clutched in his spasmodically contracted right hand.

The entries after the failure of the lights were highly disjointed, and legible only in part. From them certain investigators have drawn conclusions differing greatly from the materialistic official verdict, but such speculations have little chance for belief among the conservative. The case of these imaginative theorists has not been helped by the action of superstitious Doctor Dexter, who threw the curious box and angled stone – an object certainly self-luminous as seen in the black windowless steeple where it was found – into the deepest channel of Narragansett Bay. Excessive imagination and neurotic unbalance on Blake's part, aggravated by knowledge of the evil bygone cult whose startling traces he had uncovered, form the dominant interpretation given those final frenzied jottings. These are the entries – or all that can be made of them.

'Lights still out – must be five minutes now. Everything depends on lightning. Yaddith grant it will keep up! . . . Some influence seems beating through it . . . Rain and thunder and wind deafen . . . The thing is taking hold of my mind . . .

'Trouble with memory. I see things I never knew before. Other worlds and other galaxies . . . Dark . . . The lightning seems dark and the darkness seems light . . .

'It cannot be the real hill and church that I see in the pitch-darkness. Must be retinal impression left by flashes. Heaven grant the Italians are out with their candles if the lightning stops!

'What am I afraid of? Is it not an avatar of Nyarlathotep, who in antique and shadowy Khem even took the form of man? I remember Yuggoth, and more distant Shaggai, and the ultimate void of the black planets . . .

'The long, winging flight through the void . . . cannot cross the universe of light . . . re-created by the thoughts caught in the Shining Trapezohedron . . . send it through the horrible abysses of radiance . . .

'My name is Blake – Robert Harrison Blake of 620 East Knapp Street, Milwaukee, Wisconsin . . . I am on this planet . . .

'Azathoth have mercy! – the lightning no longer flashes – horrible – I can see everything with a monstrous sense that is not sight – light is dark and dark is light . . . those people on the hill . . . guard . . . candles and charms . . . their priests . . .

'Sense of distance gone – far is near and near is far. No light – no glass – see that steeple – that tower – window – can hear – Roderick Usher – am mad or going mad – the thing is stirring

and fumbling in the tower – I am it and it is I – I want to get out
. . . must get out and unify the forces . . . It knows where I am
. . .

  'I am Robert Blake, but I see the tower in the dark. There is
a monstrous odour . . . senses transfigured . . . boarding at
that tower window cracking and giving way . . . Iä . . . ngai . . .
ygg . . .

  'I see it – coming here – hell-wind – titan blur – black wings –
Yog-Sothoth save me – the three lobed burning eye . . .'

The Shadow from the Steeple

ROBERT BLOCH

William Hurley was born an Irishman and grew up to be a taxicab driver – therefore it would be redundant, in the face of both of these facts, to say that he was garrulous.

The minute he picked up his passenger in downtown Providence that warm summer evening, he began talking. The passenger, a tall thin man in his early thirties, entered the cab and sat back, clutching a briefcase. He gave an address on Benefit Street and Hurley started out, shifting both taxi and tongue into high gear.

Hurley began what was to be a one-sided conversation by commencing on the afternoon performance of the New York Giants. Unperturbed by his passenger's silence, he made a few remarks about the weather – recent, current, and expected. Since he received no reply, the driver then proceeded to discuss a local phenomenon, namely the reported escape, that morning, of two black panthers or leopards from the travelling menagerie of Langer Brothers Circus, currently appearing in the city. In response to a direct inquiry as to whether he had seen the beasts roaming at large, Hurley's customer shook his head.

The driver then made several uncomplimentary remarks about the local police force and their inability to capture the beasts. It was his considered opinion that a given platoon of law enforcement officers would be unable to catch a cold if immured in an ice-box for a year. This witticism failed to amuse his passenger, and before Hurley could continue his monologue they had arrived at the Benefit Street address.

Eighty-five cents changed hands, passenger and briefcase left the cab, and Hurley drove away.

He could not know it at the time, but he thus became the last man who could or would testify to seeing his passenger alive.

The rest is conjecture, and perhaps that is for the best. Certainly it is easy enough to draw certain conclusions as to what happened that night in the old house on Benefit Street, but the weight of those conclusions is hard to bear.

One minor mystery is easy enough to clear up – the peculiar silence and aloofness of Hurley's passenger. That passenger, Edmund Fiske, of Chicago, Illinois, was meditating upon the fulfilment of fifteen years of questing; the cab-trip represented the last stage of this long journey, and he was reviewing the circumstances as he rode.

Edmund Fiske's quest had begun, on August 8, 1935, with the death of his close friend, Robert Harrison Blake, of Milwaukee.

Like Fiske himself at the time, Blake had been a precocious adolescent interested in fantasy-writing, and as such became a member of the 'Lovecraft circle' – a group of writers maintaining correspondence with one another and with the late Howard Phillips Lovecraft, of Providence.

It was through correspondence that Fiske and Blake had become acquainted; they visited back and forth between Milwaukee and Chicago, and their mutual preoccupation with the weird and the fantastic in literature and art served to form the foundation for the close friendship which existed at the time of Blake's unexpected and inexplicable demise.

Most of the facts – and certain of the conjectures – in connection with Blake's death have been embodied in Lovecraft's story, 'The Haunter of the Dark', which was published more than a year after the younger writer's passing.

Lovecraft had an excellent opportunity to observe matters, for it was on his suggestion that young Blake had journeyed to Providence early in 1935, and had been provided with living-quarters on College Street by Lovecraft himself. So it

was both as friend and neighbour that the elder fantasy
writer had acted in narrating the singular story of Robert
Harrison Blake's last months.

In his story, he tells of Blake's efforts to begin a novel
dealing with survival of New England witch-cults, but mod-
estly omits his own part in assisting his friend to secure
material. Apparently Blake began work on his project and
then became enmeshed in a horror greater than any envisioned by his imagination.

For Blake was drawn to investigate the crumbling black
pile of Federal Hill – the deserted ruin of a church that had
once housed the worshippers of an esoteric cult. Early in
spring he paid a visit to the shunned structure and there
made certain discoveries which (in Lovecraft's opinion) made
his death inevitable.

Briefly, Blake entered the boarded-up Free Will Church
and stumbled across the skeleton of a reporter from the
Providence Telegram, one Edwin M. Lillibridge, who had
apparently attempted a similar investigation in 1893. The
fact that his death was not explained seemed alarming
enough, but more disturbing still was the realization that no
one had been bold enough to enter the church since that date
and discover the body.

Blake found the reporter's notebook in his clothing, and
its contents afforded a partial revelation.

A certain Professor Bowen, of Providence, had travelled
widely in Egypt, and in 1843, in the course of archaeological
investigations of the crypt of Nephren-Ka, had made an
unusual find.

Nephren-Ka is the 'forgotten pharaoh', whose name has
been cursed by the priests and obliterated from official
dynastic records. The name was familiar to the young writer
at the time, due largely to the work of another Milwaukee
author who had dealt with the semi-legendary ruler in his
tale, 'Fane of the Black Pharaoh'. But the discovery Bowen
made in the crypt was totally unexpected.

The reporter's notebook said little of the actual nature of

that discovery, but it recorded subsequent events in a precise chronological fashion. Immediately upon unearthing his mysterious find in Egypt, Professor Bowen abandoned his research and returned to Providence, where he purchased the Free Will Church in 1844 and made it the headquarters of what was called the 'Starry Wisdom' sect.

Members of this religious cult, evidently recruited by Bowen, professed to worship an entity they called the 'Haunter of the Dark'. By gazing into a crystal they summoned the actual presence of this entity and did homage with blood sacrifice.

Such, at least, was the fantastic story circulated in Providence at the time – and the church became a place to be avoided. Local superstition fanned agitation, and agitation precipitated direct action. In May of 1877 the sect was forcibly broken up by the authorities, due to public pressure, and several hundred of its members abruptly left the city.

The church itself was immediately closed, and apparently individual curiosity could not overcome the widespread fear which resulted in leaving the structure undisturbed and unexplored until the reporter, Lillibridge, made his ill-fated private investigation in 1893.

Such was the gist of the story unfolded in the pages of his notebook. Blake read it, but was nevertheless undeterred in his further scrutiny of the environs. Eventually he came upon the mysterious object Bowen had found in the Egyptian crypt – the object upon which the Starry Wisdom worship had been founded – the asymmetrical metal box with its curiously hinged lid, a lid that had been closed for countless years. Blake thus gazed at the interior, gazed upon the four-inch red-black crystal polyhedron hanging suspended by seven supports. He not only gazed *at* but also *into* the polyhedron; just as the cult-worshippers had purportedly gazed, and with the same results. He was assailed by a curious psychic disturbance; he seemed to 'see visions of other lands and the gulfs beyond the stars,' as superstitious accounts had told.

And then Blake made his greatest mistake. He closed the box.

Closing the box – again, according to the superstitions annotated by Lillibridge – was the act that summoned the alien entity itself, the Haunter of the Dark. It was a creature of darkness and could not survive light. And in that boarded-up blackness of the ruined church, the thing emerged by night.

Blake fled the church in terror, but the damage was done. In mid-July, a thunderstorm put out the lights in Providence for an hour, and the Italian colony living near the deserted church heard bumping and thumping from inside the shadow-shrouded structure.

Crowds with candles stood outside in the rain and played candles upon the building, shielding themselves against the possible emergence of the feared entity by a barrier of light.

Apparently the story had remained alive throughout the neighbourhood. Once the storm abated, local newspapers grew interested, and on July 17 two reporters entered the old church, together with a policeman. Nothing definite was found, although there were curious and inexplicable smears and stains on the stairs and the pews.

Less than a month later – at 2:35 A.M. on the morning of August 8, to be exact – Robert Harrison Blake met his death during an electrical storm while seated before the window of his room on College Street.

During the gathering storm, before his death occurred, Blake scribbled frantically in his diary, gradually revealing his innermost obsessions and delusions concerning the Haunter of the Dark. It was Blake's conviction that by gazing into the curious crystal in its box he had somehow established a linkage with the non-terrestrial entity. He further believed that closing the box had summoned the creature to dwell in the darkness of the church steeple, and that in some way his own fate was now irrevocably linked to that of the monstrosity.

All this is revealed in the last messages he set down while watching the progress of the storm from his window.

Meanwhile, at the church itself, on Federal Hill, a crowd of agitated spectators gathered to play lights upon the structure. That they heard alarming sounds from inside the boarded-up building is undeniable; at least two competent witnesses have testified to the fact. One, Father Merluzzo of the Spirito Santo Church, was on hand to quiet his congregation. The other, Patrolman (now Sergeant) William J. Monahan, of Central Station, was attempting to preserve order in the face of growing panic. Monahan himself saw the blinding 'blur' that seemed to issue, smokelike, from the steeple of the ancient edifice as the final lightning-flash came.

Flash, meteor, fireball – call it what you will – erupted over the city in a blinding blaze; perhaps at the very moment that Robert Harrison Blake, across town, was writing, 'Is it not an avatar of Nyarlathotep, who in antique and shadowy Khem even took the form of man?'

A few moments later he was dead. The coroner's physician rendered a verdict attributing his demise to 'electrical shock' although the window he faced was unbroken. Another physician, known to Lovecraft, quarrelled privately with that verdict and subsequently entered the affair the next day. Without legal authority, he entered the church and climbed to the windowless steeple where he discovered the strange asymmetrical – was it golden? – box and the curious stone within. Apparently his first gesture was to make sure of raising the lid and bringing the stone into the light. His next recorded gesture was to charter a boat, take box and curiously angled stone aboard, and drop them into the deepest channel of Narragansett Bay.

There ended the admittedly fictionalized account of Blake's death as recorded by H. P. Lovecraft. And there began Edmund Fiske's fifteen-year quest.

Fiske, of course, had known some of the events outlined in the story. When Blake had left for Providence in the spring,

Fiske had tentatively promised to join him the following autumn. At first, the two friends had exchanged letters regularly, but by early summer Blake ceased correspondence altogether.

At the time, Fiske was unaware of Blake's exploration of the ruined church. He could not account for Blake's silence, and wrote to Lovecraft for a possible explanation.

Lovecraft could supply little information. Young Blake, he said, had visited with him frequently during the early weeks of his stay; had consulted with him about his writing, and had accompanied him on several nocturnal strolls through the city.

But during the summer, Blake's neighbourliness ceased. It was not in Lovecraft's reclusive nature to impose himself upon others, and he did not seek to invade Blake's privacy for several weeks.

When he did so – and learned from the almost hysterical adolescent of his experiences in the forbidding, forbidden church on Federal Hill – Lovecraft offered words of warning and advice. But it was already too late. Within ten days of his visit came the shocking end.

Fiske learned of that end from Lovecraft on the following day. It was his task to break the news to Blake's parents. For a time he was tempted to visit Providence immediately, but lack of funds and the pressure of his own domestic affairs forestalled him. The body of his young friend duly arrived and Fiske attended the brief ceremony of cremation.

Then Lovecraft began his own investigation – an investigation which ultimately resulted in the publication of his story. And there the matter might have rested.

But Fiske was not satisfied.

His best friend had died under circumstances which even the most sceptical must admit were mysterious. The local authorities summarily wrote off the matter with a fatuous and inadequate explanation.

Fiske determined to ascertain the truth.

Bear in mind one salient fact – all three of these men,

Lovecraft, Blake, and Fiske, were professional writers and students of the supernatural or the supranormal. All three of them had extraordinary access to a bulk of written material dealing with ancient legend and superstition. Ironically enough, the use to which they put their knowledge was limited to excursions into so-called 'fantasy fiction' but none of them, in the light of their own experience, could wholly join their reading audience in scoffing at the myths of which they wrote.

For, as Fiske wrote to Lovecraft, 'the term, myth, as we know, is merely a polite euphemism. Blake's death was not a myth, but a hideous reality. I implore you to investigate fully. See this matter through to the end, for if Blake's diary holds even a distorted truth, there is no telling what may be loosed upon the world.'

Lovecraft pledged cooperation, discovered the fate of the metal box and its contents, and endeavoured to arrange a meeting with Doctor Ambrose Dexter, of Benefit Street. Doctor Dexter, it appeared, had left town immediately following his dramatic theft and disposal of the 'Shining Trapezohedron', as Lovecraft called it.

Lovecraft then apparently interviewed Father Merluzzo and Patrolman Monahan, plunged into the files of the *Bulletin*, and endeavoured to reconstruct the story of the Starry Wisdom sect and the entity they worshipped.

Of course he learned a good deal more than he dared to put into his magazine story. His letters to Edmund Fiske in the late fall and early spring of 1936 contain guarded hints and references to 'menaces from Outside'. But he seemed anxious to reassure Fiske that if there had been any menace, even in the realistic rather than the supernatural sense, the danger was now averted because Doctor Dexter had disposed of the Shining Trapezohedron which acted as a summoning talisman. Such was the gist of his report, and the matter rested there for a time.

Fiske made tentative arrangements, early in 1937, to visit Lovecraft at his home, with the private intention of doing

some further research on his own into the cause of Blake's
death. But once again, circumstances intervened. For in
March of that year, Lovecraft died. His unexpected passing
plunged Fiske into a period of mental despondency from
which he was slow to recover; accordingly, it was not until
almost a year later that Edmund Fiske paid his first visit to
Providence, and to the scene of the tragic episodes which
brought Blake's life to a close.

For somehow, always, a black undercurrent of suspicion
existed. The coroner's physician had been glib, Lovecraft had
been tactful, the press and the general public had accepted
matters completely – yet Blake was dead, and there had
been an entity abroad in the night.

Fiske felt that if he could visit the accursed church himself,
talk to Doctor Dexter and find out what had drawn him into
the affair, interrogate the reporters, and pursue any relevant
leads or clues he might eventually hope to uncover the truth
and at least clear his dead friend's name of the ugly shadow
of mental unbalance.

Accordingly, Fiske's first step after arriving in Providence
and registering at a hotel was to set out for Federal Hill and
the ruined church.

The search was doomed to immediate, irremediable disappointment. For the church was no more. It had been razed
the previous fall and the property taken over by the city
authorities. The black and baleful spire no longer cast its
spell over the Hill.

Fiske immediately took pains to see Father Merluzzo, at
Spirito Santo, a few squares away. He learned from a
courteous housekeeper that Father Merluzzo had died in
1936, within a year of young Blake.

Discouraged but persistent, Fiske next attempted to reach
Doctor Dexter, but the old house on Benefit Street was
boarded up. A call to the Physician's Service Bureau produced only the cryptic information that Ambrose Dexter,
MD, had left the city for an indeterminate stay.

Nor did a visit with the city editor of the *Bulletin* yield any better result. Fiske was permitted to go into the newspaper's morgue and read the aggravatingly short and matter-of-fact story of Blake's death, but the two reporters who had covered the assignment and subsequently visited the Federal Hill church had left the paper for berths in other cities.

There were, of course, other leads to follow, and during the ensuing week Fiske ran them all to the ground. A copy of *Who's Who* added nothing significant to his mental picture of Doctor Ambrose Dexter. The physician was Providence born, a life-long resident, 40 years of age, unmarried, a general practitioner, member of several medical societies – but there was no indication of any unusual 'hobbies' or 'other interest' which might provide a clue as to his participation in the affair.

Sergeant William J. Monahan of Central Station was sought out, and for the first time Fiske actually managed to speak to someone who admitted an actual connection with the events leading to Blake's death. Monahan was polite, but cautiously noncommittal.

Despite Fiske's complete unburdening, the polite officer remained discreetly reticent.

'There's really nothing I can tell you,' he said. 'It's true, like Mister Lovecraft said, that I was at the church that night, for there was a rough crowd out and there's no telling what some of them ones in the neighbourhood will do when riled up. Like the story said, the old church had a bad name, and I guess Sheeley could have given you many's the story.'

'Sheeley?' interjected Fiske.

'Bert Sheeley – it was his beat, you know, not mine. He was ill of pneumonia at the time and I substituted for two weeks. Then, when he died – '

Fiske shook his head. Another possible source of information gone. Blake dead, Lovecraft dead, Father Merluzzo dead, and now Sheeley. Reporters scattered, and Doctor Dexter mysteriously missing. He sighed and persevered.

'That last night, when you saw the blur,' he asked, 'can you add anything by way of details? Were there any noises?

Did anyone in the crowd say anything? Try to remember – whatever you can add may be of great help to me.'

Monahan shook his head. 'There were noises aplenty,' he said. 'But what with the thunder and all, I couldn't rightly make out if anything came from inside the church, like the story has it. And as for the crowd, with the women wailing and the men muttering, all mixed up with thunderclaps and wind, it was as much as I could do to hear myself yelling to keep in place let alone make out what was being said.'

'And the blur?' Fiske persisted.

'It was a blur, and that's all. Smoke, or a cloud, or just a shadow before the lightning struck again. But I'll not be saying I saw any devils, or monsters, or whatchamacallits as Mister Lovecraft would write about in those wild tales of his.'

Sergeant Monahan shrugged self-righteously and picked up the desk-phone to answer a call. The interview was obviously at an end.

And so, for the nonce, was Fiske's quest. He didn't abandon hope, however. For a day he sat by his own hotel phone and called up every 'Dexter' listed in the book in an effort to locate a relative of the missing doctor; but to no avail. Another day was spent in a small boat on Narragansett Bay, as Fiske assiduously and painstakingly familiarized himself with the location of the 'deepest channel' alluded to in Lovecraft's story.

But at the end of a futile week in Providence, Fiske had to confess himself beaten. He returned to Chicago, his work, and his normal pursuits. Gradually the affair dropped out of the foreground of his consciousness, but he by no means forgot it completely or gave up the notion of eventually unravelling the mystery – if mystery there was.

In 1941, during a three-day furlough from Basic Training, Pvt First Class Edmund Fiske passed through Providence on his way to New York City and again attempted to locate Dr Ambrose Dexter, without success.

During 1942 and 1943 Sgt Edmund Fiske wrote from his

stations overseas, to Dr Ambrose Dexter c/o General Delivery, Providence, RI. His letters were never acknowledged, if indeed they were received.

In 1945, in a USO library lounge in Honolulu, Fiske read a report in – of all things – a journal on astro-physics which mentioned a recent gathering at Princeton University, at which the guest speaker, Dr Ambrose Dexter, had delivered an address on 'Practical Applications in Military Technology'.

Fiske did not return to the States until the end of 1946. Domestic affairs, naturally, were the subject of his paramount consideration during the following year. It wasn't until 1948 that he accidentally came upon Dr Dexter's name again – this time in a listing of 'investigators in the field of nuclear physics' in a national weekly news-magazine. He wrote to the editors for further information, but received no reply. And another letter, dispatched to Providence, remained unanswered.

But in 1949, late in autumn, Dexter's name again came to his attention through the news columns; this time in relation to a discussion of work on the secret H-bomb.

Whatever he guessed, whatever he feared, whatever he wildly imagined, Fiske was impelled to action. It was then that he wrote to a certain Ogden Purvis, a private investigator in the city of Providence, and commissioned him to locate Doctor Ambrose Dexter. All that he required was that he be placed in communication with Dexter, and he paid a substantial retainer fee. Purvis took the case.

The private detective sent several reports to Fiske in Chicago and they were, at first, disheartening. The Dexter residence was still untenanted. Dexter himself, according to the information elicited from governmental sources, was on a special mission. The private investigator seemed to assume from this that he was a person above reproach, engaged in confidential defence work.

Fiske's own reaction was panic.

He raised his offer of a fee and insisted that Ogden Purvis
continue his efforts to find the elusive doctor.

Winter of 1950 came, and with it, another report. The
private investigator had tracked down every lead Fiske had
suggested, and one of them led, eventually, to Tom Jonas.

Tom Jonas was the owner of the small boat which had
been chartered by Doctor Dexter one evening in the late
summer of 1935 – the small boat which had been rowed to
the 'deepest channel of Narragansett Bay'.

Tom Jonas had rested his oars as Dexter threw overboard
the dully-gleaming, asymmetrical metal box with the hinged
lid open to disclose the Shining Trapezohedron.

The old fisherman had spoken freely to the private detective; his words were reported in detail to Fiske via confidential report.

'Mighty peculiar' was Jonas's own reaction to the incident.
Dexter had offered him 'twenty smackers to take the boat
out in the middle o' midnight and heave this funny-lookin'
contraption overboard. Said there was no harm in it; said it
was just an old keepsake he wanted to git rid of. But all the
way out he kep' starin' at the sort of jewel-thing set in some
iron bands inside the box, and mumblin' in some foreign
language, I guess. No, 'tweren't French or German or Italian
talk either. Polish, mebbe. I don't remember any words,
either. But he acted sort-of-drunk. Not that I'd say anything
against Doctor Dexter, understand; comes of a fine old
family, even if he ain't been around these parts since, to my
knowing. But I figgered he was a bit under the influence,
you might say. Else why would he pay me twenty smackers
to do a crazy stunt like that?'

There was more to the verbatim transcript of the old
fisherman's monologue, but it did not explain anything.

'He sure seemed glad to git rid of it, as I recollect. On the
way back he told me to keep mum about it, but I can't see no
harm in telling at this late date; I wouldn't hold anythin'
back from the law.'

Evidently the private investigator had made use of a

rather unethical stratagem – posing as an actual detective in order to get Jonas to talk.

This did not bother Fiske, in Chicago. It was enough to get his grasp on something tangible at last; enough to make him send Purvis another payment, with instructions to keep up the search for Ambrose Dexter. Several months passed in waiting.

Then, in late spring, came the news Fiske had waited for. Doctor Dexter was back; he had returned to his house on Benefit Street. The boards had been removed, furniture vans appeared to discharge their contents, and a manservant appeared to answer the door, and to take telephone messages.

Doctor Dexter was not at home to the investigator, or to anyone. He was, it appeared, recuperating from a severe illness contracted while in government service. He took a card from Purvis and promised to deliver a message, but repeated calls brought no indication of a reply.

Nor did Purvis who conscientiously 'cased' the house and neighbourhood, ever succeed in laying eyes upon the doctor himself or in finding anyone who claimed to have seen the convalescent physician on the street.

Groceries were delivered regularly; mail appeared in the box; lights glowed in the Benefit Street house nightly until all hours.

As a matter of fact, this was the only concrete statement Purvis could make regarding any possible irregularity in Doctor Dexter's mode of life – he seemed to keep electricity burning twenty-four hours a day.

Fiske promptly dispatched another letter to Doctor Dexter, and then another. Still no acknowledgement or reply was forthcoming. And after several more unenlightening reports from Purvis, Fiske made up his mind. He would go to Providence and see Dexter, somehow, come what may.

He might be completely wrong in his suspicions; he might be completely wrong in his assumption that Doctor Dexter could clear the name of his dead friend; he might be completely wrong in even surmising any connection between the two – but for fifteen years he had brooded and wondered, and it was time to put an end to his own inner conflict.

Accordingly, late that summer, Fiske wired Purvis of his intentions and instructed him to meet him at the hotel upon his arrival.

Thus it was that Edmund Fiske came to Providence for the last time; on the day that the Giants lost, on the day that the Langer Brothers lost their two black panthers, on the day that cabdriver William Hurley was in a garrulous mood.

Purvis was not at the hotel to meet him, but such was Fiske's own frenzy of impatience that he decided to act without him and drove, as we have seen, to Benefit Street in the early evening.

As the cab departed, Fiske stared up at the panelled doorway; stared at the lights blazing from the upper windows of the Georgian structure. A brass name-plate gleamed on the door itself, and the light from the windows played upon the legend, Ambrose Dexter, MD.

Slight as it was, this seemed a reassuring touch to Edmund Fiske. The doctor was not concealing his presence in the house from the world, however much he might conceal his actual person. Surely the blazing lights and the appearance of the name-plate augured well.

Fiske shrugged, rang the bell.

The door opened quickly. A small, dark-skinned man with a slight stoop appeared and made a question of the word, 'Yes?'

'Doctor Dexter, please.'

'The Doctor is not in to callers. He is ill.'

'Would you take a message, please?'

'Certainly.' The dark-skinned servant smiled.

'Tell him that Edmund Fiske of Chicago wishes to see him at his convenience for a few moments. I have come all the way from the Middle West for this purpose, and what I have to speak to him about would take only a moment or two of his time.'

'Wait, please.'

The door closed. Fiske stood in the gathering darkness and transferred his briefcase from one hand to the other.

Abruptly, the door opened again. The servant peered out at him.

'Mr Fiske – are you the gentleman who wrote the letters?'

'Letters – oh, yes, I am. I did not know the doctor ever received them.'

The servant nodded. 'I could not say. But Doctor Dexter said that if you were the man who had written to him, you were to come right in.'

Fiske permitted himself an audible sigh of relief as he stepped over the threshold. It had taken fifteen years to come this far, and now –

'Just go upstairs, if you please. You will find Doctor Dexter waiting in the study, right at the head of the hall.'

Edmund Fiske climbed the stairs, turned at the top to a doorway, and entered a room in which the light was an almost palpable presence, so intense was its glare.

And there, rising from a chair beside the fireplace, was Doctor Ambrose Dexter.

Fiske found himself facing a tall, thin, immaculately dressed man who may have been fifty but who scarcely looked thirty-five; a man whose wholly natural grace and elegance of movement concealed the sole incongruity of his aspect – a very deep suntan.

'So you are Edmund Fiske.'

The voice was soft, well-modulated, and unmistakably New England – and the accompanying handclasp warm and firm. Doctor Dexter's smile was natural and friendly. White teeth gleamed against the brown background of his features.

'Won't you sit down?' invited the doctor. He indicated a chair and bowed slightly. Fiske couldn't help but stare; there was certainly no indication of any present or recent illness in his host's demeanour or behaviour. As Doctor Dexter resumed his own seat near the fire and Fiske moved around the chair to join him, he noted the bookshelves on either side of the room. The size and shape of several volumes immedi-

ately engaged his rapt attention – so much that he hesitated
before taking a seat, and instead inspected the titles of the
tomes.

For the first time in his life, Edmund Fiske found himself
confronting the half-legendary *De Vermis Mysteriis*, the
Liber Ivonis, and the almost mythical Latin version of the
Necronomicon. Without seeking his host's permission, he
lifted the bulk of the latter volume from the shelf and riffled
through the yellowed pages of the Spanish translation of
1622.

Then he turned to Doctor Dexter, and all traces of his
carefully-contrived composure dropped away. 'Then it must
have been you who found these books in the church,' he said.
'In the rear vestry room beside the apse. Lovecraft mentioned
them in his story, and I've always wondered what became of
them.'

Doctor Dexter nodded gravely. 'Yes, I took them. I did not
think it wise for such books to fall into the hands of the
authorities. You know what they contain, and what might
happen if such knowledge was wrongfully employed.'

Fiske reluctantly replaced the great book on the shelf and
took a chair facing the doctor before the fire. He held his
briefcase on his lap and fumbled uneasily with the clasp.

'Don't be uneasy,' said Doctor Dexter, with a kindly smile.
'Let us proceed without fencing. You are here to discover
what part I played in the affair of your friend's death.'

'Yes, there are some questions I wanted to ask.'

'Please.' The doctor raised a slim brown hand. 'I am not in
the best of health and can give you only a few minutes. Allow
me to anticipate your queries and tell you what little I know.'

'As you wish.' Fiske stared at the bronzed man, wondering
what lay behind the perfection of his poise.

'I met your friend Robert Harrison Blake only once,' said
Doctor Dexter. 'It was on an evening during the latter part
of July 1935. He called upon me here, as a patient.'

Fiske leaned forward eagerly. 'I never knew that!' he
exclaimed.

'There was no reason for anyone to know it,' the doctor answered. 'He was merely a patient. He claimed to be suffering from insomnia. I examined him, prescribed a sedative, and acting on the merest surmise, asked if he had recently been subjected to any unusual strain or trauma. It was then that he told me the story of his visit to the church on Federal Hill and of what he had found there. I must say that I had the acumen not to dismiss his tale as the product of a hysterical imagination. As a member of one of the older families here, I was already acquainted with the legends surrounding the Starry Wisdom sect and the so-called Haunter of the Dark.

'Young Blake confessed to me certain of his fears concerning the Shining Trapezohedron – intimating that it was a focal point of primal evil. He further admitted his own dread of being somehow linked to the monstrosity in the church.

'Naturally, I was not prepared to accept this last premise as a rational one. I attempted to reassure the young man, advised him to leave Providence and forget it. And at the time I acted in all good faith. And then, in August, came the news of Blake's death.'

'So you went to the church,' Fiske said.

'Wouldn't you have done the same thing?' parried Doctor Dexter. 'If Blake had come to you with this story, told you of what he feared, wouldn't his death have moved you to action? I assure you, I did what I thought best. Rather than provoke a scandal, rather than expose the general public to needless fears, rather than permit the possibility of danger to exist, I went to the church. I took the books. I took the Shining Trapezohedron from under the noses of the authorities. And I chartered a boat and dumped the accursed thing in Narragansett Bay, where it could no longer possibly harm mankind. The lid was up when I dropped it – for as you know, only darkness can summon the Haunter, and now the stone is eternally exposed to light.

'But that is all I can tell you. I regret that my work in recent years has prevented me from seeing or communicating with you before this. I appreciate your interest in the affair and trust my remarks will help to clarify, in a small way, your bewilderment. As to young Blake, in my capacity as examining physician, I will gladly give you a written testimony to my belief in his sanity at the time of his death. I'll have it drawn up tomorrow and send it to your hotel if you give me the address. Fair enough?'

The doctor rose, signifying that the interview was over. Fiske remained seated, shifting his briefcase.

'Now if you will excuse me,' the physician murmured.

'In a moment. There are still one or two brief questions I'd appreciate your answering.'

'Certainly.' If Doctor Dexter was irritated, he gave no sign.

'Did you by any chance see Lovecraft before or during his last illness?'

'No. I was not his physician. In fact, I never met the man, though of course I knew of him and his work.'

'What caused you to leave Providence so abruptly after the Blake affair?'

'My interests in physics superseded my interest in medicine. As you may or may not know, during the past decade or more, I have been working on problems relative to atomic energy and nuclear fission. In fact, starting tomorrow, I am leaving Providence once more to deliver a course of lectures before the faculties of eastern universities and certain governmental groups.'

'That is very interesting to me, Doctor,' said Fiske. 'By the way, did you ever meet Einstein?'

'As a matter of fact, I did, some years ago. I worked with him on – but no matter. I must beg you to excuse me, now. At another time, perhaps, we can discuss such things.'

His impatience was unmistakable now. Fiske rose, lifting his briefcase in one hand and reaching out to extinguish a tablelamp with the other.

Doctor Dexter crossed swiftly and lighted the lamp again.

'Why are you afraid of the dark, Doctor?' asked Fiske, softly.

'I am not af – '

For the first time the physician seemed on the verge of losing his composure. 'What makes you think that?' he whispered.

'It's the Shining Trapezohedron, isn't it?' Fiske continued. 'When you threw it into the bay you acted too hastily. You didn't remember at the time that even if you left the lid open, the stone would be surrounded by darkness there at the bottom of the channel. Perhaps the Haunter didn't want you to remember. You looked into the stone just as Blake did, and established the same psychic linkage. And when you threw the thing away, you gave it into perpetual darkness, where the Haunter's power would feed and grow.

'That's why you left Providence – because you were afraid the Haunter would come to you, just as it came to Blake. And because you knew that now the thing would remain abroad forever.'

Doctor Dexter moved towards the door. 'I must definitely ask that you leave now,' he said. 'If you're implying that I keep the lights on because I'm afraid of the Haunter coming after me, the way it did Blake, then you're mistaken.'

Fiske smiled wryly. 'That's not it at all,' he answered. 'I know you don't fear that. Because it's too late. The Haunter must have come to you long before this – perhaps within a day or so after you gave it power by consigning the Shining Trapezohedron to the darkness of the Bay. It came to you, but unlike the case of Blake, it did not kill you.

'It used you. That's why you fear the dark. You fear it as the Haunter itself fears being discovered. I believe that in the darkness you look *different*. More like the old shape. Because when the Haunter came to you, it did not kill but instead, *merged*. *You* are the Haunter of the Dark!'

'Mr Fiske, really – '

'There is no Doctor Dexter. There hasn't been any such person for many years now. There's only the outer shell, possessed by an entity older than the world; an entity that is moving quickly and cunningly to bring destruction to all mankind. It was you who turned "scientist" and insinuated yourself into the proper circles, hinting and prompting and assisting foolish men into their sudden "discovery" of nuclear fission. When the first atomic bomb fell, how you must have laughed! And now you've given them the secret of the hydrogen bomb, and you're going on to teach them more, show them new ways to bring about their own destruction.

'It took me years of brooding to discover the clues, the keys to the so-called wild myths that Lovecraft wrote about. For he wrote in parable and allegory, but he wrote the truth. He has set it down in black and white time and again, the prophecy of your coming to earth – Blake knew it at the last when he identified the Haunter by its rightful name.'

'And that is?' snapped the doctor.

'Nyarlathotep!'

The brown face creased into a grimace of laughter. 'I'm afraid you're a victim of the same fantasy-projections as poor Blake and your friend Lovecraft. Everyone knows that Nyarlathotep is pure invention – part of the Lovecraft mythos.'

'I thought so, until I found the clue in his poem. That's when it all fitted in; the Haunter of the Dark, your fleeing, and your sudden interest in scientific research. Lovecraft's words took on a new meaning:

> And at last from inner Egypt came
> The strange dark one to whom the
> fellahs bowed.'

Fiske chanted the lines, staring at the dark face of the physician.

'Nonsense – if you must know, this dermatological disturbance of mine is the result of exposure to radiation at Los Alamos.'

Fiske did not heed; he was continuing Lovecraft's poem:

> ' – That wild beasts followed him and licked his
>   hands.
> Soon from the sea a noxious birth began:

Forgotten lands with weedy spires of gold
The ground was cleft and mad auroras rolled
Down on the quaking cities of man.
Then crushing what he chanced to mould in
    play
The idiot Chaos blew Earth's dust away.'

Doctor Dexter shook his head. 'Ridiculous on the face of it,'
he asserted. 'Surely, even in your – er – upset condition, you
can understand that, man! The poem has no literal meaning.
Do wild beasts lick my hands? Is something rising from the
sea? Are there earthquakes and auroras? Nonsense! You're
suffering from a bad case of what we call "atomic jitters" – I
can see it now. You're preoccupied, as so many laymen are
today, with the foolish obsession that somehow our work in
nuclear fission will result in the destruction of the earth. All
this rationalization is a product of your imaginings.'

Fiske held his briefcase tightly. 'I told you it was a parable,
this prophecy of Lovecraft's. God knows what he *knew* or
feared; whatever it was, it was enough to make him cloak
his meaning. And even then, perhaps, *they* got to him
because he knew too much.'

'*They?*'

'They from Outside – the ones you serve. You are their
Messenger, Nyarlathotep. You came, in linkage with the
Shining Trapezohedron, out of inner Egypt, as the poem
says. And the fellahs – the common workers of Providence
who became converted to the Starry Wisdom sect – bowed
before the "strange Dark one" they worshipped as the
Haunter.

'The Trapezohedron was thrown into the Bay, and soon
from the sea came this noxious birth – your birth, or
incarnation in the body of Doctor Dexter. And you taught
men new methods of destruction; destruction with atomic
bombs in which the "ground was cleft and mad auroras rolled
down on the quaking cities of man". Oh, Lovecraft knew
what he was writing, and Blake recognized you, too. And
they both died. I suppose you'll try to kill me now, so you can

go on. You'll lecture, and stand at the elbows of the laboratory men urging them on and giving them new suggestions to result in greater destruction. And finally you'll blow earth's dust away.'

'Please.' Dexter held out both hands. 'Control yourself – let me get you something! Can't you realize this whole thing is absurd?'

Fiske moved towards him, hands fumbling at the clasp of the briefcase. The flap opened, and Fiske reached inside, then withdrew his hand. He held a revolver now, and pointed it quite steadily at Doctor Dexter's breast.

'Of course it's absurd,' Fiske muttered. 'No one ever believed in the Starry Wisdom sect except a few fanatics and some ignorant foreigners. No one ever took Blake's stories or Lovecraft's, or mine for that matter, as anything but a rather morbid form of amusement. By the same token, no one will ever believe there is anything wrong with you, or with so-called scientific investigation of atomic energy, or the other horrors you plan to loose on the world to bring about its doom. And that's why I'm going to kill you now!'

'Put down that gun!'

Fiske began suddenly to tremble; his whole body shook in a spectacular spasm. Dexter noted it and moved forward. The younger man's eyes were bulging, and the physician inched towards him.

'Stand back!' Fiske warned. The words were distorted by the convulsive shuddering of his jaws. 'That's all I needed to know. Since you are in a human body, you can be destroyed by ordinary weapons. And so I do destroy you – Nyarlathotep!'

His finger moved.

So did Doctor Dexter's. His hand went swiftly behind him, to the wall masterlightswitch. A click and the room was plunged into utter darkness.

Not utter darkness – for there was a glow.

The face and hands of Doctor Ambrose Dexter glowed with a phosphorescent fire in the dark. There are presumable forms of radium poisoning which can cause such an effect, and no doubt Doctor Dexter would have so explained the phenomenon to Edmund Fiske, had he the opportunity.

But there was no opportunity. Edmund Fiske heard the click, saw the fantastic features, and pitched forward to the floor.

Doctor Dexter quietly switched on the lights, went over to the younger man's side and knelt for a long moment. He sought a pulse in vain.

Edmund Fiske was dead.

The doctor sighed, rose, and left the room. In the hall downstairs he summoned his servant.

'There has been a regrettable accident,' he said. 'That young visitor of mine – a hysteric – suffered a heart attack. You had better call the police, immediately. And then continue with the packing. We must leave tomorrow, for the lecture tour.'

'But the police may detain you.'

Doctor Dexter shook his head. 'I think not. It's a clear-cut case. In any event, I can easily explain. When they arrive, notify me. I shall be in the garden.'

The doctor proceeded down the hall to the rear exit and emerged upon the moonlit splendour of the garden behind the house on Benefit Street.

The radiant vista was walled off from the world, utterly deserted. The dark man stood in moonlight and its glow mingled with his own aura.

At this moment two silken shadows leapt over the wall. They crouched in the coolness of the garden, then slithered forwards towards Doctor Dexter. They made panting sounds.

In the moonlight, he recognized the shapes of two black panthers.

Immobile, he waited as they advanced, padding purposefully towards him, eyes aglow, jaws slavering and agape.

Doctor Dexter turned away. His face was turned in mockery to the moon as the beasts fawned before him and licked his hands.

Notebook Found in a Deserted House

ROBERT BLOCH

First off, I want to write that I never did anything wrong. Not to nobody. They got no call to shut me up here, whoever they are. They got no reason to do what I'm afraid they're going to do, either.

I think they're coming pretty soon, because they've been gone outside a long time. Digging, I guess, in that old well. Looking for a gate, I heard. Not a regular gate, of course, but something else.

Got a notion what they mean, and I'm scared.

I'd look out the windows but of course they are boarded up so I can't see.

But I turned on the lamp, and I found this here notebook so I want to put it all down. Then if I get a chance maybe I can send it to somebody who can help me. Or maybe somebody will find it. Anyway, it's better to write it out as best I can instead of just sitting here and waiting. Waiting for *them* to come and get me.

I better start by telling my name, which is Willie Osborne, and that I am 12 years old last July. I don't know where I was born.

First thing I can remember is living out Roodsford way, out in what folks call the back hill country. It's real lonesome out there, with deep woods all around and lots of mountains and hills that nobody ever climbs.

Grandma use to tell me about it when I was just a little shaver. That's who I lived with, just Grandma on account of my real folks being dead. Grandma was the one who taught me how to read and write. I never been to a regular school.

Grandma knew all kinds of things about the hills and the woods and she told me some mighty queer stories. That's what I thought they was, anyway, when I was little and living all alone with her. Just stories, like the ones in books.

Like stories about *them ones* hiding in the swamps, that was here before the settlers and the Indians both and how there was circles in swamps and big stones called alters where *them ones* used to make sacrefices to what they worshipped.

Grandma got some of the stories from her Grandma she said – about how *them ones* hid in the woods and swamps because they couldn't stand sunshine, and how the Indians kept out of their way. She said sometimes the Indians would leave some of their young people tied to trees in the forest as a sacrefice, so as to keep *them* contented and peacefull.

Indians knew all about *them* and they tried to keep white folks from noticing too much or settling too close to the hills. *Them ones* didn't cause much trouble, but they might if they was crowded. So the Indians give excuses for not settling, saying there wasn't enough hunting and no trails and it was too far off from the coast.

Grandma told me that was why not many places was settled even today. Nothing but a few farmhouses here and there. She told me *them ones* was still alive and on certain nights in the Spring and Fall you could see lights and hear noises far off on the tops of the hills.

Grandma said I had an Aunt Lucy and a Uncle Fred who lived out there right smack in the middle of the hills. Said my Pa used to visit them before he got married and once he heard *them* beating on a tree drum one night along about Hallowe'en time. That was before he met Ma and they got married and she died when I come and he went away.

I heard all kinds of stories. About witches and devils and bat men that sucked your blood and haunts. About Salem and Arkham because I never been to a city and I wanted to

hear tell how they were. About a place called Innsmouth
with old rotten houses where people hid awful things away
in the cellars and the attics. She told me about the way
graves was dug deep under Arkham. Made it sound like the
whole country was full of haunts.

She use to scare me, telling about how some of these things
looked and all but she never would tell me how *them ones*
looked no matter how much I asked. Said she didn't want me
to have any truck with such things – bad enough she and
her kin knew as much as they did – almost too much for
decent God-fearing people. It was lucky for me I didn't have
to bother with such ideas, like my own ancestor on my
father's side, Mehitabel Osborne, who got hanged for a witch
back in the Salem days.

So they was just stories to me until last year when
Grandma died and Judge Crubinthorp put me on the train
and I went out to live with Aunt Lucy and Uncle Fred in the
very same hills that Grandma use to tell about so often.

You can bet I was pretty excited, and the conductor let me
ride with him all the way and told me about the towns and
everything.

Uncle Fred met me at the station. He was a tall thin man
with a long beard. We drove off in a buggy from the little
deepo – no houses around there or nothing – right into the
woods.

Funny thing about those woods. They was so still and
quiet. Gave me the creeps they was so dark and lonesome.
Seemed like nobody had ever shouted or laughed or even
smiled in them. Couldn't imagine anyone saying anything
there excep in whispers.

Trees and all was so old, too. No animals around or birds.
Path kind of overgrown like nobody used it much ever. Uncle
Fred drove along right fast, he didn't hardly talk to me at all
but just made that old horse hump it.

Pretty soon we struck into some hills, they was awfully
high ones. They was woods on them, too, and sometimes a

brook come running down, but I didn't see no houses and it was always dark like at twilight, wherever you looked.

Lastly we got to the farmhouse – a little place, old frame house and barn in a clear space with trees all around kind of gloomy-like. Aunt Lucy come out to meet us, she was a nice sort of little middle-aged lady who hugged me and took my stuff in back.

But all this don't hold with what I'm supposed to write down here. It don't matter that all this last year I was living in the house here with them, eating off the stuff Uncle Fred farmed without ever going into town. No other farms around here for almost four mile and no school – so evenings Aunt Lucy would help me with my reading. I never played much.

At first I was scared of going into the woods on account of what Grandma had told me. Besides, I could tell as Aunt Lucy and Uncle Fred was scared of something from the way they locked the doors at night and never went into the woods after dark, even in summer.

But after a while, I got used to the idea of living in the woods and they didn't seem so scarey. I did chores for Uncle Fred, of course, but sometimes in afternoons when he was busy, I'd go off by myself. Particular by the time it was fall.

And that's how I heard one of the things. It was early October, I was in the glen right by the big boulder. Then the noise started. I got behind that rock fast.

You see, like I say, there isn't any animals in the woods. Nor people. Excep perhaps old Cap Pritchett the mailman who only comes through on Thursday afternoons.

So when I heard a sound that wasn't Uncle Fred or Aunt Lucy calling to me, I knew I better hide.

About that sound. It was far-away at first, kind of a dropping noise. Sounded like the blood falling in little spurts on the bottom of the bucket when Uncle Fred hung up a butchered hog.

I looked around but I couldn't make out nothing, and I couldn't figure out the direction the noise was from either. The noise sort of stopped for a minute and they was only twilight and trees, still as death. Then the noise started again, nearer and louder.

Sounded like a lot of people running or walking all at once, moving this way. Twigs busting under feet and scrabbling in the bushes all mixed up in the noise. I scrunched down behind that boulder and kep real quiet.

I can tell that whatever makes the noise, it's real close now, right in the glen. I want to look up but dassn't because the sound is so loud and *mean*. And also there is an awful smell like something that was dead and buried being uncovered again in the sun.

All at once the noise stops again and I can tell that whatever makes it is real close by. For a minute the woods are creepy-still. Then comes the sound.

It's a voice and it's not a voice. That is, it doesn't *sound* like a voice but more like a buzzing or croaking, deep and droning. But it *has* to be a voice because it is saying words.

Not words I could understand, but words. Words that made me keep my head down, half afraid I might be seen and half afraid I might see something. I stayed there sweating and shaking. The smell was making me pretty sick, but that awful, deep droning voice was worse. Saying over and over something like:

'E uh shub nigger ath ngaa ryla neb shoggoth.'

I can't hope to spell it out the way it sounded, but I heard it enough times to remember. I was still listening when the smell got awful thick and I guess I must have fainted because when I woke up the voice was gone and it was getting quite dark.

I ran all the way home that night, but not before I saw where the thing had stood when it talked – and it *was* a thing.

No human being can leave tracks in the mud like goat's hoofs all green with slime that smell awful – not four or eight, but a couple *hundred*!

I didn't tell Aunt Lucy or Uncle Fred. But that night when I went to bed I had terrible dreams. I thought I was back in the glen, only this time I could see the thing. It was real tall and all inky-black, without any particular shape except a lot of black ropes with ends like hoofs on it. I mean, it had a shape but it kep changing – all bulgy and squirming into different sizes. They was a lot of mouths all over the thing like puckered up leaves on branches.

That's as close as I can come. The mouths was like leaves and the whole thing was like a tree in the wind, a black tree with lots of branches trailing the ground, and a whole lot of roots ending in hoofs. And that green slime dribbling out of the mouths and down the legs was like sap!

Next day I remembered to look in a book Aunt Lucy had downstairs. It was called mythology. This book told about some people who lived over in England and France in the old days and was called Druids. They worshipped trees and thought they was alive. Maybe this thing was like what they worshipped – called a nature-spirit.

But these Druids lived across the ocean, so how could it be? I did a lot of thinking about it the next couple days, and you can bet I didn't go out to play in those woods again.

At last I figgered it out something like this.

Maybe those Druids got chased out of the forests over in England and France and some of them was smart enough to build boats and come across the ocean like old Leaf Erikson is supposed to have. Then they could maybe settle in the woods back here and frighten away the Indians with their magic spells.

They would know how to hide themselves away in the swamps and go right on with their heathen worshipping and call up these spirits out of the ground or wherever they come from.

Indians use to believe that white gods come from out of the sea a long time ago. What if that was just another way of telling how the Druids got here? Some real civilized Indians down in Mexico or South America – Aztecs or Inkas, I guess – said a white god come over in a boat and taught them all kinds of magic. Couldn't he of been a Druid?

That would explain Grandma's stories about *them ones*, too.

Those Druids hiding in the swamps would be the ones who did the drumming and pounding and lit the fires on the hills. And they would be calling up *them ones*, the tree spirits or whatever, out of the earth. Then they would make sacrefices. Those Druids always made sacrefices with blood, just like the old witches. And didn't Grandma tell about people who lived too near the hills disappearing and never being found again?

We lived in a spot just exactly like that.

And it was getting close to Hallowe'en. That was the big time, Grandma always said.

I began to wonder – how soon now?

Got so scared I didn't go out of the house. Aunt Lucy made me take a tonic, said I looked peaked. Guess I did. All I know is one afternoon when I heard a buggy coming through the woods I ran and hid under the bed.

But it was only Cap Pritchett with the mail. Uncle Fred got it and come in all excited with a letter.

Cousin Osborne was coming to stay with us. He was kin to Aunt Lucy and he had a vacation and he wanted to stay a week. He'd get here on the same train I did – the only train they was passing through these parts – on noon, October 25th.

For the next few days we was all so excited that I forgot all my crazy notions for a spell. Uncle Fred fixed up the back room for Cousin Osborne to sleep in and I helped him with the carpenter parts of the job.

Days got shorter right along, and the nights was all cold with big winds. It was pretty brisk the morning of the 25th and Uncle Fred bundled up warm to drive through the woods. He meant to fetch Cousin Osborne at noon, and it was seven miles to the station. He wouldn't take me, and I didn't beg. Them woods was too full of creaking and rustling sounds from the wind – sounds that might be something else, too.

Well, he left, and Aunt Lucy and I stayed in the house.

She was putting up preserves now – plums – for over the
winter season. I washed out jars from the well.

Seems like I should have told about them having two
wells. A new one with a big shiny pump, close to the house.
Then an old stone one out by the barn, with the pump gone.
It never had been any good, Uncle Fred said, it was there
when they bought the place. Water was all slimy. Something
funny about it, because even without a pump, sometimes it
seemed to back up. Uncle Fred couldn't figure it out, but
some mornings water would be running out over the sides –
green, slimy water that smelled terrible.

We kep away from it and I was by the new well, till along
about noon when it started in to cloud up. Aunt Lucy fixed
lunch, and it started to rain hard with thunder rolling in off
the big hills in the west.

Seemed to me Uncle Fred and Cousin Osborne was going
to have troubles getting home in the storm, but Aunt Lucy
didn't fret about it – just made me help her put up the stock.

Come five o'clock, getting dark, and still no Uncle Fred.
Then we began to worry. Maybe the train was late, or
something happened to the horse or buggy.

Six o'clock and still no Uncle Fred. The rain stopped, but
you could still hear the thunder sort of growling off in the
hills, and the wet branches kep dripping down in the woods,
making a sound like women laughing.

Maybe the road was too bad for them to get through.
Buggy might bog down in the mud. Perhaps they decided to
stay in the deepo over night.

Seven o'clock and it was pitch dark outside. No rain sounds
any more. Aunt Lucy was awful worried. She said for us to
go out and post a lantern on the fence rail by the road.

We went down the path to the fence. It was dark and the
wind had died down. Everything was still, like in the deep
part of the woods. I felt kind of scared just walking down the
path with Aunt Lucy – like something was out there in the
quiet dark, someplace, waiting to grab me.

We lit the lantern and stood there looking down the dark

road and, 'What's that?' said Aunt Lucy, real sharp. I listened and heard a drumming sound far away.

'Horse and buggy,' I said. Aunt Lucy perked up.

'You're right,' she says, all at once. And it is, because we see it. The horse is running fast and the buggy lurches behind it, crazy-like. It don't even take a second look to see something has happened, because the buggy don't stop by the gate but keeps going to the barn with Aunt Lucy and me running through the mud after the horse. The horse is all full of lather and foam, and when it stops it can't stand still. Aunt Lucy and I wait for Uncle Fred and Cousin Osborne to step out, but nothing happens. We look inside.

There isn't anybody in the buggy at all.

Aunt Lucy says, 'Oh!' in a real loud voice and then faints. I had to carry her back to the house and get her into bed.

I waited almost all night by the window, but Uncle Fred and Cousin Osborne never showed up. Never.

The next few days was awful. They was nothing in the buggy for a clue like to what happened, and Aunt Lucy wouldn't let me go along the road into town or even to the station through the woods.

The next morning the horse was dead in the barn, and of course we would of had to walk to the deepo or all those miles to Warren's farm. Aunt Lucy was scared to go and scared to stay and she allowed as how when Cap Pritchett comes by we had best go with him over to town and make a report and then stay there until we found out what happened.

Me, I had my own ideas what happened. Halloween was only a few days away from now, and maybe *them ones* had snatched Uncle Fred and Cousin Osborne for sacrefice. *Them ones* or the Druids. The mythology book said Druids could even raise storms if they wanted to with their spells.

No sense talking to Aunt Lucy, though. She was like out of her head with worry, anyway, just rocking back and forth and mumbling over and over, 'They're gone' and 'Fred always warned me' and 'No use, no use.' I had to get the meals and tend to stock myself. And nights it was hard to sleep, because

I kep listening for drums. I never heard any, though, but still it was better than sleeping and having those dreams.

Dreams about the black thing like a tree, walking through the woods and sort of rooting itself to one particular spot so it could pray with all those mouths – pray down to that old god in the ground below.

I don't know where I got the idea that was how it prayed – by sort of attaching its mouth to the ground. Maybe it was on account of seeing the green slime. Or had I really seen it? I'd never gone back to look. Maybe it was all in my head – the Druid story and about *them ones* and the voice that said 'shoggoth' and all the rest.

But then, where was Cousin Osborne and Uncle Fred? And what scared the horse so it up and died the next day?

Thoughts kep going round and round in my head, chasing each other, but all I knew was we'd be out of here by Halloween night.

Because Halloween was on a Thursday, and Cap Pritchett would come and we could ride to town with him.

Night before I made Aunt Lucy pack and we got all ready, and then I settled down to sleep. There was no noises, and for the first time I felt a little better.

Only the dreams come again. I dreamed a bunch of men come in the night and crawled through the parlour bedroom window where Aunt Lucy slept and got her. They tied her up and took her away, all quiet, in the dark, because they had cat-eyes and didn't need light to see.

The dream scared me so I woke up while it was just breaking into dawn. I went down the hall to Aunt Lucy right away.

She was gone.

The window was wide open like in my dream, and some of the blankets was torn.

Ground was hard outside the window and I didn't see footprints or anything. But she was gone.

I guess I cried then.

It's hard to remember what I did next. Didn't want break-

fast. Went out hollering 'Aunt Lucy' and not expecting any
answer. I walked to the barn and the door was open and the
cows were gone. Saw one or two prints going out the yard
and up the road, but I didn't think it was safe to follow them.

Some time later I went over to the well and then I cried
again because the water was all slimy-green in the new one,
just like the old.

When I saw that I knew I was right. *Them ones* must of
come in the night and they wasn't even trying to hide their
doings any more. Like they was sure of things.

Tonight was Halloween. I had to get out of here. If *them
ones* was watching and waiting, I couldn't depend on Cap
Pritchett showing up this afternoon. I'd have to chance it
down the road and I'd better start walking now, in the
morning, while it was still light enough to make town.

So I rummaged around and found a little money in Uncle
Fred's drawer of the bureau and Cousin Osborne's letter with
the address in Kingsport he wrote it from. That's where I'd
have to go after I told folks in town what happened. I'd have
some kin there.

I wondered if they'd believe me in town when I told them
about the way Uncle Fred had disappeared and Aunt Lucy,
and about *them* stealing the cattle for a sacrefice and about
the green slime in the well where something had stopped to
drink. I wondered if they would know about the drums and
the lights on the hills tonight and if they was going to get up
a party and come back this evening to try and catch *them
ones* and what they meant to call up rumbling out of the
earth. I wondered if they knew what a 'shoggoth' was.

Well, whether they did or not, I couldn't stay and find out
for myself. So I packed up my satchel and got ready to leave.
Must of been around noon and everything was still.

I went to the door and stepped outside, not bothering to
lock it behind me. Why should I with nobody around for
miles?

Then I heard the noise down the road.

Footsteps.

Somebody walking along the road, just around the bend.

I stood still for a minute, waiting to see, waiting to run.

Then he come along.

He was tall and thin, and looked something like Uncle Fred only a lot younger and without a beard, and he was wearing a nice city kind of suit and crush hat. He smiled when he saw me and come marching up like he knowed who I was.

'Hello, Willie,' he said.

I didn't say nothing, I was so confuzed.

'Don't you know me?' he said. 'I'm Cousin Osborne. Your cousin, Frank.' He held out his hand to shake. 'But then I guess you wouldn't remember, would you? Last time I saw you, you were only a baby.'

'But I thought you were suppose to come last week,' I said. 'We expected you on the 25th.'

'Didn't you get my telegram?' he asked. 'I had business.'

I shook my head. 'We never get nothing here unless the mail delivers it on Thursdays. Maybe it's at the station.'

Cousin Osborne grinned. 'You are pretty well off the beaten track at that. Nobody at the station this noon. I was hoping Fred would come along with the buggy so I wouldn't have to walk, but no luck.'

'You walked all the way?' I asked.

'That's right.'

'And you come on the train?'

Cousin Osborne nodded.

'Then where's your suitcase?'

'I left it at the deepo,' he told me. 'Too far to fetch it along. I thought Fred would drive me back there in the buggy to pick it up.' He noticed my luggage for the first time. 'But wait a minute – where are you going with a suitcase, son?'

Well, there was nothing else for me to do but tell him everything that happened.

So I said for him to come into the house and set down and I'd explain.

We went back in and he fixed some coffee and I made a

couple sandwiches and we ate, and then I told him about Uncle Fred going to the deepo and not coming back, and about the horse and then what happened to Aunt Lucy. I left out the part about me in the woods, of course, and I didn't even hint at *them ones*. But I told him I was scared and figgered on walking to town today before dark.

Cousin Osborne he listened to me, nodding and not saying much or interrupting.

'Now you can see why we got to go, right away,' I said. 'Whatever come after them will be coming after us, and I don't want to spend another night here.'

Cousin Osborne stood up. 'You may be right, Willie,' he said. 'But dont let your imagination run away with you, son. Try to separate fact from fancy. Your Aunt Lucy and Uncle have disappeared. That's fact. But this other nonsense about things in the woods coming after you – that's fancy. Reminds me of all the silly talk I heard back home, in Arkham. And for some reason there seems to be more of it around this time of year, at Halloween. Why, when I left – '

'Excuse me, Cousin Osborne,' I said. 'But dont you live in Kingsport?'

'Why to be sure,' he told me. 'But I did live in Arkham once, and I know the people around here. It's no wonder you were so frightened in the woods and got to imagining things. As it is, I admire your bravery. For a 12-year-old you've acted very sensibly.'

'Then lets start walking,' I said. 'Here it is almost 2 and we better get moving if we want to make town before sundown.'

'Not just yet, son,' Cousin Osborne said. 'I wouldn't feel right about leaving without looking around and seeing what we can discover about this mystery. After all, you must understand that we can't just march into town and tell the sheriff some wild nonsense about strange creatures in the woods making off with your Aunt and Uncle. Sensible folks just won't believe such things. They might think I was lying and laugh at me. Why they might even think you had something to do with your Aunt and Uncle's – well, leaving.'

'Please,' I said. 'We got to go, right now.'

He shook his head.

I didn't say any more. I might of told him a lot, about what I dreamed and heard and saw and knew – but I figgered it was no use.

Besides, there was some things I didn't want to say to him now that I had talked to him. I was feeling scared again.

First he said he was from Arkham and then when I asked him he said he was from Kingsport but it sounded like a lie to me.

Then he said something about me being scared in the woods and how could he know that? I never told him *that* part at all.

If you want to know what I really thought, I thought maybe he wasn't really Cousin Osborne at all.

And if he wasn't, then – who was he?

I stood up and walked back into the hall.

'Where are you going, son?' he asked.

'Outside.'

'I'll come with you.'

Sure enough, he was watching me. He wasn't going to let me out of his sight. He came over and took my arm, real friendly – but I couldn't break loose. No, he hung on to me. He knew I meant to run for it.

What could I do? All alone in the house in the woods with this man, with night coming on, Halloween night, and *them ones* there waiting.

We went outside and I noticed it was getting darker already, even in afternoon. Clouds had covered up the sun, and the wind was moving the trees so they stretched out their branches, like they was trying to hold me back. They made a rustling noise, just as if they were whispering things about me, and he sort of looked up at them and listened. Maybe he understood what they were saying. Maybe they were giving him orders.

Then I almost laughed, because he *was* listening to something and now I heard it too.

It was a drumming sound, on the road.

'Cap Pritchett,' I said. 'He's the mailman. Now we can ride to town with him in the buggy.'

'Let me talk to him,' he says. 'About your Aunt and Uncle. No sense in alarming him, and we don't want any scandal, do we? You just run along inside.'

'But Cousin Osborne,' I said. 'We got to tell the truth.'

'Of course, son. But this is a matter for adults. Now run along. I'll call you.'

He was real polite about it and even smiled, but all the same he dragged me back up the porch and into the house and slammed the door. I stood there in the dark hall and I could hear Cap Pritchett slow down and call out to him, and him going to the buggy and talking, and then all I heard was a lot of mumbling, real low. I peeked out through a crack in the door and saw them. Cap Pritchett was talking to him friendly, all right, and nothing was wrong.

Except that in a minute or so, Cap Pritchett waved and then he grabbed the reins and the buggy started off again!

Then I knew I'd have to do it, no matter what happened. I opened the door and ran out, suitcase and all, down the path and up the road after the buggy. Cousin Osborne he tried to grab me when I went by, but I ducked around him and yelled, 'Wait for me, Cap – I'm coming – take me to town!'

Cap slowed down and stared back, real puzzled. 'Willie!' he says. 'Why I thought you was gone. He said you went away with Fred and Lucy – '

'Pay no attention,' I said. 'He didn't want me to go. Take me to town. I'll tell you what really happened. Please, Cap, you got to take me.'

'Sure I'll take you, Willie. Hop right up here.'

I hopped.

Cousin Osborne came right up to the buggy. 'Here, now,' he said, real sharp. 'You can't leave like this. I forbid it. You're in my custody.'

'Don't listen to him,' I yelled. 'Take me, Cap please!!'

'Very well,' said Cousin Osborne. 'If you insist on being unreasonable. We'll all go. I cannot permit you to leave alone.'

He smiled at Cap 'You can see the boy is unstrung,' he said. 'And I trust you will not be disturbed by his imaginings. Living out here like this – well, you understand – he's not quite himself. I'll explain everything on the way to town.'

He sort of shrugged at Cap and made signs of tapping his head. Then he smiled again and made to climb up next to us in the buggy seat.

But Cap didn't smile back. 'No, you don't,' he said. 'This boy Willie is a good boy. I know him. I don't know you. Looks as if you done enough explaining already, Mister, when you said Willie had gone away.'

'But I merely wanted to avoid talk – you see, I've been called in to doctor the boy – he's mentally unstable – '

'Stables be damned!' Cap spit out some tobacco juice right at Cousin Osborne's feet. 'We're going.'

Cousin Osborne stopped smiling. 'Then I insist you take me with you,' he said. And he tried to climb into the buggy.

Cap reached into his jacket and when he pulled his hand out again he had a big pistol in it.

'Git down!' he yelled. 'Mister, you're talking to the United States Mail and you don't tell the Government nothing, understand? Now git down before I mess your brains all over this road.'

Cousin Osborne scowled, but he got away from the buggy, fast.

He looked at me and shrugged. 'You're making a big mistake, Willie,' he said.

I didn't even look at him. Cap said, 'Gee up,' and we went off down the road. The buggy wheels turned faster and faster and pretty soon the farmhouse was out of sight and Cap put his pistol away, and patted me on the shoulder.

'Stop that trembling, Willie,' he said. 'You're safe now.

Nothing to worry about. Be in town little over an hour or so.
Now you just set back and tell old Cap all about it.'

So I told him. It took a long time. We kep going though the
woods, and before I knew it, it was almost dark. The sun
sneaked down and hid behind the hills. The dark began to
creep out of the woods on each side of the road, and the trees
started to rustle, whispering to the big shadows that followed
us.

The horse was clipping and clopping along, and pretty soon
they were other noises from far away. Might have been
thunder and might have been something else. But it was
getting night-time for sure, and it was the night of
Halloween.

The road cut off through the hills now, and you could
hardly see where the next turn would take you. Besides, it
was getting dark awful fast.

'Guess we're in for a spell of rain,' Cap said, looking up.
'That's thunder, I reckon.'

'Drums,' I said.

'Drums?'

'At night in the hills you can hear them,' I told him. 'I
heard them all this month. It's *them ones*, getting ready for
the Sabbath.'

'Sabbath?' Cap looked at me. 'Where you hear tell about a
Sabbath?'

Then I told him some more about what had happened. I
told him all the rest. He didn't say anything, and before long
he couldn't of answered me anyway, because the thunder
was all around us, and the rain was lashing down on the
buggy, on the road, everywhere. It was pitch-black outside
now, and the only time we could see was when lightning
flashed. I had to yell to make him hear me – yell about the
things that caught Uncle Fred and come for Aunt Lucy, the
things that took our cattle and then sent Cousin Osborne
back to fetch me. I hollered out about what I heard in the
wood, too.

In the lightning flashes I could see Cap's face. He wasn't

smiling or scowling – he just looked like he believed me. And I noticed he had his pistol out again and was holding the reins with one hand even though we were racing along. The horse was so scared he didn't need the whip to keep him running.

The old buggy was lurching and bouncing, and the rain was whistling down in the wind and it was all like an awful dream but it was real. It was real when I hollered out to Cap Pritchett about that time in the woods.

'Shoggoth,' I yelled. 'What's a shoggoth?'

Cap grabbed my arm, and then the lightning come and I could see his face, with his mouth open. But he wasn't looking at me. He was looking at the road and what was ahead of us.

The trees sort of come together, hanging over the next turn, and in the black it looked as if they were alive – moving and bending and twisting to block our way. Lightning flickered up again and I could see them plain, and also something else.

Something black in the road, something that wasn't a tree. Something big and black, just squatting there, waiting, with ropy arms squirming and reaching.

'Shoggoth!' Cap yelled. But I could scarcely hear him because the thunder was roaring and now the horse let out a scream and I felt the buggy jerk to one side and the horse reared up and we was almost into the black stuff. I could smell an awful smell, and Cap was pointing his pistol and it went off with a bang that was almost as loud as the thunder and almost as loud as the sound we made when we hit the black thing.

Then everything happened at once. The thunder, the horse falling, the shot, and us hitting as the buggy went over. Cap must of had the reins wrapped around his arm, because when the horse and the buggy turned over, he went right over the dashboard head first and down into the squirming mess that was the horse – and the black thing that grabbed it. I felt myself falling in the dark, then landing in the mud and gravel of the road.

There was thunder and screaming and another sound which I had heard once before in the woods – a droning sound like a voice.

That's why I never looked back. That's why I didn't even think about being hurt when I landed – just got up and started to run down the road, fast as I could, run down the road in the storm and the dark with the trees squirming and shaking their heads while they pointed at me with their branches and laughed.

Over the thunder I heard the horse scream and I heard Cap scream, too, but I still didn't look back. The lightning winked on and off, and I ran through the trees now because the road was nothing but mud that dragged me down and sucked at my legs. After a while I began to scream, too, but I couldn't even hear myself for thunder. And more than thunder. I heard drums.

All at once I busted clear of the woods and got to the hills. I ran up, and the drumming got louder, and pretty soon I could see regular, not just when they was lightning. Because they was fires burning on the hill, and the booming of the drums come from there.

I got lost in the noise; the wind shrieking and the trees laughing and the drums pounding. But I stopped in time. I stopped when I saw the fires plain; red and green fires burning in all that rain.

I saw a big white stone in the centre of a cleared-off space on top of the hill. The red and green fires was around and behind it, so everything stood out clear against the flames.

They was men around the alter, men with long grey beards and wrinkled-up faces, men throwing awful-smelling stuff on the fires to make them blaze red and green. And they had knives in their hands and I could hear them howling over the storm. In back, squatting on the ground, more men pounded on drums.

Pretty soon something else come up the hill – two men

driving cattle. I could tell it was our cows they drove, drove them right up to the alter and then the men with the knives cut their throats for a sacrefice.

All this I could see in lightning flashes and in the fire lights, and I sort of scooched down so I couldn't get spotted by anyone.

But pretty soon I couldn't see very good any more, on account of the way they threw stuff on the fire. It set up a real thick black smoke. When this come up, the men began to chant and pray louder.

I couldn't hear words, but the sounds was like what I heard back in the woods. I couldn't see too good, but I knew what was going to happen. Two men who had led the cattle went back down the other side of the hill and when they come up again they had new sacrefices. The smoke kep me from seeing plain, but these was two-legged sacrefices, not four. I might of seen better at that, only now I hid my face when they dragged them up to the white alter and used the knives, and the fire and smoke flared up and the drums boomed and they all chanted and called in a loud voice to something waiting over on the other side of the hill.

The ground began to shake. It was storming, they was thunder and lightning and fire and smoke and chanting and I was scared half out of my wits, but one thing I'll swear to – the ground began to shake. It shook and shivered and they called out to something and in a minute something came.

It came crawling up the hillside to the alter and the sacrefice, and it was the black thing of my dreams – that black ropy, slimy jelly-thing out of the woods. It crawled up and it flowed up on its hoofs and mouths and snaky arms. And the men bowed and stood back and then it got to the alter where they was something squirming on top, squirming and screaming.

The black thing sort of bent over the alter and then I heard droning sounds over the screaming as it come down. I only watched a minute, but while I watched the black thing began to swell and *grow*.

That finished me. I didn't care any more. I had to run. I got up and I run and run and run, screaming at the top of my lungs no matter who heard.

I kep running and I kep screaming for ever, through the woods and the storm, away from that hill and that alter, and then all at once I knew where I was and I was back here at the farmhouse.

Yes, that's what I'd done – run in a circle and come back. But I couldn't go any further, I couldn't stand the night and the storm. So I run inside here. At first after I locked the door I just lay down on the floor, all tuckered out from running and crying.

But in a little while I got up and hunted me some nails and a hammer and some of Uncle Fred's boards that wasn't split up into kindling.

I nailed up the door first and then boarded up all the windows. Every last one of them. Guess I worked for hours, tired as I was. When it was all done, the storm died down and it got quiet. Quiet enough for me to lie down on the couch and go to sleep.

Woke up a couple hours ago. It was daylight. I could see it shining through the cracks. From the way the sun come in, I knew it was afternoon already. I'd slept through the whole morning, and nothing had come.

I figgered now maybe I could let myself out and make town on foot, like I'd planned yesterday.

But I figgered wrong.

Before I got started taking out the nails, I heard him. It was Cousin Osborne, of course. The man who said he was Cousin Osborne, I mean.

He come into the yard, calling 'Willie!' but I didn't answer. Then he tried the door and then the windows. I could hear him pounding and cussing. That was bad.

But then he began mumbling, and that was worse. Because it meant he wasn't out there alone.

I sneaked a look through the crack, but he already went

around to the back of the house so I didn't see him or who was with him.

Guess that's just as well, because if I'm right, I wouldn't want to see.

Hearing's bad enough.

Hearing that deep croaking, and then him talking, and then that croaking again.

Smelling that awful smell, like the green slime from the woods and around the well.

The well – they went over to the well in back. And I heard Cousin Osborne say something about, 'Wait until dark. We can use the well if you find the gate. Look for the gate.'

I know what that means now. The well must be a sort of entrance to the underground place – that's where those Druid men live. And the black thing.

They're out in back now, looking.

I been writing for quite a spell and already the afternoon is going. Peeking through the cracks I can see it's getting dark again.

That's when they'll come for me – when it's dark.

They'll break down the doors or the windows and come and take me. They'll take me down into the well, into the black places where the shoggoths are. There must be a whole world down under the hills, a world where they hide and wait to come out for more sacrefices, more blood. They don't want any humans around, except for sacrefices.

I saw what the black thing did on the alter. I know what's going to happen to me.

Maybe they'll miss the real Cousin Osborne back home and send somebody to find out what become of him. Maybe folks in town will miss Cap Pritchett and go on a search. Maybe they'll come here and find me. But if they don't come soon it will be too late.

That's why I wrote this. It's true, cross my heart, every word of it. And if anyone finds this notebook where I hide it, come and look down the well. The old well, out in back.

Remember what I told about *them ones*. Block up the well

and clean out them swamps. No sense looking for me – if I'm not here.

I wish I wasn't so scared. I'm not even scared so much for myself, but for other folks. The ones who might come after and live here and have the same thing happen – or worse.

You just got to believe me. Go to the woods if you don't. Go to the hill. The hill where they had the sacrefice. Maybe the stains are gone and the rain washed the footprints away. Maybe they got rid of the traces of the fire. But the alter stone must be there. And if it is, you'll know the truth. There should be some big round spots on that stone. Round spots about two feet wide.

I didn't tell about that. At the last, I did look back. I looked back at the big black thing that was a shoggoth. I looked back as it kep swelling and growing. I guess I told about how it could change shape, and how big it got. But you can't hardly imagine how big or what shape and I still dassn't tell.

All I say is look. Look and you'll see what's hiding under the earth in these hills, waiting to creep out and feast and kill some more.

Wait. They're coming now. Getting twilight and I can hear footsteps. And other sounds. Voices. And other sounds. They're banging on the door. And sure enough – they must have a tree or a plank to use for battering it down. The whole place is shaking. I can hear Cousin Osborne yelling, and that droning. The smell is awful, I'm getting sick, and in a minute –

Look at the alter. Then you'll understand what I'm trying to tell. Look at the big round marks, two feet wide, on each side. That's where the big black thing grabbed hold.

Look for the marks and you'll know what I saw, what I'm afraid of, what's to grab you unless you shut it up forever under the earth.

Black marks two feet wide, but they aren't just marks.

What they really are is *fingerprints!*

The door is busting o – –

Cold Print

RAMSEY CAMPBELL

'. . . for even the minions of Cthulhu dare not speak of Y'golonac; yet the time will come when Y'golonac strides forth from the loneliness of aeons to walk once more among men . . .'

Revelations of Glaaki, vol. 12

Sam Strutt licked his fingers and wiped them on his handkerchief; his fingertips were grey with snow from the pole on the bus platform. Then he coaxed his book out of the polythene bag on the seat beside him, withdrew the bus-ticket from between the pages, held it against the cover to protect the latter from his fingers, and began to read. As often happened the conductor assumed that the ticket authorized Strutt's present journey; Strutt did not enlighten him. Outside, the snow whirled down the side streets and slipped beneath the wheels of cautious cars.

The slush splashed into his boots as he stepped down outside Brichester Central and, snuggling the bag beneath his coat for extra safety, pushed his way towards the bookstall, treading on the settling snowflakes. The glass panels of the stall were not quite closed; snow had filtered through and dulled the glossy paperbacks. 'Look at that!' Strutt complained to a young man who stood next to him and anxiously surveyed the crowd, drawing his neck down inside his collar like a tortoise. 'Isn't that disgusting? These people just don't care!' The young man, still searching the wet faces, agreed abstractedly. Strutt strode to the other counter of the stall, where the assistant was handing out newspapers. 'I

say!' called Strutt. The assistant, sorting change for a customer, gestured him to wait. Over the paperbacks, through
the steaming glass, Strutt watched the young man rush
forward and embrace a girl, then gently dry her face with a
handkerchief. Strutt glanced at the newspaper held by the
man awaiting change. *Brutal Murder in Ruined Church*, he
read; the previous night a body had been found inside the
roofless walls of a church in Lower Brichester; when the
snow had been cleared from this marble image, frightful
mutilations had been revealed covering the corpse, oval
mutilations which resembled – The man took the paper and
his change away into the station. The assistant turned to
Strutt with a smile: 'Sorry to keep you waiting.' 'Yes,' said
Strutt. 'Do you realize those books are getting snowed on?
People may want to buy them, you know.' 'Do *you*?' the
assistant replied. Strutt tightened his lips and turned back
into the snow-filled gusts. Behind him he heard the ring of
glass pane meeting pane.

Good Books on The Highway provided shelter; he closed
out the lashing sleet and stood taking stock. On the shelves
the current titles showed their faces while the others turned
their backs. Girls were giggling over comic Christmas cards;
an unshaven man was swept in on a flake-edged blast and
halted, staring round uneasily. Strutt clucked his tongue;
tramps shouldn't be allowed in bookshops to soil the books.
Glancing sideways to observe whether the man would bend
back the covers or break the spines, Strutt moved among the
shelves, but could not find what he sought. Chatting with
the cashier, however, was an assistant who had praised *Last
Exit to Brooklyn* to him when he had bought it last week,
and had listened patiently to a list of Strutt's recent reading,
though he had not seemed to recognize the titles. Strutt
approached him and inquired: 'Hello – any more exciting
books this week?'

The man faced him, puzzled. 'Any more – ?'

'You know, books like this?' Strutt held up his polythene
bag to show the grey Ultimate Press cover of *The Caning-
Master* by Hector Q.

'Ah, no. I don't think we have.' He tapped his lip. 'Except –
Jean Genet?'

'Who? Oh, you mean *Jennet*. No, thanks, he's dull as
ditchwater.'

'Well, I'm sorry, sir, I'm afraid I can't help you.'

'Oh.' Strutt felt rebuffed. The man seemed not to recognize
him, or perhaps he was pretending. Strutt had met his kind
before and had them mutely patronize his reading. He
scanned the shelves again, but no cover caught his eye. At
the door he furtively unbuttoned his shirt to protect his book
still further, and a hand fell on his arm. Lined with grime,
the hand slid down to his and touched his bag. Strutt shook
it off angrily and confronted the tramp.

'Wait a minute!' the man hissed. 'Are you after more books
like that? I know where we can get some.'

This approach offended Strutt's self-righteous sense of
reading books which had no right to be suppressed. He
snatched the bag out of the fingers closing on it. 'So you like
them too, do you?'

'Oh, yes, I've got lots.'

Strutt sprang his trap. 'Such as?'

'Oh, *Adam and Evan*, *Take Me How You Like*, all the
Harrison adventures, you know, there's lots.'

Strutt grudgingly admitted that the man's offer seemed
genuine. The assistant at the cash-desk was eyeing them;
Strutt stared back. 'All right,' he said. 'Where's this place
you're talking about?'

The other took his arm and pulled him eagerly into the
slanting snow. Clutching shut their collars, pedestrians were
slipping between the cars as they waited for a skidded bus
ahead to be removed; flakes were crushed into the corners of
the windscreens by the wipers. The man dragged Strutt amid
the horns which brayed and honked, then between two store
windows from which girls watched smugly as they dressed
headless figures, and down an alley. Strutt recognized the
area as one which he had vainly combed for back-street
bookshops; disappointing alcoves of men's magazines, occa-

sional hot pungent breaths from kitchens, cars fitted with
caps of snow, loud pubs warm against the weather. Strutt's
guide dodged into the doorway of a public bar to shake his
coat; the white glaze cracked and fell from him. Strutt joined
the man and adjusted the book in its bag, snuggled beneath
his shirt. He stamped the crust loose from his boots, stopping
when the other followed suit; he did not wish to be connected
with the man even by such a trivial action. He looked with
distaste at his companion, at his swollen nose through which
he was now snorting back snot, at the stubble shifting on the
cheeks as they inflated and the man blew on his trembling
hands. Strutt had a horror of touching anyone who was not
fastidious. Beyond the doorway flakes were already obscur-
ing their footprints, and the man said: 'I get terrible thirsty
walking fast like this.'

'So that's the game, is it?' But the bookshop lay ahead.
Strutt led the way into the bar and bought two pints from a
colossal barmaid, her bosom bristling with ruffles, who
billowed back and forth with glasses and worked the pumps
with gusto. Old men sucked at pipes in vague alcoves, a radio
blared marches, men clutching tankards aimed with jovial
inaccuracy at dart-board or spittoon. Strutt flapped his
overcoat and hung it next to him; the other retained his and
stared into his beer. Determined not to talk, Strutt surveyed
the murky mirrors which reflected gesticulating parties
around littered tables not directly visible. But he was gradually surprised by the taciturnity of his table-mate; surely
these people (he thought) were remarkably loquacious, in
fact virtually impossible to silence? This was intolerable;
sitting idly in an airless backstreet bar when he could be on
the move or reading – something must be done. He gulped
down his beer and thumped the glass upon its mat. The other
started. Then, visibly abashed, he began to sip, seeming
oddly nervous. At last it was obvious that he was dawdling
over the froth, and he set down his glass and stared at it. 'It
looks as if it's time to go,' said Strutt.

The man looked up; fear widened his eyes. 'Christ, I'm

wet,' he muttered. 'I'll take you again when the snow goes off.'

'That's the game, is it?' Strutt shouted. In the mirrors, eyes sought him. 'You don't get that drink out of me for nothing! I haven't come this far – !!'

The man swung round and back, trapped. 'All right, all right, only maybe I won't find it in this weather.'

Strutt found this remark too inane to comment. He rose and, buttoning his coat, strode into the arcs of snow, glaring behind to ensure he was followed.

The last few shop-fronts, behind them pyramids of tins marked with misspelt placards, were cast out by lines of furtively curtained windows set in unrelieved vistas of red brick; behind the panes Christmas decorations hung like wreaths. Across the road, framed in a bedroom window, a middle-aged woman drew the curtains and hid the teenage boy at her shoulder. 'Hel-*lo*, there they go,' Strutt did not say; he felt he could control the figure ahead without speaking to him, and indeed had no desire to speak to the man as he halted trembling, no doubt from the cold, and hurried onward as Strutt, an inch taller than his five-and-a-half feet and better built, loomed behind him. For an instant, as a body of snow drove towards him down the street, flakes over-exposing the landscape and cutting his cheeks like transitory razors of ice, Strutt yearned to speak, to tell of nights when he lay awake in his room, hearing the landlady's daughter being beaten by her father in the attic bedroom above, straining to catch muffled sounds through the creak of bed-springs, perhaps from the couple below. But the moment passed, swept away by the snow; the end of the street had opened, split by a traffic-island into two roads thickly draped with snow, one curling away to hide between the houses, the other short, attached to a roundabout. Now Strutt knew where he was. From a bus earlier in the week he had noticed the *Keep Left* sign lying helpless on its back on the traffic island, its face kicked in.

They crossed the roundabout, negotiated the crumbling

lips of ruts full of deceptively glazed pools collecting behind
the bulldozer treads of a redevelopment scheme, and onward
through the whirling white to a patch of waste ground where
a lone fireplace drank the snow. Strutt's guide scuttled into
an alley and Strutt followed, intent on keeping close to the
other as he knocked powdered snow from dustbin lids and
flinched from back-yard doors at which dogs clawed and
snarled. The man dodged left, then right, between the close
labyrinthine walls, among houses whose cruel edges of
jagged window-panes and thrusting askew doors even the
snow, kinder to buildings than to their occupants, could not
soften. A last turning, and the man slithered on to a
pavement beside the remnants of a store, its front gaping
emptily to frame wine-bottles abandoned beneath a *Hein 57
Variet* poster. A dollop of snow fell from the awning's
skeleton to be swallowed by the drift below. The man shook,
but as Strutt confronted him, pointed fearfully to the opposite
pavements: 'That's it. I've brought you here.'

The tracks of slush splashed up Strutt's trouser legs as he
ran across, checking mentally that while the man had tried
to disorient him he had deducted which main road lay some
five hundred yards away, then read the inscription over the
shop: *American Books Bought and Sold.* He touched a railing
which protected an opaque window below street level, wet
rust gritting beneath his nails, and surveyed the display in
the window facing him: *History of the Rod* – a book he had
found monotonous – thrusting out its shoulders among
science-fiction novels by Aldiss, Tubb, and Harrison, which
hid shame-facedly behind lurid covers; *Le Sadisme au
Cinéma*; Robbe-Grillet's *Voyeur* looking lost; *The Naked
Lunch* – nothing worth his journey there, Strutt thought.
'All right, it's about time we went in,' he urged the man
inside, and with a glance up the eroded red brick at the first-
floor window, the back of a dressing-table mirror shoved
against it to replace one pane, entered also. The other had
halted again, and for an unpleasant second Strutt's fingers

brushed the man's musty overcoat. 'Come on, where's the books?' he demanded, shoving past into the shop.

The yellow daylight was made murkier by the window display and the pin-up magazines hanging on the inside of the glass-panelled door; dust hung lazily in the stray beams. Strutt stooped to read the covers of paperbacks stuffed into cardboard boxes on one table, but the boxes contained only Westerns, fantasies and American erotica, selling at half price. Grimacing at the books which stretched wide their corners like flowering petals, Strutt bypassed the hardcovers and squinted behind the counter, slightly preoccupied; as he had closed the door beneath its tongueless bell, he had imagined he had heard a cry somewhere near, quickly cut off. No doubt round here you hear that sort of thing all the time, he thought, and turned on the other: 'Well, I don't see what I came for. Doesn't anybody work in this place?'

Wide-eyed, the man gazed past Strutt's shoulder; Strutt looked back and saw the frosted-glass panel of a door, one corner of the glass repaired with cardboard, black against a dim yellow light which filtered through the panel. The bookseller's office, presumably – had he heard Strutt's remark? Strutt confronted the door, ready to face impertinence. Then the man pushed by him, searching distractedly behind the counter, fumbling open a glass-fronted bookcase full of volumes in brown paper jackets and finally extracting a parcel in grey paper from its hiding-place in one corner of a shelf. He thrust it at Strutt, muttering 'This is one, this is one,' and watched, the skin beneath his eyes twitching, as Strutt tore off the paper.

The Secret Life of Wackford Squeers – 'Ah, that's fine,' Strutt approved, forgetting himself momentarily, and reached for his wallet; but greasy fingers clawed at his wrist. 'Pay next time,' the man pleaded. Strutt hesitated; could he get away with the book without paying? At that moment, a shadow rippled across the frosted glass: a headless man dragging something heavy. Decapitated by the frosted glass and by his hunched position, Strutt decided, then realized that the shopkeeper must be in contact with Ultimate Press; he must not prejudice this contact by stealing a book. He knocked away the frantic fingers and counted out two pounds; but the other backed away, stretching out his fingers in stark fear, and crouched against the office door, from whose pane the silhouette had disappeared, before flinching almost into Strutt's arms. Strutt pushed him back and laid the notes in the space left on the shelf by *Wackford Squeers*, then turned on him: 'Don't you intend to wrap it up? No, on second thoughts I'll do it myself.'

The roller on the counter rumbled forth a streamer of brown paper; Strutt sought an undiscoloured stretch. As he parcelled the book, disentangling his feet from the rejected coil, something crashed to the floor. The other had retreated towards the street door until one dangling cuff-button had hooked the corner of a carton full of paperbacks; he froze above the scattered books, mouth and hands gaping wide, one foot atop an open novel like a broken moth, and around him motes floated into beams of light mottled by the sifting snow. Somewhere a lock clicked. Strutt breathed hard, taped the package and circling the man in distaste, opened the door. The cold attacked his legs. He began to mount the steps and the other flurried in pursuit. The man's foot was on the doorstep when a heavy tread approached across the boards. The man spun about and below Strutt the door slammed. Strutt waited; then it occurred to him that he could hurry and shake off his guide. He reached the street and a powdered breeze pecked at his cheeks, cleaning away the stale dust of the shop. He turned away his face and kicking the rind of snow from the headline of a sodden newspaper, made for the main road which he knew to pass close by.

Strutt woke shivering. The neon sign outside the window of his flat, a cliché but relentless as toothache, was garishly defined against the night every five seconds, and by this and the shafts of cold Strutt knew that it was early morning. He closed his eyes again, but though his lids were hot and heavy

his mind would not be lulled. Beyond the limits of his
memory lurked the dream which had awoken him; he moved
uneasily. For some reason he thought of a passage from the
previous evening's reading: 'As Adam reached the door he
felt Evan's hand grip his, twisting his arm behind his back,
forcing him to the floor – ' His eyes opened and sought the
bookcase as if for reassurance; yes, there was the book,
secure within its covers, carefully aligned with its fellows.
He recalled returning home one evening to find *Miss Whippe,
Old-Style Governess* thrust inside *Prefects and Fags*, strad-
dled by *Prefects and Fags*; the landlady had explained that
she must have replaced them wrongly after dusting, but
Strutt knew that she had damaged them vindictively. He
had bought a case that locked, and when she asked him for
the key had replied: 'Thanks, I think I can do them justice.'
You couldn't make friends nowadays. He closed his eyes
again; the room and bookcase, created in five seconds by the
neon and destroyed with equal regularity, filled him with
their emptiness, reminding him that weeks lay ahead before
the beginning of next term, when he would confront the first
class of the morning and add 'You know me by now' to his
usual introduction 'You play fair with me and I'll play fair
with you,' a warning which some boy would be sure to test,
and Strutt would have him; he saw the expanse of white
gym-short seat stretched tight down on which he would bring
a gym-shoe with satisfying force – Strutt relaxed; soothed by
an overwhelming echo of the pounding feet on the wooden
gymnasium floor, the fevered shaking of the wall-bars as the
boys swarmed ceilingward and he stared up from below, he
slept.

Panting, he drove himself through his morning exercises,
then tossed off the fruit juice which was always his first call
on the tray brought up by the landlady's daughter. Viciously
he banged the glass back on the tray; the glass splintered
(he'd say it was an accident; he paid enough rent to cover it,
he might as well get a little satisfaction for his money). 'Bet

you have a fab Christmas,' the girl had said, surveying the room. He'd made to grab her round the waist and curb her pert femininity – but she'd already gone, her skirt's pleats whirling, leaving his stomach hotly knotted in anticipation.

Later he trudged to the supermarket. From several front gardens came the teeth-grinding scrape of spades clearing snow; these faded and were answered by the crushed squeak of snow engulfing boots. When he emerged from the supermarket clutching an armful of cans, a snowball whipped by his face to thud against the window, a translucent beard spreading down the pane like that fluid from the noses of those boys who felt Strutt's wrath most often, for he was determined to beat this ugliness, this revoltingness out of them. Strutt glared about him for the marksman – a seven-year-old, boarding his tricycle for a quick retreat; Strutt moved involuntarily as if to pull the boy across his knee. But the street was not deserted; even now the child's mother, in slacks and curlers peeking from beneath a headscarf, was slapping her son's hand: 'I've told you, *don't* do that. – Sorry,' she called to Strutt. 'Yes, I'm sure,' he snarled, and tramped back to his flat. His heart pumped uncontrollably. He wished fervently that he could talk to someone as he had talked to the bookseller on the edge of Goatswood who had shared his urges; when the man had died earlier that year Strutt had felt abandoned in a tacitly conspiring, hostile world. Perhaps the new shop's owner might prove similarly sympathetic? Strutt hoped that the man who had conducted him there yesterday would not be in attendance, but if he were, surely he could be got rid of – a bookseller dealing with Ultimate Press must be a man after Strutt's own heart, who would be as opposed as he to that other's presence while they were talking frankly. As well as this discussion, Strutt needed books to read over Christmas, and *Squeers* would not last him long; the shop would scarcely be closed on Christmas Eve. Thus reassured, he unloaded the cans on the kitchen table and ran downstairs.

Strutt stepped from the bus into silence; the engine's throb

was quickly muffled among the laden houses. The piled snow
waited for some sound. He splashed through the tracks of
cars to the pavement, its dull coat depressed by countless
overlapping footprints. The road twisted slyly; as soon as the
main road was out of sight the side street revealed its real
character. The snow laid over the house-fronts became
threadbare; rusty protrusions poked through. One or two
windows showed Christmas trees, their ageing needles falling out, their branches tipped with luridly sputtering lights.
Strutt, however, had no eye for this but kept his gaze on the
pavement, seeking to avoid stains circled by dogs' pawmarks.
Once he met the gaze of an old woman staring down at a
point below her window which was perhaps the extent of her
outside world. Momentarily chilled, he hurried on, pursued
by a woman who, on the evidence within her pram, had
given birth to a litter of newspapers, and halted before the
shop.

Though the orange sky could scarcely have illuminated
the interior, no electric gleam was visible through the
magazines, and the torn notice hanging behind the grime
might read CLOSED. Slowly Strutt descended the steps. The
pram squealed by, the latest flakes spreading darkly across
the newspapers. Strutt stared out its inquisitive proprietor,
turned and almost fell into sudden darkness. The door had
opened and a figure blocked the doorway.

'You're not shut, surely?' Strutt's tongue tangled.

'Perhaps not. Can I help you?'

'I was here yesterday. Ultimate Press book,' Strutt replied
to the face level with his own and uncomfortably close.

'Of course you were, yes, I recall.' The other swayed
incessantly like an athlete limbering up, and his voice
wavered constantly from bass to falsetto, dismaying Strutt.
'Well, come in before the snow gets to you,' the other said
and slammed the door behind them, evoking a note from the
ghost of the bell's tongue.

The bookseller – this was he, Strutt presumed – loomed
behind him, a head taller; down in the half-light, among the

vague vindictive corners of the tables, Strutt felt an obscure compulsion to assert himself, somehow, and remarked: 'I hope you found the money for the book. Your man didn't seem to want me to pay. Some people would have taken him at his word.'

'He's not with us today.' The bookseller switched on the light inside his office. As his lined pouched face was lit up it seemed to grow; the eyes were sunk in sagging stars of wrinkles; the cheeks and forehead bulged from furrows; the head floated like a half-inflated balloon above the stuffed tweed suit. Beneath the unshaded bulb the walls pressed close, surrounding a battered desk from which overflowed fingerprinted copies of *The Bookseller* thrust aside by a black typewriter clogged with dirt, beside which lay a stub of sealing-wax and an open box of matches. Two chairs faced each other across the desk, and behind it was a closed door. Strutt seated himself before the desk, brushing dust to the floor. The bookseller paced round him and suddenly, as if struck by the question, demanded: 'Tell me, why d'you read these books?'

This was a question often aimed at Strutt by the English master in the staffroom until he had ceased to read his novels in the breaks. Its sudden reappearance caught him off guard, and he could only call on his old riposte: 'How d'you mean, why? Why not?'

'I wasn't being critical,' the other hurried on, moving restlessly around the desk, 'I'm genuinely interested. I was going to make the point that don't you want what you read about to happen, in a sense?'

'Well, maybe.' Strutt was suspicious of the trend of this discussion, and wished that he could dominate; his words seemed to plunge into the snow-cloaked silence inside the dusty walls to vanish immediately, leaving no impression.

'I mean this: when you read a book don't you make it happen before you, in your mind? Particularly if you consciously attempt to visualize, but that's not essential. You might cast the book away from you, of course. I knew a

bookseller who worked on this theory; you don't get much
time to be yourself in this sort of area, but when he could he
worked on it, though he never quite formulated – Wait a
minute, I'll show you something.'

He leapt away from the desk and into the shop. Strutt
wondered what was beyond the door behind the desk. He
half-rose but, peering back, saw the bookseller already
returning through the drifting shadows with a volume
extracted from among the Lovecrafts and Derleths.

'This ties in with your Ultimate Press books, really,' the
other said, banging the office door to as he entered. 'They're
publishing a book by Johannes Henricus Pott next year, so
we hear, and that's concerned with forbidden lore as well,
like this one; you'll no doubt be amazed to hear that they
think they may/have to leave some of Pott in the original
Latin. This here should interest you, though: the only copy.
You probably won't know the *Revelations of Glaaki*; it's a
sort of Bible written under supernatural guidance. There
were only eleven volumes – but this is the twelfth, written
by a man at the top of Mercy Hill guided through his dreams.'
His voice grew unsteadier as he continued. 'I don't know how
it got out; I suppose the man's family may have found it in
some attic after his death and thought it worth a few coppers,
who knows? My bookseller – well, he knew of the *Revelations*,
and he realized this was priceless; but he didn't want the
seller to realize he had a find and perhaps take it to the
library or the University, so he took it off his hands as part
of a job lot and said he might use it for scribbling. When he
read it – Well, there was one passage that for testing his
theory looked like a godsend. Look.'

The bookseller circled Strutt again and placed the book in
his lap, his arms resting on Strutt's shoulders. Strutt compressed his lips and glanced up at the other's face; but some
strength weakened, refusing to support his disapproval, and
he opened the book. It was an old ledger, its hinges cracking,
its yellowed pages covered by irregular lines of scrawny
handwriting. Throughout the introductory monologue Strutt

had been baffled; now the book was before him, it vaguely
recalled those bundles of duplicated typewritten sheets
which had been passed around the toilets in his adolescence.
'Revelations' suggested the forbidden. Thus intrigued, he
read at random. Up here in Lower Brichester the bare bulb
defined each scrap of flaking paint on the door opposite, and
hands moved on his shoulders, but somewhere down below
he would be pursued through darkness by vast soft footsteps;
when he turned to look a swollen glowing figure was upon
him – What was all this about? A hand gripped his left
shoulder and the right hand turned pages; finally one finger
underlined a phrase:

'Beyond a gulf in the subterranean night a passage leads
to a wall of massive bricks, and beyond the wall rises
Y'golonac to be served by the tattered eyeless figures of the
dark. Long has he slept beyond the wall, and those which
crawl over the bricks scuttle across his body never knowing
it to be Y'golonac; but when his name is spoken or read he
comes forth to be worshipped or to feed and take on the shape
and soul of those he feeds upon. For those who read of evil
and search for its form within their minds call forth evil,
and so may Y'golonac return to walk among men and await that
time when the earth is cleared off and Cthulhu rises from
his tomb among the weeds, Glaaki thrust open the crystal
trapdoor, the brood of Eihort are born into daylight, Shub-
Niggurath strides forth to smash the moon-lens, Byatis
bursts forth from his prison, Daoloth tears away illusion to
expose the reality concealed behind.'

The hands on his shoulders shifted constantly, slackening
and tightening. The voice fluctuated: 'What did you think of
that?'

Strutt thought it was rubbish, but somewhere his courage
had slipped away; he replied unevenly: 'Well, it's – not the
sort of thing you see on sale.'

'You found it interesting?' The voice was deepening; now
it was an overwhelming bass. The other swung round behind
the desk; he seemed taller – his head struck the bulb, setting

shadows peering from the corners and withdrawing, and peering again. 'You're interested?' His expression was intense, as far as it could be made out; for the light moved darkness in the hollows of his face, as if the bone structure were melting visibly.

In the murk in Strutt's mind appeared a suspicion; had he not heard from his dear dead friend the Goatswood bookseller that a black magic cult existed in Brichester, a circle of young men dominated by somebody Franklin or Franklyn? Was he being interviewed for this? 'I wouldn't say that,' he countered.

'Listen. There was a bookseller who read this, and I told him you may be the high priest of Y'golonac. You will call down the shapes of night to worship him at the times of year; you will prostrate yourself before him and in return you will survive when the earth is cleared off for the Great Old Ones; you will go beyond the rim to what stirs out of the light . . .'

Before he could consider Strutt blurted: 'Are you talking about me?' He had realized that he was alone in a room with a madman.

'No, no, I meant the bookseller. But the offer now is for you.'

'Well, I'm sorry, I've got other things to do.' Strutt prepared to stand up.

'He refused also.' The timbre of the voice grated in Strutt's ears. 'I had to kill him.'

Strutt froze. How did one treat the insane? Pacify them. 'Now, now, hold on a minute . . .'

'How can it benefit you to doubt? I have more proof at my disposal than you could bear. You will be my high priest, or you will never leave this room.'

For the first time in his life, as the shadows between the harsh oppressive walls moved slower as if anticipating, Strutt battled to control an emotion; he subdued his mingled fear and ire with calm. 'If you don't mind, I've got to meet somebody.'

'Not when your fulfilment lies here between these walls.'

The voice was thickening. 'You know I killed the bookseller –
it was in your papers. He fled into the ruined church, but I
caught him with my hands ... Then I left the book in the
shop to be read, but the only one who picked it up by mistake
was the man who brought you here ... Fool! He went mad
and cowered in the corner when he saw the mouths! I kept
him because I thought he might bring some of his friends
who wallow in physical taboos and lose the true experiences,
those places forbidden to the spirit. But he only contacted
you and brought you here while I was feeding. There is food
occasionally: young boys who come here for books in secret;
they make sure nobody knows what they read! – and can be
persuaded to look at the *Revelations*. Imbecile! He can no
longer betray me with his fumbling – but I knew you would
return. Now you will be mine.'

Strutt's teeth ground together silently until he thought his
jaws would break; he stood up, nodding, and handed the
volume of the *Revelations* towards the figure; he was poised,
and when the hand closed on the ledger he would dart for
the office door.

'You can't get out, you know; it's locked.' The bookseller
rocked on his feet, but did not start towards him; the shadows
now were mercilessly clear, and dust hung in the silence.
'You're not afraid – you look too calculating. Is it possible
that you still do not believe? All right' – he laid his hand on
the doorknob behind the desk – 'do you want to see what is
left of my food?'

A door opened in Strutt's mind, and he recoiled from what
might lie beyond. 'No! No!' he shrieked. Fury followed his
involuntary display of fear; he wished he had a cane to
subjugate the figure taunting him. Judging by the face, he
thought, the bulges filling the tweed suit must be of fat; if
they should struggle, Strutt would win. 'Let's get this clear,'
he shouted, 'we've played games long enough! You'll let me
out of here or I – ' but he found himself glaring about for a
weapon. Suddenly he thought of the book still in his hand.
He snatched the matchbox from the desk, behind which the

figure watched, ominously impassive. Strutt struck a match, then pinched the boards between finger and thumb and shook out the pages. 'I'll burn this book!' he threatened.

The figure tensed, and Strutt went cold with fear of his next move. He touched the flame to paper, and the pages curled and were consumed so swiftly that Strutt had only the impression of bright fire and shadows growing unsteadily massive on the walls before he was shaking ashes to the floor. For a moment they faced each other, immobile. After the flames a darkness had rushed into Strutt's eyes. Through it he saw the tweed tear loudly as the figure expanded.

Strutt threw himself against the office door, which resisted. He drew back his fist, and watched with an odd timeless detachment as it shattered the frosted glass; the act seemed to isolate him, as if suspending all action outside himself. Through the knives of glass, on which gleamed drops of blood, he saw the snowflakes settle through the amber light, infinitely far; too far to call for help. A horror filled him of being overpowered from behind. From the back of the office came a sound; Strutt spun and as he did so closed his eyes, terrified to face the source of such a sound – but when he opened them he saw why the shadow on the frosted pane yesterday had been headless, and he screamed. As the desk was thrust aside by the towering naked figure, on whose surface still hung rags of the tweed suit, Strutt's last thought was an unbelieving conviction that this was happening because he had read the *Revelations*; somewhere, someone had *wanted* this to happen to him. It wasn't playing fair, he hadn't done anything to deserve this – but before he could scream out his protest his breath was cut off, as the hands descended on his face and the wet red mouths opened in their palms.

The Sister City

BRIAN LUMLEY

This manuscript attached as 'Annex "A"' to report number M-Y-127/52, dated August 7, 1952.

Towards the end of the war, when our London home was bombed and both my parents were killed, I was hospitalized through my own injuries and forced to spend the better part of two years on my back. It was during this period of my youth – I was only seventeen when I left the hospital – that I formed, in the main, the enthusiasm which in later years developed into a craving for travel, adventure, and knowledge of Earth's elder antiquities. I had always had a wanderer's nature but was so restricted during those two, dreary years that when my chance for adventure eventually came I made up for wasted time by letting that nature hold full sway.

Not that those long, painful months were totally devoid of pleasures. Between operations, when my health would allow it, I read avidly in the hospital's library, primarily to forget my bereavement, eventually to be carried along to those worlds of elder wonder created by Walter Scott in his enchanting *Arabian Nights*.

Apart from delighting me tremendously, the book helped to take my mind off the things I had heard said about me in the wards. It had been put about that I was different; allegedly the doctors had found something strange in my physical makeup. There were whispers about the peculiar qualities of my skin and the slightly extending horny carti-

lage at the base of my spine. There was talk about the fact
that my fingers and toes were ever so slightly webbed and
being, as I was, so totally devoid of hair, I became the
recipient of many queer glances.

These things plus my name, Robert Krug, did nothing to
increase my popularity at the hospital. In fact, at a time
when Hitler was still occasionally devastating London with
his bombs, a surname like Krug, with its implications of
Germanic ancestry, was probably more a hindrance to friendship than all my other peculiarities put together.

With the end of the war I found myself rich; the only heir
to my father's wealth, and still not out of my teens. I had left
Scott's Jinns, Ghouls, and Efreets far behind me but was
returned to the same *type* of thrill I had known with the
Arabian Nights by the popular publication of Lloyd's *Exca-
vations on Sumerian Sites*. In the main it was that book
which was responsible for the subsequent awe in which I
ever held those magical words 'Lost Cities'.

In the months that followed, indeed through all my
remaining – formative – years, Lloyd's work remained a
landmark, followed as it was by many more volumes in a
like vein. I read avidly of Layard's *Nineveh and Babylon* and
Early Adventures in Persia, Susiana, and Babylonia. I
dwelled long over such works as Budge's *Rise and Progress
of Assyriology* and Burckhardt's *Travels in Syria and the
Holy Land*.

Nor were the fabled lands of Mesopotamia the only places
of interest to me. Fictional Shangri-La and Ephiroth ranked
equally beside the reality of Mycenae, Knossos, Palmyra and
Thebes. I read excitedly of Atlantis and Chichen-Itza, never
bothering to separate fact from fancy, and dreamed equally
longingly of the Palace of Minos in Crete and Unknown
Kadath in the Cold Waste.

What I read of Sir Amery Wendy-Smith's African expedition in search of dead G'harne confirmed my belief that
certain myths and legends are not far removed from historical fact. If no less a person than that eminent antiquarian

and archaeologist had equipped an expedition to search for a
jungle city considered by most reputable authorities to be
purely mythological ... Why! His failure meant nothing
compared with the fact that he had *tried* ...

While others, before my time, had ridiculed the broken
figure of the demented explorer who returned alone from the
jungles of the Dark Continent I tended to emulate his
deranged fancies – as his theories have been considered – re-
examining the evidence for Chyria and G'harne and delving
ever deeper into the fragmentary antiquities of legendary
cities and lands with such unlikely names as R'lyeh, Ephiroth, Mnar, and Hyperborea.

As the years passed my body healed completely and I grew
from a fascinated youth into a dedicated man. Not that I
ever guessed what drove me to explore the ill-lit passages of
history and fantasy. I only knew that there was something
fascinating for me in the re-discovery of those ancient worlds
of dream and legend.

Before I began those far-flung travels which were destined
to occupy me on and off for four years I bought a house in
Marske, at the very edge of the Yorkshire moors. This was
the region in which I had spent my childhood and there had
always been about the brooding moors a strong feeling of
affinity which was hard for me to define. I felt closer to *home*
there somehow – and infinitely closer to the beckoning past.
It was with a genuine reluctance that I left my moors but
the inexplicable lure of distant places and foreign names
called me away, across the seas.

First I visited those lands that were within easy reach,
ignoring the places of dreams and fancies but promising
myself that later – later!!

Egypt, with all its mystery! Djoser's step-pyramid at Sag-
gara, Imhotep's Masterpiece; the ancient mastabas, tombs of
centuries-dead kings; the inscrutably smiling sphinx; the
Sneferu pyramid at Meidum and those of Chephren and
Cheops at Giza; the mummies, the brooding Gods ...

Yet in spite of all its wonder Egypt could not hold me for

long. The sand and heat were damaging to my skin which
tanned quickly and roughened almost overnight.

Crete, the Nymph of the beautiful Mediterranean ...
Theseus and the Minotaur; the Palace of Minos at Knossos
... All wonderful – but that which I sought was not there.

Salamis and Cyprus, with all their ruins of ancient civilizations, each held me but a month or so. Yet it was in Cyprus
that I learned of yet another personal peculiarity; my queer
abilities in water ...

I became friendly with a party of divers at Famagusta.
Daily they were diving for amphorae and other relics of the
past offshore from the ruins of Salonica on the south-east
coast. At first the fact that I could remain beneath the water
three times as long as the best of them, and swim further
without the aid of fins or snorkel, was only a source of
amazement to my friends; but after a few days I noticed that
they were having less and less to do with me. They did not
care for the hairlessness of my body or the webbing, which
seemed to have lengthened, between my toes and fingers.
They did not like the bump low at the rear of my bathing-
costume or the way I could converse with them in their own
tongue when I had never studied Greek in my life.

It was time to move on. My travels took me all over the
world and I became an authority on those dead civilizations
which were my one joy in life. Then, in Phetri, I heard of the
Nameless City.

Remote in the desert of Araby lies the Nameless City,
crumbling and inarticulate, its low walls nearly hidden by
the sands of uncounted ages. It was of this place that Abdul
Alhazred the mad poet dreamed on the night before he sang
his inexplicable couplet:

> 'That is not dead which can eternal lie,
> And with strange aeons even death may die.'

My Arab guides thought I, too, was mad when I ignored
their warnings and continued in search of that City of Devils

Their fleet-footed camels took them off in more than necessary haste for they had noticed my skin's scaly strangeness
and certain other unspoken things which made them uneasy
in my presence. Also, they had been nonplussed, as I had
been myself, at the strange fluency with which I used their
tongue.

Of what I saw and did in Kara-Shehr I will not write. It
must suffice to say that I learned of things which struck
chords in my sub-conscious; things which sent me off again
on my travels to seek Sarnath the Doomed in what was once
the land of Mnar . . .

No man knows the whereabouts of Sarnath and it is better
that this remain so. Of my travels in search of the place and
the difficulties which I encountered at every phase of my
journey I will therefore recount nothing. Yet my discovery of
the slime-sunken city, and of the incredibly aged ruins of
nearby Ib, were major links forged in the lengthening chain
of knowledge which was slowly bridging the awesome gap
between this world and my ultimate destination. And I,
bewildered, did not even know where or what that destination was.

For three weeks I wandered the slimy shores of the still
lake which hides Sarnath and at the end of that time, driven
by a fearful compulsion, I once again used those unnatural
aquatic powers of mine and began exploring beneath the
surface of that hideous morass.

That night I slept with a small green figurine, rescued
from the sunken ruins, pressed to my bosom. In my dreams I
saw my mother and father – but dimly, as if through a mist –
and they beckoned to me . . .

The next day I went again to stand in the centuried ruins
of Ib and as I was making ready to leave I saw the inscribed
stone which gave me my first clue. The wonder is that I could
read what was written on that weathered, aeon-old pillar;
for it was written in a curious cuneiform older even than the
inscriptions on Geph's broken columns, and it had been
pitted by the ravages of time.

It told nothing of the beings who once lived in Ib, or anything of the long-dead inhabitants of Sarnath. It spoke only of the destruction which the men of Sarnath had brought to the beings of Ib – and of the resulting doom that came to Sarnath. This doom was wrought by the Gods of the beings of Ib but of those Gods I could learn not a thing. I only knew that reading that stone and being in Ib had stirred long-hidden memories, perhaps even *ancestral* memories, in my mind. Again that feeling of closeness to home, that feeling I always felt so strongly on the moors in Yorkshire, flooded over me. Then, as I idly moved the rushes at the base of the pillar with my foot, yet more chiselled inscriptions appeared. I cleared away the slime and read on. There were only a few lines but those lines contained my clue:

'Ib is gone but the Gods live on. Across the world is the Sister City, hidden in the earth, in the barbarous lands of Zimmeria. There The People flourish yet and there will The Gods ever be worshipped; even unto the coming of Cthulhu . . .'

Many months later in Cairo, I sought out a man steeped in elder-lore, a widely acknowledged authority on forbidden antiquities and prehistoric lands and legends. This sage had never heard of Zimmeria but he did know of a land which had once had a name much similar. 'And where did this Cimmeria lie?' I asked.

'Unfortunately,' my erudite adviser answered, consulting a chart, 'most of Cimmeria now lies beneath the sea but originally it lay between Vanaheim and Nemedia in ancient Hyperborea.'

'You say *most* of it is sunken?' I queried. 'But what of the land which lies *above* the sea?' Perhaps it was the eagerness in my voice which caused him to glance at me the way he did. Again, perhaps it was my queer aspect; for the hot suns of many lands had hardened my hairless skin most peculiarly and a strong web now showed between my fingers.

'Why do you wish to know?' he asked. 'What is it you are seeking?'

'Home.' I answered instinctively, not knowing what prompted me to say it.

'Yes . . .' he said, studying me closely. 'That might well be . . . You are an Englishman, are you not? May I inquire from which part?'

'From the North-East,' I said, reminded suddenly of my moors. 'Why do you want to know?'

'My friend, you have searched in vain,' he smiled, 'for Cimmeria, or that which remains of it, encompasses all of that North-Eastern part of England which is your homeland. Is it not ironic? In order to find your home you have left it . . .'

That night fate dealt me a card which I could not ignore. In the lobby of my hotel was a table devoted solely to the reading habits of the English residents. Upon it was a wide variety of books, paperbacks, newspapers, and journals, ranging from *The Reader's Digest* to *The News of The World*, and to pass a few hours in relative coolness I sat beneath a soothing fan with a glass of iced water and idly glanced through one of the newspapers. Abruptly, on turning a page, I came upon a picture and an article which, when I had scanned the thing through, caused me to book a seat on the next flight to London.

The picture was poorly reproduced but was still clear enough for me to see that it depicted a small, green figurine – *the duplicate of that which I had salvaged from the ruins of Sarnath beneath the still pool . . .*

The article, as best I can remember, read like this:

'Mr Samuel Davies, of 17 Heddington Crescent, Radcar, found the beautiful relic of bygone ages pictured above in a stream whose only known source is the cliff-face at Sarby-on-the-Moors. The figurine is now in Radcar Museum, having been donated by Mr Davies, and is being studied by the curator, Prof. Gordon Walmsley of Goole. So far Prof. Walmsley has been unable to throw any light on the figurine's origin but the Wendy-Smith Test, a scientific means of checking the age of archaeological fragments, has shown it to be over ten thousand years old. The green figurine does not appear to have any connection with any of the better known civilizations of ancient England and is thought to be a find of rare importance. Unfortunately, expert pot-holers have given unanimous opinions that the stream, where it springs from the cliffs at Sarby, is totally untraversable.'

The next day, during the flight, I slept for an hour or so and again, in my dreams, I saw my parents. As before they appeared to me in a mist – but their beckonings were stronger than in that previous dream and in the blanketing vapours around them were strange *figures*, bowed in seeming obeisance, while a chant of teasing familiarity rang from hidden and nameless throats . . .

I had wired my housekeeper from Cairo, informing her of my returning, and when I arrived at my house in Marske I found a solicitor waiting for me. This gentleman introduced himself as being Mr Harvey, of the Radcar firm of Harvey, Johnson, and Harvey, and presented me with a large sealed envelope. It was addressed to me, *in my father's hand*, and Mr Harvey informed me his instructions had been to deliver the envelope into my hands on the attainment of my twenty-first birthday. Unfortunately I had been out of the country at the time, almost a year earlier, but the firm had kept in touch with my housekeeper so that on my return the agreement made nearly seven years earlier between my father and Mr Harvey's firm might be kept. After Mr Harvey left I dismissed my woman and opened the envelope. The manuscript within was not in any script I had ever learned at school. This was the language I had seen written on that aeon-old pillar in ancient Ib; nonetheless I knew instinctively that it had been my father's hand which had written the thing. And of course, I could read it as easily as if it were in English. The many and diverse contents of the letter made it, as I have said, more akin to a manuscript in its length and it is not my purpose to completely reproduce it. That would take too long and the speed with which The First Change is taking place does not permit it. I will merely set down the specially significant points which the letter brought to my attention.

In disbelief I read the first paragraph – but, as I read on, that disbelief soon became a weird amazement which in turn became a savage joy at the fantastic disclosure revealed by those timeless hieroglyphs of Ib. *My parents were not dead!* They had merely gone away; gone home . . .

That time nearly seven years ago, when I had returned home from a school reduced to ruins by the bombing, our London home had been purposely sabotaged by my father. A powerful explosive had been rigged, primed to be set off by the first air-raid siren, and then my parents had gone off in secrecy back to the moors. They had not known, I realized, that I was on my way home from the ruined school where I boarded. Even now they were unaware that I had arrived at the house just as the radar defences of England's military services had picked out those hostile dots in the sky. That plan which had been so carefully laid to fool men into believing that my parents were dead had worked well; but it had also nearly destroyed me. And all this time I, too, had believed them killed. But why had they gone to such extremes? What *was* that secret which it was so necessary to hide from our fellow men – and where were my parents now? I read on . . .

Slowly all was revealed. We are not *indigenous* to England, my parents and I, and they had brought me here as an infant from our homeland, a land quite near yet paradoxically far away. The letter went on to explain how *all* the children of our race are brought here as infants, for the atmosphere of our homeland is not conducive to health in the young and unformed. The difference in my case had been that my mother was unable to part with me. That was the awful thing! Though all the children of our race must wax and grow up *away* from their homeland, the elders can only rarely depart from their native clime. This fact is determined by their physical *appearance* throughout the greater period of their life-spans. *For they are not, for the better part of their lives, either the physical or mental counterparts of ordinary men.*

This means that children have to be left on doorsteps, at the entrances of orphanages, in churches and in other places where they will be found and cared for; for in extreme youth there is little difference between my race and the race of men. As I read I was reminded of those tales of fantasy I had once loved; of ghouls and fairies and other creatures who left their young to be reared by human beings and who stole human children to be brought up in their own likenesses.

Was *that*, then, my destiny? Was I to be a ghoul? I read on. I learned that the people of my race can only leave our native country twice in their lives; once in youth – when, as I have explained, they are brought here of necessity to be left until they attain the approximate age of twenty-one years – and once in later life, when *changes* in their appearances make them compatible to *outside* conditions. My parents had just reached this latter stage of their – development – when I was born. Because of my mother's devotion they had forsaken their *duties* in our own land and had brought me personally to England where, ignoring The Laws, they stayed with me. My father had brought certain treasures with him to ensure an easy life for himself and my mother until that time should come when they would be *forced* to leave me, the Time of the Second Change, when to stay would be to alert mankind of our existence.

That time had eventually arrived and they had covered up their departure back to our own, secret land by blowing up our London home; letting the authorities and I (though it must have broken my mother's heart) believe them dead of a German bomb raid.

And how could they have done otherwise? They dared not take the chance of telling me *what I really was*; for who can say what effect such a disclosure would have had on me, I who had barely begun to show my *differences*? They had to hope I would discover the secret myself, or at least the

greater part of it, which I have done! But to be doubly sure
my father left his letter.

The letter also told how not many *foundlings* find their
way back to their own land. Accidents claim some and others
go mad. At this point I was reminded of something I had
read somewhere of two inmates of Oakdeene Sanatorium
near Glasgow who are so horribly mad *and so unnatural in
aspect* that they are not even allowed to be seen and even
their nurses cannot abide to stay near them for long. Yet
others become hermits in wild and inaccessible places and,
worst of all, still others suffer more hideous fates and I
shuddered as I read what those fates were. But there *were*
those few who did manage to get back. These were the lucky
ones, those who returned to claim their rights; and while
some of them were *guided* back – by adults of the race during
second visits – others made it by instinct or luck. Yet horrible
though this overall plan of existence seemed to be, the letter
explained its logic. For my homeland could not support many
of my kind and those perils of lunacy, brought on by inexplicable physical changes, and accidents and those *other fates* I
have mentioned acted as a system of selection whereby only
the fittest in mind and body returned to the land of their
birth.

But there; I have just finished reading the letter through a
second time – and already I begin to feel a stiffening of my
limbs . . . My father's manuscript has arrived barely in time.
I have long been worried by my growing *differences*. The
webbing on my hands now extends almost to the small, first
knuckles and my skin is fantastically thick, rough and
ichthyic. The short tail which protrudes from the base of my
spine is now not so much an oddity as an *addition*; an extra
limb which, in the light of what I now know, is not an oddity
at all but the most natural thing in my world! My hairlessness, with the discovery of my destiny, has also ceased to be
an embarrassment to me. I am different to men, true, but is
that not as it should be? *For I am not a man . . .*

Ah, the lucky fates which caused me to pick up that

newspaper in Cairo! Had I not seen that picture or read that article I might not have returned so soon to my moors and I shudder to think what might have become of me then. What would I have done after The First Change had altered me? Would I have hurried, disguised and wrapped in smothering clothes, to some distant land — there to live the life of a hermit? Perhaps I would have returned to Ib or the Nameless City, to dwell in ruins and solitude until my appearance was again capable of sustaining my existence among men. And what after that — after The Second Change?

Perhaps I would have gone mad at such inexplicable alterations in my person. Who knows but there might have been another inmate at Oakdeene? On the other hand my fate might have been worse than all these; for I may have been drawn to dwell in the depths, to be one with the Deep Ones in the worship of Dagon and Great Cthulhu, as have others before me.

But no! By good fortune, by the learning gained on my far journeys and by the help given me by my father's document I have been spared all those terrors which others of my kind have known. I will return to Ib's Sister City, to Lh-yib, in that land of my birth *beneath* these Yorkshire moors; that land from which was washed the green figurine which guided me back to these shores, that figurine which is the duplicate of the one I raised from beneath the pool at Sarnath. I will return to be worshipped by those whose ancestral brothers died at Ib on the spears of the men of Sarnath; those who are so aptly described on the Brick Cylinders of Kadatheron; those who chant voicelessly in the abyss. I will return to Lh-yib!

For even now I hear my mother's voice; calling me as she did when I was a child and used to wander these very moors. 'Bob! Little Bo! Where are you?'

Bo, she used to call me and would only laugh when I asked her why. But why not? Was Bo not a fitting name? Robert — Bob — Bo? What odds? Blind fool that I have been! I never really pondered the fact that my parents were never quite

like other people; not even towards the end . . . Were not my
ancestors worshipped in grey stone Ib before the coming of
men, in the earliest days of Earth's evolution? I should have
guessed my identity when first I brought that figurine up out
of the slime; *for the features of the thing were as my own
features will be after The First Change, and engraved upon
its base in the ancient letters of Ib – letters I could read
because they were part of my native language, the precursor
of all languages – was my own name!*
    Bokrug:
    *Water-Lizard God of the people of Ib and Lh-yib, the Sister
City!*

Note:

Sir,
    Attached to this manuscript, 'Annex "A"' to my report, was a
brief note of explanation addressed to the NECB in Newcastle
and reproduced as follows:

                                        Robert Krug,
                                        Marske,
                                        Yorks.,
                                        Evening – July 19, '52
Secretary and Members,
NECB, Newcastle-on-Tyne.

Gentlemen of the North-East Coal-Board:

    My discovery while abroad, in the pages of a popular science
magazine, of your Yorkshire Moors Project, scheduled to commence next summer, determined me, upon the culmination of
some recent discoveries of mine, to write you this letter. You
will see that my letter is a protest against your proposals to drill
deep into the moors in order to set off underground explosions in
the hope of creating pockets of gas to be tapped as part of the
country's natural resources. It is quite possible that the under-
taking envisioned by your scientific advisers would mean the
destruction of two ancient races of sentient life. The prevention
of such destruction is that which causes me to break the laws of
my race and thus announce the existence of them and their

servitors. In order to explain my protest more fully I think it necessary that I tell my whole story. Perhaps upon reading the enclosed manuscript you will suspend indefinitely your projected operations.

Robert Krug . . .

POLICE REPORT M-Y-127/52

Alleged Suicide

Sir,

I have to report that at Dilham, on the 20th July 1952, at about four-thirty P.M., I was on duty at the Police Station when three children (statements attached at Annex 'B') reported to the Desk Sgt that they had seen a 'funny man' climb the fence at 'Devil's Pool', ignoring the warning notices, and throw himself into the stream where it vanishes into the hillside. Accompanied by the eldest of the children I went to the scene of the alleged occurrence, about three-quarters of a mile over the moors from Dilham, where the spot that the 'funny man' allegedly climbed the fence was pointed out to me. There *were* signs that someone had recently gone over the fence; trampled grass and grass-stains on the timbers. With slight difficulty I climbed the fence myself but was unable to decide whether or not the children had told the truth. There was no evidence in or around the pool to suggest that anyone had thrown himself in – but this is hardly surprising as at that point, where the stream enters the hillside, the water rushes steeply downwards into the earth. Once in the water only an extremely strong swimmer would be able to get back out. Three experienced pot-holers were lost at this same spot in August last year when they attempted a partial reconnoitre of the stream's underground course.

When I further questioned the boy I had taken with me, I was told that a *second* man had been on the scene prior to the incident. This other man had been seen to limp as though he was hurt, into a nearby cave. This had occurred shortly before the 'funny man' – described as being green and having a short, flexible tail – came out of the same cave, went over the fence and threw himself into the pool.

On inspecting the said cave I found what appeared to be an animal-hide of some sort, split down the arms and legs and up the belly, in the manner of the trophies of big-game hunters. This object was rolled up neatly in one corner of the cave and is now in the found-property room at the Police Station in Dilham.

Near this hide was a complete set of good-quality gent's clothing, neatly folded and laid down. In the inside pocket of the jacket I found a wallet containing, along with fourteen pounds in one-pound notes, a card bearing the address of a house in Marske; namely, 11 Sunderland Crescent. These articles of clothing, plus the wallet, are also now in the found-property room.

At about six-thirty P.M. I went to the above address in Marske and interviewed the housekeeper, one Mrs White, who provided me with a statement (attached at Annex 'C') in respect of her partial employer, Robert Krug. Mrs White also gave me two envelopes, one of which contained the manuscript attached to this report at Annex 'A'. Mrs White had found this envelope, sealed, with a note asking her to deliver it, when she went to the house on the afternoon of the 20th about half an hour before I arrived. In view of the inquiries I was making and because of their nature, i.e. – an investigation into the possible suicide of Mr Krug, Mrs White thought it was best that the envelope be given to the police. Apart from this she was at a loss what to do with it because Krug had forgotten to address it. As there was the possibility of the envelope containing a suicide note or dying declaration I accepted it.

The other envelope, which was unsealed, contained a manu-script in a foreign language and is now in the property room at Dilham.

In the two weeks since the alleged suicide, despite all my efforts to trace Robert Krug, no evidence has come to light to support the hope that he may still be alive. This, plus the fact that the clothing found in the cave has since been identified by Mrs White as being that which Krug was wearing the night before his disappearance, has determined me to request that my report be placed in the 'unsolved' file and that Robert Krug be listed as missing.

Sgt J. T. Miller,
Dilham,
Yorks.

August 7, 1952

Note:

Sir,
Do you wish me to send a copy of the manuscript at Annex 'A' – as requested of Mrs White by Krug – to the Secretary of the North-East Coal-Board?

Inspector I. L. Ianson,
Yorkshire County Constabulary,
Radcar,
Yorks.

Dear Sgt Miller,

In answer to your note of the 7th. Take no further action on the Krug case. As you suggest, I have had the man posted as missing, believed a suicide. As for his *document*; well, the man was either mentally unbalanced or a monumental hoaxer; possibly a combination of both. Regardless of the fact that certain things in his story are matters of indisputable fact, the majority of the thing appears to be the product of a diseased mind.

Meanwhile I await your progress-report on that other case. I refer to the baby found in the church pews at Eely-on-the-Moor last June. How are you going about tracing the mother?

Cement Surroundings

BRIAN LUMLEY

1

It will never fail to amaze me how certain allegedly Christian people take a perverse delight in the misfortunes of others. Just how true this is was brought forcibly home to me by the totally unnecessary whispers and rumours which were put about following the disastrous decline of my closest living relative.

There were those who concluded that just as the moon is responsible for the tides, and in part the slow movement of the Earth's upper crust, so was it also responsible for Sir Amery Wendy-Smith's *behaviour* on his return from Africa. As proof they pointed out my uncle's sudden fascination for seismography – the study of earthquakes – a subject which so took his fancy that he built his own instrument, a model which does not incorporate the conventional concrete base, to such an exactitude that it measures even the most minute of the deep tremors which are constantly shaking this world. It is that same instrument which sits before me now, rescued from the ruins of the cottage, at which I am given to casting, with increasing frequency, sharp and fearful glances. Before his disappearance my uncle spent hours, seemingly without purpose, studying the fractional movements of the stylus over the graph.

For my own part I found it more than odd the way in which, while Sir Amery was staying in London after his return, he shunned the underground and would pay abortive taxi fares rather than go down into what he termed 'those black tunnels'. Odd, certainly – but I never considered it a sign of insanity.

Yet even his few really close friends seemed convinced of his madness, blaming it upon his living too close to those dead and nigh-forgotten civilizations which so fascinated him. But how could it have been otherwise? My uncle was both antiquarian and archaeologist. His strange wanderings to foreign lands were not the result of any longing for personal gain or acclaim. Rather were they undertaken out of a love of the life, for any fame which resulted – as frequently occurred – was more often than not shrugged off on to the ever-willing personages of his colleagues. They envied him, those so-called contemporaries of his, and would have emulated his successes had they possessed the foresight and inquisitiveness with which he was so singularly gifted – or, as I have now come to believe, with which he was cursed. My bitterness towards them is directed by the way in which they cut him after the dreadful culmination of that last, fatal expedition. In earlier years many of them had been 'made' by his discoveries but on that last trip those 'hangers-on' had been the uninvited, the ones out of favour, to whom he would not offer the opportunity of fresh, stolen glory. I believe that for the greater part their assurances of his insanity were nothing more than a spiteful means of belittling his genius.

Certainly that last safari was his *physical* end. He who before had been straight and strong, for a man his age, with jet hair and a constant smile, was seen to walk with a pronounced stoop and had lost a lot of weight. His hair had greyed and his smile had become rare and nervous while a distinct tic jerked the flesh at the corner of his mouth.

Before these awful deteriorations made it possible for his erstwhile 'friends' to ridicule him, before the expedition, Sir Amery had deciphered or translated – I know little of these things – a handful of decaying, centuried shards known in

archaeological circles as the *G'harne Fragments*. Though he
would never fully discuss his findings I know it was that
which he learned which sent him, ill-fated, into Africa. He
and a handful of personal friends, all equally learned gentlemen, ventured into the interior seeking a legendary city
which Sir Amery believed had existed centuries before the
foundations were cut for the pyramids. Indeed, according to
his calculations, Man's primal ancestors were not yet conceived when G'harne's towering ramparts first reared their
monolithic sculptings to pre-dawn skies. Nor with regard to
the age of the place, if it existed at all, could my uncle's
claims be disproved. New scientific tests on the *G'harne
Fragments* had shown them to be pre-triassic and their very
existence, in any form other than centuried dust, was impossible to explain.

It was Sir Amery, alone and in a terrible condition, who
staggered upon an encampment of savages five weeks after
setting out from the native village where the expedition had
last had contact with civilization. No doubt the ferocious
men who found him would have done away with him there
and then but for their superstitions. His wild appearance
and the strange tongue in which he screamed, plus the fact
that he had emerged from an area which was 'taboo' in their
tribal legends, stayed their hands. Eventually they nursed
him back to a semblance of health and conveyed him to a
more civilized region from where he was slowly able to make
his way back to the outside world. Of the expedition's other
members nothing has since been seen or heard and only I
know the story, having read it in the letter my uncle left me.
But more of that later.

Following his lone return to England, Sir Amery developed
those eccentricities already mentioned and the merest hint
or speculation on the part of outsiders with reference to the
disappearance of his colleagues was sufficient to start him
raving horribly of such inexplicable things as 'a buried land
where Shudde-M'ell broods and bubbles, plotting the destruc-

tion of the human race and the release from his watery
prison of Great Cthulhu . . .' When he was asked *officially* to
account for his missing companions he said that they had
died in an earthquake and though, reputedly, he was asked
to clarify his answer, he would say no more . . .

Thus, being uncertain as to how he would *react* to questions about his expedition, I was loth to ask him of it.
However, on those rare occasions when he saw fit to talk of
it without prompting I listened avidly for I, as much as if not
more so than others, was eager to have the mystery cleared
up.

He had been back only a few months when he suddenly
left London and invited me up to his cottage, isolated here
on the Yorkshire moors, to keep him company. This invitation was a thing strange in itself as he was one who had
spent months in absolute solitude in various far-flung desolate places and liked to think of himself as something of a
hermit. I accepted, for I saw the perfect chance to get a little
of that solitude which I find particularly helpful to my
writing.

2

One day, shortly after I had settled in, Sir Amery showed me
a pair of strangely beautiful pearly spheres. They measured
about four inches in diameter and though he had been unable
to positively identify the material from which they were
made, he was able to tell me that it appeared to be some
unknown combination of calcium, chrysolite, and diamond-
dust. *How* the things had been made was, as he put it,
'anybody's guess'. The spheres, he told me, had been found at
the site of dead G'harne – the first intimation he had offered
that he had actually *found* the place – buried beneath the
earth in a lidless, stone box which had borne upon its queerly

angled sides certain utterly alien engravings. Sir Amery was anything but explicit with regard to those *designs*, merely stating that they were so loathsome in what they suggested that it would not do to describe them too closely. Finally, in answer to my probing questions, he told me they depicted monstrous sacrifices to some unnameable, cthonian deity. More he refused to say but directed me, as I seemed so 'damnably eager', to the works of Commodus and the hag-hidden Caracalla. He mentioned that also upon the box, along with the pictures, were many lines of sharply cut characters much similar to the cuneiform etchings of the *G'harne Fragments* and, in certain aspects, having a disturbing likeness to the almost unfathomable *Pnakotic Manuscripts*. Quite possibly, he went on, the container had been a toy-box of sorts and the spheres, in all probability, were once the baubles of a child of the ancient city; certainly children – or young ones – were mentioned in what he had managed to decipher of the odd writing on the box.

It was during this stage of his narrative that I noticed Sir Amery's eyes were beginning to glaze over and his speech was starting to falter – almost as though some strange, psychic block were affecting his memory. Without warning, like a man suddenly gone into a hypnotic trance, he began muttering of Shudde-M'ell and Cthulhu, Yog-Sothoth and Yibb-Tstll – 'alien *Gods* defying description' – and of mythological places with equally fantastic names: Sarnath and Hyperborea, R'lyeh and Ephiroth and many more . . .

Eager though I was to learn more of that tragic expedition I fear it was I who stopped Sir Amery from saying on. Try as I might, on hearing him babbling so, I could not keep a look of pity and concern from showing on my face which, when he saw it, caused him to hurriedly excuse himself and flee to the privacy of his room. Later, when I looked in at his door, he was engrossed with his seismograph and appeared to be relating the markings on its graph to an atlas of the world which he had taken from his library. I was concerned to note that he was quietly arguing with himself.

Naturally, being what he was and having such a great interest in peculiar, ethnic problems, my uncle had always possessed – along with his historical and archaeological source books – a smattering of works concerning elder-lore and primitive and doubtful religions. I mean such works as the *Golden Bough* and Miss Murray's *Witch Cult*. But what was I to make of those *other* books which I found in his library within a few days of my arrival? On his shelves were at least nine works which I know are so outrageous in what they suggest that they have been mentioned by widely differing authorities over a period of many years as being damnable, blasphemous, abhorrent, unspeakable, and literary lunacy. These included the *Cthaat Aquadingen* by an unknown author, Feery's *Notes on the Necronomicon*, the *Liber Miraculorem*, Eliphas Lévi's *History of Magic* and a faded, leather-bound copy of the hideous *Cultes des Goules*. Perhaps the worst thing I saw was a slim volume by Commodus which that 'Blood Maniac' had written in A.D. 183 and which was protected from further fragmentation by lamination.

And moreover, as if these books were not puzzling enough, there was that *other* thing!! What of the indescribable, droning *chant* which I often heard issuing from Sir Amery's room in the dead of night? This first occurred on the sixth night I spent with him and I was roused from my own uneasy slumbers by the morbid accents of a language it seemed impossible for the vocal cords of Man to emulate. Yet my uncle was weirdly fluent with it and I scribbled down an oft-repeated sentence-sequence in what I considered the nearest written approximation of the spoken words I could find. These words – *or sounds* – were:

Ce'haiie ep-ngh fl'hur G'harne fhtagn,
Ce'haiie fhtagn ngh Shudde-M'ell.
Hai G'harne orr'e ep fl'hur,
Shudde-M'ell ican-icanicas fl'ur orr'e G'harne . . .

Though at the time I found the thing impossible to pronounce as I heard it, I have since found that with each
passing day, oddly, the pronunciation of those lines becomes
easier – as if with the approach of some obscene horror I
grow more capable of expressing myself in the horror's terms.
Perhaps it is just that lately in my dreams, I have found
occasion to speak those very words and, as all things are far
simpler in dreams, my fluency has passed over into my
waking hours. But that does not explain the tremors – the
same inexplicable tremors which so terrorized my uncle. Are
the shocks which cause the ever-present quiverings of the
seismograph stylus merely the traces of some vast, subterrene cataclysm a thousand miles deep and five thousand
miles away – *or are they caused by something else?* Something so outré and fearsome that my mind freezes when I am
tempted to study the problem too closely . . .

3

There came a time, after I had been with him for a number
of weeks, when it seemed plain that Sir Amery was rapidly
recovering. True, he still retained his stoop – though to me
it seemed no longer so pronounced – and his so-called
eccentricities, but he was more his old self in other ways.
The nervous tic had left his face completely and his cheeks
had regained something of their former colour. His improvement, I conjectured, had much to do with his never-ending
studies of the seismograph: for I had established by that time
that there was a definite connection between the measure-
ments of that machine and my uncle's illness. Nevertheless,
I was at a loss to understand why the internal movements of
the Earth should so determine the state of his nerves. It was
after a trip to his room, to look at that instrument, that he

told me more of dead G'harne. It was a subject I should have attempted to steer him away from . . .

'The fragments,' he said, 'told the location of a city the name of which, G'harne, is only known in legend and which has in the past been spoken of on a par with Atlantis, Mu, and R'lyeh. A myth and nothing more. But if you give a legend a location you strengthen it somewhat – and if that location yields up relics of the past, of a civilization lost for aeons, then the legend becomes history. You'd be surprised how much of the world's history has in fact been built up that way.

'It was my hope, a hunch you might call it, that G'harne had been real – and with the deciphering of the fragments I found it within my power to *prove*, one way or the other, G'harne's elder existence. I have been in some strange places, Paul, and have listened to even stranger stories. I once lived with an African tribe who declared they knew the secrets of the lost city and their story-tellers told me of a land where the sun never shines; where Shudde-M'ell, hiding deep in the honeycombed ground, plots the dissemination of evil and madness throughout the world and plans the resurrection of other, even worse abominations!

'He hides there in the earth and awaits the time when the stars will be *right*, when his horrible hordes will be *sufficient* in number, and when he can infest the entire world with his loathsomeness, and cause the *return* of others more loathsome yet! I was told stories of fabulous star-born creatures who inhabited the Earth millions of years before Man appeared and who were still here, in certain dark places, when he eventually evolved. I tell you, Paul,' his voice rose, '*that they are here even now – in places undreamed of!* I was told of sacrifices to Yog-Sothoth and Yibb-Tstll that would make your blood run cold and of weird rites practised beneath prehistoric skies before the old Egypt was born. These things I've heard make the works of Albertus Magnus

and Grobert seem tame and de Sade himself would have
paled at the hearing.'

My uncle's voice had been speeding up progressively with
each sentence, but now he paused for breath and in a more
normal tone and at a reduced rate he continued:

'My first thought on deciphering the fragments was of an
expedition. I may tell you I had learned of certain things I
could have dug for here in England – you'd be surprised
what lurks beneath the surface of some of those peaceful
Cotswold hills – but that would have alerted a host of so-
called "experts" and amateurs alike so I decided on G'harne.
When I first mentioned an expedition to Kyle and Gordon
and the others I must have produced quite a convincing
argument for they all insisted on coming along. Some of
them though, I'm sure, must have considered themselves
upon a wild goose chase for, as I've explained, G'harne lies
in the same realm as Mu or Ephiroth – or at least it did –
and they must have seen themselves as questing after a
veritable Lamp of Aladdin; but despite all that they came.
They could hardly afford *not* to come, for if G'harne *was* real
. . . why! Think of the lost glory . . . They would never have
forgiven themselves. And that's why I can't forgive *myself*;
but for my meddling with the fragments they'd all be here
now, God help them . . .'

Again Sir Amery's voice had become full of some dread
excitement and feverishly he continued.

'Heavens, but this place sickens me! I can't stand it much
longer. It's all this grass and soil. Makes me shudder! Cement
surroundings are what I need – and the thicker the cement
the better . . . Yet even the cities have their drawbacks . . .
Undergrounds and things . . . Did you ever see Pickman's
Subway Accident, Paul? By God, what a picture . . . And the
night . . . That *night*! If you could have *seen* them – coming
up out of the diggings! If you could have felt the tremors . . .
Why! The very ground rocked and danced as they rose . . .
We'd disturbed them, d'you see? They may have even

thought they were under *attack* and up they came . . . My God! What could have been the reason for such *ferocity*? Only a few hours before I had been congratulating myself on finding the spheres, and then . . . And then . . .'

Now he was panting and his eyes, as before, had partly glazed over. His voice had undergone a strange change of timbre and his accents were slurred and alien.

· *'Ce'haiie, Ce'haiie* . . . The city may be buried but whoever named the place *dead* G'harne didn't know the half of it. *They were alive!*. They've been alive for millions of years; perhaps they *can't* die . . . And why shouldn't that be? They're Gods aren't they, of a sort? . . . Up they come in the night . . .'

'Uncle, please!' I said.

'You needn't look at me so, Paul, or think what you're thinking either . . . There's stranger things happened, believe me. Wilmarth of Miskatonic could crack a few yarns, I'll be bound! You haven't read what Johansen wrote! Dear Lord, *read the Johansen narrative! Hai ep fl'hur* . . . Wilmarth . . . The old babbler . . . What is it he knows which he won't tell? Why was that which was found at those Mountains of Madness so hushed up, eh? What did Pabodie's equipment draw up out of the earth? *Tell me those things, if you can?* Ha, ha, ha! *Ce'haiie, Ce'haiie – G'harne icanica* . . .'

Shrieking now, and glassy-eyed he stood, with his hands gesticulating wildly in the air. I do not think he saw me at all, or anything, except – in his mind's eye – a horrible recurrence of what he imagined had been. I took hold of his arm to calm him but he brushed my hand away, seemingly without knowing what he was doing.

'Up they come, the rubbery things . . . Goodbye Gordon . . . Don't scream so – the shrieking turns my mind . . . Thank heavens it's only a dream! . . . A nightmare just like all the others I've been having lately . . . It *is* a dream, isn't it? Goodbye Scott Kyle, Leslie . . .'

Sudenly, eyes bulging, he spun wildly round.

'*The ground is breaking up! So many of them . . . I'm
falling . . .* It's not a dream! *Dear God!* IT'S NOT A DREAM!
No! Keep off, d'you hear! Aghhh! *The slime* . . . Got to run!
. . . Run! . . . Away from those – voices? – away from the
sucking sounds and the chanting . . .'

Without warning he broke into a chant himself and the
awful *sound* of it, no longer distorted by distance or the
thickness of a stout door, would have sent a more timid
listener into a faint. It was similar to what I had heard
before in the night and the words do not seem so evil on
paper, almost ludicrous in fact, but to hear them issuing
from the mouth of my own flesh and blood – and with such
unnatural *fluency* . . .

> 'Ep ep fl'hur G'harne,
> G'harne fhtagn Shudde-M'ell hyas Negg'h.'

While chanting these incredible mouthings Sir Amery's
feet had started to pump up and down in a grotesque parody
of running. Suddenly he screamed anew and with startling
abruptness leapt past me and ran full tilt into the wall. The
shock knocked him off his feet and he collapsed in a heap on
the floor.

I was worried that my meagre ministrations might not be
adequate, but to my immense relief he regained consciousness a few minutes later. Shakily he assured me that he was
'all right, just shook up a bit' and, supported by my arm, he
retired to his room.

That night I found it impossible to close my eyes so I
wrapped myself in a blanket and sat outside my uncle's room
to be on hand if he were disturbed in his sleep. He passed a
quiet night, however, and paradoxically enough, in the
morning, he seemed to have got the thing out of his system
and was positively improved.

Modern doctors have known for a long time that in certain
mental conditions a cure may be obtained by inciting the

patient to *re-live* the events which caused his illness. Perhaps
my uncle's outburst of the previous night had served the
same purpose, or at least, so I thought, for by that time I had
worked out new ideas on his abnormal behaviour. I reasoned
that if he had been having recurrent nightmares and had
been in the middle of one on that fateful night of the
earthquake, when his friends and colleagues were killed, it
was only natural that his mind should temporarily become
somewhat unhinged upon waking and discovering the car-
nage. And if my theory were correct, it also explained his
seismic obsessions . . .

4

A week later came another grim reminder of Sir Amery's
condition. He had seemed so much improved, though he still
occasionally rambled in his sleep, and had gone out into the
garden 'to do a bit of trimming'. It was well into September
and quite chill, but the sun was shining and he spent the
entire morning working with a rake and hedge clippers. We
were doing for ourselves and I was thinking about preparing
the mid-day meal when a singular thing happened. I distinctly felt the ground move fractionally under my feet and
heard a low rumble. I was sitting in the living room when it
happened and the next moment the door to the garden burst
open and my uncle rushed in. His face was deathly white
and his eyes bulged horribly as he fled past me to his room. I
was so stunned by his wild appearance that I had barely
moved from my chair by the time he shakily came back into
the room. His hands trembled as he lowered himself into an
easy chair.

'It was the ground . . . I thought for a minute that the
ground . . .' He was mumbling, more to himself than to me,
and visibly trembling from head to toe as the after-effect of

the shock hit him. Then he saw the concern on my face and tried to calm himself. 'The ground. I was sure I felt a tremor – but I was mistaken. It must be this place. All that open space . . . I fear I'll really have to make an effort and get away from here. There's altogether too much soil and not enough cement! Cement surroundings are the thing . . .'

I had had it on the tip of my tongue to say that I too had felt the shock but upon learning that he believed himself mistaken I kept quiet. I did not wish to needlessly add to his already considerable disorders.

That night, after Sir Amery had retired, I went through into his study – a room which, though he had never said so, I knew he considered inviolate – to have a look at the seismograph. Before I looked at the machine, however, I saw the *notes* spread out on the table beside it. A glance was sufficient to tell me that the sheets of white foolscap were covered by fragmentary jottings in my uncle's heavy handwriting and when I looked closer I was sickened to discover that they were a rambling jumble of seemingly disassociated – yet apparently *linked* – occurrences connected in some way with his weird delusions. These notes have since been delivered permanently into my possession and are as reproduced here:

HADRIAN'S WALL
A.D. 122–128. Limestone Bank. (Gn'yah of the *Fragments*)??? *Earth tremors* interrupted the diggings and that is why cut, basalt blocks were left in the uncompleted ditch with wedge holes ready for splitting.

W'nyal-Shash (MITHRAS)
Romans had their own deities *but it wasn't Mithras* that the disciples of Commodus, the Blood Maniac, sacrificed to at Limestone Bank! And that was the same area where, fifty years earlier, a great block of stone was unearthed and discovered to be covered with *inscriptions* and *engraven pictures!* Silvanus the centurion defaced it and buried it again. A skeleton, positively identified as Silvanus's by the signet ring on one of its fingers,

has been lately found *beneath the ground (deep)* where once stood a Vicus Tavern at Housesteads Fort – but we don't know *how* he vanished! Nor were Commodus's followers any too careful. According to Caracalla they also vanished overnight – *during an earthquake!*

AVEBURY
(Neolithic *A'byy* of the *Fragments* and *Pnakotic Ms*???) Reference Stukeley's book, *A Temple to the British Druids*, incredible ... Druids, indeed ... But Stukeley nearly had it when he said Snake Worship! *Worms, more like it!*

COUNCIL OF NANTES
(9th century) The council didn't know what they were doing when they said: 'Let the *stones* also which, deceived by the derision of the *demons*, they worship amid ruins and in wooded places, where they both make their vows and bestow their *offerings*, be *dug up* from the very foundations, and let them be cast into such places as never will their devotees be able to find them again . . .' I've read that paragraph so many times that it's become imprinted upon my mind! *God only knows what happened to the poor devils who tried to carry out the Council's orders* . . .

DESTRUCTION OF GREAT STONES
In the 13th and 14th centuries the Church also attempted the removal of certain stones from Avebury because of *local superstitions* which caused the country folk to take part in *heathen worship* and *witchcraft* around them! In fact some of the stones *were* destroyed – by fire and douching – 'because of the *devices* upon them'.

INCIDENT
1920–5. Why was a big effort made to bury one of the great stones? An *earth-tremor* caused the stone to slip, trapping a workman. *No effort appears to have been made to free him* ... The 'accident' happened at dusk and two other men *died of fright!* Why did other diggers flee the scene? And what was the titanic *thing* which one of them saw wriggling away *into the ground*? Allegedly thing left monstrous *smell* behind it ... *By their SMELL shall ye know them* ... Was it a member of another nest of the timeless ghouls?

THE OBELISK
Why was Stukeley's huge obelisk broken up? The pieces were
buried in the early 18th century but in 1833 Henry Browne
found burnt *sacrifices* at the site . . . And nearby, at Silbury hill
. . . *My God! That devil-mound!* There are some things, even
amidst these horrors, which don't bear thinking of – and while
I've still got my sanity Silbury Hill better remain one of them!

AMERICA: INNSMOUTH
1928. What actually happened and why did the Federal government drop depth charges off Devil Reef in the Atlantic coast just
out of Innsmouth? Why were half Innsmouth's citizen's banished? What was their connection with Polynesia and what also
lies buried in the lands *beneath the sea*?

WIND WALKER
(Death-Walker, Ithaqua, Wendigo etc . . .) Yet *another* horror –
though of a different *type*! And such *evidence*! Alleged *human
sacrifices* in Manitoba. Unbelievable circumstances surrounding
Norris Case! Spencer of Quebec University literally *affirmed* the
validity of the case . . . And at . . .

But that is as far as the notes go and when I first read
them I was glad such was the case. It was quickly becoming
all too apparent that my uncle was far from well and still
not quite right in his mind. Of course, there was always the
chance that he had written those notes *before* his seeming
improvement, in which case his plight was not necessarily
as bad as it appeared.

Having put the notes back exactly as I found them I turned
my attention to the seismograph. The line on the graph was
straight and true and when I dismantled the spool and
checked the chart I saw that it had followed that almost
unnaturally unbroken smoothness for the last twelve days.
As I have said, that machine and my uncle's condition were
directly related and this proof of the quietness of the earth
was undoubtedly the reason for his comparative well-being
of late. But here was yet another oddity . . . Frankly I was
astonished at my findings for I was certain I had felt a tremor

– indeed I had *heard* a low rumble – and it seemed impossible
that both Sir Amery and myself should suffer the same,
simultaneous sensory illusion. I rewound the spool and then,
as I turned to leave the room, I noticed that which my uncle
had missed. It was a small brass screw lying on the floor.
Once more I unwound the spool and saw the countersunk
hole which I *had* noticed before but which had not made an
impression of any importance upon my mind. Now I guessed
that it was meant to house that screw. I am nothing where
mechanics are concerned and could not tell what that small
integer played in the workings of the machine; nevertheless
I replaced it and again set the instrument in order. I stood
then, for a moment, to ensure that everything was working
correctly and for a few seconds noticed nothing abnormal. It
was my ears which first warned of the change. There had
been a low, clockwork hum and a steady, sharp scraping
noise before. The hum was still attendant but in place of the
scraping sound was a jerky scratching which drew my
fascinated eyes to the stylus.

That small screw had evidently made all the difference in
the world. No wonder the shock we had felt in the afternoon,
which had so disturbed my uncle, had gone unrecorded. The
instrument had not been working correctly *then – but now it
was . . . Now it could be plainly seen that every few minutes
the ground was being shaken by tremors which, though they
were not so severe as to be felt, were certainly strong enough
to cause the stylus to wildly zigzag over the surface of the
revolving graph paper . . .*

I felt in a far more shaken state than the ground when I
finally retired that night. Yet I could not really decide the
cause of my nervousness. Just why should I feel so apprehensive about my discovery? True, I knew the effect of the now –
correctly? – working machine upon my uncle would probably
be unpleasant and might even cause another of his 'out-
bursts' but was that knowledge all that unsettled me? On

reflection I could see no reason whatever why any particular
area of the country should receive more than its usual quota
of earth-tremors. Eventually I concluded that the machine
was either faulty or far too sensitive and went to sleep
assuring myself that the strong shock we had felt had been
merely coincidental to my uncle's condition. Still, I noticed
before I dozed off that the very air itself seemed charged with
a strange tension and the slight breeze which had wafted the
late leaves during the day had gone completely, leaving in
its passing an absolute quiet in which, during my slumbers,
I fancied all night that the ground trembled beneath my bed
. . .

5

The next morning I was up early. I was short of writing
materials and had decided to catch the lone morning bus into
Radcar. I left before Sir Amery was awake and during the
journey I thought back on the events of the previous day and
decided to do a little research while I was in the town. In
Radcar I had a bite to eat and then I called at the offices of
the *Radcar Recorder* where a Mr McKinnen, a sub-editor,
was particularly helpful. He spent some time on the office
telephones making extensive inquiries on my behalf. Eventually I was told that for the better part of a year there had
been no tremors of any importance in England, a point I
would obviously have argued had not further information
been forthcoming. I learned that there *had* been some *minor
shocks* and that these had occurred at places as far as Goole,
a few miles away (that one within the last twenty-four hours)
and at Tenterden near Dover. There had also been a very
minor tremor at Ramsey in Huntingdonshire. I thanked Mr
McKinnen profusely for his help and would have left then –
but, as an afterthought, he asked me if I would be interested

in checking through the paper's international files. I gratefully accepted and was left on my own to study a great pile
of interesting translations. Of course, most of it was useless
to me but it did not take me long to sort out what I was after.
At first I had difficulty believing the evidence of my own
eyes. I read that in August there had been 'quakes in Aisne
of such severity that one or two houses had collapsed and a
number of people had been injured. These shocks had been
likened to those of a few weeks earlier at Agen in that they
seemed to be caused more by some *settling of the ground*
than by an actual tremor. In early July there had also been
shocks in Calahorra, Chinchon, and Ronda in Spain. The
trail went as straight as the flight of an arrow and lay across
– *or rather under* – the Straits of Gibraltar to Xauen in
Spanish Morocco, where an entire street of houses had
collapsed. Farther yet, to . . . But I had had enough. I dared
look no more; I did not wish to know – not even remotely –
the whereabouts of dead G'harne . . .

Oh! I had seen more than sufficient to make me forget
about my original errand. My book could wait, for now there
were more important things to do. My next port of call was
the town library where I took down Nicheljohn's *World Atlas*
and turned to that page with a large, folding map of the
British Isles. My geography and knowledge of England's
counties are passable and I had noticed what I considered to
be an oddity in the seemingly unconnected places where
England had suffered those *minor 'quakes*. I was not mistaken. Using a second book as a straight edge I lined up
Goole in Yorkshire and Tenterden on the south coast and
saw, with a tingle of monstrous foreboding, that the line
passed very close to, if not directly through, Ramsey in
Huntingdonshire. With dread curiosity I followed the line
north and, through suddenly fevered eyes, saw that it passed
within only a mile or so of the cottage on the moors! I turned
more pages with unfeeling, rubbery fingers until I found the
leaf showing France. For a moment I paused – then I

fumblingly found Spain and finally Africa. For a long while
I just sat there in numbed silence, occasionally turning the
pages, automatically checking names and locations . . . My
thoughts were in a terrible turmoil when I eventually left
the library and I could feel upon my spine the chill, hopping
feet of some abysmal dread from the beginning of time. My
previously wholesome nervous system had already started to
crumble . . .

During the journey back across the moors in the evening
bus, the drone of the engine lulled me into a kind of half-
sleep in which I heard again something Sir Amery had
mentioned – something he had murmured aloud while sleeping and presumably dreaming. He had said:

'They don't like water . . . England's safe . . . Have to go
too deep . . .' The memory of those words shocked me back to
wakefulness and filled me with a further icy chill which got
into the very marrow of my bones. Nor were these feelings of
horrid foreboding misleading, for awaiting me at the cottage
was that which went far to completing the destruction of my
entire nervous system . . .

As the bus came round the final wooded bend which hid
the cottage from sight *I saw it!* The place had collapsed. I
simply could not take it in! Even knowing all I knew – with
all my slowly accumulating evidence – it was too much for
my tortured mind to comprehend. I left the bus and waited
until it had threaded its way through the parked police cars
before crossing the road. The fence to the cottage had been
knocked down to allow an ambulance to park in the queerly
tilted garden. Spotlights had been set up, for it was almost
dark, and a team of rescuers were toiling frantically at the
incredible ruins. As I stood there, aghast, I was approached
by a police officer and having stumblingly identified myself
was told the following story.

A passing motorist had actually seen the collapse and the
tremors attendant to it had been felt in nearby Marske. The
motorist had realized there was little he could do on his own

and had speeded into Marske to report the thing. Allegedly
the house had gone down like a pack of cards. The police and
an ambulance had been on the scene within minutes and
rescue operations had begun immediately. Up to now it
appeared that my uncle had been *out* when the collapse
occurred for as yet there had been no trace of him. There had
been a strange, poisonous *odour* about the place but this had
vanished soon after the work had started. The rescuers had
cleared the floors of all the rooms except the study and
during the time it took the officer to bring me up to date
even more debris was being frantically hauled away.

Suddenly there was a lull in the excited babble of voices. I
saw that the gang of rescue workers were standing looking
down at something. My heart gave a wild leap and I scram-
bled over the debris to see what they had found.

There, where the floor of the study had been, was that
which I had feared and more than half expected. It was
simply a hole. A gaping *hole* in the floor – *but from the angles
at which the floorboards lay, and the manner in which they
were scattered about, it looked as though the ground, rather
than sinking, had been pushed up from below* . . .

6

Nothing has since been seen or heard of Sir Amery Wendy-
Smith and though he is listed as being *missing* I know in
fact that he is dead. He is gone to worlds of ancient wonder
and my only prayer is that his soul wanders on *our* side of
the threshold. For in our ignorance we did Sir Amery a great
injustice – I and all the others who thought he was out of his
mind. All his queer ways – I understand them all now, but
the understanding has come hard and will cost me dear. No,
he was not mad. He did the things he did out of self-
preservation and though his precautions came to nothing in

the end, it was fear of a nameless evil and not madness which prompted them.

But the worst is still to come. I myself have yet to face a similar end. I know it, for no matter what I do the tremors haunt me. Or is it only in my mind? No! There is little wrong with my mind. My nerves are gone but my mind is intact. I *know* too much! *They* have visited me in dreams, as I believe *they* must have visited my uncle, and what *they* have read in my mind has warned *them* of *their* danger. *They* dare not allow me to investigate, for it is such meddling which may one day fully reveal *them* to men – *before they are ready* . . . God! Why has that ancient fool Wilmarth at Miskatonic not answered my telegrams? There must be a way out! Even now *they* dig – those dwellers in darkness . . .

But no! This is no good. I must get a grip of myself and finish this narrative. I have not had time to try to tell the authorities the truth but even if I had I know what the result would have been. 'There's something wrong with all the Wendy-Smith blood' they would say. But this manuscript will tell the story for me and will also stand as a warning to others. Perhaps when it is seen how my – *passing* – so closely parallels that of Sir Amery, people will be curious; with this manuscript to guide them perhaps men will seek out and destroy Earth's elder madness before it destroys them . . .

A few days after the collapse of the cottage on the moors, I settled here in this house on the outskirts of Marske to be close at hand if – though I could see little hope of it – my uncle should turn up again. But now some dread power keeps me here. I *cannot* flee . . . At first *their* power was not so strong, but now . . . I am no longer able even to leave this desk and I know the end must be coming fast. I am rooted to this chair as if grown here and it is as much as I can do to type! But I must . . . I must . . . And the ground movements are much stronger now. That hellish, damnable, mocking stylus – leaping so crazily over the paper.

I had been here only two days when the police delivered to

me a dirty, soil-stained envelope. It had been found in the ruins of the cottage – near the lip of that curious hole – and was addressed to me. It contained those notes I have already copied and a letter from Sir Amery which, if its awful ending is anything to go on, he must have still been writing when the horror came for him ... When I consider, it is not surprising that the envelope survived the collapse. *They* would not have known what it was, and so would have had no interest in it. *Nothing* in the cottage was purposely damaged – nothing *inanimate*, that is – and so far as I have been able to discover the only missing items are those terrible spheres, *or what remained of them* ... But I must hurry ... I cannot escape and all the time the tremors are increasing in strength and frequency ... No! I will not have time. No time to write all I wanted to say ... The shocks are too heavy ... To o hea vy ...Int erfer in g with m y t yping ... I will finis h this i n th e only way rem ain ing to me and staple S ir Amer y's lette r to this man usc ript ... now ...

Dear Paul.

In the event of this letter ever getting to you, there are certain things I must ask you to do for the safety and sanity of the world. It is absolutely necessary that these things be explored and *dealt with* – though how that may be done I am at a loss to say. It was my intention, for the sake of my own sanity, to forget what happened at G'harne. I was wrong to try and hide it. At this very moment there are men digging in strange, forbidden places and who knows what they may unearth? Certainly all these horrors must be tracked down and rooted out – but not by bumbling amateurs. It must be done by men who are ready for the ultimate in hideous, cosmic horror. Men with weapons. Perhaps flame-throwers would do the trick ... Certainly a scientific knowledge of war would be a necessity ... Devices could be made to track the enemy ... I mean specialized seismological instruments ... If I had the time I would prepare a dossier, detailed and explicit, but it appears that this letter will have to suffice as a guide to tomorrow's horror-hunters. You see, *I now know for sure that they are after me*! And there's nothing I can do about it. It's too late! At first even I, just like so many others, believed myself to be just a little bit mad. I refused to admit to myself that what I had *seen* happen had ever happened at all! To admit *that* was to admit lunacy! But it's real all right . . . It *did* happen – and *will again*!

Heaven only knows what's been wrong with my seismograph but the damn thing's let me down in the worst possible way! Oh, *they* would have got me eventually, but I might at least have had time to prepare a proper warning . . . I ask you to think, Paul . . . Think of what has happened at the cottage . . . I can write of it as though it had *already happened*; because I know *it must! It will!* It is Shudde-M'ell, come for his spheres . . . Paul, look at the manner of my death, for if you are reading this then I am either dead or disappeared – which means the same thing. Read the enclosed notes carefully, I beg you. I haven't the time to be more explicit but these old notes of mine should be of some help . . . If you are only half so inquiring as I believe you to be, you will surely soon come to recognize a fantastic horror, which, I repeat, the whole world must be *made* to believe in . . . The ground is really shaking now but, knowing it is the end, I am steady in my horror . . . Not that I expect my present calm state of mind to last . . . I think that by the time *they* actually come for me my mind will have snapped completely. I can imagine it now . . . The floor splintering, erupting, to admit *them*. Why! Even *thinking* of it my senses recoil at the terror of the thought . . . There will be a hideous *smell, a slime, a chanting* and gigantic *writhing* and . . . And then . . .

Unable to escape, I await the thing . . . I am trapped by the same hypnotic power that claimed the others at G'harne. What monstrous memories! How I awoke to see my friends and companions sucked dry of their life's blood by wormy, vampirish *things* from the cesspools of time! Gods of alien dimensions . . . I was hypnotized then by this same terrible force, unable to move to the aid of my friends or even to save myself! Miraculously, with the passing of the moon behind the wisps of cloud, the hypnotic effect was broken. Then, screaming and sobbing, temporarily out of my mind, I fled; hearing behind me the vile and slobbering *sucking* sounds and the droning, demoniac chanting of Shudde-M'ell and his hordes.

Not knowing that I did it, in my mindlessness I carried with me those hell-spheres . . . Last night I dreamed of them. And in my dreams I saw again the inscriptions on that stone box. Moreover, *I could read them*! All the fears and *ambitions* of those hellish things were there to be read as clearly as the headlines in a daily newspaper! 'Gods' they may or may not be but one thing is sure; the greatest setback to their plans for conquest of the Earth *is their terribly long and complicated reproductory cycle*! Only a handful of young are born every thousand years; but, considering how *long* they have been here, the time must be drawing ever nearer when their numbers will be *sufficient*! Naturally, this tedious build up of their numbers makes them loth to lose even a single member of their hideous spawn. *And that is why they have tunnelled these many thousands of miles, even under deep oceans, to retrieve the spheres!* I had wondered why they could be following me – and now I know. I also know *how*. Can you not guess how they know where I am, Paul, or why they are coming? Those spheres are like a beacon to them; a siren voice calling. *And just as any other parent – though more out of awful ambition, I fear, than any type of emotion we could understand – they are merely answering the call of their young!*

But they are too late! A few minutes ago, just before I began this letter, the things *hatched* . . . Who would have guessed that they were *eggs* – or that the container they were in *was an incubator*? I can't blame myself for not knowing it. I even tried to have the spheres X-rayed once, damn them, but they reflected the rays! And the shells were so *thick*! Yet at the time of hatching they just splintered into tiny fragments. The creatures inside were no bigger than walnuts . . . Taking into account the *size* of an adult they must have a fantastic growth rate. Not that those two will ever grow! I shrivelled them with a cigar . . . *And you should have heard the mental screams from those beneath!*

If only I could have known earlier, *definitely*, that it was not madness, there might have been a way to escape this horror . . . But no use now . . . My notes – look into them, Paul, and do what I should have done. Complete a detailed dossier and present it to the authorities. Wilmarth may help and perhaps Spencer of Quebec University . . . Haven't much time now . . . Cracks in ceiling . . .

That last shock . . . ceiling coming away in chunks . . . coming up. Heaven help me, they're coming up . . . I can feel them groping inside my mind as they come –

Sir,

Reference this manuscript found in the ruins of number 17 Anwick Street, Marske, Yorkshire, following the earth-tremors of September this year and believed to be a 'fantasy' which the writer, Paul Wendy-Smith, had completed for publication. It is more than possible that the so-called disappearances of both Sir Amery Wendy-Smith and his nephew, the writer, were nothing more than promotion stunts for this story . . . It is well known that Sir Amery is/was interested in seismography and perhaps some prior intimation of the two 'quakes supplied the inspiration for his nephew's tale. Investigations continuing . . .

Sgt J. Williams.
Yorks. County Constabulary.
October 2, 1933.

The Deep Ones

JAMES WADE

'Diviner than the dolphin is nothing yet created; for indeed they
were aforetime men, and lived in cities along with mortals.'
— Oppian: HALIEUTICA (A.D. 200)

I had never met Dr Frederick Wilhelm before I went to work
at his Institute for Zoological Studies, located in a remote
cove on the California coast some miles north of San Simeon
and Piedres Blancas, not far from the Big Sur area; but of
course I had heard of his studies. The Sunday supplements
picked Wilhelm up years ago, which was only natural: what
more potentially sensational subject could a journalist hope
for than the idea that man shared the earth with another,
older, and perhaps more intelligent species; a species overlooked or ignored by modern science, but with which communication might someday be established?

It wasn't a worn-out gambit like flying saucer people, or
spiritualism, or trolls hidden under the hills, of course.
Wilhelm's subject was the dolphin, that ocean mammal
glimpsed centuries ago by superstitious sailors and trans-
mogrified into myths of mermaids, sirens, all the fabulous
sea-dwelling secret races of legend. Now, it appeared, the
superstitions might not be far wrong.

Preliminary tests had showed long ago that our ocean-
going distant cousins harboured a high degree of pure
intelligence and potential for communication, unsuspected
because of their watery habitat and their lack of hands or

any other prehensile apparatus for producing artefacts. Wilhelm's researches had not been the first, but his speculations were certainly the most daring, and he had parlayed his preoccupation into a career, attracting both government and private foundation funds to set up the institute towards which I found myself jogging in a rented jeep over rutted, sandy roads beside the sinuous green Pacific one starkly sunlit afternoon in April a year ago.

Although I knew of Frederick Wilhelm and his institute, I wasn't sure just how or what he knew of me. In a sense, I could easily see how my field, extrasensory perception and telepathy, might tie in with his work; but his initial letters and wires to me had never spelled out in any detail what he expected of our collaboration. His messages, indeed, had seemed at once euphoric and evasive, confining themselves mostly to grandiloquent descriptions of his basic purposes and facilities, plus details on the financial aspects of our association.

I will admit that the amount of money Dr Wilhelm offered was a strong factor in my accepting a job the exact nature of which remained unclear. As research coordinator of a small Eastern foundation devoted to parapsychological studies overlooked by the Rhine group at Duke, I had had my fill of skimped budgets and starvation wages. Wilhelm's offer had come as an opportunity golden in more ways than one, so I had lost little time in packing my bags for the trip to sunny California.

Actually, the location of Wilhelm's experiments gave me more pause than any of the other doubtful aspects of his offer. I confess that I have always had an antipathy to California, despite the little time I recall having spent there. Perhaps I had read too much in the works of mordant satirists like Waugh and Nathanael West, but to me there has always seemed something decadent and even sinister about this self-eulogizing Pacific paradise.

The impression had not been allayed by my arrival via

plane in gritty, galvanic Los Angeles, or by a stroll through that tiny downtown park where predatory homosexuals, drug derelicts, and demented fanatics of all kinds congregate under the bloated, twisted palms, like so many patients in the garden of Dr Caligari's madhouse. To some, Gothic battlements or New England backwaters represent the apex of spiritual horror and decay; for me, the neon-lit, screaming depravity of Los Angeles filled the bill. As the comedian Fred Allen once remarked, California is a great place if you're an orange.

These thoughts and others tangled in my mind as I guided my jeep over the rough beachside path which, I had been assured by the jovial car rental agent in San Simeon, would take me unfailingly to the Institute for Zoological Studies. ('Ain't no place else the road goes, after you turn off left at the first orange juice stand – you know, the kind where the stand is built to look just like a great big orange. Jest keep on goin', and don't stop for hippies or high water till the road ends!')

As I glanced rather nervously around, I could see on my left a sort of encampment of bleached white tents and dark, darting figures down by the wavering lace of surf at the water's edge. Were these the hippies my guide had referred to, those sardonic jesters on the periphery of our society, razzing and reviling all the standards and values of three thousand civilized years? Or had he been spoofing me; were these only a gaggle of middle-class youngsters out for an afternoon of beachside sun, sand, and sex as a respite from the abrasive grind of our precariously affluent society?

Even as these trite and puerile thoughts chased through my head, suddenly the vestigial road took a sharp turn over a rise and I found myself startlingly close up (a zoomlens effect) to what could only be the famous Institute for Zoological Studies.

2

'What, actually, do you know about dolphins – or porpoises,
as they are sometimes called?' queried Dr Frederick Wilhelm, his eyes invisible behind thick lenses that caught the
light from filtered globes under gold-tinted shades in his
plush office. We had just settled down over a late afternoon
cocktail, expertly crafted by Wilhelm himself, after my first
rapid tour of the Institute, conducted by its director immediately after meeting my arriving jeep.

Wilhelm had been cordial and almost courtly, though it
seemed a bit odd for him to start me off on a junket around
his establishment before I had had a chance even to drop my
luggage at my quarters and freshen up a bit after the long
drive. I put it down to the vanity of a self-made scientific
pioneer jockeying a cherished hobby horse down the home
stretch in the big race.

The impression I'd received on the whirlwind tour was
superficial and a bit bewildering: the long, low, white-
plastered cement buildings straggling along the shoreline
seemed crammed with more sound, lighting, recording, pho-
tographic, and less identifiable computerized equipment than
would be needed to study the entire passenger list of Noah's
ark, let alone one minor sub-species of marine mammal.

About Wilhelm himself, there was nothing odd, though: a
big, rumpled, greying penguin of a man, he moved and spoke
with the disarming enthusiasm of a schoolboy just discovering that there is such a thing as science. As he hurried me
from lab to lab at a breathless pace, he explained, 'We'll see
the dolphin pools tomorrow morning. Josephine – my
research assistant Josephine Gilman – is working there now;
she'll join us later for drinks and dinner.'

As I had learned from correspondence with Dr Wilhelm,

his senior staff (now totalling three, himself included, with my arrival) had quarters at the Institute, while the dozen or so technicians and laboratory assistants employed here made the trip to and from San Simeon billets in a Volkswagen micro-bus each day.

Now as I sat with Wilhelm in the dim, richly decorated office over an acridly enticing martini, I heard the bus pull away, and realized that I was alone in the sprawling complex of buildings with its director and the unsurmised Josephine Gilman.

'What do you actually know about dolphins?' Wilhelm was saying.

'About what any layman knows,' I found myself replying frankly. 'I know that research started back in the 1950s, and indicated that dolphin brain size and specialized adaptations made probable a high degree of intelligence, along with sensory equipment suggesting a possibility of communication with man. So far as I recall, up to date nothing conclusive has come of it all, despite a lot of effort. I bought Dr Lilly's books on his research in the Virgin Islands, but all this has happened so fast I haven't gone very far into them, though I have them with me, in my suitcase.'

'Don't bother with Lilly,' Dr Wilhelm broke in, refilling my glass from a crystal shaker with the etched classical design of a boy riding a dolphin. 'I can show you things here that Lilly never even dreamed of.'

'But the big mystery to me,' I had the temerity to mention, 'is what I'm here for. Do you want me to try and hypnotize your dolphins, or read their minds?'

'Not exactly,' Wilhelm answered. 'At least, not at the present stage. The way I actually plan for you to begin is to hypnotize a human subject, to see whether such a person may become more sensitive to the thought-patterns of the animal.

'We've done a lot of work, following up Lilly's leads, in recording and analysing the sounds these beasts make, both under water and in the air: clicks, beats, whistles, a wide gamut of noises – some of them above the sound spectrum audible to humans. We've taped these sounds, coded them, and fed them into computers, but no pattern of language has emerged, outside of certain very obvious signals for pain, distress, mating – signals many kinds of animals make, but which can't be called real language. And although dolphins will sometimes mimic human speech with a startling clarity, it usually seems to be mere parroting, without real understanding.

'Yet at the same time, our encephalographs show patterns of electrical output in dolphin brains similar to those that occur during human speech, and in parts of the brain analogous to our speech centres – all this while no vocalization of any kind is going on, subsonic or supersonic, airborne or waterborne.

'This led me to a theory that the basic means of dolphin communication may be telepathic, and the conviction that we'll never get in touch with them any other way.'

I was somewhat taken aback. 'Do you have a telepathically sensitive and experienced person on the staff, or are you going to hire such a person?' I queried.

'Even better than that,' rapped Dr Wilhelm triumphantly, his twin-moon spectacles jiggling with emphasis. 'We have a person sensitive and experienced over many months with the animals themselves – someone who knows how dolphins think, feel, and react; someone who has lived with dolphins so closely that she might almost be accepted among them as a dolphin herself.'

'He means me, Mr Dorn.' Through an open door leading to a dusky hallway stepped lightly the lithe figure of a woman.

3

Glancing sidelong at her across the candle-lit dinner table an hour later, I decided that Josephine Gilman was striking but not beautiful. Fairly young, with a trim figure, she missed real distinction due to the muddy colouring and rather swarthy texture of her skin, and especially the staring protuberance of her eyes.

Nor was her manner entirely prepossessing. Her melodramatic entrance of Dr Wilhelm's office that afternoon I could forgive, even with its implication that she had been listening outside for some time. But in subsequent conversation she had proved as much a monomaniac as her employer on the subject of their experiments, and with far less sense of humour – a fitting Trilby to Wilhelm's benign, avuncular Svengali.

'But of course,' she was addressing me over our coffee, 'you know all the old Greek and Roman stories about dolphins, Mr Dorn. How they herded fish to help fishermen, saved drowning persons, and sometimes even fell in love with attractive boys and carried them off to sea on their backs. There's a long history of friendly relations between our species, even though the latter-type incident seems based on – shall we say, a misunderstanding?'

'I don't know about that, Miss Gilman,' I riposted. 'From what I've seen in California already, some of our modern youth would try anything once.'

'Surf, sand, and sex,' Dr Wilhelm interjected, like a slogan. 'I know what you mean. We have some of that type camped out down the beach right now, just south around the bend. Hippies, they call themselves these days. But to get back to dolphins, a more intelligent species. I'm not entirely sure that their good "PR", so to speak, through the ages really rings true,' Wilhelm continued. 'Sometimes I even imagine it resembles the way superstitious people used to refer to the fairies and trolls as "the Good Folk" to flatter them, out of fear of what they might do. So we get the modern nursery-rhyme and Walt Disney type of fairy instead of the hidden troll races, the menacing, stunted, displaced hill-dwellers that were their real origin.'

Josephine Gilman picked up her coffee cup and daintily shrugged, as if to express disagreement.

'No, Jo, there's something to it,' Wilhelm insisted, getting up and lumbering over to a big bookcase in the shadowed corner of the room. 'Let me give you an example from a non-Western tradition.' He searched for a book on one of the upper shelves.

'Sir Arthur Grimble was a colonial governor in the Gilbert Islands not so long ago. He visited an atoll called – what was it? – Butaritari, where there was supposed to be a man who could call dolphins.' Wilhelm located the book he sought and fumbled it open.

'Grimble writes, let's see, here it is: "His spirit went out of his body in a dream; it sought out the porpoise folk in their home under the western horizon and invited them to a dance, with feasting, in Kuma village. If he spoke the words of the invitation aright (and very few had the secret of them) the porpoises would follow him with cries of joy to the surface."

'Well, Grimble had him try it. The place was dead quiet that afternoon under the palm trees, the way he describes it, and the children had been gathered in under the thatches, the women were absorbed in plaiting garlands of flowers, and the men were silently polishing their ceremonial orna-ments of shell. The makings of a feast lay ready in baskets. Suddenly – wait till I find it – "a strangled howl burst from the dreamer's hut. He dashed into the open and stood a while clawing at the air," says Grimble, and "whining on a queer high note like a puppy's. The words came out 'Teiraki!

Teiraki!' which means 'Arise! Arise!' Our friends from the
west . . . Let us go down and greet them.

'"A roar went up from the village, and everyone rushed
over to the beach on the atoll's ocean side. They strung
themselves out and splashed through the shallows, all wearing the garlands woven that afternoon. Breast deep the
porpoises appeared, 'gambolling towards us at a fine clip'.
Everyone was screaming hard. When the porpoises reached
the edge of the reef they slackened speed, spread out, and
started cruising back and forth in front of the human line.
Then suddenly they vanished."'

Dr Wilhelm brought the book to the table, sat down, and
finished his remaining coffee. 'Grimble thought they had
gone away. But in a moment the dreamer pointed downwards, muttering, "The King out of the West comes to greet
me." There, not ten yards away, was the great shape of a
porpoise, "poised like a glimmering shadow in the glass-
green water. Behind it followed a whole dusky flotilla of
them."

'The porpoises seemed to be hung in a trance. Their leader
came slowly to the caller's legs. "As we approached the
emerald shallows, the keels of the creatures began to take
the sand: they flapped gently, as if asking for help. The men
leaned down to throw their arms around the great barrels
and ease them over the ridges. They showed no sign of alarm.
It was as if their single wish was to get to the beach."

'When the water stood only thigh-deep, the men crowded
around the porpoises, ten or more to each beast. Then "Lift!"
shouted the dreamer, and the ponderous black shapes were
half dragged, half carried, unresisting, to the lip of the tide.
There they settled down, those beautiful, dignified shapes,
utterly at peace, while all hell broke loose around them.'

Wilhelm's glasses caught the twin candle flames from the
table; his eyes were impossible to see. Was this wild account,
I found myself wondering, the real basis for his belief in the
possibility of man's telepathic communication with dolphins?

'Men, women, and children,' he continued, 'leaping and

posturing with shrieks that tore the sky, stripped off their garlands and flung them around the still bodies, in a sudden and dreadful fury of boastfulness and derision. "My mind," says Grimble, "still shrinks from that last scene – the raving humans, the beasts so triumphantly at rest." There, what do you think of that?' He closed the book.

'It seems,' I responded, 'that the islanders made the dolphins the object of some sort of religious ritual, and that the dolphins enjoyed the proceedings. Sounds like something our hippie neighbours might go in for.'

'You're wrong about that part,' Josephine Gilman told me solemnly. 'Those people out on the beach there hate the dolphins. Either that, or they're afraid of them.'

4

The next morning dawned damp and cloudy. As I breakfasted in the glass-enclosed patio outside my quarters, which overlooked the surging grey-green waves of the Pacific across a narrow stretch of sand, I saw Dr Wilhelm sauntering along the beach on what seemed a morning constitutional. Suddenly I was aware that he was not alone; slogging across the sand to meet him came a fantastic figure: a booted, bearded, fur-clad man with bulbous features and tangled masses of hair surmounted by a big, bright-red beret – a coarse caricature, he appeared to me, of the well-known bust of the composer Wagner. One of the hippies!

Some impulse, perhaps simply curiosity, moved me to bolt down the eggs and toast which the early-arriving housekeeper had brought me on a tray, and to rush out on to the beach through the storm-door of my entryway and join that strange colloquy shaping up under the striated silver-grey clouds as Wilhelm closed with his odd visitor.

My employer's stance seemed brusque and unfriendly as

he listened to whatever the bearded man was saying to him. I slowed and approached the pair, as if on a casual stroll; until I came up to them, all I could hear was the sibilance of surf hissing over the sand almost at our feet.

'Good morning, Mr Dorn,' Wilhelm snapped, obviously not pleased to see me. 'Perhaps you ought to meet Mr Alonzo Waite, since he's our neighbour. Mr Waite is the high priest, or whatever he calls himself, of that hippie bunch down the way.'

'I call myself nothing,' the other responded quickly. 'My disciples have awarded me the title of *guru*, or spiritual leader, since I have spent more time in mystic exercises than they. But I neither seek nor accept any pre-eminence among them. We are all fellow pilgrims on the sacred quest for truth.' His voice was hollow, deep, strangely impressive; and his words, while eccentric, seemed more urbanely cultivated than I had expected.

'All very well, perhaps,' Wilhelm put in testily, 'but your quest for truth seems determined to interfere with mine.'

'I am simply warning you, as I have warned you before, that your work with the dolphins is potentially very dangerous, to yourselves and others. You should give up these studies and release the beasts before great harm results.'

'And on what evidence do you base this remarkable prophecy?' Wilhelm inquired acidly. 'Tell Mr Dorn; I've heard all this before.'

Waite's cavernous voice descended even deeper. 'As you may know, the League for Spiritual Discovery has been working with mind-expanding substances – not drugs, in the proper sense – that produce intuitions and perceptions unattainable to the ordinary brain. We are not of that group, but we too claim that such states are true ecstatic trances, comparable or superior to those that have always played such a vital part in all the Eastern religions, and which modern science would do well to recognize and investigate.'

'This is more Mr Dorn's field than mine,' Wilhelm said

uneasily. 'He's in parapsychology. I know nothing about such matters, but none of this sounds at all plausible to me.'

'But what has all this to do with dolphins?' I asked the bearded *guru*.

'Our dreams and visions lately have been troubled by the presence of great, white, menacing shapes, cutting across and blocking out the sacred colour patterns and animated mandalas that lead us to greater spiritual understanding,' Waite boomed. 'These are vibrations emanating from the creatures you have penned here, which you call dolphins, but which we know by an older name. These creatures are evil, strong and evil. As your experiments have progressed, so have the disturbing manifestations intensified. These vibrations are terribly destructive, not only mentally but physically. For your own good, I warn you to desist before it is too late.'

'If what we're doing upsets your pipe-dreams,' Wilhelm remarked with ill-concealed contempt, 'why don't you move elsewhere and get out of range?'

The tall, bearded man blinked and gazed into the distance. 'We must remain and concentrate our psychic powers on combating the evil vibrations,' he said quietly. 'There are certain spiritual exercises and ceremonies we can undertake that may help curb or deflect the danger for a while. In fact, we are planning such a ceremony for tonight. But the only sure way to safety is for you to release these ancient, wickedly wise creatures, and to give up your experiment.'

Waite stood solemnly staring out to sea, a grotesque, foreboding, and somehow dignified figure in his oversize beret and flapping fur robe.

5

'A scene right out of a Hollywood science-fiction thriller,' Wilhelm muttered angrily as he led me through the barn-like, high-ceilinged main laboratory and out a rear door. He couldn't seem to get the encounter on the beach out of his mind, and it bothered him more that I could well understand. As for me, I had put Waite down as just a typical California nut, though more intelligent than most, and doubted that we would have any real trouble with him.

'You've seen our sound recording equipment, both atmospheric and underwater,' Wilhelm said, finally changing the subject. 'Now you must see where most of it is used, and where your own work will be concentrated.'

The back of the lab looked out over the beach; near the water's edge stood a smaller windowless structure – long, low, and plastered with white cement like the others. Wilhelm led the way to it and opened its single heavy metal door with a key from his pocket.

The inside was taken up mostly by a sunken tank that resembled a small indoor swimming pool. The narrow verge that surrounded the tank on three sides was cluttered with electrical control panels, head sets, and other paraphernalia connected with the main tape recording and computer banks in the big lab. The ocean side of the building consisted mostly of a sort of sea gate that could be opened on a cove communicating with the ocean itself, as I learned later, so that the water might be cleaned and freshened at need. Harsh fluorescent lamps played over the glittering surface of the pool, sending rippling whorls of reflected light into every corner of the room; there was a low hissing sound from the steam radiators run by thermostats that kept both the air and water temperatures constant and controllable.

But none of this attracted my immediate attention; for here I was at last confronted with the subject of the experiment itself: a lithe, bulky yet graceful shape – mottled grey above, dirty white below, with a long saw-toothed snout and deep-set, intelligent eyes – hung motionless in the shallow water on its slowly fanning flippers.

And not alone, for the dolphin shared its pool with Josephine Gilman, clad in a bright red bathing suit that set off her striking figure in an arresting manner. Indeed, I found myself staring more intently at Josephine than at her aquatic companion.

'Hi.' Josephine's greeting was bland, but suggested a veiled irony, as if she were conscious of my covert gaze.

'Jo has been more or less living in this pool for the last two and a half months,' Dr Wilhelm explained. 'The purpose is to get into complete rapport with Flip – that's the dolphin – and encourage any attempts at communication on his part.'

'Flip,' Josephine interjected, 'is short for Flipper, of course, the dolphin hero of that old movie and TV series that was the first sign of popular awareness of the animal's intelligence.'

Jo laughed, heaving herself adroitly on to the tiled edge of the pool. 'The show was just a sea-going Lassie, of course.' She reached out for and wrapped herself snugly within a heavy terry-cloth towel. 'Anybody for coffee? It's a bit chilly today for these early morning aquatics.'

As Jo served coffee from a sideboard silex, Wilhelm was priming me with data on Flip.

'He's a prime specimen of *Tursiops truncata*, though a bit smaller than average – about six and a half feet, actually. The brain weighs an average of 1,700 grams, 350 grams more than the human brain, with comparable density of cell count.

'We've had this fellow for over a year now, and though he'll make every noise they're noted for – barks, grunts, clicks and scrapes and whistles – and even mimic human speech, we can't dope out a language pattern. Yet they must talk to each other. My first interest in delphinology was aroused by a report on sonar charts that Navy boats made near Ponape in the south Pacific. The charts showed orderly discipline in their undersea movements over a distance amounting to miles; and something more: a pattern or formation of mathematically precise movements that suggests either elaborate play or some sort of ritual.'

'Maybe,' I interrupted facetiously, 'they were practising for the ceremony that so impressed Gov. Grimble.'

'Anyway,' said Jo, putting aside her cup and straightening a strap on her bathing suit, 'in ten weeks I haven't got to first base with Flip here, and now you're supposed to get us on to the proper wave length. Also, you'll have to provide some hints about what to look for and concentrate on in telepathic communication attempts. Frankly, I don't put much faith in it; but if Fred wants to try, I'll co-operate with as few mental reservations as possible.'

Remembering a passage from Dr Lilly's pioneer book on dolphins, I asked Wilhelm: 'Have you implanted electrodes in the beast's brain for pleasure-stimulus experiments?'

'We're beyond all that,' Wilhelm replied impatiently. 'It's been known for years that they'll learn the most complex reaction patterns almost immediately to achieve the stimulus, far beyond what any lower animal can manage. Besides, it's crude – a kind of electrical masturbation, or LSD, like our friends out there on the beach favour. It doesn't show a proper respect for our basic equality with the dolphin – or his superiority over us, as the case may be.'

While this conversation progressed, my attention was gradually distracted by the animal itself, floating in the pool beside us. It was obviously following our talk, though I assumed without any degree of verbal comprehension. The single visible eye, set in a convoluted socket behind the rather menacing snout, moved from one to the other of us with lively interest. I even caught myself reading human

expressions into it: proprietary interest when turned on
Josephine Gilman, tolerant amusement in regard to Dr
Wilhelm, and towards myself, what? Resentment, animosity,
jealousy? What fancies were these I was weaving, under the
glaring lights of a scientific laboratory?

'You'll have to get better acquainted with Flip,' Wilhelm
was saying. 'If you're to help us learn to interpret delphinese,
you and he should become good friends.'

There was a commotion in the water; Flip turned abruptly
to his left and swam off semi-submerged, emitting as he did
so the first dolphin sound I had ever heard: a shrill whistle
of derision.

6

That evening after dinner, Josephine Gilman and I walked
on the beach under a moon that shone only intermittently
through scurrying clouds. Dr Wilhelm was in his office
writing up notes, and the housekeeper-cook, last to leave of
the staff each evening, was just rattling off towards San
Simeon in the Institute's Land Rover.

I found that I didn't know what to make of my feelings
towards Jo. When I had seen her in the pool with the dolphin
that morning, she had attracted me intensely, seeming in
her proper element. But at dinner, in a frilly cocktail gown
that somehow didn't suit her, she once more repelled me
with her sallow skin, her bulging, humourless eyes.

'Tomorrow the hypnosis sessions are to begin,' I reminded
her as we paced slowly towards the surf's edge. 'Are you sure
you really want to undergo this? After all, you say you have
no confidence in this approach, and that may inhibit your
response to it.'

'I'll do as Fred thinks best, and I'll assume what he
assumes, temporarily at least. I've become quite good at that,

within limits. Did you know he once wanted me to marry him? That's where I drew the line, though.'

'No.' I was embarrassed by her abrupt interjection of personal matters.

'I think it was for convenience, mostly. His first wife had died, we were working together, we shared the same interests – even the fact that we had to stay here together overnight, to watch over the work 24 hours a day when that was necessary – well, it would have made things easier, but I told him no.'

'How did you first become interested in – delphinology, is that the word?' I sought to change the subject. We had reached the point beyond which the waves retreated, leaving streaks of hissing, iridescent foam half visible in the gloom.

'Actually, I've always been fascinated by the sea and things that live underwater. I used to spend half my time at the aquarium back home in Boston – either there or down at the harbour.'

'Your family comes from Boston?'

'Not originally. My father was in the Navy, and we lived there a long time, ever since Mother died. His family came from a run-down seaport mill-town called Innsmouth, up past Marblehead. The Gilmans are an old family there. They were in whaling and the East Indies trade as far back as two hundred years ago, and I suppose that's where my oceanographic interests come from.'

'Do you often go back there?'

'I've never been there, strange as it seems. The whole place almost burned to the ground back in the 1920s, before I was born. My father said it was a dead, depressing place, and made me promise years ago to keep away from it – I don't know exactly why. That was just after his last trip there, and on his next voyage he was lost overboard from a destroyer he commanded. No one ever knew how; it was calm weather.'

414 Tales of the Cthulhu Mythos

'Weren't you ever curious about why he warned you away from – what was it, Innsville?' I faltered.

'Yes, especially after he died. I looked up the newspapers from around the time of the big fire – the Boston libraries had almost nothing else on Innsmouth – and found one story that might have had some bearing. It was full of preposterous hints about how the people of Innsmouth had brought back some sort of hybrid heathen savages with them from the South Seas years ago, and started a devil-worship cult that brought them sunken treasure and supernatural power over the weather. The story suggested that the men had interbred with their Polynesian priestesses or whatever, and that was one reason why people nearby shunned and hated them.'

I thought of Josephine's swarthy skin and strange eyes, and wondered.

We had covered a mile or more from the Institute, and were suddenly aware that the darkness ahead was laced with a faint flickering, as of a fire on the beach to the south. At the same time, a sort of low mumble or glutinous chant became audible from the same direction. All at once, a high hysterical wail, reverberating in shocking ecstasy, burst forth on the night air, prolonging itself incredibly – now terror-stricken, now mockingly ironic, now mindlessly animal – rising and falling in a frenzy that suggested only delirium or insanity raised to the highest possible human – or inhuman – pitch.

Without thought or volition, Josephine and I found ourselves clinging together and kissing with an abandon that echoed the wild caterwauling down the beach.

The hippies, it seemed, were holding their promised ritual to exorcize the evil influence of the sinister creatures from the sea.

7

The next few days can most conveniently be summarized through extracts from the clinical journal which I began to keep from the outset of our attempt to establish telepathic contact with the dolphin Flip through hypnosis of a human subject:

April 20. This morning I placed Josephine under light hypnosis, finding her an almost ideally suggestible subject. I implanted post-hypnotic commands intended to keep her alert and concentrating on the dolphin's mind to catch any message emanating from it. After I awakened her, she went back into the tank with Flip and spent the rest of the day there, playing the number of games they have devised together. It is remarkable to observe how devoted the animal is to her, following her about the pool and protesting with loud barkings and bleatings whenever she leaves it. Flip will accept his food, raw whole fish, only from her hands.

I asked Dr Wilhelm whether there was any danger from those wicked-looking hundred-toothed jaws, which snap down on the fish like a huge, lethal pair of shears. He said no; in neither history nor legend has there ever been a report of a dolphin attacking or even accidentally injuring a human. Then he quoted something from Plutarch – his erudition is profound, if one-sided – which I looked up in the library later. Here it is: 'To the dolphin alone, beyond all others, Nature has granted what the best philosophers seek: friendship for no advantage . . .'

April 22. Still no results. Wilhelm wants me to try deeper hypnosis and stronger suggestion. In fact, he proposed leaving Josephine in a trance for periods of a day or more, with just enough volition to keep her head above water in the tank. When I protested that this was dangerous, since in such a state she might well drown inadvertently, Wilhelm gave me an odd look and said, 'Flip wouldn't let her . . .'

April 25. Today, in the absence of any progress whatsoever, I agreed to try Wilhelm's second-stage plan, since Jo agrees. I put

her to sleep by the pool's edge while Flip watched curiously. (I
don't think this dolphin likes me, although I've had no trouble
making friends with the others in the bigger tank up on the
north beach.) After implanting in her subconscious the strongest
admonitions to be careful in the water, I let her re-enter the pool
for a few hours. Her demeanour, of course, is that of a sleep
walker or a comatose person. She sits on the lip of the pool or
wades about in it abstractedly. Flip seems puzzled and resentful
that she won't play their usual games with him.

When I was helping Jo out of the pool after an hour or so of
this, the dolphin zoomed past at terrific speed, and I was sure he
was about to snap at my arm, thus making me the first dolphin-
bitten human in history; but he apparently changed his mind at
the last moment and veered away, quacking and creaking
angrily, his single visible eye glaring balefully . . .

April 27. Dr Wilhelm wants to increase the period with Jo in the
pool under hypnosis. This is because when she woke up yesterday she said she remembered vague, strange impressions that
might be telepathic images or messages. I'm almost certain that
these are pseudo-memories, created by her subconscious to
please Dr Wilhelm, and I have strongly protested any intensifi-
cation of this phase of the experiment.

Those hippie orgies on the beach south of here go on almost
every night till all hours. The three of us are losing sleep and
getting on edge, especially Jo, who tires easily after the longer
periods under hypnosis.

April 28. Jo had an especially vivid impression of some sort of
scenes or pictures transmitted to her during hypnosis after I
brought her out of the trance this afternoon. At Wilhelm's
suggestion I put her under again to help her remember, and we
taped some inconclusive question-and-answer exchanges. She
spoke of a ruined stone city under the sea, with weedy arches
and domes and spires, and of sea creatures moving through the
sunken streets. Over and over she repeated a word that sounded
like 'Arlyah'. It's all imagination, I'm sure, plus memories of
poems by Poe or cheap horror fiction – maybe even the story
Wilhelm read us about Gilbert Island porpoises and their 'King
out of the West'. Yet Wilhelm was excited, and so was Josephine
when she woke up and heard the tape played back. Both of them
wanted me to put her in a deep trance and leave her in the pool
around the clock. I consider this to be a nonsensical idea and
told them so.

April 29. This morning Wilhelm pressed me again. I told him I couldn't be responsible for what might happen, and he answered: 'No, of course not; I am responsible for whatever goes on at this Institute myself.' Then he showed me a kind of canvas harness or breeches buoy affair he'd rigged up in the pool, securely anchored to the verge, where Jo could be strapped and still move around without any danger of drowning under hypnosis. I gave in and agreed to try the idea for a while.

April 30. Everything went off without any difficulty, and at least Jo and Wilhelm are convinced that what they call her 'messages' are getting sharper and more concrete. To me, what she recalls under light hypnosis is just nonsense or fantasy, mixed in perhaps with those odd rumours concerning her father's home town Innsmouth, which she told me about earlier. Nevertheless, the two of them want to keep it up another day or so, and I agreed, since there seems to be no actual danger involved.

8

'No danger involved!' If, when I wrote those words, I had had even an inkling of what I know now, I would have halted the experiment immediately; either that or left this oceanside outpost on the edge of the unknown, threatened by fanatic superstition from the outside and a stiff-necked scientific *hubris* from within. But though the hints were there, recognizable in hindsight, still at the time I saw nothing, felt nothing but a vague, unplaceable malaise, and so did nothing; and thus I must share the guilt for what happened.

Late on the evening of April 30, soon after I had written the journal entry quoted above, Dr Wilhelm and I were roused from our rooms by the sound of a scream which, though faint and muffled by distance, we at once recognized as Jo's voice, not the subhuman caterwauling of our drug-debauched neighbours.

Ask me now why we had left Jo Gilman alone in the dolphin's tank that evening and I must admit that it appears

to be criminal negligence or inexcusable folly. But Wilhelm
and I had stood watch over her alternately the night before
as she hung half-submerged in her canvas harness and
dreamed her strange dreams under the glare of the fluorescent tubes. The harness held her head and thorax well clear
of the water; and Flip, lolling quiescent in the tank, seemed
to drowse too (though dolphins never sleep, since they must
keep surfacing to breathe, like whales). Thus this second
night, at her own prior urging, Wilhelm and I had retired for
dinner and then sought some relaxation in our rooms.

The scream, which jolted us both out of a vague torpor
induced by loss of sleep, came at about 10 P.M. Dr Wilhelm's
room was nearer the main lab than mine; thus, despite his
greater age and bulk, he was ahead of me reaching the heavy
iron door of the beachside aquarium. As I approached the
building, I could see him fumbling with the lock, his hands
trembling. I was taken aback when he wheezed breathlessly
at me over his shoulder: 'Wait here!'

I had no choice, for he slipped inside and clanged the door
shut behind him. The lock operated automatically, and since
only Wilhelm and the chief lab technician – now miles away
in San Simeon – had keys, I was forced to obey.

I can recall and relive in minute detail the agony and
apprehension of that vigil, while the sibilant surf piled up
only yards away under a freshening wind, and the half-full
moon shone down with an ironic tranquillity upon that
silent, windowless, spectral white structure.

I had glanced at my watch as I ran along the beach, and
can verify that it was almost exactly ten minutes after
Wilhelm had slammed the door that he again opened it –
slowly, gratingly, the aperture framing, as always, a rectangle of harsh, glaring light.

'Help me with her,' Wilhelm muttered from within, and
turned away.

I stepped inside. He had removed Jo Gilman's limp form
from the water and had wrapped it in several of the capacious

beach robes that were always at hand near the tank. Glancing beyond the inert figure, I was startled to see Jo's canvas
harness strung out dismembered across the winking surface
of the water; and even part of her bright red bathing suit,
which seemed entangled with the shredded canvas. The
shadowy shape of the dolphin Flip I glimpsed too, fully
submerged and strangely immobile in a far corner of the
pool.

'To her room,' Wilhelm murmured as we lifted Jo. Somehow, staggering and sidling in the shifting sand, we gained
the dormitory building, groped open the door, and stumbled
through Jo's apartment (I had never been inside, but Wilhelm seemed to know his way), finally dropping her muffled
body unceremoniously on to the narrow folding bed.

'I'll call a doctor,' I mumbled, lurching towards the door.

'No, don't!' Wilhelm rapped, adjusting the dim bedside
lamp. 'She's not really hurt – as a zoologist, I'm doctor
enough myself to know that. Bring a tape recorder from the
lab. I think she's still hypnotized, and she may be able to tell
us what happened.'

'But you saw – ' I began breathlessly.

'I saw only what you saw,' he grated, glaring at me though
lenses that picked up the muted glow of the bed lamp. 'She
was clinging to the edge of the pool when I went in there,
only partly conscious, out of her harness, and – get the tape
machine, man!'

Why I obeyed blindly I still do not understand, but I found
myself again blundering along the beach, Wilhelm's key ring
in my hand, and then fumbling a portable tape recorder from
the orderly storage cabinets of the main laboratory.

When I lugged the machine back to Josephine's room, I
found that Dr Wilhelm had somehow manoeuvred her into
an incongruous frilly lounging robe and got her under the
bed covers. He was massaging her wrists with a mechanical
motion, and scanning her face anxiously. Her eyes were still
closed, her breathing harsh and irregular.

'Is she in hypnosis or shock?' he inquired edgily.

'Either, or perhaps both,' I shot back. 'At this point, the symptoms would be similar.'

'Then set up the machine.'

It soon appeared that the deep mesmeric state into which I had placed Jo Gilman that morning still held. I was able to elicit responses from her by employing the key words that I use to trigger the state of trance, so easily invoked these days as to be almost disconcerting.

'Jo, can you hear me? Tell us what happened to you,' I urged her gently. The colour began to return to her face; she sighed deeply and twisted under the bedclothes. For what happened next, I have the evidence not only of my own recollections, but a transcription typed up next day from the tape machine, whose microphone Dr Wilhelm now held beside her pillow with tense expectancy. This is a summary – omitting some of her repetitions, and the urgings on our part – of what we heard muttered by the bruised lips of that comatose woman writhing uneasily on her cot in a dimly lit room beside the glittering, moon-drenched Pacific, close on to midnight of May Eve:

'Must get out . . . must get out and unify the forces. Those who wait in watery Arlyah (Sp.?), those who walk the snowy wastes of Leng, whistlers and lurkers of sullen Kadath – all shall rise, all shall join once more in praise of Great Clooloo (Sp.?), of Shub-Niggurath, of Him Who is not to be Named . . .

'You will help me, fellow breather of air, fellow holder of warmth, storer of seed for the last sowing and the endless harvest – (Unpronounceable name; possibly Y'ha-nthlei) shall celebrate our nuptials, the weedy labyrinth shall hold our couch, the silent strutters in darkness will welcome us with high debauch and dances upon their many-segmented legs . . . their ancient, glittering eyes are gay . . . And we shall dwell amidst wonder and glory for ever . . .'

The speaker gasped and seemed to struggle to awaken. My

apprehensions had crystallized into certainty: 'She's hysterical,' I whispered.

'No – no, not hysterical,' Dr Wilhelm hissed, trying in his elation to keep his voice subdued. 'Not hysterical. She's broken through. Don't you see what this is? Don't you see that she's echoing ideas and images that have been projected to her? Can't you understand? What we've just heard is her attempt to verbalize in English what she's experienced today – the most astonishing thing any human being has ever experienced: communication from another intelligent species!'

9

Of the rest of that night I remember little. The twin shocks of Jo Gilman's hysterical seizure – for so I interpreted not only her unconscious ranting but also the initial scream, and her struggle out of the restraining apparatus – plus the unreasoning interpretation placed upon these events by my employer, served to unnerve me to the extent that when Jo sank gradually into normal slumber I excused myself to Dr Wilhelm and reeled off to my own room a little before midnight, for ten hours of uninterrupted – if not undisturbed – sleep.

It was a distinct surprise to me when I joined the others at staff luncheon next day to find that a reticence amounting almost to a conspiracy of silence had already grown up in regard to the events of the preceding night. Jo, although pale and shaken, referred to what had happened as her 'LSD trip' before the other staff members, and Dr Wilhelm merely spoke of an abortive phase of 'Operation Dolphin' which had been given up.

In any event, Jo completely abandoned her previous intimacy with Flip; indeed, I never once saw her in the aquarium building again; at least, not until a certain climactic occasion, the facts about which I almost hesitate to affirm, even at this juncture.

Suddenly, all research efforts seemed to be shifted hastily to the crowded pens of young dolphins on the north beach, and I was called upon to interpret sonar charts and graphs recording patterns of underwater movement that might – or might not – indicate a telepathic herd-communion between individuals and groups of animals, both free and in captivity.

This, although a plausibly rational shift in experimental emphasis, somehow failed to convince me; it seemed merely a coverup (on the part of Josephine as well as Wilhelm), masking a fear, an uncertainty, or some unsurmised preoccupation I failed to grasp. Perhaps these further extracts from my journal will make clear my uneasiness during this period:

May 7. Jo is still distant and evasive with me. Today as we worked together coding patterns of dolphin movement for the computer, she suddenly fell silent, stopped work, and began to stare straight ahead. When I passed my hand in front of her face, I confirmed that her stare was unfocused, and she had actually fallen into a trance again, from which I am able to awaken her with the same key words we used when she was regularly under hypnosis.

I was horrified, for such involuntary trances may well be a symptom of deep psychic disturbance, over which I can only blame myself for giving in to Dr Wilhelm's rash obstinacy. When she woke up, however, she would admit only to having a headache and dozing off for a moment. I did not press the issue then.

May 8. The above entry was written in the late afternoon. Since Jo seemed herself at dinner, I determined to go to her room later for a serious talk about the dangerous state into which she has fallen. But when I reached the door of her apartment I was surprised to hear voices, as it seemed, in muttered conversation inside.

I stood there for a few moments, irresolute whether to knock or not. Suddenly I realized that although what I heard was divided into the usual give-and-take exchanges of conversation, with pauses and variations in the rhythm and tempo of the participating voices, in actuality the timbre was that of only one speaker; Josephine Gilman herself.

I was shocked – had her state deteriorated into schizophrenia? Might she indeed be picking up telepathic messages; and if so, from whom? I could distinguish no words in the muttered stream of speech. Cautiously I tried the door. It was locked, and I tiptoed away along the outer corridor as if I were a thief, or an ordinary eavesdropper . . .

May 10. I still cannot believe that what Jo said on the tape after her so-called hysterical seizure was really a remembered telepathic transmission from Flip; and despite what Dr Wilhelm said that night, I don't know whether he still believes it either. I have studied the transcript over and over, and think I have found a clue. Something about one of the phrases she spoke seemed hauntingly familiar: 'Their ancient, glittering eyes are gay.'

Recalling Wilhelm's remarkable memory, I mentioned it to him, and he agreed immediately: 'Yes, it's from Yeats. I recognized that almost at once.'

'But that means the so-called message, or part of it at least, must have come from her own subconscious memory of a poem.'

'Perhaps. But after all, it was Yeats who wrote the line about "that dolphin-torn, that gong-tormented sea." Perhaps he's their favourite poet.'

This flippancy irritated me. 'Dr Wilhelm,' I answered angrily, 'do you really believe that that tape was a telepathic transmission from Flip?'

He sobered. 'I don't know, Dorn. Maybe we'll never know. I thought so at first, but perhaps I was carried away. I almost hope so – it was a pretty unsettling experience. But one thing I do know: you were right; that particular line of approach is too dangerous, at least with a subject as highly strung as Jo. Perhaps we can devise a safer way to resume the research with hypnosis later, but just now I don't see how. We're only lucky that she didn't suffer any real harm.'

'We don't know that either,' I replied. 'She's started hypnotizing herself.'

Wilhelm didn't answer . . .

May 20. For over a week, I have not observed Jo fall into one of her trances in the daytime. However, she always retires early, pleading exhaustion, so we don't know what may go on at night. Several times I have deliberately paused outside her door during the evening, and once I thought I heard that strange muffled conversation again, but softer or more distant.

The research is now mechanical and curiously artificial: I don't see that we're accomplishing anything, nor is there any special need for me to be here at all. The old enthusiasm and vigour seem to have gone out of Wilhelm, too. He has lost weight and appears older, apprehensive, as if waiting for something . . .

May 24. I sat late on the patio last night, looking out towards the ocean, which was invisible, since there was no moon. At about nine o'clock I thought I saw something white moving down by the water's edge, proceeding south in the general direction of the main lab. Curiously disturbed, I followed.

It was Jo of course, either under hypnosis or walking in her sleep. (Here indeed was a scene from a horror film for Wilhelm to snort at!) I took her arm and was able to guide her back to the dormitory building. The door to her apartment was open, and I put her to bed without resistance. However, when I tried to awaken her by the usual mesmeric methods, I failed. After a while, though, she seemed to fall into ordinary slumber, and I left, setting the lock on the hall door to catch automatically.

Wilhelm was working late in his study, but I could see no reason to tell him about this incident. I shall probably not tell Jo either, since it might upset her nerves even more. I realize that I have become extremely fond of her since her 'LSD trip', in a tender, protective way unlike my initial physical attraction for her. And this knowledge makes me recognize, too, that something must be done to help her. All I can think of is to call in a psychiatrist, but Wilhelm has already denied the need for this, and I know Jo will follow his lead.

I must keep alert for more evidence to convince the pair of them that such a step is urgently indicated.

For the past few weeks our hippies have abated their nocturnal ceremonies, but last night after I left Jo's room I could hear that inhuman chanting and shouting start up, and see from my patio the reflections from their distant fire on the beach.

Again I did not sleep well.

10

It was past mid-June, with no change in the tense but tenuous situation at the Institute, when I had my momentous interview with the hippie *guru*, Alonzo Waite.

The moon shone brightly that evening, and I sat as usual on my glass-fronted patio, nursing a last brandy and trying to put my thoughts and ideas into some sort of order for the hundredth time. Jo Gilman had as usual retired early, and Dr Wilhelm had driven into town for some sort of needed supplies, so I was in effect alone in the Institute. Perhaps Waite knew this somehow, for he came unerringly up the beach to my door, his fur cloak flapping dejectedly around his shanks, even though my apartment showed no light. I rose somewhat hesitantly to admit him.

He seated himself in a canvas chair, refused brandy, and abstractedly removed the soiled red beret from his unshorn locks. In the faint glow of the hurricane lamp I had lit, his dark eyes were distant and withdrawn; I wondered whether he were under the influence of drugs.

'Mr Dorn,' my visitor began, in the resonant tones I well remembered, 'I know that you as a man of science cannot approve or understand what my companions and I are trying to do. Yet because your field is exploration of the lesser-known aspects of the human mind, I have hopes that you may give me a more sympathetic hearing than Dr Wilhelm has done.

'I, too, am a scientist, or was – don't smile! A few years ago, I was assistant professor in clinical psychology at a small school in Massachusetts called Miskatonic University, a place you've possibly never even heard of. It's in an old colonial town called Arkham, quite a backwater, but better known in the days of the Salem witch trails.

'Now, extravagant as the coincidence may seem – if it is really a coincidence – I knew your co-worker Josephine Gilman by sight when she was a student there, though she would certainly not recognize me, or even recall my name perhaps, in the guise I have now adopted.' He shrugged slightly and glanced down at his eccentric getup, then continued.

'You probably don't remember the scandal that resulted in my leaving my post, since it was hushed up, and only a few sensational newspapers carried the item. I was one of those early martyrs to science – or to superstition, if you like; but whose superstition? – fired for drug experiments with students in the early days of LSD research. Like others who became better known, and who sometimes exploited their discoveries for personal profit or notoriety, I was convinced that the mind-expanding drugs gave humanity an opening into a whole new world of psychic and religious experience. I never stopped to wonder in those days whether the experience would involve beauty alone, or also encompass terror. I was a pure scientist then, I liked to think, and to me whatever was was good – or at least neutral – raw material for the advancement of human understanding. I had much to learn.

'The drug underground at Miskatonic University was a little special. The school has one of the most outstanding collections of old books on out-of-the-way religious practices now extant. If I mention the medieval Arab treatise called the *Necronomicon* in its Latin version, you won't have heard of it; yet the Miskatonic copy is priceless, one of only three acknowledged still to exist – the others are in the Harvard and Paris libraries.

'These books tell of an ancient secret society or cult that believes the earth and all the known universe were once ruled by vast alien invaders from outside space and time, long before man evolved on this planet. These entities were so completely foreign to molecular matter and protoplasmic life that for all intents and purposes they were supernatural – supernatural and evil.'

Waite may once have been a college professor, I reflected, but judging by his portentous word choice and delivery, he would have made an even better old-time Shakespearean actor or revival preacher. His costume helped the effect, too.

'At some point,' the bearded *guru* continued, 'these usurpers were defeated and banished by even stronger cosmic opponents who, at least from our limited viewpoint, would appear benevolent. However, the defeated Old Ones could not be killed, not even permanently thwarted. They live on, imprisoned, but always seeking to return and resume their sway over the space-time universe, pursuing their immemorial and completely unknowable purposes.

'These old books record the lore that has been passed on to man from human and pre-human priesthoods that served these imprisoned deities, who constantly strive to mould and sway the thoughts of men by dreams; moving them to perform the rites and ceremonies by means of which the alien entities may be preserved, strengthened, and at last released from their hated bondage.

'All this goes on even today, and has influenced half the history of human science and religion in unacknowledged ways. And of course, there are rival cults that seek to prevent the return of the Old Ones, and to stymie the efforts of their minions.

'To be brief, the visions induced by LSD in the Miskatonic students, together with the results of certain experiments and ceremonies we learned from the old books, confirmed the reality of this fantastic mythology in a very terrible way. Even now I could not be persuaded to tell any living person some of the things I have seen in my visions, nor even to hint at the places my spirit has journeyed during periods of astral detachment. There were several disappearances of group members who dared too much, and several mental breakdowns, accompanied by certain physical changes that necessitated placing the victim in permanent seclusion. These occurrences, I assure you, were not due to any human agency whatever, no matter what the authorities may have chosen to believe.

'Though there was no evidence of foul play, the group was discovered and expelled, and I lost my job. After that some of us came here and formed a community dedicated to thwarting the efforts of evil cultists to free the Great Old Ones, which would mean in effect the death or degradation of all men not sworn to serve them. This is the aim of our present efforts to achieve spiritual knowledge and discipline through controlled use of hallucinogenic agents. Believe me, we have seen more than enough of the horrors connected with these matters, and our sympathies are all on the other side. Unfortunately, there are opposing groups, some of them right here in California, working in parallel ways to effect directly contrary results.'

'An interesting story,' I put in impatiently, disgusted by what I regarded as insane ramblings, 'but what has all this to do with our research here, and the fact that you knew Miss Gilman as a college student?'

'Josephine's family comes from Innsmouth,' Waite rumbled forebodingly. 'That blighted town was once one of the centres of this cosmic conspiracy. Before the Civil War, mariners from Innsmouth brought back strange beliefs from their South Pacific trading voyages – strange beliefs, strange powers, and strange, deformed Polynesian women as their brides. Later, still stranger things came out of the sea itself in response to certain ceremonies and sacrifices.

'These creatures, half human and half amphibians of unknown batrachian strains, lived in the town and interbred with the people there, producing monstrous hybrids. Almost all the Innsmouth people became tainted with this unhuman heritage, and as they grew older many went to live underwater in the vast stone cities built there by the races that serve Great Cthulhu.'

I repeated the strange name falteringly; somehow it rang a bell in my memory. All this was oddly reminiscent, both of what Jo had told me and of her delirious words on the tape, which Wilhelm half believed represented a message from the mind of an undersea race.

'Cthulhu,' Waite repeated sepulchrally, 'is the demonic deity imprisoned in his citadel amidst the prehuman city of R'lyeh, sunken somewhere in mid-Pacific by the power of his enemies aeons ago; asleep but dreaming forever of the day of release, when he will resume sway over the earth. And his dreams over the centuries have created and controlled those undersea races of evil intelligence who are his servants.'

'You can't mean the dolphins!' I exclaimed.

'These and others – some of such aspect that only delirious castaways have ever seen them and lived. These are the sources of the legendary hydras and harpies, Medusa and mermaids, Scylla and Circe, which have terrified human beings from the dawn of civilization, and before.

'Now you can guess why I have constantly warned Dr Wilhelm to give up his work, even though he is nearer success that he realizes. He is meddling in things more terrible than he can well imagine when he seeks communication with these Deep Ones, these minions of the blasphemous horror known as Cthulhu.

'More than this – the girl through whom he seeks this communication is one of the Innsmouth Gilmans. No, don't interrupt me! I knew it as soon as I saw her at the university; the signs are unmistakable, though not far advanced yet: the bulging, ichthyic eyes, the rough skin around the neck where incipient gill-openings will gradually develop with age. Some day, like her ancestors, she will leave the land and live underwater as an ageless amphibian in the weedy cities of the Deep Ones, which I glimpse almost daily, in my visions and in my nightmares alike.

'This cannot be coincidence – there is manipulation somewhere in bringing this girl, almost wholly ignorant of her

awful heritage, into intimate, unholy contact with a creature
that can end what slim chances she may ever have had of
escaping her monstrous genetic destiny!'

11

Although I did my best to calm Alonzo Waite by assuring
him that all attempts to establish hypnotic rapport between
Jo and Flip had ended, and that the girl had even taken an
aversion to the animal, I did not tell him any of the other
puzzling aspects of the matter, some of which seemed to fit
in strangely with the outlandish farrago of superstition and
hallucination that he had been trying to foist upon me.

Waite did not seem much convinced by my protestations,
but I wanted to get rid of him and think matters over again.
Obviously the whole of his story was absurd; but just as
obviously he believed it. And if others believed it too, as he
claimed, then this might explain in some measure the odd
coincidences and the semi-consistent pattern that seemed to
string together so many irrelevancies and ambiguities.

But after Waite left, I decided that there were still pieces
missing from the puzzle. Thus when Jo Gilman knocked on
my door a little before eleven o'clock, I was not only surprised
(she never came out at night any more, since her sleep-
walking episode) but glad of the opportunity to ask her some
questions.

'I couldn't sleep and felt like talking,' Jo explained, with
an air of rather strained nonchalance, as she settled in the
same chair Waite had used. 'I hope I'm not disturbing you.'
She accepted a brandy and soda, and lit a cigarette. I had a
sudden, detached flash of vision that saw this scene as a
decidedly familiar one: drinks and cigarettes, a girl in a
dressing gown in the beachside apartment of a bachelor. But
our conversation didn't fall into the cliché pattern; we talked

of sonar graphs and neuron density, of supersonic vibrations, computer tapes, and the influence of water temperature on dolphin mating habits.

I watched Jo carefully for any signs of falling into that autohypnotic state in which she held conversations with herself, but could see none; she seemed closer to normal than had been the case for many weeks. At the same time, I was annoyed to realize that I had become more conscious than before of the physical peculiarities which that idiot Waite had attributed to a biologically impossible strain in her ancestry.

The conversation had been entirely prosaic until I seized the opportunity of a short silence to ask one of the questions that had begun to intrigue me: 'When did you first hear about Dr Wilhelm's studies, and how did you happen to come to work for him?'

'It was right after my father drowned. I had to drop out of graduate school back in Massachusetts and start making my own living. I had heard about Fred's research, and of course I was fascinated from the start, but I never thought of applying for a job here until my Uncle Joseph suggested it.'

'Your father's brother?'

'Yes, a funny little old fellow; I always thought when I was a child that he looked just like a frog. He spends about half the year at the old family place in Innsmouth and half in Boston. He seems to have all the money he needs, though I've never seen any of it. My father once asked him jokingly what he did for a living, and Uncle Joe just laughed and said he dove for Spanish doubloons.

'Anyway, a few weeks after I left school and came back to Boston, Uncle Joe showed me a story about Dr Wilhelm's work with the delphinidae – I think it was in the *Scientific American*. Joe knew of my studies in oceanography, of course, and he said he knew an authority in the field who would write me a good recommendation. It must have been a good one, all right, because in less than six weeks here I was. That was over two years ago, now.'

If Alonzo Waite needed a further link in his wild theory of conspiracy, here was perfect raw material!

'You know,' Jo went on with apparently casual lightness, 'I told you a long time ago that Dr Wilhelm asked me to marry him. That was over six months ago. At the time I thought it was a bad idea, but now I rather wish I had taken him up on it.'

'Why? Afraid of becoming an old maid? I might have something to say about that one of these days.'

'No.' Her voice remained as calm and casual as before. 'The reason is that – dating from right around the time that Fred Wilhelm rescued me from my LSD trip in that dolphin tank – I've been pregnant. At least, that's the timetable that the doctor in San Simeon has figured.'

12

'Then it's Fred?' My remark sounded stupid, clumsy; like something that hypothetical beachside couple I had imagined might be discussing in some tawdry charade illustrating California's vaunted 'New Morality'.

'Figure it out for yourself,' Jo answered with a nervous laugh. 'It's either you or Fred. I don't remember a thing until I woke up the next morning feeling like a used punching bag.'

'Wilhelm was alone with you for at least ten minutes before he let me into the aquarium. And he was alone with you in your apartment after I went to bed three hours later. I never was alone with you that evening.'

'That's what I assumed from what you both told me next day. Besides, I never turned you down – maybe only because you didn't ask me.'

'Jo,' I said, getting out of my chair; and didn't know what to say next.

'No, whatever it is, forget it,' she murmured. 'Whatever you were going to say, it's too late. I've got to think in an entirely different frame of reference now.'

'What are you going to do?'

'I think I'm going to marry Fred – that is, if he's still interested. From there we'll see. There's more now than just me to worry about, and that seems the right move – the only move – to start with.'

We didn't say much more. Jo felt drowsy all of a sudden and I walked her back to her apartment. Afterwards, I strolled on the beach. A brisk wind arose around midnight, and clouds covered what moon there was. I felt numb; I hadn't known, or anyway admitted to myself, how I felt about Jo until now. I loved her too. But if Wilhelm, the old satyr, had made her pregnant while she was under hypnosis, then what she planned was probably best for all concerned. But how unlike Wilhelm such an act appeared! The gentlemanly, scholarly enthusiast, with his grandfatherly grey hair and amusing penguin shape – he might become infatuated with and propose to a young woman, especially someone who shared his enthusiasms. That was in character. But a dastardly attack like the one Jo suspected? He must be insane.

I heard the Land-Rover chugging up the sandy road; Dr Wilhelm was returning. I'd find it hard to face him tomorrow. In fact, that might just be the best time for me to offer him my resignation, although I had no future prospects. Maybe I could get my old job back. At any rate, nobody needed me around here any more, that much was crystal clear.

I went back to my room and had several more brandies. Before I fell asleep, I became aware that the hippies were launching one of their wild orgies down on the south beach. From what Waite had said, they were holding ceremonies to keep the nice, normal, sane world safe for nice, normal, sane people.

If there were any left these days.

13

I don't think I had slept as much as an hour when something sent me bolt upright in bed, wide awake. It may have been a sound, or it may have been some sort of mental message – (ironic, since this was my field of study, that I had never observed, much less experienced, a fully convincing instance of telepathic communication).

In any case, something was wrong, I was sure of that; and if my premonition proved right, I knew where to go to find it: the beach by the main laboratory. I dressed hurriedly and dashed out on the shifting sands.

The wind, now near gale force, had swept the clouds away from the sickle moon, which shone starkly on the beach and glared upon an ocean of crinkled tinfoil. I could see two figures moving towards the windowless building at the water's edge where Flip, the neglected subject of our old experiment, was still kept in isolation. They converged and entered the building together, after a moment's hesitation over the locks.

As I dashed in pursuit, the gusty wind brought me snatches of the hippie ceremony; I made out drums and cymbals beaten wildly, as well as that same muffled chanting and the high, floating wail of ecstasy or terror, or both.

The harsh white light of fluorescent tubes now streamed through the open door leading to the dolphin tank, and I heard another sound inside as I approached: the clank of machinery and the hum of an electric motor. Dr Wilhelm was raising the sea gate on the ocean side of the building, the gate that was sometimes used to change the water in the tank while Flip was held under restraint by the daytime lab assistants. No one could be holding him now; was Wilhelm about to release the animal, to satisfy some vague, belated qualm of conscience?

But as I panted up to the open door, I realized that more than this was afoot. In a momentary glimpse just before the storm cut out our power lines, I took in the whole unbelievable scene: the massive sea gate was fully raised now, allowing turbulent waves to surge into the floodlighted pool, and even to splash violently over its rim, inundating the observation deck and its elaborate equipment.

The dolphin, pitting his powerful muscles against the force of the incoming water, was relentlessly beating his way out to sea. Of Dr Wilhelm there was no sign; but, perched on the broad, smooth back of the great sea beast itself, her naked body partly covered by her soaked, streaming hair, sat Josephine Gilman, bolt upright, bestriding her strange mount like the old Grecian design of the boy on the dolphin, that enigmatic emblem of the marriage of earth to ocean.

Then the lights failed, but the waves pounded on, and the distant delirious chanting reached a peak of hysteria that sustained itself incredibly, unendingly.

I can recall no more.

14

Josephine's body was never found; nor was there any reason that I should ever have expected that it would be. When the lab crew arrived next morning, they repaired the power line and raised the sea gate again. Dr Wilhelm's mangled body was caught beneath it. The gate had fallen when the power failed, and had crushed Wilhelm as he attempted to follow the fantastic pair he had liberated into the open sea.

On the neat desk in Dr Wilhelm's office, where I had first met Josephine Gilman on the evening of my arrival, lay a manila envelope addressed to me. It contained a typed letter and a roll of recording tape. I found the envelope myself, and I have not shown it to the police, who seem to believe my story that Wilhelm and Josephine were swept out to sea when the gate was accidently raised during an experiment.

This is what the letter said:

Dear Dorn:

When you read this I shall be dead, if I am lucky. I must release the two of them to go back to the ocean depths where they belong. For you see, I now believe everything that grotesque person Alonzo Waite told me.

I lied to you once when you asked me whether I had implanted electrodes in the brain of the test dolphin. I did implant one electrode at an earlier stage of my work, when I was doing some studies on the mechanism of sexual stimulation in the animal. And when our experiments in telepathic communication seemed to be inconclusive, I was criminally foolish enough to broadcast a remote signal to activate that stimulus, in a misguided attempt to increase the rapport between the subject and the animal.

This was on the afternoon of April 30, and you can guess – reluctantly enough – what happened that evening. I assume full responsibility and guilt, which I will expiate in the only way that seems appropriate.

When I got to the pool ahead of you on that awful night, I saw at a glance what must have just occurred. Josephine had been ripped from her canvas sling, still hypnotized, and badly mauled. Her suit was torn almost off her, but I wrapped her in a robe and somehow got her into bed without your guessing what had really happened. The hypnosis held, and she never realized either. From then on, though, she was increasingly under telepathic contact and even control by that beast in the pool, even though she consciously and purposely avoided him.

Tonight when I got back from town she told me about her pregnancy, but in the middle of talking she fell into the usual trance and started to walk out on the beach. I locked her in her room and sat down to write this, since you have a right to know the truth, although there is nothing more that can be done after tonight.

I think we each loved Josephine in our own way, but now it is too late. I must let her out to join her own – she was changing – and when the baby is born – well, you can imagine the rest.

I myself would never have believed any of this, except for the tape. Play it and you'll understand everything. I didn't even think of it for a couple of weeks, fool that I was. Then I remembered that all during the time Jo spent hypnotized in the pool with the dolphin, I had ordered the microphones left open to record whatever might happen. The tapes were routinely filed by date the next day, and had never been monitored. I found the reel for April 30 and copied the part that I enclose with this letter.

Goodbye – and I'm sorry.

                                        Frederick C. Wilhelm

Many hours passed – hours of stunned sorrow and disbelief – before I dared bring a tape machine to my room and listen to the recording Wilhelm had left for me. I debated destroying the reel unheard; and afterwards I did erase the master tape stored in the main laboratory.

But the need to know the truth – a scientific virtue that is sometimes a human failing – forced me to listen to the accursed thing. It meant the end for me of any peace of mind or security in this life. I hope that Jo and Flip have found some measure of satisfaction in the strange, alien world so forebodingly described by the *guru* Waite, and that Frederick Wilhelm has found peace. I can neither look for nor expect either.

This is what I transcribed from that tape after many agonizing hours of replaying. The time code indicates that it was recorded at about 9:35 on the evening of April 30, a scant few minutes before Josephine's agonized scream sent Wilhelm and me dashing belatedly to rescue her from that garishly illuminated chamber where the ultimate horror took place:

'My beloved, my betrothed, you must help me. I must get out and unify the forces. Those who wait in watery R'lyeh, those who walk the snowy wastes of Leng, whistlers and lurkers of sullen Kadath – all shall rise, all shall join once more in praise of Great Cthulhu, of Shub-Niggurath, of Him Who is not to be Named. You shall help me, fellow breather of air, fellow holder

of warmth, another storer of seed for the last sowing and the
endless harvest. Y'ha-nthlei shall celebrate our nuptials, the
weedy labyrinths shall hold our couch, the silent strutters in
darkness will welcome us with high debauch and dances upon
their many-segmented legs ... their ancient, glittering eyes are
gay. And we shall dwell amidst wonder and glory for ever.'

Merely a repetition, you say; merely an earlier version of
that meaningless rant that Josephine repeated an hour later
under hypnosis in her bedroom, a garbled outpouring of
suppressed fragments and fears from the subconscious mind
of one who unreasoningly dreaded her family background in
a shunned, decadent seaport a continent away?

I wish I could believe that too, but I cannot. For these wild
words were spoken, not by a mentally unbalanced woman in
deep hypnotic trance, *but in the quacking, bleating, inhuman
tones that are the unmistakable voice of the dolphin itself,
alien servant of still more alien masters; the Deep Ones of
legend, pre-human (and perhaps soon post-human) intelli-
gences behind whose bland, benign exterior lurks a threat to
man which not all man's destructive ingenuity can equal, or
avert.*

The Return of the Lloigor

COLIN WILSON

My name is Paul Dunbar Lang, and in three weeks' time I shall be seventy-two years old. My health is excellent, but since one can never know how many more years lie ahead, I shall set down this story on paper, and perhaps even publish it, if the fit takes me. In my youth, I was a confirmed believer in the Baconian authorship of Shakespeare's plays, but I took care never to mention my views in print, out of fear of my academic colleagues. But age has one advantage; it teaches one that the opinions of other people are not really very important; death is so much more real. So if I publish this, it will not be out of desire to convince anyone of its truth; but only because I don't care whether it is believed or not.

Although I was born in England – in Bristol – I have lived in America since I was twelve years old. And for nearly forty years, I have taught English literature at the University of Virginia in Charlottesville. My *Life of Chatterton* is still the standard work on its subject, and for the past fifteen years I have been the editor of *Poe Studies*.

Two years ago in Moscow, I had the pleasure of meeting the Russian writer Irakli Andronikov, who is known mainly for his 'literary research stories', a genre he may be said to have created. It was Andronikov who asked me if I ever met W. Romaine Newbold, whose name is involved with the Voynich manuscript. Not only had I never met Professor Newbold, who died in 1927, but I had never heard of the

manuscript. Andronikov outlined the story. I was fascinated.
When I returned to the States, I hastened to read Newbold's
The Cipher of Roger Bacon (Philadelphia, 1928), and Profes-
sor Manly's two articles on the subject.

The story of the Voynich manuscript is briefly this. It was
found in an old chest in an Italian castle by a rare book
dealer, Wilfred M. Voynich, and brought to the United States
in 1912. With the manuscript, Voynich also found a letter
that asserted that it had been the property of two famous
scholars of the 17th century, and that it had been written by
Roger Bacon, the Franciscan monk who died about 1294. The
manuscript was 116 pages long, and was apparently written
in cipher. It was clearly some kind of scientific or magical
document, since it contained drawings of roots or plants. On
the other hand, it also contained sketches that looked amaz-
ingly like illustrations from some modern biological textbook of minute cells and organisms – for example, of sper-
matozoa. There were also astronomical diagrams.

For nine years, professors, historians, and cryptographers
tried to break the code. Then, in 1921, Newbold announced
to the American Philosophical Society in Philadelphia that
he had been able to decipher certain pages. The excitement
was immense; it was regarded as a supreme feat of American
scholarship. But the excitement increased when Newbold
disclosed the contents of the manuscript. For it seemed that
Bacon must have been many centuries ahead of his time. He
had apparently invented the microscope some four hundred
years before Leewenhoeck, and had shown a scientific
acumen that surpassed even that of his namesake Francis
Bacon in the sixteenth century.

Newbold died before completing his work, but his 'discoveries' were published by his friend Roland Kent. It was at
this point that Professor Manly took up the study of the
manuscript, and decided that Newbold's enthusiasm had led
him to deceive himself. Examined under a microscope, it was
seen that the strange nature of the characters was not

entirely due to a cipher. The ink had peeled off the vellum as it dried, so that the 'shorthand' was actually due to ordinary wear and tear over many centuries. With Manly's announcement of his discovery in 1931, interest in the 'most mysterious manuscript in the world' (Manly's phrase) vanished, Bacon's reputation sank, and the whole thing was quickly forgotten.

Upon my return from Russia, I visited the university of Pennsylvania, and examined the manuscript. It was an odd sensation. I was not disposed to view it romantically. In my younger days, I had often felt my hair stirring as I handled a letter in Poe's handwriting, and I had spent many hours sitting in his room at the University of Virginia, trying to commune with his spirit. As I got older, I became more matter of fact – a recognition that geniuses are basically like other men – and I stopped imagining that inanimate objects are somehow trying to 'tell a story'.

Yet as soon as I handled the Voynich manuscript, I had a nasty sensation. I cannot describe it more precisely than that. It was not a sense of evil or horror or dread – just nastiness; like the sensation I used to have as a child passing the house of a woman who was reputed to have eaten her sister. It made me think of murder. This sensation stayed with me during the two hours while I examined the manuscript, like an unpleasant smell. The librarian obviously did not share my feeling. When I handed the manuscript back to her, I said jokingly: 'I don't like that thing.' She merely looked puzzled; I could tell she had no idea of what I meant.

Two weeks later, the two photostat copies I had ordered arrived in Charlottesville. I sent one to Andronikov, as I had promised, and had the other one bound for the university library. I spent some time poring over it with a magnifying glass, reading Newbold's book and Manly's articles. The sensation of 'nastiness' did not return. But when, some months later, I took my nephew to look at the manuscript, I again experienced the same feeling. My nephew felt nothing.

While we were in the library, an acquaintance of mine introduced me to Averel Merriman, the young photographer whose work is used extensively in expensive art books of the kind published by Thames and Hudson. Merriman told me that he had recently photographed a page of the Voynich manuscript in colour. I asked if I might see it. Later that afternoon, I called on him in his hotel room and saw the photograph. What was my motive? I believe it was a sort of morbid desire to find out if the 'nastiness' would come over in a colour photograph. It didn't. But something more inter- esting did. It so happened that I was thoroughly familiar with the page Merriman had photographed. And so now, looking at it carefully, I felt sure that it was, in some subtle way, different from the original. I stared at it for a long time before I realized why. The colouring of the photograph – developed by a process invented by Merriman – was slightly 'richer' than that of the original manuscript. And when I looked at certain symbols indirectly – concentrating on the line just above them – they appeared to be somehow 'com- pleted', as if the discoloration left by the flakes of ink had become visible.

I tried not to show my excitement. For some reason, I felt intensely secretive, as if Merriman had just handed me the clue to hidden treasure. A kind of 'Mr Hyde' sensation came over me – a feeling of cunning, and a kind of lust. I asked him casually how much it would cost to photograph the whole manuscript in this way. He told me several hundred dollars. Then my idea came to me. I asked if, for a much larger sum – say a thousand dollars – he would be willing to make me large 'blow-ups' of the pages – perhaps four to a page. He said he would, and I wrote him a cheque on the spot. I was tempted to ask him to send me the photographs one by one, as he did them, then felt that this might arouse his curiosity. To my nephew Julian I explained as we left that the library of the University of Virginia had asked me to have the photographs made – a pointless lie that puzzled

me. Why should I lie? Had the manuscript some dubious
influence of which I had become a victim?

A month later, the registered parcel arrived. I locked the
door of my study, and sat in the armchair by the window as
I tore off the wrappings. I took a random photograph from
the middle of the pile, and held it out to the light. I wanted
to shout with pleasure at what I saw. Many of the symbols
seemed to be 'completed', as if their broken halves were
joined by a slightly darkened area of the vellum. I looked at
sheet after sheet. It was impossible to doubt. The colour
photography somehow showed up markings that were invisible even to a microscope.

What followed now was routine work, although it took
many months. The photographs were taped, one after the
other, to a large drawing board, and then traced. The
tracings were transferred, with the utmost care, to heavy
drawing paper. Then, working with deliberate slowness, I
sketched in the 'invisible' part of the symbols, completing
them. When the whole thing was finished, I bound it into a
large folio, and then settled down to study it. I had completed
more than half the symbols – which were, of course, four
times their natural size. Now, with the aid of a kind of
painstaking detective work, I was able to complete nearly all
the others.

Only then, after ten months' work, did I allow myself to
consider the main part of my task – the question of
deciphering.

To begin with, I was totally in the dark. The symbols were
complete – but what were they? I showed some of them to a
colleague who had written a book on the deciphering of
ancient languages. He said they bore some resemblance to
later Egyptian hieroglyphics – of the period when all resemblance to 'pictures' had vanished. I wasted a month pursuing
this false trail. But fate was on my side. My nephew was
about to return to England, and he asked me to let him have
a photograph of a few pages of the Voynich manuscript. I

experienced a deep reluctance, but could hardly refuse. I was still being thoroughly secretive about my work, rationalizing this by telling myself that I merely wanted to ensure that no one stole my ideas. Finally, I decided that perhaps the best way of preventing Julian from feeling curiosity about my labours was to make as little fuss as possible. So two days before he was due to sail, I presented him with a photograph of a page of the manuscript, and with my reconstructed version of yet another page. I did this casually, as if it were a matter that hardly interested me.

Ten days later, I received a letter from Julian that made me congratulate myself on my decision. On the boat, he had made friends with a young member of the Arab Cultural Association, who was travelling to London to take up a post. One evening, by chance, he showed him the photographs. The actual page of the Voynich manuscript meant nothing to the Arab; but when he saw my 'reconstruction', he said immediately: 'Ah, this is some form of Arabic.' Not modern Arabic; and he was unable to read it. But he had no doubt that the manuscript had originated in the Middle East.

I rushed to the university library and found an Arabic text. A glance at it showed me the Arab had been right. The mystery of the Voynich script was solved: it seemed to be medieval Arabic.

It took me two weeks to learn to read Arabic – although, of course, I could not understand it. I prepared to settle down to a study of the language. If I worked at it for six hours a day, I calculated that I should be able to speak it fluently in about four months. However, this labour proved to be unnecessary. For once I had mastered the script well enough to translate a few sentences into English letters, I realized that it was not written in Arabic, but in a mixture of Latin and Greek.

My first thought was that someone had gone to a great deal of trouble to hide his thoughts from prying eyes. Then I realized that this was an unnecessary assumption. The Arabs were, of course, among the most skilled doctors in Europe in the Middle Ages. If an Arab physician were to write a manuscript, what would be more likely than that he should do so in Latin and Greek, using Arab script?

I was now so excited that I could barely eat or sleep. My housekeeper told me continually that I needed a holiday. I decided to take her advice, and take a sea voyage. I would go back to Bristol to see my family, and take the manuscript with me on the boat, where I could work undisturbed all day long.

Two days before the ship sailed, I discovered the title of the manuscript. Its title page was missing, but there was a reference on the fourteenth page that was clearly to the work itself. It was called *Necronomicon*.

The following day, I was seated in the lounge of the Algonquin Hotel in New York, sipping a martini before dinner, when I heard a familiar voice. It was my old friend Foster Damon, of Brown University, in Providence. We had met years before when he was collecting folk songs in Virginia, and my admiration for his poetry, as well as for his works on Blake, had kept us in fairly close contact ever since. I was delighted to meet him in New York. He was also staying at the Algonquin. Naturally, we had dinner together. Halfway through the meal, he asked me what I was working on.

'Have you ever heard of the *Necronomicon*?' I asked him, smiling.

'Of course.'

I goggled at him. 'You have? Where?'

'In Lovecraft. Isn't that what you meant?'

'Who on earth is Lovecraft?'

'Don't you know? One of our local writers in Providence. He died about thirty years ago. Haven't you come across his name?'

Now a memory stirred somewhere in my head. When I had been investigating Mrs Whitman's house in Providence – for my book *The Shadow of Poe* – Foster had mentioned Love-craft, with some such comment as: 'You ought to read Lovecraft. He's the best American writer of horror stories since Poe.' I can remember saying that I thought Bierce deserved that title, and then forgetting about it.

'Do you mean that this word *Necronomicon* actually occurs in Lovecraft?'

'I'm pretty sure of it.'

'And where do you suppose Lovecraft got it?'

'I always assumed he invented it.'

My interest in food vanished. This was the kind of development that no one could have foreseen. For, as far as I knew, I was the first person to read the Voynich manuscript. Or was I? How about the two scholars of the 17th century? Had one of them deciphered it and mentioned its name in his writings?

Obviously, the first thing to do was to check Lovecraft, and find out whether Foster's memory had served him correctly. I found myself praying that he was mistaken. After the meal, we took a taxi to a bookshop in Greenwich Village, and there I was able to locate a paperback of Lovecraft stories. Before we left the shop Foster riffled through its pages, then placed his finger on one of them:

'There it is. "*Necronomicon*, by the mad Arab Abdul Alhazred."'

There it was, impossible to doubt. In the taxi, on the way home, I tried not to show how shattered I felt. But soon after we got back, I excused myself and went to my room. I tried to read Lovecraft, but could not concentrate.

The next day, before sailing, I searched Brentano's for Lovecraft books, and managed to find two in hard covers, as well as several paperbacks. The hard-cover books were *The Shuttered Room* and *Supernatural Horror in Literature*, In the first of these, I found a lengthy account of the *Necro-nomicon*, together with several quotations. But the account states 'While the book itself, and most of its translators, and

its author, are all imaginary, Lovecraft here employed . . .
*his techniques of inserting actual historical fact in the middle
of large areas of purely imaginary lore.'*

Purely imaginary . . . Could it perhaps be a mere matter
of coincidence of names? *Necronomicon* – the book of dead
names. Not a difficult title to invent. The more I thought of
it, the more likely it seemed that this was the correct
explanation. And so before I went on board that afternoon, I
was already feeling a great deal easier in my mind. I ate a
good dinner, and read myself to sleep afterwards with
Lovecraft.

I am not sure how many days went by before I began to
experience a gradually increasing fascination with this new
literary discovery. I know that my first impression was
simply that Lovecraft was a skilful constructor of weird
stories. Perhaps it was my work on the translation of the
Voynich manuscript that altered my approach to him. Or
possibly it was simply the realization that Lovecraft had
been uniquely obsessed by this strange world of his own
creation – uniquely even when compared with such writers
as Gogol and Poe. He made me think of certain writers on
anthropology, however lacking in literary skill, yet made
impressive by the sheer authenticity of their material.

With several hours a day in which to work, I quickly
completed my translation of the Voynich manuscript. Long
before the end, I had become aware that it was a fragment,
and that there were mysteries involved that went beyond
the cipher – a code within a code, as it were. But what struck
me most powerfully – so that I sometimes had the utmost
difficulty in restraining myself from rushing into the corridor
and talking to the first person I met – was the incredible
scientific knowledge revealed by the manuscript. Newbold
had not been entirely wrong about this. The author simply
knew far more than any 13th-century monk – or Mahomme-
dan scholar, for that matter – could possibly know. A long
and obscure passage about a 'god' or demon who is somehow

a vortex filled with stars is followed by a passage in which
the primal constituent of matter is described as energy (using
the Greek *dynamis* and *energeia*, as well as the Latin *vis*) *in
limited units*. This sounds like a clear anticipation of the
quantum theory. Again, the seed of man is described as being
made up of units of power, each of which endows man with a
lifelong characteristic. This certainly sounds remarkably
like a reference to the genes. The drawing of a human
spermatozoon occurs in the midst of a text that refers to the
Sefer Yezirah, the Book of Creation in the Kabala. Several
slighting references to the *Ars Magna* of Raymond Lull
support the notion that the author of the work was Roger
Bacon – a contemporary of the mathematical mystic,
although in one place in the text, he refers to himself under
the name of Martinus Hortulanus, which might be translated
Martin Gardener.

What, in the last analysis, is the Voynich manuscript? It
is a fragment of a work that professes to be a complete
scientific account of the universe: its origin, history, geography (if I may use the term), mathematical structure and
hidden depths. The pages I possessed contained a preliminary digest of this material. In parts, it was terrifyingly
knowledgeable; in other places, it seemed to be a typical
medieval *mélange* of magic, theology, and pre-Copernican
speculation. I got the impression that the work may have
had several authors, or that the part I possessed was a digest
of some other book that was imperfectly understood by
Martin the Gardener. There are the usual references to
Hermes Trismegistus and the Emerald Tablet, to Cleopatra's
book on gold making, the *Chrysopeia*, to the gnostic serpent
Ouroboros, and to a mysterious planet or star called Torman-
tius, which was spoken of as the home of awe-inspiring
deities. There were also many references to a 'Khian language' which, from their context, obviously have no connection with the Aegean island of Chios, Homer's birthplace.

It was this that set me upon the next stage of my discovery.

In Lovecraft's *Supernatural Horror in Literature*, in the short section on Arthur Machen, I came across a reference to the 'Chian language', connected in some way with a witchcraft cult. It also mentioned 'dôls', 'voolas' and certain 'Aklo letters'. The latter caught my attention; there had been a reference in the Voynich manuscript to the 'Aklo inscriptions'. I had at first supposed Aklo to be some kind of corruption of the Kabalistic 'Agla', a word used in exorcism; now I revised my opinion. To appeal to coincidence beyond a certain point is a sign of feeble-mindedness. The hypothesis that now presented itself to my mind was this: that the Voynich manuscript was a fragment or a summary of a much longer work called the *Necronomicon*, perhaps of Kabalistic origin. Complete copies of this book exist, or have existed, and word of mouth tradition may have been kept alive by secret societies such as Naundorff's infamous Church of Carmel, or the Brotherhood of Tlön described by Borges. Machen, who spent some time in Paris in the 1880s, almost certainly came into contact with Naundorff's disciple, the Abbé Boullan, who is known to have practised black magic. (He appears in Huysmans' *La Bas*.) This could explain the traces of the *Necronomicon* to be found in his work. As to Lovecraft – he may have come across it or the verbal traditions concerning it, on his own, or perhaps even through Machen.

In that case, there might be copies of the work hidden away in some garret, or perhaps in another chest in an Italian castle. What a triumph if I could locate it, and publish it together with my translation of the Voynich manuscript! Or even if I could definitely prove that it had existed.

This was the daydream that preoccupied me during my five days on the Atlantic. And I read and reread my translation of the manuscript, hoping to discover some clue that might lead me to the complete work. But the more I read, the less clear it became. On a first reading, I had sensed an over-all pattern, some dark mythology, never stated openly,

but deducible from hints. As I reread the work, I began to
wonder whether all this had not been my imagination. The
book seemed to dissolve into unrelated fragments.

In London, I spent a futile week in the British Museum,
searching for references to the *Necronomicon* in various
magical works, from Basil Valentine's *Azoth* to Aleister
Crowley. The only promising reference was a footnote in E.
A. Hitchcock's *Remarks on Alchemy* (1865) to 'the now
unattainable secrets of the Aklo tablets'. But the book
contained no other reference to these tablets. Did the word
'unattainable' mean that the tablets were known to be
destroyed? If so, how did Hitchcock come to know about it?

The gloom of a London October, and the exhaustion that
came from a persistent sore throat, had almost persuaded me
to take a plane back to New York, when my luck changed.
In a bookshop in Maidstone I met Fr. Anthony Carter, a
Carmelite monk and editor of a small literary magazine. He
had met Machen in 1944 – three years before the writer's
death, and had later devoted an issue of his magazine to
Machen's life and work. I accompanied Fr Carter back to the
Priory near Sevenoaks, and as he drove the baby Austin at a
sedate thirty miles an hour, he talked to me at length about
Machen. Finally, I asked him whether, to his knowledge,
Machen had ever had contact with secret societies or black
magic. 'Oh, I doubt it,' he said, and my heart sank. Another
false trail . . . 'I suspect he picked up various odd traditions
near his birthplace, Melincourt. It used to be the Roman Isca
Silurum.'

'Traditions?' I tried to keep my voice casual. 'What sort of
traditions?'

'Oh you know. The sort of thing he describes in *The Hill of
Dreams*. Pagan cults and that sort of thing.'

'I thought that was pure imagination.'

'Oh no. He once hinted to me that he'd seen a book that
revealed all kinds of horrible things about that area of
Wales.'

'Where? What kind of book?'

'I've no idea. I didn't pay too much attention. I believe he saw it in Paris — or it might have been Lyons. But I remember the name of the man who showed it to him. Staislav de Guaita.'

'Guaita!' I couldn't keep my voice down, and he almost steered us off the road. He looked at me with mild reproach.

'That's right. He was involved in some absurd black magic society. Machen pretended to take it all seriously but I'm sure he was pulling my leg . . .'

Guaita was involved in the black magic circle of Boullan and Naundorff. It was one more brick in the edifice.

'Where is Melincourt?'

'In Monmouthshire, I belive. Somewhere near Southport. Are you thinking of going?'

My train of thought must have been obvious. I saw no point in denying it.

The priest said nothing until the car stopped in the tree-shaded yard behind the Priory. Then he glanced at me and said mildly: 'I wouldn't get too involved if I were you.'

I made a non-committal noise in my throat, and we dropped the subject. But a few hours later, back in my hotel room, I remembered this comment and was struck by it. If he believed that Machen had been pulling his leg about his 'pagan cults', why warn me not to get too involved? Did he really believe in them, but prefer to keep this to himself? As a Catholic, of course, he was bound to believe in the existence of supernatural evil . . .

I had checked in the hotel's Bradshaw before going to bed. There was a train to Newport from Paddington at 9:55, with a change for Caerleon at 2:30. At five minutes past ten, I was seated in the dining car, drinking coffee, watching the dull, soot-coloured houses of Ealing give way to the green fields of Middlesex, and feeling a depth and purity of excitement that was quite new to me. I cannot explain this. I can only say that, at this point in my search, I had a clear intuition that the important things were beginning. Until now, I had been slightly depressed, in spite of the challenges of the Voynich manuscript. Perhaps this was due to a faint distaste for the subject matter of the manuscript. I am as romantic as the next man – and I think most people are healthily romantic at bottom – but I suppose all this talk of black magic struck me ultimately as degrading nonsense – degrading to the human intellect and its capacity for evolution. But on this grey October morning, I felt something else – the stirring of the hair that Watson used to experience when Holmes shook him awake with 'The game's afoot, Watson.' I still had not the remotest idea what the game might consist of. But I was beginning to experience an odd intuition of its seriousness.

When I grew tired of looking at the scenery, I opened the book bag and took out a *Guide to Wales*, and two volumes by Arthur Machen; some selected stories, and the autobiographical *Far Off Things*. This latter led me to expect to find a land of enchantment in Machen's part of Wales. He writes: 'I shall always esteem it as the greatest piece of fortune that has fallen to me, that I was born in the heart of Gwent.' His descriptions of the 'mystic tumulus', the 'giant rounded billow' of the Mountain of Stone, the deep woods and the winding river, made it sound like the landscape of a dream. And in fact, Melincourt is the legendary seat of King Arthur, and Tennyson sets his *Idylls of the King* there.

The *Guide to Wales*, which I had picked up at a second-hand bookshop in the Charing Cross Road, described Southport as a little country market town 'amid a pleasant, undulating and luxuriant landscape of wood and meadow'. I had half an hour to spare between trains, and decided to look at the town. Ten minutes was enough. Whatever may have been its charms in 1900 (the date of the *Guide*), it is now a typical industrial town with cranes on the skyline and the hooting of trains and boats. I drank a double whisky in the hotel next to the station, to fortify myself in the event of a similar disappointment in Caerleon. And even this did little to relieve the impact of the dreary, modernized little town in which I found myself an hour later, after a short journey through the suburbs of Southport. The town is dominated by an immense red-brick monstrosity, which I guessed correctly to be a mental institution. And Chesterton's 'Usk of mighty murmurings' struck me as a muddy stream whose appearance was not improved by the rain that now fell from the slate-grey sky.

I checked into my hotel – an unpretentious place, without central heating – at half past three, looked at the flowered wallpaper in my bedroom – at least one survival from 1900 – and decided to walk out in the rain.

A hundred yards along the main street, I passed a garage with a hand-printed notice 'Cars for Hire'. A short, bespectacled man was leaning over the engine of a car. I asked him whether there was a driver available.

'Oh yes, sir.'

'This afternoon?'

'If you like, sir. Where did you want to go?'

'Just to look at the countryside.'

He looked incredulous. 'You a tourist are you, sir?'

'I suppose so, in a way.'

'I'll be right with you.'

His air as he wiped his hands suggested that he thought this was too good to miss. Five minutes later, he was waiting in front of the building, wearing a leather motoring jacket of a 1920-ish vintage, and driving a car of the same period. The headlights actually vibrated up and down to the chatter of its engine.

'Where to?'

'Anywhere. Somewhere towards the north – towards Monmouth.'

I sat huddled in the back, watching the rain, and feeling distinct signs of a cold coming on. But after ten minutes, the car warmed up, and the scenery improved. In spite of modernization and the October drizzle, the Usk valley

remained extremely beautiful. The green of the fields was
striking, even compared to Virginia. The woods were, as
Machen said, mysterious and shadowy, and the scenery
looked almost too picturesque to be genuine, like one of those
grandiose romantic landscapes by Asher Durand. And to the
north and north-east lay the mountains, hardly visible
through the smoky clouds; the desolate landscape of *The
White People* and *The Novel of the Black Seal* – both very
fresh in my mind. Mr Evans, my driver, had the tact not to
speak, but to allow me to soak up the feeling of the landscape.

I asked my driver whether he had ever seen Machen, but I
had to spell the name before Mr Evans even recognized it.
As far as I could tell, Machen seemed completely forgotten
in his native town.

'You studyin' him, are you, sir?'

He used the word 'studying' as if it were some remote and
ritualistic activity. I acknowledged that I was; in fact, I
exaggerated slightly and said that I thought of writing a
book on Machen. This aroused his interest; whatever might
have been his attitude to dead writers, he had nothing but
respect for living ones. I told him that several of Machen's
stories were set in the desolate hills that lay ahead of us, and
I added casually:

'What I really want to find out is where he picked up the
legends he used in his stories. I'm fairly sure he didn't invent
them. Do you know of anyone around here who might know
about them – the vicar, for example.'

'Oh no. The vicar wouldn't know anythin' about legends.'
He made it sound as if legends were a thoroughly pagan
activity.

'Can you think of anyone who might?'

'Let's see. There's the Colonel, if you could get on the right
side of him. He's a funny chap, is the Colonel. If he don't like
you, you'd be wastin' your breath.'

I tried to find out more about this Colonel – whether he
was an antiquary, perhaps; but Evans's statements remained

Celtically vague. I changed the subject to the scenery, and
got a steady stream of information that lasted all the way
back to Melincourt. At Mr Evans's suggestion, we drove as
far north as Raglan, then turned west and drove back with
the Black Mountains on our right, looking bleaker and more
menacing at close quarters than from the green lowlands
around Melincourt. In Pontypool, I stopped and bought a
book about the Roman remains at Melincourt, and a second-
hand copy of Giraldus Cambrensis, the Welsh historian and
geographer, a contemporary of Roger Bacon.

Mr Evans's taxi rates proved to be surprisingly reasonable
and I agreed to hire him for a whole day as soon as the
weather improved. Then, back in the hotel, with a potation
called grog, consisting of brown rum, hot water, lemon juice,
and sugar, I read the London newspapers, and made cautious
inquiries about the Colonel. The line of approach proving
barren – the Welsh are not forthcoming with strangers – I
looked him up in the phone book. Colonel Lionel Urquart,
The Leasowes, Melincourt. Then, fortified by my grog, I went
into the icy phone kiosk and dialled his number. A woman's
voice with an almost incomprehensible Welsh accent said
the Colonel was not at home, then said he might be, and she
would go and look.

After a long wait, a harsh, British upper-class voice barked
into the phone: 'Hello, who is it?' I identified myself, but
before I could finish, he snapped: 'I'm sorry, I never give
interviews.' I explained quickly that I was a professor of
literature, not a journalist.

'Ah, literature. What kind of literature?'

'At the moment, I'm interested in the local legends. Someone mentioned that you knew a great deal about them.'

'Ah, they did, eh? Well, I suppose I do. What did you say
your name was?'

I repeated it, and mentioned the University of Virginia,
and my major publications. There were odd mumbling noises

at the other end of the line, as if he were eating his moustache and finding it hard to swallow. Finally, he said:

'Look here . . . supposing you come over here a bit later this evening, around nine? We can have a drink and talk.'

I thanked him, and went back to the lounge, where there was a good fire, and ordered another rum. I felt I deserved congratulations, after Mr Evans's warnings about the Colonel. Only one thing worried me. I still had no idea of who he was, or what kind of legends interested him. I could only guess that he was the local antiquary.

At half past eight, after an ample but unimaginative supper of lamb chops, boiled potatoes, and some unidentifiable green vegetable, I set out for the Colonel's house, having inquired the way from the desk clerk, who was obviously intrigued. It was still raining and windy, but my cold was held at bay by the grog.

The Colonel's house was outside the town, halfway up a steep hill. There was a rusty iron gate, and a driveway full of pools of muddy water. When I rang the doorbell, ten dogs began to bark at once, and one approached the door on the other side and snarled discouragingly. A plump Welsh woman opened the door, slapped the Doberman Pinscher that growled and slavered, and led me past a pack of yelping dogs – several, I noticed, with scars and torn ears – into a dimly lit library smelling of coal smoke. I'm not sure what sort of a man I expected to meet, – probably tall and British, with a sunburned face and bristly moustache – but he proved rather a surprise. Short and twisted – a riding accident had broken his right hip – his dark complexion suggested mixed blood, while the receding chin gave him a slightly reptilian look. On first acquaintance, a definitely repellent character. His eyes were bright and intelligent, but mistrustful. He struck me as a man who could generate considerable resentment. He shook my hand and asked me to sit down. I sat near the fire. A cloud of smoke immediately bellowed out, making me choke and gasp.

'Needs sweeping,' said my host. 'Try that chair.' A few moments later, something fell down the chimney along with a quantity of soot, and before the flames made it unrecognizable, I thought I recognized the skeleton of a bat. I surmised – correctly, as it turned out – that Colonel Urquart had few visitors, and therefore few occasions to use the library.

'Which of my books have you come across?' he asked me.

'I . . . er . . . to be quite honest, I only know them by hearsay.'

I was relieved when he said drily: 'Like most people. Still, it's encouraging to know you're interested.'

At this point, looking past his head, I noticed his name on a spine of a book. It seemed a rather luridly designed dust jacket, and the title, *The Mysteries of Mu*, was quite clearly visible in scarlet letters. So I added quickly:

'Of course, I don't know a great deal about Mu. I remember reading a book by Spence . . .'

'Total charlatan!' Urquart snapped, and I thought his eyes took on a reddish tinge in the firelight.

'And then,' I added, 'Robert Graves has some curious theories about Wales and the Welsh . . .'

'Lost tribes of Israel, indeed! I've never heard such an infantile and far-fetched idea! Anyone could tell you it's nonsense. And besides, I've proved conclusively that the Welsh are survivors from the lost continent of Mu. I have evidence to prove it. No doubt you've come across some of it.'

'Not as much as I could have wished,' I said, wondering what I'd let myself in for.

At this point he interrupted himself to offer me a whisky, and I had to make a quick decision – whether to plead another appointment and escape, or to stick it out. The sound of rain on the windows decided me. I would stick it out.

As he poured the whisky, he said, 'I think I can guess what you are thinking. Why Mu rather than Atlantis?'

'Why, indeed,' I said, in a bemused way. I wasn't even

aware, at that stage, that Mu was supposed to have been situated in the Pacific.

'Quite. I asked myself exactly that question twenty years ago, when I first made my discoveries. Why Mu, when the major relics lie in South Wales and Providence?'

'Providence? Which Providence?'

'Rhode Island. I have proof that it was the centre of the religion of the survivors from Mu.

'Relics. This, for example.' He handed me a chunk of green stone, almost too heavy to hold in one hand. I had never seen such stone before, although I know a little about geology. Neither had I seen anything like the drawing and inscription cut into it, except once in a temple in the jungles of Brazil. The inscription was in curved characters, not unlike Pitman's shorthand; the face in the midst of them could have been a devil mask, or a snake god, or a sea monster. As I stared at it, I felt the same distaste – the sense of *nastiness* – that I had experienced on first seeing the Voynich manuscript. I took a large swallow of my whisky. Urquart indicated the 'sea monster'.

'The symbol of the people of Mu. The Yambi. This stone is their colour. It's one of the ways to learn where they've been – water of that colour.'

I looked at him blankly. 'In what way?'

'When they destroy a place, they like to leave behind pools of water – small lakes, if possible. You can always tell them because they look slightly different from an ordinary pool of water. You get this combination of the green of stagnation, and that bluey-grey you can see here.'

He turned to the bookshelf and took down an expensive art book with a title like *The Pleasures of Ruins*. He opened it and pointed at a photograph. It was in colour.

'Look at this – Sidon in Lebanon. The same green water. And look at this: Anuradhapura in Ceylon – the same green and blue. Colours of decay and death. Both places they destroyed at some point. There are six more that I know of.'

I was fascinated and impressed in spite of myself; perhaps it was the stone that did it.

'But how did they do that?'

'You make the usual mistake – of thinking of them as being like ourselves. They weren't. In human terms, they were formless and invisible.'

'Invisible?'

'Like wind or electricity. You have to understand they were *forces* rather than beings. They weren't even clear separate identities, as we are. That's stated in Churchward's Naacal tablets.'

He proceeded to talk, and I shall not attempt to set down all he said. A lot of it struck me as sheer nonsense. But there was a crazy logic in much of it. He would snatch up books off his shelves and read me passages – most of these, as far as I could see, by all kinds of cranks. But he would then take up a textbook of anthropology or palaeontology, and read some extract that seemed to confirm what he had just said.

What he told me, in brief, was this. The continent of Mu existed in the South Pacific between twenty thousand and twelve thousand years ago. It consisted of two races, one of which resembled present-day man. The other consisted of Urquart's 'invisible ones from the stars'. These latter, he said, were definitely aliens on our earth, and the chief among them was called Ghatanothoa, the dark one. They sometimes took forms, such as the monster on the tablet – who was a representation of Ghatanothoa – but existed as 'vortices' of power in their natural state. They were not benevolent, in our sense, for their instincts and desires were completely unlike ours. A tradition of the Naacal tablets has it that these beings created man, but this, Urquart said, must be incorrect, since archaeological evidence proved that man had evolved over millions of years. However, the men of Mu were certainly their slaves, and were apparently treated with what we would consider unbelievable barbarity. The Lloigor, or star-beings, could amputate limbs without causing death, and did this at the least sign of rebelliousness. They could also cause cancer-like tentacles to grow on their human slaves, and also used this as a form of punishment. One picture in the Naacal tablets shows a man with tentacles growing from both eye sockets.

But Urquart's theory about Mu had an extremely original touch. He told me that there was one major difference between the Lloigor and human beings. The Lloigor were deeply and wholly pessimistic. Urquart pointed out that we could hardly imagine what this meant. Human beings live on hopes of various kinds. We know we have to die. We have no idea where we came from, or where we are going to. We know that we are subject to accident and illness. We know that we seldom achieve what we want; and if we achieve it, we have ceased to appreciate it. All this we know, and yet we remain incurably optimistic, even deceiving ourselves with absurd, patently nonsensical, beliefs about life after death

'Why am I talking to you,' said Urquart, 'although I know perfectly well that no professor has an open mind, and every one I've had any dealings with has betrayed me? Because I think that you might be the exception – you might grasp the truth of what I'm saying. But why should I want it known, when I have to die like everyone else? Absurd, isn't it? Yet we're *not* reasonable creatures. We live and act on an unreasonable reflex of optimism – a mere reflex, like your knee kicking when somebody taps it. It's obviously completely stupid. Yet we live by it.'

I found myself impressed by him, in spite of my conviction that he was slightly mad. He was certainly intelligent.

He went on to explain that the Lloigor, although infinitely more powerful than men, were also aware that optimism would be absurd in this universe. Their minds were a unity, not compartmentalized like ours. There was no distinction in them between conscious, subconscious and superconscious mind. So they saw things clearly all the time, without the possibility of averting the mind from the truth, or forgetting. Mentally speaking, the closest equivalent to them would be one of those suicidal romantics of the 19th century, steeped in gloom, convinced that life is a pit of misery, and accepting this as a basis for everyday life. Urquart denied that the Buddhists resemble the Lloigor in their ultimate pessimism – not merely because of the concept of Nirvana, which offers a kind of absolute, equivalent to the Christian God, but because no Buddhist really lives in the constant comtemplation of his pessimism. He accepts it intellectually, but he does not feel it with his nerves and bones. The Lloigor *lived* their pessimism.

Unfortunately – and here I found it hard to follow Urquart – the earth is not suitable for such pessimism, on a subatomic level. It is a young planet. All its energy processes are still in the uphill stage, so to speak; they are evolutionary, making for complexification, and therefore, the destruction of negative forces. A simple example of this is the way that so many of the romantics died young; the earth simply will not tolerate subversive forces.

Hence the legend that the Lloigor created men as their slaves. For why should all-powerful beings require slaves? Only because of the active hostility, so to speak, of the earth itself. To counteract this hostility, to carry out their simplest purposes, they needed creatures who worked on an optimistic basis. And so men were created, deliberately shortsighted creatures, incapable of steadily contemplating the obvious truth about the universe.

What had then happened had been absurd. The Lloigor had been increasingly weakened by their life on earth. Urquart said that the documents offer no reason for the Lloigor's leaving their home, probably situated in the Andromeda nebula. They had gradually become less and less an active force. And their slaves had taken over, becoming the men of today. The Naacal tablets and other works that have come down from Mu are the creation of these men, not of the original 'gods'. The earth has favoured the evolution of its ungainly, optimistic children, and weakened the Lloigor. Nevertheless, these ancient powers remain. They have retreated under the earth and sea, in order to concentrate their power in stones and rocks, whose normal metabolism they can reverse. This has enabled them to cling to the earth for many thousands of years. Occasionally, they accumulate enough energy to erupt once again into human life, and the results are whole cities destroyed. At one time, it was the whole continent – Mu itself – and later still, Atlantis. They had always been particularly virulent when they had been able to find traces of their previous slaves. They are responsible for many archaeological mysteries – great ruined cities of South America, Cambodia, Burma, Ceylon, North Africa, even Italy. And then, according to Urquart, the two great ruined cities of North America, Grudèn Itzà, now sunk beneath the swampland around New Orleans, and Nam-Ergest, a flourishing city that once stood on the land where the Grand Canyon now yawns. The Grand Canyon, Urquart said, was not created by earth erosion, but by a tremendous underground explosion followed by a 'hail of fire'. He suspects that, like the great Siberian explosion, it was produced by some kind of atomic bomb. To my question of why there were no signs of an explosion around the Grand Canyon, Urquart had two replies: that it had taken place so long ago that most signs of it had been destroyed by natural forces, and second, that to any unprejudiced observer, it is plain enough that the Grand Canyon is an immense and irregular crater.

After two hours of this, and several helpings of his excellent whisky, I felt so confused that I had completely lost track of the questions I wanted to ask. I said I had to go to bed and think about it all, and the Colonel offered to run me home in his car. One of my questions came back to me as I climbed into the passenger seat of the ancient Rolls-Royce.

'What did you mean about the Welsh being survivors of Mu?'

'What I said. I am certain – I have evidence to prove – that they are descendants of the slaves of the Lloigor.'

'What kind of evidence?'

'All kinds. It would take another hour to explain.'

'Couldn't you give me some hint?'

'All right. Look in the local paper in the morning. Tell me what strikes you?'

'But what am I to look for?'

He was amused by my refusal to 'wait and see'. He should have known that old men are less patient than children.

'The crime figures.'

'Can't you tell me more?'

'All right.' We were parked outside the hotel by now, and it was still raining heavily. At this hour of the night, there was no sound but the fall of rain and the gurgling of water in the gutters. 'You'll find that the crime rate in this area is about three times that of the rest of England. The figures are so high that they're seldom published. Murder, cruelty, rape, every possible kind of sexual perversion – this area has the highest in the British Isles.'

'But why?'

'I've told you. The Lloigor achieve the strength to reappear every now and then.' And to make it clear that he wanted to go home, he leaned over and opened my door for me. Before I had reached the door of the hotel, he had driven off.

I asked the caretaker on duty if I could borrow a local newspaper; he produced me one from his cubbyhole, which he said I could keep. I went up to my room, undressed, and climbed into bed – there was a hot water bottle in it. Then I glanced through the newspaper. At first sight, I could see no evidence for Urquart's assertion. The headline was about a strike in the local dockyard, and the lead stories were about a local cattle show in which the judges had been accused of accepting bribes, and about a Southport girl swimmer who had almost broken the record for the cross-channel swim. On the middle page, the editorial was on some question of Sunday observance. It looked innocent enough.

Then I began to notice the small paragraphs, tucked away next to the advertisements or among the sports news. The headless body that had been found floating in the Bryn Mawr reservoir has been tentatively identified as a teenage farm girl from Llandalffen. A fourteen-year-old boy sentenced to a corrective institution for inflicting injuries on a sheep with a hatchet. A farmer petitioning for divorce on the grounds that his wife seemed to be infatuated with her imbecile stepson. A vicar sentenced to a year in prison for offences against choir boys. A father who had murdered his daughter and her boyfriend out of sexual jealousy. A man in the old folks home who had incinerated two of his companions by pouring paraffin on their beds and setting them alight. A twelve-year-old boy who had offered his twin sisters, age seven, ice cream with rat poison sprinkled on it, and then laughed uncontrollably in the juvenile court. (The children luckily survived with bad stomach aches.) A short paragraph saying that the police had now charged a man with the three Lovers' Lane murders.

I jotted these down in the order I read them. It was quite a chronicle for a peaceful rural area, even allowing that Southport and Cardiff, with their higher crime rates, were fairly close. Admittedly, it was not too bad a record compared to most places in America. Even Charlottesville can produce a crime record that would be regarded as a major crime wave in England. Before falling asleep, I pulled on my dressing gown, and found my way to the lounge, where I had seen a copy of Whitaker's *Almanac*, and looked up the English crime rate. A mere 166 murders in 1967 – three murders to every million people of the population; American's murder rate is about twenty times as high. Yet here, in a single issue of a small local newspaper, I had found mention of nine murders – although admittedly, some of them dated back a long way. (The Lovers' Lane murders were spread over eighteen months.)

I slept very badly that night, my mind running constantly on invisible monsters, awful cataclysms, sadistic murderers, demoniac teenagers. It was a relief to wake up to bright sunshine and a cup of morning tea. Even so, I found myself stealing a look at the maid – a pale-faced little thing with dull eyes and stringy hair – and wondering what irregular union had produced her. I had breakfast and the morning paper sent up to my room, and read it with morbid interest.

Again, the more lurid news was carefully tucked away in small paragraphs. Two eleven-year-old schoolboys were accused of being implicated in the murder of the headless girl, but claimed that a tramp 'with smouldering eyes' had actually decapitated her. A Southport druggist forced to resign from the town council when accused of having 'carnal knowledge' of his fourteen-year-old assistant. Evidence suggesting that a deceased midwife had been a successful baby farmer in the manner of the infamous Mrs Dyer of Reading. An old lady of Llangwm seriously injured by a man who accused her of witchcraft – of causing babies to be born with deformities. An attempt on the life of the mayor of Chepstow by a man with some obscure grudge . . . I omit more than half of the list, for the crimes are as dull as they are sordid.

There was no doubt that all this brooding on crime and corruption was having its effect on my outlook. I had always liked the Welsh, with their small stature and dark hair and pale skins. Now I found myself looking at them as if they were troglodytes, trying to find evidence of secret vices in their eyes. And the more I looked, the more I saw it. I observed the number of words beginning with two L's, from Lloyd's Bank to Llandudno, and thought of the Lloigor with a shudder. (Incidentally, I thought the word familiar and found it on page 258 of the Lovecraft *Shuttered Room* volume, listed as the god 'who walks the winds among the star spaces'. I also found Ghatanothoa, the Dark God, mentioned there, although not as the chief of the 'star dwellers'.)

It was almost intolerable, walking along the sunlit street, looking at the rural population going about their everyday business of shopping and admiring one another's babies, to feel this awful secret inside me, struggling to get out. I wanted to dismiss the whole thing as a nightmare, the invention of one half-crazed mind; then I had to acknowledge that it all followed logically from the Voynich manuscript and the Lovecraft gods. Yes, there could hardly be any doubt: Lovecraft and Machen had simply obtained some knowledge of an ancient tradition, that may have existed before any known civilization on earth.

The only other alternative was some elaborate literary hoax, organized between Machen, Lovecraft, and Voynich, who must be regarded as a forger, and that was impossible. But what an alternative! How could I believe in it and still feel sane, here in this sunlit high street, with the lilting sound of Welsh in my ears? Some evil, dark world, so alien from ours that human beings cannot even begin to understand it; strange powers whose actions seem incredibly cruel and vengeful, yet who are simply driven by abstract laws of their being that would be incomprehensible to us. Urquart, with his reptilian face and his morose intelligence. And above all, unseen forces bending the minds of these apparently innocent people around me, making them corrupt and depraved.

I had already decided what I would do that day. I would get Mr Evans to drive me out to the 'Grey Hills' mentioned by Machen, and take some photographs, and make some discreet inquiries. I even had a compass with me – one I usually kept in my car in America – in case I managed to *lose* my way.

There was a small crowd gathered outside Mr Evans's garage and an ambulance stood by the pavement. As I approached, two attendants came out, carrying a stretcher. I saw Mr Evans standing gloomily inside the small shop attached to the garage, watching the crowd. I asked him:

'What happened?'

'Chap upstairs committed suicide in the night. Gassed himself.'

As the ambulance pulled away, I asked, 'Don't you think there's rather a lot of that around here?'

'Of what?'

'Suicides, murders, and so on. Your local paper's full of it.'

'I suppose so. It's the teenagers nowadays. They do what they like.'

I saw there was no point in pursuing the subject. I asked him whether he was free to drive me to the Grey Hills. He shook his head.

'I promised I'd wait around to make a statement to the police. You're welcome to use the car if you want it.'

And so I bought a map of the area, and drove myself. I stopped for ten minutes to admire the medieval bridge, mentioned by Machen, then drove slowly north. The morning was windy, but not cold, and the sunlight made the scene look totally different from the previous afternoon. Although I looked out carefully for signs of Machen's Grey Hills, I saw nothing in the pleasant, rolling landscape that seemed to answer that description. Soon I found myself passing a signpost that announced Abergavenny ten miles away. I decided to take a look at the place. By the time I arrived there, the sunlight had so far dispelled the night vapours from my head that I drove round the town – unremarkable enough architecturally – and then walked up to look at the ruined castle above it. I spoke to a couple of natives, who struck me as more English than Welsh in type. Indeed, the town is not many miles away from the Severn Valley and A. E. Housman's Shropshire.

But I was reminded of the myth of the Lloigor by a few sentences in the local guide book about William de Braose, Lord of Brecheiniog (Brecon), 'whose shadow broods darkly

over the past of Abergavenny', whose 'foul deeds' had apparently shocked even the lawless English of the 12th century.
I made a mental note to ask Urquart how long the Lloigor
had been present in South Wales, and how far their influence
extended. I drove on northwest, through the most attractive
part of the valley of the Usk. At Crickhowell, I stopped in a
pleasantly old-fashioned pub and drank a cool pint of mild
ale, and fell into conversation with a local who proved to
have read Machen. I asked him where he supposed the 'Grey
Hills' to be situated, and he told me confidently that it was
directly to the north, in the Black Mountains, the high, wild
moorland between the valleys of the Usk and the Wye. So I
drove on for another half an hour, to the top of the pass
called the Bwlch, where the scenery is among the finest of
Wales, with the Brecon Beacons to the west, and woodland
and hills to the south, with glimpses of the Usk reflecting
the sunlight. But the Black Mountains to the east looked
anything but menacing, and their description did not corre-
spond to the page in Machen that I was using as a guide. So
I turned south once again, through Abergavenny (where I
ate a light lunch) and then through minor roads to Llandalffen, the road climbing steeply again.

It was here that I began to suspect that I was approaching
my objective. There was a barrenness about the hills that
suggested the atmosphere of *The Novel of the Black Seal*. But
I kept an open mind, for the afternoon had become cloudy,
and I suspected it might be pure imagination. I stopped the
car by the roadside, close to a stone bridge, and got out to
lean on the parapet. It was a fast-flowing stream, and the
glassy power of the current fascinated me until I felt almost
hypnotized by it. I walked down by the side of the bridge,
digging in my heels to keep my balance on the steep slope,
and went down to a flat rock beside the stream. This was
almost an act of bravado, for I felt a distinct discomfort,
which I knew to be partly self-induced. A man of my age

tends to feel tired and depressed after lunch, particularly when he has been drinking.

I had my polaroid camera round my neck. The green of the grass and the grey of the sky made such a contrast that I decided to take a picture. I adjusted the light meter on the front of the camera, and pointed the camera upstream; then I pulled out the photograph, and slipped it under my coat to develop. A minute later, I stripped off the negative paper. The photograph was black. Obviously, it had somehow been exposed to light. I raised the camera and took a second shot, tossing the first one into the stream. As I pulled the second photograph from the camera, I had a sudden intuitive certainty that it would also be black.

I looked nervously around, and almost tripped into the stream as I saw a face looking down at me from the bridge above. It was a boy, or a youth, leaning on the parapet, watching me. My timing device stopped buzzing. Ignoring the boy, I stripped the paper off the photograph. It was black. I swore under my breath, and tossed it into the stream. Then I looked up the slope, to calculate the easiest way back, and saw the youth standing at the top. He was dressed in shabby brown clothes, completely nondescript. His face was thin and brown, reminding me of gypsies I had seen on the station in Newport. The brown eyes were expressionless. I stared back at him without smiling, at first only curious as to what he wanted.

But he made no apologetic movement, and I felt suddenly afraid that he wanted to rob me – perhaps of the camera, or the traveller's cheques in my wallet. Another look at him convinced me that he would not know what to do with either. The vacant eyes and the protruding ears indicated that I was dealing with an imbecile. And then, with sudden total certainty, I knew what he had in mind as clearly as if he had told me. He meant to rush at me down the slope, and knock me backwards into the water. But why? I glanced at the water. It was very fast, and perhaps waist deep – perhaps a little more – but not deep enough to drown a grown man. There were rocks and stones in it, but none large enough to hurt me if I was dashed against it.

Nothing like this had ever happened to me before – at least, for the past fifty years. Weakness and fear flowed over me, so that I wanted to sit down. Only my determination not to betray fear prevented me. I made an effort, and scowled at him in an irritable manner, as I have occasionally scowled at my students. To my surprise, he smiled at me – although I think it was a smile of malice rather than of amusement – and turned away. I lost no time in scrambling up the bank to a less vulnerable position.

When I reached the road a few seconds later he was gone. The only cover within fifty yards was the other side of the bridge, or behind my car. I bent to peer under the car, to see if his feet were visible; they weren't. I overcame my panic, and went to look over the other parapet of the bridge. He wasn't there either. The only other possibility was that he had slipped under the bridge, although the water seemed to be flowing too fast. In any case, I was not going to look down there. I went back to the car, forcing myself not to hurry, and only felt safe when I was in motion.

At the top of the hill, it struck me that I had forgotten which way I was travelling. My alarm had completely erased all memory of which way I had approached the bridge, and I had parked in a gateway, at right angles to the road. I stopped on a lonely stretch of road to look at my compass. But its black pole swung gently in circles, apparently indifferent to direction. Tapping made no difference. It was not broken; the needle was still mounted on its pivot. It was simply de-magnetized. I drove on until I found a signpost, discovered I was going in the right direction, and made my way to Pontypool. The problem of the compass disturbed me vaguely, but not unduly. It was only later, when I thought about it, that I realized that it should be impossible to de-magnetize a compass without removing the needle and

heating it, or banging it about pretty vigorously. It had been
working at lunch time, when I had glanced at it. It came to
me then that the affair of the compass, like the boy, had been
intended as a warning. A vague, indifferent warning, like a
sleeping man brushing at a fly.

All this sounds absurd and fanciful; and I freely admit
that I was half inclined to dismiss it myself. But I am
inclined to trust my intuitions.

I was feeling shaken, enough to take a long swallow from
my brandy flask when I arrived back at the hotel. Then I
called the desk and complained about the coldness of my
room, and within ten minutes a chambermaid was making a
coal fire in a grate I had not even noticed. Seated in front of
it, smoking a pipe and sipping brandy, I began to feel better.
After all, there was no evidence that these 'powers' were
actively hostile – even admitting for a moment that they
existed. As a young man I was scornful about the supernatural, but as I have got older, the sharp line that divided the
credible from the incredible had tended to blur; I am aware
that the whole world is slightly incredible.

At six o'clock, I suddenly decided to go and see Urquart. I
didn't bother to ring, for I had come to think of him as an
ally, not as a stranger. So I walked in the thin drizzle to his
house, and rang the front doorbell. Almost immediately, it
opened, and a man came out. The Welshwoman said 'Goodbye, doctor,' I stood and stared at her, feeling sudden fear.

'Is the Colonel all right?'

The doctor answered me. 'Well enough, if he takes care. If
you're a friend of his, don't stay with him too long. He needs
sleep.'

The Welshwoman let me in without question.

'What happened?'

'Little accident. He fell down the cellar steps and we didn't
find him for a couple of hours.'

As I went upstairs, I noticed some of the dogs in the
kitchen. The door was open, yet they had not barked at the

sound of my voice. The upstairs corridor was damp and badly carpeted. The Doberman lay outside a door. It looked at me in a weary, subdued way, and did not stir as I went in past it.

Urquart said: 'Ah, it's you, old boy. Nice of you to come. Who told you?'

'Nobody. I came to see you for a talk. What happened?'

He waited until his housekeeper closed the door.

'I got pushed down the cellar steps.'

'By whom?'

'You shouldn't have to ask that.'

'But what happened?'

'I went down to the cellar to get some garden twine. Halfway down the steps – a nasty, stifling feeling – I think they can produce some sort of gas. Then a definite push sideways. There's quite a drop down to the coal. Twisted my ankle, and thought I'd broken a rib. Then the door closed and latched. I shouted like a madman for two hours before the gardener heard me.'

I didn't doubt his word now, or think him a crank. 'But you're in obvious danger here. You ought to move to some other part of the country.'

'No. They're a lot stronger than I thought. But after all I was below the ground, in the cellar. That may be the explanation. They can reach above ground, but it costs them more energy than it's worth. Anyway, there's no harm done. The ankle's only sprained and the rib isn't broken after all. It was just a gentle warning – for talking to you last night. What's been happening to you?'

'So that's it!' My own experiences now connected up. I told him what had happened to me.

He interrupted me to say, 'You went down a steep bank – you see, just like me into the cellar. A thing to avoid.' And when I mentioned the compass, he laughed without much humour. 'That's easy from them. I told you, they can permeate matter as easily as a sponge soaks up water. Have a drink?'

I accepted, and poured him one too. As he sipped, he said, 'That boy you mentioned – I think I know who it is. The grandson of Ben Chickno. I've seen him around.'

'Who is Chickno?'

'Gypsy. Half his family are idiots. They all interbreed. One of his sons got five years for involvement in a murder – one of the nastiest that ever happened around here. They tortured an old couple to find out where they kept their money, then killed then. They found some of the stolen goods in the son's caravan, but he claimed they had been left there by a man on the run. He was lucky to escape a murder charge. And incidentally, the judge died a week after sentencing the son. Heart attack.'

I knew my Machen better than Urquart did, and the suspicion that now came to me was natural. For Machen speaks of intercourse between certain half-imbecilic country people and his strange powers of evil. I asked Urquart, 'Could this old man – Chickno – be connected with the Lloigor?'

'It depends what you mean by connected. I don't think he's important enough to know much about them. But he's the kind of person they like to encourage – a degenerate old swine. You want to ask Inspector Davison about him; he's the head of the local force. Chickno's got a string of convictions as long as your arm – arson, rape, robbery with violence, bestiality, incest. Just a thorough degenerate.'

Mrs Dolgelly brought in his supper at this point, and intimated that it was time for me to go. At the door, I asked, 'Is this man's caravan anywhere nearby?'

'About a mile away from the bridge you mentioned. You're not thinking of going there, I hope?'

Nothing was further from my thoughts, and I said so.

* * *

That evening, I wrote a long letter to George Lauerdale at Brown University. Lauerdale writes detective stories under a pseudonym, and has been responsible for two anthologies of modern poetry. I knew him to be writing a book about Lovecraft, and I needed his advice. By now, I had a feeling of being totally involved in this business. I no longer had any doubts. So was there any evidence of the Lloigor in the Providence area? I wanted to know if anyone had theories about where Lovecraft obtained his basic information. Where had he seen or heard of the *Necronomicon*? I took care to hide my real preoccupations in my letter to Lauerdale: I explained simply that I had succeeded in translating a large part of the Voynich manuscript, and that I had reason to believe that it was the *Necronomicon* referred to by Love-craft; how could Lauerdale account for this? I went on to say that there was evidence that Machen had used real legends of Monmouthshire in his stories, and that I suspected similar legends underlying Lovecraft's work. Had he any knowledge of any such local legends? For example, were there any unpleasant stories connected with Lovecraft's 'shunned house' on Benefit Street in Providence . . .?

The day after Urquart's accident, a curious thing happened, which I shall mention only briefly, since it had no sequel. I have already mentioned the chambermaid, a pale-faced girl with stringy hair and thin legs. After breakfast, I went up to my room, and found her apparently unconscious on the hearthrug. I tried to call the desk, but got no reply. She seemed small and light, so I decided to move her on to the bed, or into the armchair. This was not difficult; but as I lifted her, it was impossible not to become aware that she seemed to be wearing little or nothing under the brown overall-smock. This made me wonder; the weather was cold. Then, as I laid her down, she opened her eyes, and stared up at me with a cunning delight that convinced me that she had been shamming, and one of her hands caught the wrist that was trying to disengage itself from her, with the unmistakable intention of prolonging our contact.

But it was all done a little too crudely, and I started up. As I did so, I heard a step outside the door and quickly opened it. A rough-looking man with a gypsy-ish face was standing there, and he looked startled to see me. He started to say: 'I was looking for . . .' then he saw the girl in the room.

I said quickly, 'I found her unconscious on the floor. I'll get a doctor.' My only intention was to escape downstairs, but the girl overheard me and said, 'No need for that,' jumping up off the bed. The man turned and walked off, and she followed him a few seconds later without attempting an excuse. It took no particular subtlety to see what had been planned; he was supposed to open the door and find me in the act of making love to her. I cannot guess what was supposed to happen then; perhaps he would demand money. But I think it more likely that he would have attacked me. There was a definite family resemblance to the youth who had stared at me from the bridge. I never saw him again, and the girl seemed disposed to avoid me thereafter.

The episode made me more certain than ever that the gypsy family was more intimately involved with the Lloigor than Urquart realized. I rang his home, but was told that he was sleeping. I spent the rest of the day writing letters home, and examining the Roman remains in the town.

That evening, I saw Chickno for the first time. On the way to Urquart's, I had to pass a small public house, with a notice in the window: *No gypsies.* Yet in the doorway of the pub stood an old man dressed in baggy clothes – a harmless-looking old man – who watched me pass with his hands in his pockets. He was smoking a cigarette which dangled loosely from his lips. He was unmistakably a gypsy.

I told Urquart about the episode of the chambermaid, but he seemed inclined to dismiss it; at worst, he thought they might have intended to blackmail me. But when I mentioned the old man, he became more interested, and made me describe him in detail. 'That was Chickno all right. I wonder what the devil he wants.'

'He looked harmless,' I said.

'About as harmless as a poison spider.'

The encounter with Chickno disturbed me. I hope I am no more of a physical coward than the next man; but the youth by the bridge, and the chambermaid business made me realize that we are all pretty vulnerable physically. If the chambermaid's boyfriend – or brother, or whoever it was – had chosen to hit me in the stomach, he could have beaten me into unconsciousness, or broken all my ribs without my making a sound. And no court would have convicted a man trying to defend a girl's 'honour', especially when she alleged that she woke up from a faint to find herself being ravished . . . The thought gave me a most unpleasant sensation in the stomach, and a real fear that I was playing with fire.

This fear explains the next event that I must describe. But I should mention that Urquart was out of bed on the third day, and that we drove out together through the Grey Hills, trying to find out whether there was any substance in Machen's mention of underground caves that were supposed to house his malicious troglodytes. We questioned the vicar in Llandalffen, and in two nearby villages, and talked to several farmworkers we met, explaining that we were interested in pot-holing. No one questioned our unlikely excuse, but no one had any information, although the minister in Llandalffen said he *had* heard stories of rumours of openings in hillsides, concealed by boulders.

Urquart was exhausted after his day of limping around with me, and went home at six o'clock, intending to get an early night. On my way home, I thought – or perhaps imagined – that a gypsy-ish looking man followed me for several hundred yards. Someone resembling the youth was hanging around the entrance to the hotel, and walked away as I appeared. I began to feel a marked man. But after supper, feeling more comfortable, I decided to walk to the pub where I had seen old Chickno, and inquire discreetly whether he was known there.

When I was still a quarter of a mile from the place, I saw him standing in the doorway of a dairy, watching me, with no attempt to disguise the fact. I knew that if I ignored him, my feeling of insecurity would increase, and that it might cost me a sleepless night. So I did what I sometimes do to the monsters in nightmares – walked up to him and accosted him. I had the satisfaction of seeing, for a moment, that I had taken him by surprise. The watery eyes glanced away quickly – the action of a man who usually had something on his conscience.

Then, as I came up to him, I realized that the direct approach would be pointless – 'Why are you following me?' He would react with the instinctive cunning of a man who is usually on the wrong side of the law, and flatly deny it. So instead, I smiled and said, 'Pleasant evening.' He grinned at me and said, 'Oh ay.' Then I stood beside him and pretended to be watching the world go past. I had another of my intuitive insights. He was slightly uncomfortable to be in the position of the hunter, so to speak; he was more used to being the quarry.

After a few moments, he said, 'You're a stranger 'round here.' The accent was not Welsh; it was harsher, more northern.

'Yes, I'm an American,' I said. After a pause, I added, 'You're a stranger too, from the sound of your accent.'

'Ay. From Lancashire.'

'What part?'

'Downham.'

'Ah, the village of the witches.' I had given a course on the Victorian novelists, and recalled *The Lancashire Witches* by Ainsworth.

He grinned at me, and I saw that he hadn't a whole tooth

in his head; the stumps were brown and broken. At close
quarters, I could see that I had been completely mistaken to
think he looked harmless. Urquart's description of a poison
spider was not all that far out. To begin with, he was much
older than he looked at a distance – over eighty, I would
have guessed. (Rumour had it later that he was over a
hundred. Certainly his eldest daughter was sixty-five.) But
age had not softened him or made him seem benevolent.
There was a loose, degenerate look about him, and a kind of
unpleasant vitality, as if he could still enjoy inflicting pain
or causing fear. Even to talk with him was a slightly
worrying sensation, like patting a dog you suspect has rabies.
Urquart had told me some pretty disgusting rumours about
him, but I could now believe them all. I recalled a story
about the small daughter of a farm labourer who had
accepted his hospitality one rainy night, and found it hard to
keep my disgust from showing.

We stood there for several minutes more, looking at the
lighted street and the few teenagers carrying portable radios
who sauntered past, ignoring us.

"Old out your 'and,' he said.

I did so. He stared at it with interest. Then he traced with
his thumb the lines across the base of my right thumb.

'Long life line.'

'I'm glad to hear that. Can you see anything else?'

He looked at me and grinned maliciously. 'Nuthin' that'd
interest you.'

There was something unreal about this interview. I
glanced at my watch. 'Time for a drink.' I started to walk
away, then said, as if the idea had just occurred to me, 'Care
to join me?'

'I don't mind if I do.' But the smile was so frankly insulting
that anyone without ulterior motive would have taken offence. I knew what he was thinking – that I was afraid of
him and wanted to try to win him over. There was some

truth in the first part; none in the second. I felt that his failure to understand me gave me a slight advantage.

We walked to the pub I had intended to visit. Then I saw the notice in the window, and hesitated.

'Don't worry. That doesn't apply to me,' he said.

A moment later, I saw why. The bar was half full. Several labourers were playing darts. Chickno made straight for the seat under the dartboard and sat down. A few of the men looked angry, but none said anything. They put the darts on the windowsill, and went back to the bar. Chickno grinned. I could see he enjoyed showing his power.

He said he would have a rum. I went to the bar, and the landlord served me without looking me full in the face. People moved unobtrusively to the other side of the bar, or at least as far from us as they conveniently could without being obvious. Clearly, Chickno was feared. Perhaps the death of the judge who sentenced his son had something to do with it; later, Urquart told me of other things.

One thing made me feel less worried. He could not hold his drink. I had bought him a single rum, in case he thought I was trying to get him drunk, but he looked at it and said 'Bit small, that,' so I ordered a second. He had drunk the first before I brought the second over. And ten minutes later, his eyes had lost some of their cunning and sharpness.

I decided I had nothing to lose by frankness. 'I've heard about you, Mr Chickno. I'm most interested to meet you.'

He said, 'Ay. 'Appen you are.' He sipped thoughtfully at the second rum, and sucked at a hollow tooth. Then he said: 'You look a sensible fellow. Why do you stay where you're not wanted?'

I didn't pretend to misunderstand.

'I'm leaving soon – probably at the end of the week. But I came here to try and find something. Have you heard of the Voynich manuscript?' He obviously hadn't. So in spite of a feeling that I was wasting my breath – he was looking past me blankly – I told him briefly about the history of the

manuscript, and how I had deciphered it. I ended by saying
that Machen had also seemed to know the work, and that I
suspected that its other half, or perhaps another copy, might
be in this part of the world. When he answered, I saw that I
had been mistaken to think him stupid or inattentive.

'So you want me to believe you're in this part lookin' for a
manuscript? Is that all?' he said.

The tone had a Lancashire bluntness, but was not hostile.
I said, 'That's the reason I came here.'

He leaned across the table, and breathed rum on me. 'Look
'ere, mister, I know a lot more than you think. I know
everything about you. So let's not 'ave any of this. You may
be a college professor, but you don't impress me.' I had a
strong impression that I was looking at a rat or a weasel – a
feeling that he was dangerous, and ought to be destroyed,
like a dangerous snake – but I made an effort to keep this
out of my eyes. I suddenly knew something else about him;
he *was* impressed by the fact that I was a professor, and was
enjoying his position of virtually giving me orders to go away
and mind my own business.

So I drew a deep breath and said politely, 'Believe me, Mr
Chickno, my main interest is in that manuscript. If I could
find that, I'd be perfectly happy.'

He drained his rum, and for a moment I thought he was
going to walk out. But he only wanted another. I went to the
bar and got him a double, and another Haig for myself.

When I sat down again, he took a good swallow of the rum.
'I *know* why you're 'ere, mister. I know about your book as
well. I'm not a vindictive sort of bloke. All I'm saying is that
nobody's interested in you. So why don't you go back to
America? You won't find the rest of your book round 'ere, I
can tell you that.'

Neither of us said anything for a few minutes. Then I
decided to try complete frankness. 'Why do they want me to
go?'

For a moment, he didn't take in what I had said. Then his

face became sober and serious – but only briefly. 'Better not to talk of it.' But after a moment, he seemed to think better of his suggestion. His eyes were malicious again. He leaned forward to me. 'They're not interested in you, mister. They couldn't care less about you. It's 'im they don't like.' His head jerked vaguely – I gathered he meant Urquart. 'He's a fool. He's had plenty of warning, and you can tell him from me, they won't bother to warn him next time.'

'He doesn't think they have any power. Not enough to harm him,' I said.

He seemed unable to make up his mind whether to smile or sneer. His face contorted, and for a moment I had the illusion that his eyes had turned red, like a spider's. Then he spat out: 'Then he's nothing but a bleeding — fool, and he deserves what he gets.'

While I felt a twinge of fear, I also felt a touch of triumph. He had started to talk. My frankness had paid off. And unless he suddenly became cautious again, I was close to finding out some of the things I wanted to know.

He controlled himself, then said, less violently, 'First of all, he's a fool because he doesn't really know anything. Not a bloody thing.' He tapped my wrist with a bent forefinger.

'I suspected that,' I said.

'You did, did you? Well, you were right. All this stuff about Atlantis.' There was no doubt that scorn was real. But what he said next shocked me more than anything so far. He leaned forward, and said with an odd sincerity: 'These things aren't out of a fairy story, you know. They're not playing games.'

And I understood something that had not been clear to me so far. He knew 'them', knew them with the indifferent realism of a scientist referring to the atomic bomb. I think that, up to this point, I had not really believed in 'them'; I had been hoping that it was all some odd delusion; or that, like ghosts, they could not impinge on human affairs to any practical extent. His words made me understand my mistake.

'These things.' My hair stirred, and I felt the cold flowing down my legs to my feet.

'What *are* they doing, then?'

He emptied the glass, and said casually. 'That's nuthin' to do wi' you, mate. You can't do anything about it. Nobody can.' He set down the glass. 'You see, this is their world anyway. We're a mistake. They want it back again.' He caught the eye of the barman, and pointed to his glass.

I went over and collected another rum for him. Now I wanted to leave as soon as possible, to speak to Urquart. But it would be difficult, without running the risk of offending him.

Chickno solved my problem. After his third double rum, he abruptly ceased to be intelligible. He muttered things in a language which I took to be Romany. He mentioned a 'Liz Southern' several times, pronouncing it 'Sowthern', and it was only later that I recalled that this was the name of one of the Lancashire witches, executed in 1612. I never found out what he was saying, or whether he was, in fact, referring to the witch. His eyes became glassy, although he obviously thought he was still communicating something to me. Finally, I had the eerie impression that it was no longer old Chickno who was talking to me, but that he was possessed by some other creature. Half an hour later, he was dozing with his head on the table. I crossed to the barman.

'I'm sorry about this.' I pointed to old Chickno.

'That's all right,' he said. I think he had gathered by then that I was not a friend of the gypsy's. 'I'll phone his grandson. He'll take him home.'

I rang Urquart's house from the nearest phone box. His housekeeper said he was asleep. I was tempted to go over and wake him, then decided against it, and went back to the hotel, wishing I had someone to talk to.

I tried to sort out my thoughts, to see some meaning in what Chickno had said. If he didn't deny the reality of the Lloigor, then why was Urquart so wrong? But I had drunk too much, and I felt exhausted. I fell asleep at midnight, but slept badly, haunted by nightmares. At two in the morning, I woke up with a horrible sense of the evil reality of the Lloigor, although it was mixed up in my mind with my nightmares about the Marquis de Sade and Jack the Ripper. My sense of danger was so strong that I switched on the light. This improved things. Then I decided that I had better write down my conversation with Chickno and give it to Urquart to read, in case he could add some of the missing parts to the jigsaw. I wrote it down in detail.

My fingers numb with the cold, I slept again, but was awakened by a faint trembling of the room, which reminded me of an earthquake tremor I experienced once in Mexico. Then I slept again until morning.

Before going in to breakfast, I inquired at the desk for mail. There was a reply to my letter from Lauerdale at Brown, and I read it as I ate my kippers.

Much of the letter was literary – a discussion of Lovecraft and his psychology. But there were pages that held far more interest for me. Lauerdale wrote: 'I myself am inclined to believe, on the evidence of letters, that one of the most important experiences in Lovecraft's early life was a visit to Cohasset, a rundown fishing village between Quonochontaug and Weekapaug in Southern Rhode Island. Like Lovecraft's "Innsmouth", this village was later to vanish from the maps. I have been there, and its description corresponds in many ways to Lovecraft's description of Innsmouth – which Lovecraft placed in Massachusetts: "more empty houses than people", the air of decay, the stale fish smell. There was actually a character known as Captain Marsh living in Cohasset in 1915, when Lovecraft was there, who had spent some time in the South Seas. It may have been he who told the young Lovecraft the stories of evil Polynesian temples and undersea people. The chief of these legends – as mentioned also by Jung and Spence – is of gods from the stars (or demons) who were once lords of this earth, who lost their power through the practice of evil magic, but who will one day return and take over the earth again. In the version quoted by Jung, these gods are said to have created human beings from sub-human monsters.

'In my own opinion, Lovecraft derived the rest of the "mythos" from Machen, perhaps from Poe, who occasionally hints at such things. 'MS Found in a Bottle', for example. I found no evidence that there were ever sinister rumours connected with the "shunned house" in Benefit Street, or any other house in Providence. I shall be extremely interested to read what you have to say about Machen's sources. While I think it is just possible that Machen heard some story about some "arcane" volume of the sort you mention, I can find no evidence that Lovecraft had first-hand acquaintance with such a book. I am sure that any connection between his *Necronomicon* and the Voynich MS is, as you suggest, coincidence.'

My hair stirred as I read the sentence about gods 'who will one day return and take over the earth again', as also about the reference to Polynesian legends. For, as Churchward has written: 'Easter Island, Tahiti, Samoas, . . . Hawaii and the Marquesas are the pathetic fingers of that great land, standing today as sentinels of a silent grave.' Polynesia is the remains of Mu.

All this told me little more than I knew already, or had guessed. But my encounter with Chickno raised a practical problem: how far was Urquart actually in danger? He might be right that the Lloigor had no power in themselves, or very little; but Chickno and his family were a different matter. Even taking the most sceptical view of all, that this whole thing was pure imagination and superstition, Chickno represented a very real danger. For some reason, they hated Urquart.

The desk clerk touched my sleeve: 'Telephone, sir.'

It was Urquart. I said, 'Thank heavens you rang. I've got to talk to you.'

'You've heard, then?'

'Heard what?'

'About the explosion? Chickno's dead.'

'What! Are you sure?'

'Pretty sure. Although they can't find much of him.'

'I'll be over right away.'

That was the first I heard of the great Llandalffen explosion. I have on my desk a volume called *Stranger than Logic* by the late Frank Edwards, one of those slightly unreliable compilations of mysteries and wonders. It has a section headed 'The Great Llandalffen Explosion', and what he says, substantially, is that the explosion was atomic, and was probably due to a fault in the engines of an 'unidentified flying object'; he quotes the rocket scientist Willy Ley to the effect that the Siberian crater of 1908 may have been an explosion of anti-matter, and draws parallels between the Llandalffen explosion and the Podkamennaya Tunguska fall. This I flatly hold to be absurd. I saw the area of the explosion, and there was not nearly enough damage for an atomic explosion, even a small one.

However, I am running ahead of my story. Urquart met me halfway to his house, and we drove out to Llandalffen. What had happened was simply that there had been a tremendous explosion at about four o'clock that morning; it may have been this that shook me awake in the early hours. The area is deserted, luckily, but a farm labourer in a cottage three miles away was thrown out of bed by the explosion. The strangest feature of the whole affair is that it made so little actual noise; the farm labourer thought it was an earth tremor, and went back to sleep. Two men in the village, returning home from a party, said they heard the explosion as a dull sound like distant thunder or blasting, and wondered whether a plane might have crashed with a load of bombs. The farm labourer pedalled out to investigate at seven in the morning, but found nothing. However, he mentioned it to the farmer who employed him, and the two drove over in the farmer's car a little after nine. This time, the farmer turned off down the side road, and drove towards the gypsy caravans, which were about two miles further on. Their first find was not, as Mr Edwards states, a part of a human body, but part of the foreleg of a donkey, which lay in the middle of the road. Beyond this, they discovered that stone walls and trees had been flattened. Bits of the caravan and other relics were scattered for hundreds of yards around the focus of the explosion, the two-acre field in which the caravans had stood.

I saw the field myself – we were allowed to approach by the inspector of police from Llandalffen, who knew Urquart. My first impression was that it had been an earthquake rather than an ordinary explosion. An explosion produces a crater, or clears a more-or-less flattened area, but the ground here was torn and split open as if by a convulsion from underneath. A stream flowed through the field, and it had now turned the area into a lake. On the other hand, there were certain signs that are characteristic of an explosion. Some trees were flattened, or reduced to broken stumps, but others were untouched. The wall between the field and the main road was almost intact, although it ran along the top of a raised mound or dyke, yet a wall much further away in the next field had been scattered over a wide area.

There were also, of course, the disfigured human and animal relics that we had expected to find; shreds of skin, fragments of bone. Few of them were identifiable; the explosion seemed to have fragmented every living creature in the field. The donkey's leg found by the farmer was the largest segment recovered.

I was soon feeling severely sick, and had to go and sit in the car, but Urquart limped around for over an hour, picking up various fragments. I heard a police sergeant ask him what he was looking for, and Urquart said he didn't know. But I knew; he was hoping for some definite evidence to connect the gypsies with Mu. And somehow, I was certain that he wouldn't find it.

By now there must have been a thousand sightseers around the area, trying to approach closely enough to find out what had happened. Our car was stopped a dozen or more times as we tried to drive away. Urquart told everyone who asked him that he thought a flying saucer had exploded.

In fact, we were both fairly certain what had happened. I believe that old Chickno had gone too far – that he told me too much. Urquart thinks that his chief mistake was to think of the Lloigor as somehow human, and of himself as their servant, entitled to take certain liberties. He failed to realize that he was completely dispensable, and that his naïve tendency to boast and present himself as an ambassador of the Lloigor made him dangerous to them.

We reached this conclusion after I had described my talk with Chickno to Urquart. When I had finished reading him my notes, Urquart said, 'No wonder they killed him.'

'But he didn't say much, after all.'

'He said enough. And perhaps they thought we could guess more than he said.'

We had lunch in the hotel, and regretted it. Everyone seemed to know where we had been, and they stared at us and tried to overhear our conversation. The waiter spent so much time hanging about in the area of our table that the manager finally had to reprimand him. We ate as quickly as we could and went back to Urquart's house. There was a fire in the library again, and Mrs Dolgelly brought in coffee.

I can still remember every moment of that afternoon. There was a sense of tension and foreboding, of physical danger. What had impressed Urquart most was old Chickno's scorn when I told him that Urquart thought 'they' had no real power. I still remember that stream of contemptuous bad language that had made several people in the pub turn their heads. And Chickno had been proved right. 'They' had plenty of power – several kinds of power. For we reached the conclusion that the devastation of the gypsy encampment was neither earthquake nor explosion, but some kind of mixture of both. An explosion violent enough to rip apart the caravans would have been heard clearly in Southport and Melincourt, and most certainly in Llandalffen, barely five miles away. The clefts and cracks in the earth suggested a convulsion of the ground. But a convulsion of the ground would not have torn apart the caravans. Urquart believed – and I finally agreed with him – that the caravans and their inhabitants *had* been literally torn apart. But in that case, what was the purpose of the convulsion of the earth? There were two possible explanations. This had happened as the 'creatures' forced their way from underground. Or the 'earthquake' was a deliberate false trail, a red herring. And the consequences that followed from such a supposition were so frightening that we poured ourselves whiskies, although it was only mid-afternoon. It meant that 'they' were anxious to provide an apparently natural explanation for what had happened. And that meant they had a reason for secrecy. And, as far as we could see, there could only be one reason: they had 'plans', plans for the future. I recalled Chickno's words: 'This is their world anyway ... They want it back again.'

The frustrating thing was that, in all his books on occultism and the history of Mu, Urquart had nothing that suggested an answer. It was hard to fight off a paralysed feeling of hopelessness, of not knowing where to begin. The evening paper increased the depression, for it stated confidently that the explosion had been caused by nitro-glycerine! The 'experts' had come up with a theory that seemed to explain the facts. Chickno's son and son-in-law had worked in stone quarries in the north, and were used to handling explosives. Nitro-glycerine was occasionally used in these quarries because of its cheapness and because it is easy to manufacture. According to the newspaper report, Chickno's sons were suspected of stealing quantities of glycerine, and of nitric and sulphuric acid. Their intention, said the report, was to use them for blowing safes. They must have manufactured fairly large quantities of the nitro-glycerine, and some kind of earth tremor set it off.

It was an absurd explanation; it would have taken a ton of nitro-glycerine to do so much damage. In any case, a nitro-glycerine explosion leaves behind characteristic signs; there were no such signs in the devastated field. A nitro-glycerine explosion can be heard; no one heard it.

And yet the explosion was never seriously questioned, although there was later an official investigation into the disaster. Presumably because human beings are afraid of mysteries for which there is absolutely no explanation, the mind needs some solution, no matter how absurd, to reassure it.

There was another item in the evening paper that at first seemed irrelevant. The headline ran: 'Did explosion release mystery gas?' It was only a short paragraph, which stated that many people in the area had awakened that morning with bad headaches and a feeling of lassitude, apparently signs of an impending attack of influenza. These had cleared up later in the day. Had the explosion released some gas, asked the reporter, that produced these symptoms. The newpaper's 'scientific correspondent' added a note saying that sulphur dioxide could produce exactly these symptoms and that several people had noticed such a smell in the night. Nitro-glycerine, of course, contains a small quantity of sulphuric acid, which would account for the smell . . .

Urquart said, 'Soon find out about that, anyway,' and rang the Southport weather bureau. They rang us back ten minutes later with the answer; the wind had been blowing from the northeast in the night. And Llandalffen lies to the north of the site of the explosion.

And still neither of us saw the significance of the item. We wasted hours searching through my translation of the Voynich manuscript for clues, then through thirty or so books of Mu and related subjects.

And then, about to reach down another volume on Lemuria and Atlantis, my eye fell on Sacheverell Sitwell's book *Poltergeists*. I stopped and stared. My mind groped for some fact I had half forgotten. Then it came.

'My God, Urquart,' I said, 'I've just thought of something. Where do these creatures get their energy?' He looked at me blankly. 'Is it their own natural energy? You need a physical body to generate physical energy. But how about poltergeists . . .' And then he understood, too. 'Poltergeists' take energy from human beings, usually from adolescent girls. One school of thought believes that poltergeists have no independent existence; they are some kind of psychic manifestation from the unconscious mind of the adolescent, an explosion of frustration or craving for attention. The other school believes that they are 'spirits' who need to borrow energy from an emotionally disturbed person; Sitwell cites cases of poltergeist disturbances in houses that have remained empty for long periods.

Could this be why so many people in the area felt tired and 'fluey' when they woke up – because the energy for the explosion came *from them*?

If this was so, then the danger was not as serious as we had believed. It meant that the Lloigor had no energy of their own; they had to draw it from people – presumably sleeping people. Their powers were therefore limited.

The same thought struck us both at the same time. Except, of course, that the world is full of people . . .

Nevertheless, we both felt suddenly more cheerful. And in this new frame of mind, we faced our fundamental task; to make the human race aware of the Lloigor. They were not indestructible, or they would not have bothered to destroy Chickno for talking about them. It might be possible to destroy them with an underground nuclear explosion. The fact that they had remained dormant for so many centuries meant that their power was limited. If we could produce definite proof of their existence, then the possibility of countering the menace was high.

The obvious starting point was the Llandalffen explosion: to make the public aware that it pointed unmistakably to the reality of these hidden forces. In a way, Chickno's death was the best thing that could have happened; they had shown their hand. We decided to visit the explosion site again in the morning, and to compile a dossier on it. We would interview the citizens of Llandalffen and find out whether any of them really *had* smelled sulphur dioxide in the night, and whether they would persist in the story when we pointed out that the wind was blowing in the opposite direction. Urquart knew a few Fleet Street journalists who had taken a vague interest in the occult and supernatural; he would contact them and hint at a big story.

When I returned to my hotel late that night, I felt happier than for many days. And I slept deeply and heavily. When I woke up, it was already long past breakfast time, and I felt exhausted. I attributed this to my long sleep, until I tried to walk to the bathroom, and found that my head throbbed as if I had picked up a flu germ. I took two aspirins, had a shave, then went downstairs. To my relief, no one else showed signs of a similar exhaustion. Coffee and buttered toast in the lounge refreshed me slightly; I decided that I was suffering from ordinary strain. Then I rang Urquart.

Mrs Dolgelly said, 'I'm afraid he's not up yet, sir. He's not feeling too well this morning.'

'What's the matter with him?'

'Nothing much. He just seems very tired.'

'I'll be right over,' I said. I told the desk to ring me a taxi; I was far too tired to walk.

Twenty minutes later, I was sitting at Urquart's bedside. He looked and felt even worse than I did.

'I hate to suggest this,' I said, 'feeling as we both do, but I think we'd better get out of this place as soon as possible.'

'Couldn't we wait until tomorrow?' he asked.

'It will be worse tomorrow. They'll exhaust us until we die of the first minor illness we pick up.'

'I suppose you're right.'

Although it all seemed too troublesome for words, I managed to get back to the hotel, pack my bags, and order a taxi to the station in Cardiff, where we could catch a London train at three o'clock. Urquart encountered more difficulty than I did; Mrs Dolgelly showed unexpected strength of mind and refused to pack a case for him. He rang me, and I dragged myself back there again, wanting nothing so much as to climb back into bed. But the effort revived me; before midday, the headache had vanished, and I was feeling less exhausted, although oddly light-headed. Mrs Dolgelly believed my explanation of an urgent telegram that made our journey a matter of life and death, although she was convinced that Urquart would collapse on the way to London.

That night, we slept in the Regent Palace Hotel. And in the morning, we both woke up feeling perfectly normal. It was Urquart who said, as we waited for our egg and bacon at breakfast, 'I think we're winning, old boy.'

But neither of us really believed it.

And from this point on, my story ceases to be a continuous narrative, and becomes a series of fragments, and a record of frustration. We spent weeks in the British Museum searching for clues, and later in the Bibliothèque Nationale. Books on cults in the South Seas indicate that many traditions of the Lloigor survive there, and it is well known that they will one day return and reclaim their world. One text quoted by Leduc and Poitier says that they will cause a 'tearing madness' to break out among those they wish to destroy, and their footnote says that 'tearing', as used in this context, means to tear with the teeth, like a man eating a chicken leg. Von Storch has records of a Haitian tribe in which the men folk became possessed of a demon that led many of them to kill wives and children by tearing at their throats with their teeth.

Lovecraft also provided us with an important hint. In 'The Call of Cthulhu' he mentions a collection of press cutings, all of which reveal that the 'entombed old ones' are becoming more active in the world. Later the same day, I happened to meet a girl who worked for a press cutting agency, who told me that her job was simply to read through dozens of newspapers every day, looking out for mention of the names of clients. I asked her if she could look for items of 'unusual' interest – anything hinting at the mysterious or supernatural – and she said she saw no reason why not. I gave her a copy of Charles Fort's *Lo!* to give her an idea of the kind of items I wanted.

Two weeks later, a thin buff envelope arrived, with a dozen or so press clippings in it. Most of them were unimportant – babies with two heads and similar medical curiosities, a man killed in Scotland by an enormous hail stone, reports of an abominable snowman seen on the slopes of Everest – but two or three were more relevant to our search. We immediately contacted several more press cutting agencies in England, America, and Australia.

The result was an enormous amount of material, which finally occupied two enormous volumes. It was arranged under various headings: explosions, murders, witchcraft (and the supernatural in general), insanity, scientific observations, miscellaneous. The details of the explosion near Al Kazimiyah in Iraq are so similar to those of the Llandalffen disaster – even to the exhaustion of the inhabitants of Al Kazimiyah – that I have no doubt that this area is another stronghold of the Lloigor. The explosion that changed the course of the Tula Gol near Ulan Bator in Mongolia actually led the Chinese to accuse Russia of dropping an atomic bomb. The strange insanity that destroyed ninety per cent of the inhabitants of the southern island of Zaforas in the Sea of Crete is still a mystery upon which the Greek military government refuses to comment. The massacre at Panagyu-rishte in Bulgaria on the night of March 29, 1968, was blamed, in the first official reports, upon a 'vampire cult' who 'regarded the nebula in Andromeda as their true home'. These are some of the major events that convinced us that the Lloigor are planning a major attack on the inhabitants of the earth.

But there were literally dozens — eventually hundreds — of less important items that fitted the pattern. The marine creature that dragged away a trout fisherman in Loch Eilt led to several newspaper articles about 'prehistoric surviv-als'; but the Glasgow edition of the *Daily Express* (May 18, 1968) printed a story of a witch cult and their worship of a sea-devil with an overpowering smell of decay that recalled Lovecraft's Innsmouth. An item about the Melksham stran-gler led me to spend some days there, and I have a signed statement by Detective Sergeant Bradley agreeing that the words the killer used repeatedly before he died were 'Ghatan-othoa', 'Nug' (another elemental described in Lovecraft) and 'Rantegoz'. (Rhan Tegoth, the beast god, also mentioned in Lovecraft?) Robbins (the strangler) claimed that he was possessed by a 'power from underground' when he killed the three women and amputated their feet.

It would be pointless to continue this list. We hope to have a number of selected items from it — some five hundred in all — published in a volume that will be sent to every member of Congress and every member of the British House of Commons.

There are certain items that will not be published in this volume, and which are perhaps the most disturbing of all. At 7:45 on December 7, 1967, a small private aircraft piloted by R. D. Jones of Kingston, Jamaica, left Fort Lauderdale, Florida, for Kingston. There were three passengers aboard. The journey of about 500 kilometres should have taken two hours. By ten o'clock, Jones's wife, waiting at the airfield, became alarmed and suggested a search. All attempts at radio contact failed. The search began during the morning. At 1:15, Jones radioed the field for permission to land, apparently unaware of the anxiety he was causing. When asked where he had been, he looked puzzled, and said 'Flying, of course.' When told the time, he was amazed. *His own watch showed 10:15.* He said he had been flying in low cloud most of the way, but that he had no cause for alarm. Weather reports showed that it was an exceptionally clear day for December, and that he should have encountered no cloud. (*Gleaner*, Dec. 8, 1967.)

The other four cases of which we possess details are similar to this first one, except that one case, the *Jeannie*, concerned a coastguard vessel off the west coast of Scotland, not an aeroplane. In this instance, the three men on board had encountered heavy 'fog', discovered the radio was not working, and that, for some reason, their watches had stopped. They assumed that it was some odd magnetic disturbance. However, the vessel's other instruments worked well enough, and in due course, the boat reached Stornoway on Lewis – having been missing for twenty-two hours instead of the three or four assumed by the crew. The naval training plane *Blackjack*, off the Baja peninsula, southern California, holds the record; it was missing for three days and five hours. The crew thought it had been away from base for seven hours or so.

We have been unable to discover what explanation was advanced by the navy for this curious episode, or by the coastguard of Great Britain for the *Jeannie* interlude. It was probably assumed that the crew got drunk at sea and fell asleep. But there is one thing we soon learned beyond all doubt: human beings do not wish to know about things that threaten their feeling of security and 'normality'. This was also a discovery made by the late Charles Fort; he devoted his life to analysing it. And I suppose the books of Fort present classic instance of what William James called 'a certain blindness in human beings'. For he invariably gives newspaper references for the incredible events he cites. Why had no one ever taken the trouble to check his references – or some of them – and then write a statement admitting his honesty or denouncing him as a fraud? Mr Tiffany Thayer once told me that critical readers take the view that there was some 'special circumstance' in each case Fort quotes which invalidates it – an unreliable witness here, an inventive reporter there, and so on. And it never strikes anyone that to use this explanation to cover a thousand pages full of carefully assembled facts amounts to pure self-delusion.

Like most people, I have always made the assumption that my fellow human beings are relatively honest, relatively open-minded, relatively curious. If anything were needed to reassure me about the curiosity about the apparently inexplicable, I would only have to glance at any airport bookstall, with its dozen or so paperbacks by Frank Edwards, et al., all bearing titles like *World of the Weird*, *A Hundred Events Stranger than Fiction*, and so on. It comes as a shock to discover that all this is not proof of a genuine open-mindedness about the 'supernatural' but only of a desire to be titillated and shocked. These books are a kind of occult pornography, part of a game of 'let's make believe the world is far less dull than it actually is'.

On August 19, 1968, Urquart and myself invited twelve 'friends' to the rooms we had taken at 83 Gower Street – the house in which Darwin lived immediately after his marriage. We felt the Darwin association was appropriate, for we had no doubt that the date would long be remembered by everyone present. I shall not go into detail except to say that there were four professors – three from London, one from Cambridge – two journalists, both from respectable newspapers, and several members of the professions, including a doctor.

Urquart introduced me, and I read from a prepared statement, elaborating where I felt it to be necessary. After ten minutes, the Cambridge professor cleared his throat, said 'Excuse me,' and hurried out of the room. I discovered later that he thought he had been the victim of a practical joke. The others listened to the end, and for a great deal of the time, I was aware that they were also wondering whether this was all a joke. When they realized that it was not, they became definitely hostile. One of the journalists, a young man just down from university, kept interrupting with: 'Are we to understand . . .' One of the ladies got up and left, although I heard later that this was less from disbelief than because she suddenly noticed that there were now thirteen people in the room and thought it unlucky. The young journalist was carrying two of Urquart's books on Mu, and he quoted from these with deadly effect. Urquart is certainly no master of the English language, and there was a time when I would have seen in them mainly an excuse for witty sarcasm.

But what was amazing to me was that no one present seemed to accept our 'lecture' as a *warning*. They argued about it as though it were an interesting theory, or perhaps an unusual short story. Finally, after an hour of quibbling about various newspaper cuttings, a solicitor stood up and made a speech that obviously conveyed the general feeling, beginning: 'I think Mr Hough (the journalist) has expressed the misgiving we all feel . . .' His main point, which he kept repeating, was that there was *no definite evidence*. The Llandalffen explosion could have been due to nitro-glycerine or even the impact of a shower of meteors. Poor Urquart's books were treated in a manner that would have made me wince even in my most sceptical days.

There is no point in going on. We tape-recorded the whole meeting, and had it typed and duplicated, hoping that one day it will be regarded as almost unbelievable evidence of human blindness and stupidity. And then nothing more happened. The two newspapers decided not to print even a critical account of our arguments. A number of people got wind of the meeting and came to see us – bosomy ladies with ouija boards, a thin man who thought the Loch Ness monster was a Russian submarine, and a number of assorted cranks. This was the point where we decided to move to America. We still entertained some absurd hope that Americans would prove more open-minded than the English.

It did not take long to disillusion us – although it is true that we found one or two people who were at least willing to suspend judgement on our sanity. But on the whole, the results were negative. We spent an interesting day at the almost defunct fishing village of Cohasset – Lovecraft's Innsmouth; long enough to discover that it is as active a centre of Lloigor activity as Llandalffen, perhaps more so, and that we would be in extreme danger if we remained there. But we managed to locate Joseph Cullen Marsh, grandson of Lovecraft's Captain Marsh, who now lived in Popasquash. He told us that his grandfather had died insane, and believed that he had possessed certain 'occult' books and manuscripts, which had been destroyed by his widow. This may have been where Lovecraft actually saw the *Necronomicon*. He also mentioned that Captain Marsh referred to the Ancient Old Ones as 'the Masters of Time' – an interesting comment in view of the case of the *Jeannie*, the *Blackjack* and the rest.

Urquart is convinced that the manuscripts were not destroyed – on the curious grounds that such ancient works have a character of their own, and tend to avoid destruction. He is conducting an enormous correspondence with Captain Marsh's heirs, and his family solicitors, in an attenpt to pick up the trail of the *Necronomicon*.

In the present stage . . .

Editor's Note. The above words were written by my uncle a few minutes before he received the telegram from Senator James R. Pinckney of Virginia, an old schoolfriend, and probably one of those my uncle mentions as being 'willing to suspend judgement on his sanity.' The telegram read: 'Come to Washington as soon as possible, bring cuttings. Contact

me at my home. Pinckney.' Senator Pinckney has confirmed
to me that the Secretary of Defense had agreed to spend
some time with my uncle, and that, if impressed, he might
conceivably have arranged an interview with the President
himself.

My uncle and Colonel Urquart were unable to get on the
three-fifteen flight from Charlottesville to Washington; they
went to the airport on a 'stand-by' basis, hoping for cancella-
tions. There was only one cancellation, and after some
argument, Colonel Urquart agreed with my uncle that they
should stick together rather than go to Washington by
different routes. At this point, Captain Harvey Nichols
agreed to fly them to Washington in a Cessna 311, of which
he was one-quarter owner.

The plane took off from a side runway at 3:43 on February
19, 1969; the sky was perfectly clear, and weather reports
were excellent. Ten minutes later, the airfield received the
mystifying signal 'running into low cloud'. He should have
been by then somewhere in the area of Gordonsville, and the
weather over this area was exceptionally clear. Subsequent
attempts to contact the plane by radio failed. At five o'clock,
I was informed that radio contact had been lost. But during
the next few hours, hope revived as widespread inquiries
failed to discover any reports of a crash. By midnight, we all
assumed that it would only be a matter of time before the
wreck was reported.

It has never been reported. In the two months that have
elapsed since then, nothing further has been heard of my
uncle or of the plane. It is my opinion – supported by many
people of wide experience in flying – that the plane had an
instrument failure, and somehow flew out over the Atlantic,
where it crashed.

My uncle had already arranged for the publication of this
book of selections from his press-cutting albums with the
Black Cockerell Press of Charlottesville, and it seems appropriate that these notes of his should be used as an
introduction.

In the newspaper stories that have appeared about my uncle in the past two months, it has often been assumed that he was insane or, at least, suffering from delusions. This is not my own view. I met Colonel Urquart on a great many occasions, and it is my own opinion that he was thoroughly untrustworthy. My mother described him to me as 'an extremely shifty character'. Even my uncle's account of him – at their first meeting – bears this out. It would be charitable to assume that Urquart believed everything he wrote in his books, but I find this hard to accept. They are cheap and sensational, and in parts obviously pure invention. (For example, he never mentions the name of the Hindu monastery – or even its location – where he made his amazing 'finds' about Mu; neither does he mention the name of the priest who is supposed to have taught him to read the language of the inscriptions.)

My uncle was a simple and easy-going man, almost a caricature of the absent-minded professor. This is revealed in his naïve account of the meeting at 83 Gower Street, and the reaction of his audience. He had no notion of the possibilities of human duplicity that are, in my opinion, revealed in the writings of Colonel Urquart. And typically, my uncle does not mention that it was he who paid for the Colonel's passage across the Atlantic, and for the rooms at 83 Gower Street. The Colonel's income was extremely small, while my uncle was, I suppose, comparatively well-off.

And yet there is, I think, another possibility that must be taken into account – suggested by my uncle's friend Foster Damon. My uncle was loved by his students and colleagues for his sense of dry humour, and has been many times compared to Mark Twain. And the resemblance did not end there: he also shared Twain's deep vein of pessimism about the human race.

I knew my uncle well in the last years of his life, and saw much of him even in the last months. He knew I did not believe his stories about the 'Lloigor', and that I thought

Urquart a charlatan. A fanatic would have tried to convince me, and perhaps refused to speak to me when I declined to be convinced. My uncle continued to treat me with the same good humour as ever, and my mother and I both noticed that his eyes often twinkled as he looked at me. Was he congratulating himself on having a nephew who was too pragmatic to be taken in by his elaborate joke?

I like to think so. For he was a good and sincere man, and is mourned by innumerable friends.

— Julian F. Lang. 1969.

Biographical

ROBERT BLOCH (1917–   ) began to write at 18 and is the author of hundreds of stories and a score of books, including *Psycho*, *Pleasant Dreams*, *The Scarf*, *The Dead Beat*, and *The Opener of the Way*, his first book, published under the imprint of Arkham House in 1945. Born in Chicago, he grew up in Milwaukee, lived for a while in upstate Wisconsin, but is currently a resident of California where he writes teleplays for such shows as *Thriller* and *Alfred Hitchcock Presents*. He has been widely published in paperback here and abroad. He was a correspondent of H. P. Lovecraft, and is one of the few members of the old Lovecraft circle still actively writing. He has contributed to a wide range of magazines, from *Weird Tales* to *Playboy*, and is as well known for his memorable sense of humour as he is for his tales of mystery and horror.

RAMSEY CAMPBELL (1946–   ) has the same background as the Beatles – Liverpool, England. He was early influenced in his writing by the work of H. P. Lovecraft, and his tales were set in the Arkham country, though he was readily persuaded to construct a fictional British milieu – the Severn Valley at Brichester – for his tales in the Lovecraft tradition. His first book, *The Inhabitant of the Lake and Less Welcome Tenants*, was published by Arkham House when he was but 18; a second, *Demons at Daylight*, followed. His work has appeared in anthologies in America and in his native England and has also made its appearance in Continental countries.

AUGUST DERLETH (1909–71) was one of the most versatile and prolific of authors, with close to 150 books to his credit, and many thousands of contributions to magazines and newspapers in America and elsewhere. His special contributions to the domain of the macabre were many, but perhaps the principal one was his establishment of Arkham House three decades ago. An early correspondent of H. P. Lovecraft – from 1925 onwards – his principal work in the Lovecraft tradition was done after Lovecraft's death. In the field of the macabre he published *Someone in the Dark*, *Something Near*, *Not Long for This World*, *Lonesome Places*, *Mr George and Other Odd Persons*, *Colonel Markesan and Less Pleasant People* (with Mark Schorer), *The Mask of Cthulhu*, *The Trail of Cthulhu*, and, with H. P. Lovecraft, *The Lurker at the Threshold* and *The Survivor and Others*. He edited many anthologies, including *Sleep No More*, *Who Knocks?*, The Sleeping and the Dead, *The Night Side*, *Over the Edge*, *Travellers by Night*, *When Evil Wakes*, *On the Other Side of the Moon*, *Beyond Time and Space*, *Strange Ports of Call*, and *Dark Things*.

In addition to H. P. Lovecraft – whose work, thanks primarily to his efforts, is now published around the world – he introduced in book form the macabre fiction of such writers as Ray Bradbury, A. E. Van Vogt, Clark Ashton Smith, Henry S. Whitehead, Donald Wandrei, Robert Bloch, Robert E. Howard, Frank Belknap Long, Fritz Leiber, Zealia Bishop, Seabury Quinn, Carl Jacobi, Joseph Payne Brennan, E. Hoffman Price, Arthur J. Burks, J. Ramsey Campbell, Manly Wade Wellman, Greye La Spina, and Brian Lumley, and reprinted in America the outstanding weird tales of Algernon Blackwood, J. Sheridan LeFanu, H. Russell Wakefield, A. E. Coppard, Arthur Machen, L. P. Hartley, Cynthia Asquith, William Hope Hodgson, S. Fowler Wright, Margery Lawrence, Lord Dunsany, and Colin Wilson.

ROBERT E. HOWARD (1906–36) was born and lived all his relatively short life in Texas. He began to write at the age of 15, and soon invented such popular characters as Conan the

Cimmerian, Solomon Kane, King Kull, and Bran Mak Morn. He was particularly effective in the kind of story known as 'sword and sorcery' fiction. He wrote sports stories, historical adventure, Oriental tales, detective, pirate, and other adventure stories, and, of course, weird fiction and verse. His stories about a Western character named Breckenridge Elkins are among his best work. His first book was *A Gent from Bear Creek*, published in England in 1937, the year after he took his own life. His first collection of weird stories was *Skull-Face and Others*. His books include *Always Comes Evening*, a collection of poetry, *The Dark Man and Others*, *Conan the Conqueror*, *The Sword of Conan*, *King Conan*, *The Coming of Conan*, *Conan the Barbarian*, and *Tales of Conan*.

HENRY KUTTNER (1914–58) was a Californian who wrote outstanding fiction in the domain of the macabre and that division of fantasy classified as science fiction. He wrote under many pen-names, of which the most popular was Lewis Padgett, and contributed to many magazines, including *Charm*, *Weird Tales*, *Strange Stories*, *Astounding Science-Fiction*, and others. His first book, a mystery novel, *The Brass Ring*, was published in 1946. Many paperback collections of his admirable short stories have appeared since his death.

FRANK BELKNAP LONG (1903–   ) is a charter member of the old Kalem Klub, the first Lovecraft Circle. His work is widely known in the genre of the macabre, and his short stories have appeared widely in both magazines and in paperback books. His work has been anthologized in America and elsewhere, both under his own name and under pen-names. His books include two of poems – *A Man from Genoa* and *The Goblin Tower* – and *The Hounds of Tindalos*, *The Horror from the Hills*, *Mars Is My Destination*, *The Day of the Robot*, and others.

HOWARD PHILLIPS LOVECRAFT (1890–1937) has since his early death been recognized as one of the world masters of the macabre. He was born in and spent most of his life in and around Providence, Rhode Island, with but brief excursions to older cities on the North American continent, indulging antiquarian tastes. Chronic illness in youth led him to omnivorous reading, and his solitary nature directed him towards astronomy, amateur press work, and an active imagination in the development of which he sought to compensate for his solitude by the creation of the memorable pantheon of mythical lands and beings that became the Cthulhu Mythos, to which most of his stories belong. His work has been collected into several volumes – *The Outsider and Others*, *Beyond the Wall of Sleep*, *Marginalia*, *The Lurker at the Threshold* (with August Derleth), *Something About Cats and Other Pieces*, *The Survivor and Others* (with August Derleth), *The Shuttered Room and Other Pieces*, *Collected Poems*, *The Dark Brotherhood and Other Pieces*, and *Selected Letters* – in five volumes, which began publication in 1965. His complete fiction has been published in the United States in three companion volumes – *The Dunwich Horror and Others*, *At the Mountains of Madness and Other Novels*, and *Dagon and Other Macabre Tales*. Lovecraft's work has been widely published, broadcast, and filmed, and his haunting stories have been published in England, Germany, France, Spain, Portugal, Denmark, Italy, Argentina, and other countries, including some behind the Iron Curtain.

BRIAN LUMLEY (1937–   ) was born at Horden, County Durham, England. His introduction to the Cthulhu Mythos came not by way of Lovecraft, but by way of Robert Bloch – in a short story reprinted in a British magazine, when Lumley was but eleven. He began writing early, and also did art work for the fanzines. He was married at 20, and began writing Mythos tales in earnest while he was stationed with his wife and daughter in West Germany with the Royal

British Military Force. His first professional work appeared in *The Arkham Collector*, and his first collection, *The Caller of the Black*, was published by Arkham House.

J. VERNON SHEA (1912–   ) is the son of a professional magician. Though born in Kentucky, he has spent most of his life in Pennsylvania and Ohio. He was in the Army Medical Corps in World War II. He began to write at 14. His work has been published in various magazines, and in the anthology, *Over the Edge*. He has edited two anthologies in the domain of the macabre – *Strange Desires* and *Strange Barriers*.

CLARK ASHTON SMITH (1893–1961) was born in mining country, at Auburn, California, east of Sacramento, and lived there for most of his life, previous to his marriage to Carol Dorman, when he moved to Pacific Grove, where he died. Smith was a poet of great distinction before most of his contemporary *fantaisistes* had begun to make their reputations, though he came into his own as a writer of memorable macabre short stories and freshly imaginative science fiction in the 1920s and 1930s. In addition to writing, Smith painted and created unique and fantastic sculptures – many of them of fabled beings in the Cthulhu Mythos, now much sought after by collectors. He published widely in many magazines, including *The London Mercury*, *Munsey's*, *The Yale Review*, *Strange Tales*, *Smart Set*, *Poetry*, *The Black Cat*, *The Arkham Sampler*, *Weird Tales*, *Amazing Stories*, and others. During his lifetime he published seven collections of poems – *The Star-Trender and Other Poems*, *Ebony and Crystal*, *Sandalwood*, *Odes and Sonnets*, *Nero and Other Poems*, *The Dark Château*, *Spells and Philtres* – and four of short stories – *Out of Space and Time*, *Lost Worlds*, *Genius Loci and Other Tales*, and *The Abominations of Yondo*. Since his death his books include *Poems in Prose* and *Tales of Science and Sorcery*. A final collection of short fiction, *Other Dimensions*, and his *Selected Poems* were also published by Arkham House.

JAMES WADE (1930–   ) was born in Illinois. After Army service in Korea, he settled in Seoul in 1960. He has been a college music professor, voluntary agency executive and journalist; he was adviser to the information programme of the Korean government. His book, *One Man's Korea*, appeared in Seoul in 1967, and his articles have seen print in *Musical America*, *High Fidelity*, *Variety*, the *St Louis Post-Dispatch*, and many other periodicals in Korea, England, and the United States. His symphonic and chamber music has been performed in many countries, including the United States. He has completed an opera based on Richard E. Kim's best-selling novel of the Korean War, *The Martyred*. His infatuation with fantasy began at the age of six. In his teens he began writing stories under the influence of Poe, Lovecraft, Blackwood, John Collier and others. *The Deep Ones* is the first of his Mythos stories to be published.

COLIN WILSON (1931–   ) is one of the most versatile authors currently producing. He is one of the most prolific writers alive, writing with authority and intelligence on an astonishing variety of subjects, ranging from philosophy to music. He made his literary bow in 1956 with a challenging 'inquiry into the nature of the sickness of mankind in the mid-twentieth century', titled *The Outsider*, which a reviewer in *The Listener* held to be 'The most remarkable book upon which the reviewer has ever had to pass judgement'. Since its publication, Mr Wilson has published in rapid succession an astounding collection of books, including *Religion and the Rebel*, *The Strength to Dream*, *Beyond the Outsiders*, *Introduction to the New Existentialism*, *An Encyclopedia of Murder*, *Rasputin and the Fall of the Romanovs*, *Brandy for the Damned*, *Ritual in the Dark*, *The Glass Cage*, *The Mind Parasites*, and many others. His interest in Lovecraft and the Cthulhu Mythos began with his chance introduction to *The Outsider and Others*; this led him to write about Lovecraft in *The Strength to Dream*, and, in response to correspondence with August Derleth, he wrote *The Mind Parasites*, his first venture into the Mythos. He has since written another novel belonging to the Mythos, *The Philosopher's Stone*.

Cabal
Clive Barker

The nightmare had begun . . .

Boone now knew for sure there was no place on this earth for him, no happiness here, not even with Lori. Just as certain, there was no salvation possible for him in Heaven. He would let Hell claim him then, let Death take him there.

But Death itself seemed to shrink from him. No wonder, if he had indeed been the monster who had shattered and violated so many others' lives. And Decker had shown him the hellish proof of the photographs where the victims were forever stilled, splayed in the last obscene moment of their torture.

Neither Heaven, nor Hell, nor Earth was possible. It could only be Midian then – that awful legendary place which gathered to itself in its monstrous embrace the half-dead, the Nightbreed . . .

Cabal is like no other novel: a horror story, a love story, a story of death and vengeance, and of the ultimate clash between two very different monstrosities. Only Clive Barker, internationally acclaimed author of *Weaveworld*, could have produced this master-work.

ISBN 0 00 617666 6

The Animal Hour
Andrew Klavan

From the author of the terrifying *Don't Say a Word*.

Nancy Kincaid was sure of one thing as she stepped on to the crowded New York subway – it was going to be a lousy day. The commuters stood packed tightly in the aisle, their smells mingled in her nostrils, their bodies jostled together. A lone trumpeter on the platform played a tune, 'Nobody's Sweetheart'. For Nancy, it struck an all too poignant chord. No one loved her, she was a girl bound by routine, on her way to her dreary old office, to begin another dull old week.

But Nancy had forgotten that it was Hallowe'en. Hallowe'en, when all is not what it seems, when the October sun sets, when the sky deepens its blue. The night of the Hallowe'en Parade, the 'Animal Hour' – a time when familiarity is no more, when no one knows who Nancy Kincaid is, for suddenly Nancy finds she no longer exists . . .

ISBN 0 586 21845 9

☐	MAGICIAN Raymond E. Feist	0-586-21783-5	£6.99
☐	SILVERTHORN Raymond E. Feist	0-586-06417-6	£4.99
☐	A DARKNESS AT SETHANON Raymond E. Feist	0-586-06688-8	£5.99
☐	THE SILVER BRANCH Patricia Kennealy	0-586-21248-5	£4.99
☐	THE ELVENBANE A. Norton/M. Lackey	0-586-21687-1	£5.99
☐	MASTER OF WHITESTORM Janny Wurts	0-586-21068-7	£4.99
☐	THE DRAGON AND THE GEORGE Gordon R. Dickson	0-586-21326-0	£4.99
☐	BLACK TRILLIUM May/Bradley/Norton	0-586-21102-0	£4.99

These books are available from your local bookseller or can be ordered direct from the publishers.

To order direct just tick the titles you want and fill in the form below:

Name: _____

Address: _____

_____

Postcode: _____

Send to: HarperCollins Mail Order, Dept 8, HarperCollins *Publishers*, Westerhill Road, Bishopbriggs, Glasgow G64 2QT.

Please enclose a cheque or postal order or your authority to debit your Visa/Access account –

Credit card no: _____

Expiry date: _____

Signature: _____

– to the value of the cover price plus:

UK & BFPO: Add £1.00 for the first and 25p for each additional book ordered.

Overseas orders including Eire, please add £2.95 service charge.

Books will be sent by surface mail but quotes for airmail despatches will be given on request.

24 HOUR TELEPHONE ORDERING SERVICE FOR ACCESS/VISA CARDHOLDERS –

TEL: GLASGOW 041-772 2281 or LONDON 081-307 4052